THE NAMELESS DAY

Sara Douglass was born in Penola, South Australia, and spent her early working life as a nurse. Rapidly growing tired of starched veils, mitred corners and irascible anaesthetists, she worked her way through three degrees at the University of Adelaide, culminating in a PhD in early modern English history.

Her first three books make up the AXIS TRILOGY: *BattleAxe*, *Enchanter* and *StarMan*. THE WAYFARER REDEMPTION, her second trilogy is also set in Tencendor: *Sinner*, *Pilgrim* and *Crusader*.

Sara now lives in Bendigo where she divides her time between writing and tending her garden.

Sara Douglass' website can be found at:
www.saradouglass.com

Also by Sara Douglass

Voyager

SARA DOUGLASS

THE NAMELESS DAY
The Crucible: Book One

HarperCollins*Publishers*

Voyager
An imprint of HarperCollins*Publishers*
77–85 Fulham Palace Road,
Hammersmith, London W6 8JB

www.voyager-books.com

Published by *Voyager* 2001
1 3 5 7 9 8 6 4 2

A catalogue record for this book
is available from the British Library

ISBN 0 00 710845 1

Typeset in Adobe Garamond

Printed and bound in Great Britain by
Omnia Books Ltd, Glasgow

Contents

In memory of my most devoted fan,

MICHAEL GODWIN

10th September 1981 – 16th March 1998

Author's Note

Time travel is not only theoretically possible, travel into our future has already been achieved (albeit on a tiny scale of a few seconds or minutes). Travel into our past is more problematic. How would interfering with our past affect our present? Some physicists argue that sending someone into the past creates a "parallel universe" — the mere presence of someone in a past time alters that world's future to such an extent that a *different* future is necessarily created: a parallel universe (or world) to the one we live in.

The three books of "The Crucible" are set, not in the medieval Europe of our past, but in the medieval Europe of a parallel universe: the insertion of even one fictional character amongst a host of historical characters necessarily creates that parallel world. Thus, while there are many similarities between our past and the world of "The Crucible", there are also many differences. The entire period of the Hundred Years War, for example, has been compressed so that the Battle of Poitiers is fought at a later date than in our past, and Joan of Arc appears at an earlier date.

Although some dates and "facts" have altered, the spirit of "The Crucible" remains identical to that of our medieval

Europe. Something strange happened in the fourteenth century ... something very, very odd. The fourteenth century was an age of unprecedented catastrophe for western Europe: widespread famine due to climate change, economic collapse, uncontrollable heresies, social upheaval, endemic war and, to compound the misery, the physical and psychological devastation of the Black Death. In all of recorded history there has never been before or since a period of such utter disaster: one half of Europe's population died due to the effects of famine, war and the Black Death. As a result, Europeans emerged from the fourteenth century profoundly — and frighteningly — changed. Medieval Europe had been an intensely spiritual society: the salvation of the soul was paramount. Post-fourteenth century Europe abandoned spirituality for secularism, materialism and worldliness. Its peoples embraced technology and science, and developed the most aggressively invasive mentality of world history. Why this profound shift from the internal quest for spiritual salvation to a craving for world domination? Was it just the end result of over a hundred years of catastrophe ... or was there another reason?

"The Crucible" presents an explanation couched in a medieval understanding of the world rather than in terms more familiar to our modern sensibilities. Medieval Europe was a world of evil incarnate, a world where demons and angels walked the same fields as men and women; a world where the armies of God and of Satan arrayed themselves for the final battle ... we now live in the aftermath of that battle, but are we sure who won?

Sara Douglass
Bendigo, 2000

Prologue

The Friday within the Octave of All Saints
to the Nameless Day
In the twenty-first year of the reign of Edward III
(7th November to Tuesday 23rd December 1348)

— St Angelo's Friary, Rome —

"Brother Wynkyn? Brother Wynkyn? Sweet Jesu, Brother, you're not going to leave us *now*?"

Brother Wynkyn de Worde slapped shut the weighty manuscript book before him and turned to face Prior Bertrand. "I have no choice, Bertrand. I must leave."

Bertrand took a deep breath. *Sweet Saviour, how could he possibly dissuade Brother Wynkyn?*

"My friend," he said, earning himself a sarcastic glance from Wynkyn. "Brother Wynkyn ... the pestilence rages across Christendom. If you leave the safety of Saint Angelo's —"

"What safety? Of the seventeen brothers who prayed here five weeks ago, now there is only you and me and two others left. Besides, if I choose to hide within these 'safe' walls a far worse pestilence will ravage Christendom than that which currently rages. I must go. Get out of my way."

"Brother, the roads are choked with the dying and the

brigands who pick their pockets and pluck the rings from their fingers." Prior Bertrand moderated his voice, trying to reason with the old man. Brother Wynkyn had ever been difficult. Bertrand knew that Wynkyn had even shouted down the Holy Father once, and Bertrand realised there was no circumstance in which he could hope for respect from someone who was powerful enough to cow a pope. "How can you possibly overcome all the difficulties and the dangers roaming the roads between here and Nuremberg? Stay, I beg you."

"I would condemn the earth to a slow descent into insanity if I stayed here." Wynkyn lowered the book — he needed both arms to lift it — and several loose pages of closely-written script into a flat-lidded oaken casket bound with brass. It was only just large enough to take the book and the pages. Once he had shut the casket, Wynkyn locked it with a key that hung from a chain on his belt.

Bertrand watched wordlessly for some minutes, and then tried again. "And if you die on the road?"

Wynkyn shot his prior an angry glance. "I will *not* die on the road! God and the angels protect me and my purpose."

"As they have protected all the other innocent souls who have died in the past weeks and months? Wynkyn, *nothing* protects mankind against the evil of this pestilence!"

Wynkyn carefully checked the casket to ensure its security. He turned his back to Bertrand.

"Rome is dying," Bertrand said, his voice now soft. "Corpses lie six deep in the streets, and the black, bubbling pestilence seeks new victims on every breath of wind. God has shown us the face of wrath for our sins, and the angels have fled. If you leave the friary now you will surely die."

Still Wynkyn did not answer.

"Brother," Bertrand said, desperation now filling his voice. "Why must you leave? What is of such importance that you must risk almost certain death?"

Wynkyn turned about and locked eyes with the prior. "Because if I don't leave, then it is almost certain death for Christendom," he said. "Either get out of my way, Bertrand, or aid me to carry this casket to my mule."

Bertrand's eyes filled with tears. He made a hopeless gesture with his hand, but Wynkyn's gaze did not waver.

"Well?" Wynkyn said.

Bertrand took a deep, sobbing breath, and then grasped a handle of the casket. "I wish peace walk with you, Wynkyn."

"Peace has never walked with me," Wynkyn said as he grabbed the other handle. "And it never will."

Wynkyn de Worde had undertaken the journey between Rome and Nuremberg over one hundred times in the past fifty or so years, but never had he done so before with such a heavy heart. He had been twenty-three in 1296 when the then pope, the great Boniface VIII, had sent him north for the first time.

Twenty-three, and entrusted with a secret so horrifying, that it, and the nightmarish responsibility it carried with it, would have killed most other men. But Wynkyn was a special man, strong and dedicated, sure of the right of God, and with a faith so unshakeable that Boniface understood why the angels had selected him as the man fit to oversee the Cleft.

"Reveal this secret to any other man," Boniface had told the young Dominican, "and you can be sure that the angels themselves will ensure your death."

Already privy to the ghastly secret, Wynkyn knew truth when he heard it.

Boniface had leaned back in his chair, satisfied. Since the beginnings of the office of the pope in the Dark Ages, its incumbents kept the secret of the Cleft, entrusting it only to the single priest the angels had said was strong enough to endure. As this priest approached the end of his life, the angels gave the pope the name of a new priest, young and strong, and this young priest would accompany the older priest on the man's final few journeys to the Cleft. From the older, dying priest the younger one learned the incantations that he would need ... and he also learned the true meaning of courage, for without it he would not endure.

These priests, the Select, spent their lives teetering on the edge of hell.

In 1298 Boniface informed Wynkyn de Worde that he was the angels' choice as the new Select. Then, having learned from his predecessor, Wynkyn performed his duty willingly and without mishap for five years. He thought his life would take the same path as the scores of priests who had preceded him ... but he, like the angels, had underestimated the power and cunning of pure evil.

Who could have thought the papacy could fail so badly? Wynkyn had not anticipated it; the angels certainly had not. In 1303 the great and revered Pope Boniface VIII died, and Wynkyn had no way of knowing that the forces of darkness and disorder would seize this opportunity to throw the papacy into chaos. In the subsequent papal election a man called Clement V took the papal throne. Outwardly pious, it quickly became apparent to Wynkyn, as to everyone else, that Clement was the puppet of the French king, Philip IV. The new pope moved the papacy to the French-controlled town of Avignon, allowing Philip to dictate the papacy's activities and edicts. There, successive popes lived in luxury and corruption, mouthing the orders of French kings instead of the will of God.

When a new pope was enthroned, either the first among archangels, St Michael, or the current Select revealed to him the secret of the Cleft, but neither St Michael nor Wynkyn approached Clement. How could they allow the fearful secrets of the angels to fall into the hands of the French monarchy? *Sweet Jesu*, Wynkyn had thought as he spent sleepless nights wondering what to do, *a French king could seize control of the world had he this knowledge in hand! He could command an army so vile that even the angels of God would quail before it.*

So both Wynkyn and the angels kept the secret against the day that the popes rediscovered God and moved themselves and the papacy back to Rome. After all, surely it could not be long? Could it?

But the seductiveness of evil was stronger than Wynkyn

and the angels had anticipated. When Clement V died, the pope who succeeded him also preferred the French monarch's bribes and the sweet air of Avignon to the word of God and the best interests of His Church on earth. And so also the pope after that one …

Every year Wynkyn travelled north to the Cleft in time for the summer and winter solstices, and then travelled back to Rome to await his next journey; he could not bear to live his entire life at the Cleft, although he knew some of his predecessors, stronger men than he, had done so.

He received income enough from what Boniface had left at his disposal to continue his work, and the prior and brothers of his friary, St Angelo's, were too in awe of him to inquire closely into his movements and activities.

Brother Wynkyn de Worde also had the angels to assist his work. As they should, for their lusts had necessitated the Cleft.

But now here Wynkyn was, an ancient man in his mid-seventies, and it seemed that the popes would never return to Rome. God's wrath had boiled over, showering Europe with a pestilence such as it had never previously endured. Wynkyn had always travelled north with a heavy heart — his mission could engender no less in any man — but this night, as he carefully led his mule through the dead and dying littering the streets of Rome, he felt his soul shudder under the weight of his despair.

He was deeply afraid, not only for what he knew he would find awaiting him at the Cleft, but because he *did* fear he might die … and then who would follow him? Who would there be to tend the Cleft?

"I should have told," he muttered. But who was there to tell? Who to confide in? The popes were dissolute and corrupt, and there was no one else. No one.

Who else was there?

God and the angels had relied on the papacy, and now the popes had betrayed God Himself for a chest full of gold coin from the French king.

Damn the angels! If it wasn't for their sins in the first instance …

It took Wynkyn almost seven weeks to reach Nuremberg; that he even reached the city at all he thanked God's benevolence.

Every town, every hamlet, every cottage he'd passed had been in the grip of the black pestilence. Hands reached out from windows, doorways and gutters, begging the passing friar for succour, for prayers, or, at the least, for the last rites, but Wynkyn had ignored them.

They were all sinners, for why else had God's wrath struck them, and Wynkyn was consumed by his need to get north as fast as he could.

Far worse than the outstretched hands of the dying were the grasping hands of the bandits and outlaws who thronged the roadways and passes. But Wynkyn was sly — God's good gift — and whenever the bandits saw that Wynkyn clasped a cloth to his mouth, and heard the desperate racking of his cough, they backed away, making the sign of the cross.

Yet even Wynkyn could not remain immune to the grasping fingers of the pestilence forever. Not at his age.

On Ember Saturday Wynkyn de Worde had approached a small village two days from Nuremberg. By the roadside lay a huddle of men and women, dying from the plague. One of them, a woman — God's curse to earth! — had risen to her feet and stumbled towards the friar riding by, but as she leaned on his mule's shoulder, begging for aid, Wynkyn kicked her roughly away.

It was too late. Unbeknown to the friar, as he extended his hand to ward her off the deadly kiss of the pestilence sprang from her mouth to his hand during the virulence of her pleas. He planted his foot in the hateful woman's chest, and when he raised his hand to his face to make the sign of the cross the pestilence leaped unseen from his hand to his mouth.

The deed was done, and there was nothing the angels could do but moan.

The peal of mourning bells covered Nuremberg in a melancholy pall; even this great northern trading city had not escaped the ravages of the pestilence. The only reason Wynkyn managed access through the gates was that the town desperately needed men licensed by God to administer the last rites to the mass of dying. But Wynkyn did not pause to administer the last rites to anyone. He made his way to the Dominican friary in the eastern quarter of the city, his mule stumbling with weakness from his journey, and demanded audience with the prior.

The friary had been struck as badly by the pestilence as had Nuremberg itself, and the brother who met Wynkyn at the friary gate informed him that the prior had died these three nights past.

"Brother Guillaume now speaks with the prior's voice," the brother said.

Wynkyn showed no emotion — death no longer surprised nor distressed him — and requested that the friar take him to Brother Guillaume. "And help me carry this casket, brother, for I am passing weary."

The brother nodded. He knew Wynkyn well.

Brother Guillaume greeted Wynkyn with ill-disguised distaste and impatience. He had never liked this autocratic friar from Rome, and neither he nor any other friar in his disease-ridden community could spare the time to attend Wynkyn's demands.

"A meal only," Wynkyn said, noting Guillaume's reaction, "and a request."

"And that is?"

Wynkyn nodded towards the casket. "I leave in the morning for the forest north of the city. If I should not return within a week, I request that you send that casket — unopened — to my home friary."

Guillaume raised his eyebrows in surprise. "Your *home* friary? But, Brother Wynkyn, that would surely be impossible!"

"Easily enough accomplished!" Wynkyn snapped, and Guillaume flinched at the brother's sudden anger. "There are sufficient merchant bands travelling through Nuremberg who could take the casket on for a suitable price."

Wynkyn reached inside his habit and pulled out a small purse he had bound about his waist. "Take these gold pieces. It will be enough and more to pay for the casket's journey."

"But ... but this pestilence has stopped all traffic, and —"

"For the love of God, Guillaume, do as I say!"

Guillaume stared, shaken by Wynkyn's distress.

"Surely the pestilence will pass eventually, and when it does, the merchants will resume their trade, as they always do. Please, do as I ask."

"Very well then." Guillaume indicated a stool, and Wynkyn sat down. "But surely you will return. You have always done so before."

Wynkyn sighed, and rubbed his face with a trembling hand. "Perhaps."

And perhaps not, Guillaume thought, as he recognised the feverish glint in the old brother's eyes, and the unhealthy glow in his cheeks.

Guillaume backed away a few steps. "I will send a brother with food and ale," he said, and scurried for the door.

"Thank you," Wynkyn said to the empty air.

That night Wynkyn sat in a cold cell by the open casket, his hand on the closed book on his lap. Because there was no one else, Wynkyn carefully explained to the book the disaster that had befallen mankind generally, and the Keeper of the Cleft specifically. The popes had abandoned the directions of God and the angels for the directions of the French king. They did not know the secrets and mysteries of the Cleft or of the book itself, for neither angels nor Wynkyn dared reveal it to them. Through his ignorance, the current pope — Clement VI — had not selected the man to follow Wynkyn.

And a woman — a woman! — had passed the pestilence to Wynkyn!

In the past few hours, as he sat in his icy cell shaking with fever, Wynkyn had refused to come to terms with the fact that he was dying. There was no one to follow him; thus how could he die?

How could he die, when that would mean the demons would run free?

In his decades of service to God and the angels, Wynkyn had never come this close to despair: not when he had first heard of his mission; not even when he had seen what awaited him at the Cleft.

Not even when the first demon he encountered had turned and spoken his name and pleaded for its life.

But now ... now, this silent misery in a cold and comfortless friary cell ... *this* was despair.

Wynkyn lowered his head and wept, a hand still on the closed book, his shoulders shaking with both his grief and his fever.

Peace.

At first Wynkyn did not respond, then, when the heavenly voice repeated itself, he slowly raised his face.

Two arm spans away the far wall of the cell glowed. Most of the light was concentrated in the centre of the wall in the vague form of a winged man, his arms outstretched.

As Wynkyn watched, round-eyed with wonder, the archangel, still only a vague glowing outline, stepped from the wall and placed his hands about Wynkyn's upturned face.

Peace, Brother Wynkyn.

"Blessed Saint Michael!" Wynkyn would have fallen to his knees, but the pressure of the archangel's hands kept him in his seat.

The archangel very slightly increased the pressure of his hands, and love and joy flowed into Wynkyn's being.

"Blessed Saint Michael," Wynkyn whispered, his eyes watering from the archangel's glow. He blinked his tears away. "I am dying —"

For an instant, an instant so fleeting he knew he must have imagined it, Wynkyn thought he felt rage sweep through the archangel.

But then it was gone, as if it had never been.

"— and there is none to follow me. Saint Michael, what can we do?"

There is not one named, Wynkyn, but that does not mean one can never be. We shall have to make one, you and I and the full majesty of my brothers.

"Saint Michael?"

Take up that book you hold, and fold back the pages to the final leaf.

Slowly, Wynkyn did as the archangel asked.

He gasped. The book revealed an incantation he had never seen before ... and how many years had he spent examining every scratch within its pages?

With our heavenly power and your voice, we can between us forge your successor.

Wynkyn quickly scanned the incantation. He frowned a little as its meaning sank in. "But it will take years, and in the meantime —"

Trust. Are you ready?

Wynkyn took a deep breath, fighting back the urge to cough as he did so. "Aye, my lord. I am ready."

The glow increased about the archangel, and as it did, Wynkyn saw with the angel's eyes.

Images flooded chaotically before him: bodies writhing and plunging, lost in the evils of lust, the thoughts of the flesh triumphing over the meditations of the soul.

Horrible sinners all! Where are they who do not sin ... ah! There! There!

Wynkyn blinked. There a man who lowered himself reluctantly to his wife's body, and his wife, most blessed of women, who turned her face aside in abhorrence and who closed her eyes against the repugnant thrusting of her husband. This was not an act of lust, but of duty. This was a husband and a wife who endured the unbearable for only one reason: the engendering of a child.

God's child indeed. Speak, Wynkyn, speak the incantation now!

He hesitated, because as St Michael voiced his command, Wynkyn realised that the cell — impossibly — was crowded with all the angels of heaven. About the friar thronged a myriad glowing forms, their faces intense and raging and their eyes so full of furious power that Wynkyn wondered that the walls of the friary did not explode in fear.

Speak! St Michael commanded, and the cell filled with the celestial cry of the angels: *Speak! Speak! Speak!*

Wynkyn spoke, his feverish tongue fumbling over some of the words, but that did not matter, because even as he fumbled, he felt the power of the incantation and the power of all the angels flood creation.

St Michael lifted his hands from Wynkyn's face and shrieked, and with him shrieked the heavenly host.

The man shrieked also, his movements now most horrid and vile. His wife screamed and tried desperately to push away her husband.

But it was too late.

Far, far too late.

Wynkyn's successor had been conceived.

The friar blinked. The archangel and his companions had gone, as had the incantation on the page before him.

He was alone again in his cell, and all that was left was to die.

Or, perhaps, to try and perform his duty one last time.

Wynkyn set out the next morning just after Matins, shivering in the cold, dawn air. It lacked but a few days until the Nativity of the Lord Jesus Christ — although Wynkyn doubted there would be much joy and celebration this year — and winter had central Europe in a tight grip.

He coughed and spat out a wad of pus- and blood-stained phlegm.

"I will live yet," Wynkyn murmured. "Just a few more days."

And he grasped his staff the tighter and shuffled onto the almost deserted road beyond the city's northern gate.

It had not been shut the previous night. No doubt the gatekeeper's corpse lay swelling with the gases of putrefaction somewhere within the gatehouse.

The wind was bitter beyond the shelter of the streets and walls, and Wynkyn had to wrap his cloak tightly about himself. Even so, he could not escape the bone-chilling cold, and he shivered violently as he forced one foot after the other on the deserted road.

"Pray to God I have the time," he whispered, and for the next several hours, until the sun was well above the horizon, he muttered prayer after prayer, using them not only for protection against the devilry in the air, but also as an aid in his journey.

If he concentrated on the prayers, then he might not notice the crippling cold.

Even the sun rising towards noon did not warm the air, nor impart any cheer to the surrounding countryside.

The fields were deserted, ploughs standing bogged in frozen earth, and the doors of abandoned hovels creaked to and fro in the wind.

There was no evidence of life at all: no men, no women, no dogs, no birds.

Just a barren and dead landscape.

"Devilry, devilry," Wynkyn muttered between prayers. "Devilry, devilry!"

By mid-afternoon Wynkyn was aching in every joint, and shaking with fatigue. His cough had worsened, and pain hammered with insistent and cruel fists behind his forehead.

"I am so old," he whispered, halting for a rest beneath a twisted tree stripped bare of all its leaves. "Too old for this. Too old."

A fit of coughing made the friar double over in agony, and when Wynkyn raised himself and wiped bleary tears from his eyes, he only stared in resignation at what he saw glistening on the ground between his feet.

No phlegm at all now. Just blood ... and thick yellow pus.

An hour before dusk, almost frozen yet still shaking with fever, Wynkyn turned onto an all but hidden small track that led north-east. Stands of shadowed trees had sprung up to either side of the road in the last mile, and the track led deeper into the woods.

The trees had been stripped of leaves by the winter cold, and moisture and fungus crept along their black branches and hung down from knobbly twigs. Boulders reared out of the moss-covered ground, tilting trees on sharp angles. Cold air eddied between trees and boulders, carrying with it a thin fog that tangled among the treetops.

No one ever ventured into these forbidding woods. Not only was their very appearance more than dismal, but legend had it that demons and sprites lingered among the trees, as did goblins among the rocks, all more than ready to snatch any foolish souls who ventured into their domain.

Wynkyn would have chuckled if he had had the energy. For hundreds of years the Church had cautioned people away from these woods with their tales of red-eyed demons. Red-eyed demons there were none, but Wynkyn knew the reality was worse than the stories.

These woods nurtured the Cleft.

He struggled along the track, stopping every ten or twelve steps to lean against the trunk of a tree and cough.

Wynkyn knew he was dying, and now the only question left in his mind was whether or not he could open the Cleft and dispose of this year's crop of horror before he commended his soul to God.

After another mile the ground began to rise to either side of the path. Yet another half mile and Wynkyn, his legs so weak he had to lean heavily on a staff to keep upright, found himself at the mouth of a gorge. The hills to either side were not over tall — perhaps some six or seven hundred feet — but the gorge floor dropped down into ... well, into hell itself.

This was the Cleft, the earth's vile equivalent of the suppurating cleft that lay between the legs of every daughter of Eve.

Wynkyn began to laugh, a harsh yet whispery sound. As loathsomeness would be sunk into the cleft of every one of the daughters of Eve, so he, Wynkyn de Worde, would see to it that loathsomeness would be sunk into this Cleft.

Every cleft led to hell, one way or the other.

Wynkyn's laughter turned into an agonising, wet, bubbling cough, and he sank to his knees and would have fallen completely had it not been for his grip on his staff. The pestilence had run riot in his lungs, and now Wynkyn was very close to drowning in his own pus and blood.

Time was passing too fast. He did not have long.

Praise God he knew the incantations by heart!

Wynkyn forced himself to raise his head. He spat out an amount of pus, hawked, spat again, then wiped his mouth with a shaking arm.

It was time.

Slowly he spoke the words, his eyes fixed on the Cleft.

When he finished, it first appeared that nothing had changed. The gorge spread before him in the twilight, a twisted wasteland of boulders and shadows and the hunched shapes of low, scrubby bushes.

But in an instant all altered. Flames licked out from behind boulders, and vegetation burst into fire. There was a roaring, rending sound, and clouds of sulphuric effluvium billowed into the air.

Wails and screams, and even the thin, white, despairing arms of those trapped within, rose and fell from the gate to hell.

Wynkyn chuckled. The Cleft had opened.

But his work was not yet done. He turned slightly so that he could see the path behind him.

"Come," he said, and clicked his fingers. "Come."

There was a momentary stillness, then from the forest lining the path walked forth children, perhaps some thirty or thirty-five, all between the ages of two and six.

Not one of them was human and all were horribly deformed; the twistings of their bodies reflecting the twistings of their souls.

Wynkyn bared his teeth. They were abominable! Devilish! And to the Devil they must be sent.

He lifted his hand, trying to control its shaking, and began to speak the incantation that would force them down into —

A convulsion racked his body, and his voice wavered and stilled.

Another convulsion swept over him, and Wynkyn de Worde collapsed to the ground.

One of the children, a boy of about six, stepped forth to within a few paces of the friar.

Wynkyn rolled over slightly, his face contorted, and began to whisper again.

The boy smiled.

Wynkyn's voice bubbled to a close. He lifted a hand trying desperately to conjure words out of air, but nothing came of it, and his hand fell back to the ground, failing him as badly as his voice.

"You're dying," said the boy, his voice a mixture of relief and joy.

He turned and looked at the crowd of his fellows. "The Keeper dies!" he said.

Behind him Wynkyn writhed and twisted, fighting uselessly against his illness. He tried to breathe, but could not … he could not … the fluids in his lungs had bubbled to his very throat and …

The boy turned back to Wynkyn as the friar made an horrific gurgling. The old man was trembling, and odorous fluids were running from his mouth and nose.

His eyes were wide and staring … and very, very afraid.

"If I had the strength," the boy said in a voice surprisingly mature for his age, "I would throw you into the Cleft myself."

But he could not, and so the boy stood there, his fellows now ranged behind him in a curious and joyful semicircle, and watched as Wynkyn de Worde struggled into death.

They waited for some time after his last breath. Making sure.

They waited until the Cleft closed of its own accord, tired of waiting for the incantation that would have fed it.

They waited until the boy at their head leaned down and retrieved the key that hung from the dead friar's belt.

They waited until the curse of the Nameless Day was past.

"Hail our freedom!" he cried, and then burst into laughter. "We are freed of the angels' curse. Freed into *life*!"

And he thrust the key nightward in an obscene gesture towards Heaven.

It was a cold night.

Worse, it was the most feared time of year, for all knew that during the winter solstice the worlds of mankind and demon touched and a passage between them became possible. In ancient times the people had called this day and night period the Nameless Day, for to name it would only have been to give it power. Even though the people now had the word of God to comfort them, they remembered the beliefs of their ancestors, and each year feared that *this* Nameless Day might witness the escape of Satan's imps into their world.

The villagers of Asterladen — those the pestilence had spared — huddled about a roaring fire inside the church. It was the only stone building in the village, and the only building with stout doors which the villagers could lock securely.

It was the safest place they could find, and the only sound which could comfort them was the murmured prayers of their parish priest.

Rainard, his wife Aude, and their infant daughter were particularly unlucky. That afternoon they had remained behind in the fields when the other villagers left, trying to discover the brooch that Aude had dropped in the mud.

It was her only piece of finery, a simple brooch made of worn bronze which had been passed down through her family for generations, and Aude was singularly proud of it. Normally she would not have worn it out to the fields, but there was to be a field dance that afternoon, and the lord had promised ale, and Aude wanted to look her best.

Despite her age and her many years spent childbearing, Aude was a vain creature and proud of her looks. But between the dancing and the ale, the brooch had somehow slipped from her breast to be trodden down into the earth. She and Rainard — he berating her the entire time for her foolishness in wearing her only piece of jewellery into the field even for a Yuletide dance — had searched for hours, but the brooch was nowhere to be found.

Too late they realised the onset of dusk, and the absence of every other soul.

They hurried back to the village, breathless and fearful, and had beaten on the doors of the church until their fists were bruised and bloody.

But the priest had called them demons, and the villagers safe inside the church had screamed and refused to believe that the voices of their well-known friends were human at all.

So Rainard and Aude and their infant daughter, whom Aude had left swaddled and safe in their cottage while they were out in the fields, had to survive the night on their own.

Rainard built up a good fire in the central hearth of their cottage, and he and his wife huddled as close to it as they could, listening all the while to the moans and cries in the wind outside.

"There'll be no harm," Aude muttered, convincing neither her husband nor herself. She threw a concerned glance to her daughter, lying asleep in her cradle.

"We *would* be safe if not for your cursed trinket," Rainard said.

Aude bared her yellowing teeth, but said nothing. She grieved deeply for her lost brooch, and wondered if somehow Rainard had been involved in its loss.

What if he had seized it in order to sell it next market day in Nuremberg? Like as not he would squander *her* money on a new couplet of pigs, or some such! Yes, perhaps he had it even now, tucked away in some —

There was a sudden noise on the wind, the sound of a distant door being forced open, and then of feet scuffling past the back wall of their cottage.

Some of the feet clicked, as if they were clawed.

"Rainard!" Aude squeaked, and leapt into her husband's arms.

He shoved her to one side, and seized an axe he had to the ready.

More feet scampered past, bolder now, and the couple thought they heard the sound of three or four more doors in neighbouring cottages being forced open.

"*Rainard!*" Aude screamed, grabbing at his arm.

And then the door of their hovel squeaked and fell open.

Rainard and Aude stared, not believing their eyes.

A child, a boy, stood there. He was weeping, and covered with dirt and abrasions.

Nonetheless, he was the most beautiful child the peasants had ever seen.

"Who are you?" Rainard said, wondering how the child had escaped the prowling demons.

The boy gulped, and began to cry. "I'm lost," he eventually said.

Rainard and Aude looked at each other. They'd heard tales of these waifs, orphaned by the pestilence, turned out of their homes by neighbours who thought the children harboured pestilence themselves.

But although this boy was cold and dirty, he was also obviously healthy. His eyes shone clear and bright, and his skin, if dirty, was not feverish.

"What is your name?" Aude said.

"I have no name," the boy said.

"Then where are your parents?" Rainard said.

"My mam is dead, and my father deserted us years ago," the boy said. "Before I was born. I know not where he is. Please, I am hungry. Will you feed me?"

There was a shuffling behind him, and two girls, perhaps three and four respectively, silently joined the boy.

"How many of you are there?" Rainard asked.

"Us, and two more, both girls," said the boy. "Please, we have all lost our parents, and are hungry. Will you feed us?"

Rainard and Aude shared a look. They were poor and had barely enough to feed themselves, but they also had souls, and cared deeply for children. God knew there were few enough left in this time of pestilence.

"We'll take you," Rainard said, pointing to the boy, "and one of the girls. The others can find homes soon enough with some of the other families."

The boy smiled, his face almost angelic. "I do thank you," he said.

He moved over to the cradle, and both Rainard and Aude stiffened.

But the boy did nothing more than reach in and gently touch the sleeping girl's forehead. "She will lead a charmed life," he said.

Over that night and the next two days twelve villages in the region north of Nuremberg found themselves sheltering hungry orphans. No one was particularly puzzled by the appearance of the children: communication between villages was poor, and there was no one to learn of the somewhat surprising number of hungry, soulful-looking children who appeared at doors asking for shelter in the time of the Nativity in the year of the black pestilence.

This was a time of unheard-of disease and death, and there must surely be orphaned children wandering about all over the land.

All the children were taken in and nourished, and loved, and raised. None of these children bit the hands that fed them; to these work-worn hands they gave back love and gratefulness and good works.

All of these children eventually left their adopted homes to lead particularly bounteous lives.

ROME

"Margrett, my sweetest Margrett! I must goe!
most dere to mee that neuer may be soo;
as Fortune willes, I cannott itt deny."
"*then know thy loue, thy Margrett, shee must
dye.*"

A Jigge (for Margrett)
Medieval English ballad

I

The Friday after Plough Monday
In the forty-ninth year of the reign of Edward III
(16th January 1377)

A dribble of red wine ran down Gerardo's stubbled chin, and he reluctantly — and somewhat unsteadily — rose from his sheltered spot behind the brazier.

It was time to close the gates.

Gerardo had been the gatekeeper at the northern gate of Rome, the Porta del Popolo, for nine years, and in all of his nine years he'd never had a day like this one. In his time he'd closed the gates against raiders, Jewish and Saracen merchants, tardy pilgrims and starving mobs come to the Holy City to beg for morsels and to rob the wealthy. He'd opened the gates to dawns, Holy Roman armies, traders and yet more pilgrims.

Today, he had opened the gate at dawn to discover a pope waiting.

Gerardo had just stood, bleary eyes blinking, mouth hanging open, one hand absently scratching at the reddened and itching lice tracks under his coarse woollen robe. He hadn't instantly recognised the man or his vestments, nor the banners carried by the considerable entourage stretching out behind the pope. And why should he? No pope had made

Rome his home for the past seventy years, and only one had made a cursory visit — and that years before Gerardo had taken on responsibility for the Porta del Popolo.

So he had stood there and stared, blinking like an addle-headed child, until one of the soldiers of the entourage shouted out to make way for His Holiness Pope Gregory XI. Still sleep-befuddled, Gerardo had obligingly shuffled out of the way, and then stood and watched as the pope, fifteen or sixteen cardinals, some sundry officials of the papal curia, soldiers, mercenaries, priests, monks, friars, general hangers-on, eight horse-drawn wagons and several score of laden mules entered Rome to the accompaniment of murmured prayers, chants, heavy incense and the flash of weighty folds of crimson and purple silks in the dawn light.

None among this, the most richest of cavalcades, thought to offer the gatekeeper a coin, and Gerardo was so fuddled he never thought to ask for one.

Instead, he stood, one hand still on the gate, and watched the pageant disappear down the street.

Within the hour Rome was in uproar.

The pope was home! Back from the terrible Babylonian Captivity in Avignon where the traitor French kings had kept successive popes for seventy years. The pope was *home*!

Mobs roared onto streets and swept over the Ponte St Angelo into the Leonine City and up the street leading to St Peter's Basilica. There Pope Gregory, a little travel weary but strong of voice, addressed the mob in true papal style, admonishing them for their sins and pleading for their true repentance ... as also for the taxes and tithes they had managed to avoid these past seventy years.

The mob was having none of it. They wanted assurance the pope wasn't going to sally back out the gate the instant they all went back to home and work. They roared the louder, and leaned forward ominously, fists waving in the air, threats of violence rising above their upturned faces. *This pope was going to remain in Rome where he belonged.*

The pope acquiesced (his train of cardinals had long since

fled into the bolted safety of St Peter's). He promised to remain, and vowed that the papacy had returned to Rome.

The mob quietened, lowered their fists and cheered. Within the hour they'd trickled back to their residences and workshops, not to begin their daily labour, but to indulge in a day of celebration.

Now Gerardo sighed, and shuffled closer to the gate. He had drunk too much of that damn rough Corsican red this day — as had most of the Roman mob, some of whom were still roaming the streets or standing outside the walls of the Leonine City (the gates to *that* had been shut many hours since) — and he couldn't wait to close these cursed gates and head back to his warm bed and comfortable wife.

He grabbed hold of the edge of one of the gates, and pulled it slowly across the opening until he could throw home its bolts into the bed of the roadway. He was about to turn for the other gate when a movement in the dusk caught his eye. Gerardo stared, then slowly cursed.

Some fifty or sixty paces down the road was a man riding a mule. Gerardo would have slammed the gates in the man's face but for the fact that the man wore the distinctive black hooded cloak over the white robe of a Dominican friar, and if there was one group of clergy Gerardo was more than reluctant to annoy it was the Dominicans.

Too many of the damn Dominicans were Father Inquisitors (and those that were not had ambitions to be), and Gerardo didn't fancy a slow death roasting over coals for irritating one of the bastards.

Worse, Gerardo couldn't charge the friar the usual coin for passage through the gate. Clergy thought themselves above such trivialities as paying gatekeepers for their labours.

So he stood there, hopping from foot to foot in the deepening dusk and chill air, running foul curses through his mind, and waited for the friar to pass.

The poor bastard looked cold, Gerardo had to give him that. Dominicans affected simple dress, and while the cloak over the robe might keep the man's body warm enough, his feet were clad in sandals that left them open to the winter's rigour. As the friar drew closer, Gerardo could see that his hands were white and shaking as they gripped the rope of the mule's halter, and his face was pinched and blue under the hood of his black cloak.

Gerardo bowed his head respectfully.

"Welcome, brother," he murmured as the friar drew level with him. *I bet the sanctimonious bastard won't be slow in downing the wine this night*, he thought.

The friar pulled his mule to a halt, and Gerardo looked up.

"Can you give me directions to the Saint Angelo friary?" the friar asked in exquisite Latin.

The friar's accent was strange, and Gerardo frowned, trying to place it. Not Roman, nor the thick German of so many merchants and bankers who passed through his gate. And certainly not the high piping tones of those French pricks. He peered at the man's face more closely. The friar was about twenty-eight or nine, and his face was that of the soldier rather than the priest: hard and angled planes to cheek and forehead, short black hair curling out from beneath the rim of the hood, a hooked nose, and penetrating light brown eyes over a traveller's stubble of dark beard.

Sweet St Catherine, perhaps he *was* a Father Inquisitor!

"Follow the westerly bend of the Tiber," said Gerardo in much rougher Latin, "until you come to the bridge that crosses over to the Castel Saint Angelo — but do not cross. The Saint Angelo friary lies tucked to one side of the bridge this side of the river. You cannot mistake it." He bowed deeply.

The friar nodded. "I thank you, good man." One hand rummaged in the pouch at his waist, and the next moment he tossed a coin at Gerardo. "For your aid," he said, and kicked his mule forward.

Gerardo grabbed the coin and gasped, revising his opinion of the man as he stared at him disappearing into the twilight.

The friar hunched under his cloak as his exhausted mule stumbled deeper into Rome. For years he had hungered to visit this most holy of cities, yet now he couldn't even summon a flicker of interest in the buildings rising above him, in the laughter and voices spilling out from open doorways, in the distant rush and tumble of the Tiber, or in the twinkling lights of the Leonine City rising to his right.

He didn't even scan the horizon for the silhouette of St Peter's Basilica.

Instead, all he could think of was the pain in his hands and feet. The cold had eaten its terrible way so deep into his flesh and joints that he thought he would limp for the rest of his life.

But of what use were feet to a man who wanted only to spend his life in contemplation of God? And, of course, in penitence for his foul sin — a sin so loathsome that he did not think he'd ever be able to atone for it enough to achieve salvation.

Alice! Alice! How could he ever have condemned her to the death he had?

He should *welcome* the pain, because it would focus his mind on God, as on his sinful soul. The flesh was nothing; it meant nothing, just as this world meant nothing. On the other hand, his soul was everything, as was contemplation of God and of eternity. Flesh was corrupt, spirit was pure.

The friar sighed and forced himself to throw his cloak away from hands and feet. Comfort was sin, and he should not indulge in it.

He sighed again, ragged and deep, and envied the life of the gatekeeper. Rough, honest work spent in the city of the Holy Father. Service to God.

What man could possibly desire anything else?

Prior Bertrand was half sunk to his arthritic knees before the cross in his cell, when there came a soft tap at the door.

Bertrand closed his eyes in annoyance, then painfully raised himself, grabbing a bench for support as he did so. "Come."

A young boy of some twelve or thirteen years entered, dressed in the robes of a novice.

He bowed his head and crossed his hands before him. "Brother Thomas Neville has arrived," he said.

Bertrand raised his eyebrows. The man had made good time! And to arrive the same day as Pope Gregory ... well, a day of many surprises then.

"Does he need rest and food before I speak with him, Daniel?" Bertrand asked.

"No," said another voice, and the newcomer stepped out from the shadows of the ill-lit passageway. He was limping badly. "I would prefer to speak with you now."

Bertrand bit down an unbrotherly retort at the man's presumptuous tone, then gestured Brother Thomas inside.

"Thank you, Daniel," Bertrand said to the novice. "Perhaps you could bring some bread and cheese from the kitchens for Brother Thomas."

Bertrand glanced at the state of the friar's hands and feet. "And ask Brother Arno to prepare a poultice."

"I don't need —" Brother Thomas began.

"Yes," Bertrand said, "you *do* need attention to your hands and feet ... your feet especially. If you were not a cripple before you entered service, then God does not demand that you become one now." He looked back at the novice. "Go."

The novice bowed again, and closed the door behind him.

"You have surprised me, brother," Bertrand said, turning to face his visitor, who had hobbled into the centre of the sparsely furnished cell. "I did not expect you for some weeks yet."

Bertrand glanced over the man's face and head; he'd travelled so fast he'd not had the time to scrape clean his chin or tonsure. That would be the next thing to be attended to, after his extremities.

"I made good time, Brother Prior," Thomas said. "A group of obliging merchants let me share their vessel down the French and Tuscany coasts."

A courageous man, thought Bertrand, *to brave the uncertain waters of the Mediterranean. But that is as befits his background.* "Will you sit?" he said, and indicated the cell's only stool, which stood to one side of the bed.

Thomas sat down, not allowing any expression of relief to mark his face, and Bertrand lowered himself to the bed. "You have arrived on an auspicious day, Brother Thomas," he said.

Thomas raised his eyebrows.

Bertrand stared briefly at the man's striking face before he responded. There was an arrogance and pride there that deeply disturbed the prior. "Aye, an auspicious day indeed. At dawn Gregory disembarked himself, most of his cardinals, and the entire papal curia, from his barges on the Tiber and entered the city."

"The pope has returned?"

Bertrand bowed his head in assent.

Brother Thomas muttered something under his breath that to Bertrand's aged ears sounded very much like a curse.

"Brother Thomas!"

The man's cheeks reddened slightly. "I beg forgiveness, Brother Prior. I only wish I had pushed my poor mule the faster so I might have been here for the event. Tell me, has he arrived to stay?"

"Well," Bertrand slid his hands inside the voluminous sleeves of his robe. "I would hear about your journey first, Brother Thomas. And then, perhaps, I can relate our news to you."

Best to put this autocratic brother in his place as soon as possible, Bertrand thought. *I will not let him direct the conversation.*

Thomas made as if to object, then bowed his head in acquiescence. "I left Dover on the Feast of Saint Benedict, and crossed to Harfleur on the French coast. From there . . ."

Bertrand listened with only a portion of his attention as Thomas continued his tale of his journey, nodding now and then with encouragement. But the tale interested him not. It was this man before him who commanded his thoughts.

Brother Thomas was a man of some interest, with an unusual background for a friar, although not for more worldly men. The Prior General of England, Richard Thorseby, had been extremely reluctant to admit Thomas

Neville into the Order of Preachers — the Dominicans — and had examined Thomas at great length before finally, and most unwillingly, allowing him to take his vows.

Men like Thomas were usually trouble.

On the other hand, Thomas could be extremely useful to the advancement of the Dominicans — if he was handled correctly.

Bertrand smiled politely as Thomas told an amusing anecdote about ship life with the rowdy merchants, but let his train of thought continue.

Why had Thomas chosen the Dominicans? The mendicant orders, of which the Dominicans were the most powerful, were orders which took their vows of chastity, poverty and obedience very seriously. Indeed, 'mendicant' was the ancient Latin word meaning 'to beg'. Friars remained poor all their lives, were not allowed to own property or live luxurious lives ... unlike many of the higher clergy within the Roman Church.

If Thomas had chosen to join the more regular orders of the Church, Bertrand thought, *he could have been a bishop within two years, a cardinal in ten, and could have aspired to be pope within twenty. Yet he chose poverty and humbleness above power and riches. Why?*

Piety?

From one of the Nevilles?

From what he knew of the Nevilles, Bertrand could not believe that one of their family would have chosen piety above power, but then one never knew the wondrous workings of the Lord.

"And so now you hope to continue your studies here," Bertrand said as Thomas' tale drew to a close.

"My colleagues at Oxford —"

Bertrand nodded. Thomas had spent two of the past five years teaching as a Master at one of the Oxford colleges.

"— spoke of nothing else but the wonders of your library. Some say," and Thomas spread his hands almost apologetically, as if he did not truly believe what some had said, "that Saint Angelo's library is more extensive than that administered by the clergy of Saint Peter's itself."

"Nevertheless, you are here, Brother Thomas. You must have believed *some* of what you had heard." Bertrand shifted slightly on the hard bed. His hips and shoulders ached in the chill air of his cell, and he berated himself for wishing this young man would leave so he could crawl beneath the blanket.

"But it is true," Bertrand continued. "We do have a fine library. For many generations our friary has been well funded by successive popes —" Bertrand did not explain why, and Thomas did not ask, "— and much of this benevolent patronage has been put to building one of the finest libraries in Rome and, I dare say, within Christendom itself. You are welcome, Brother Thomas, to use our facilities as you wish."

Thomas bowed his head again, and smiled. "You are weary, Brother Prior, and I have taken up too much of your time. Perhaps we can talk again in the morning?"

Bertrand nodded. "We break our fast after Prime prayers, Brother Thomas. You may speak with me then. Do you wish Daniel to show you your cell now?"

"I thank you," Thomas said, "but Daniel has already pointed out its location to me, and there is something else I wish to do before I retire."

"Yes?"

Thomas took a deep breath, and from the expression on his face Bertrand suddenly realised that it *was* piety that had impelled Thomas to take holy orders.

"I would pray before the altar of Saint Peter's, Brother Prior. To prostrate myself to God's will before the bones of the great Apostle has always been one of my dearest desires."

"Then for the Virgin's sake, brother, let Arno see to your feet before you go. I'll not have the pope say that it was one of my brothers who left blood smeared all over the sacred floor of Saint Peter's!"

After the celebrations of the day, Rome had darkened and quieted, and the streets were deserted. Thomas walked from the friary over the bridge crossing the Tiber — more comfortably now that Arno had daubed herbs on his ice-bitten feet, and wrapped them in thick, soft bandages inside his sandals — then halted on the far side, staring at the huge rounded shape of the Castel St Angelo from which the friary took its name. Thomas had heard that it was once the tomb of one of the great pagan Roman emperors, but the archangel Michael had appeared one day on its roof and from then on the monument had been converted to a more holy and Christian purpose: a fort, guarding the entrance to the domain of the popes in Rome, the Leonine City.

Thomas turned his head and stared west towards St Peter's Basilica built into the hill of the Leonine City, and surrounded by lesser buildings and palaces housing, once again, the papal curia and the person of the Holy Father himself. Lights glinted in many of the windows in the papal palace, but even the excitement of a once-again resident pope could not diminish Thomas' wonder at seeing the great structure of St Peter's Basilica rising into the night.

Thomas' eyes flickered once more to the Castel St Angelo. Legend had it that a long-dead pope had caused a tunnel to be built from the papal palace next to St Peter's into the basements of the fort; an escape route into a well-fortified hidey-hole, should the Roman mobs ever get too unruly. Given the widespread reputation of the Romans for spontaneous and catastrophic violence, Thomas wondered if the first chore Gregory had undertaken once ensconced in his apartments was to personally dust away the spider webs and rats' nests from the tunnel entrance.

Thomas grinned at the thought, then automatically — and silently — castigated himself for such irreverence. He looked at the gate in the wall of the Leonine City. It was closed, but several guards were on duty, and Thomas hoped they'd let him through.

They did. A single Dominican could harm no one, and Thomas' obvious piety and insistence that he be allowed to pray before St Peter's shrine impressed them as much as it had Bertrand.

The pressing of a coin into each of their hands dispelled any lingering doubts.

Beyond the gate Thomas walked slowly up the street leading to St Peter's.

The Basilica was massive. Since the Emperor Constantine had first erected the Basilica in the fourth century, it had been added to, renovated, restored and enlarged, but it was still one of the most sacred sites for any Christian: the monument erected over the tomb of St Peter, first among Christ's Apostles. Here pilgrims flocked in their tens of thousands every year. Here the penitent begged for their salvation. Here kings and emperors crawled on hands and knees begging forgiveness for their sins.

Here was the heart of functional Christendom now that Jerusalem was lost to the infidels.

Thomas faltered to a halt some hundred paces from the atrium leading to the Basilica, and his eyes filled with tears. For so long he had wanted to worship at St Peter's shrine. Initially as a child, having watched his beloved parents die from the corruption of a return of the great pestilence; through all the years of his youth — years wasted in blasphemy and anger — and finally, to this man grown into the realisation that his life must be dedicated to God and furthering God's mission here on earth.

It had been a long, difficult, fraught journey, but here he was at last.

At last.

Thomas resumed his slow walk towards the Basilica. At the end of the street thirty-five wide steps rose towards a marble platform before an irregular huddle of buildings: several huge archways, a tower, and tall brick apartments with colonnaded balconies. These buildings formed a wall to either side of the entrance archways into the vast court that served as the atrium of St Peter's.

After an instant's hesitation, Thomas climbed the steps and crossed the platform. Immediately before him were the three archways, the paved atrium stretching beyond them.

Normally, Thomas knew, it would have been full of stalls

and traders selling pilgrim badges, relics, genuine holy water, splinters from the true cross and threads from Christ's robe, but tonight the stalls were empty, their canvas roofs flapping in the breeze. For this day, at least, the pope had ordered the Leonine City emptied of traders, street merchants and hawkers.

The court was even empty of pilgrims, and Thomas' spirits rose. He would have St Peter's to himself.

As he approached the entrance into the Basilica he prayed that the pope had retired to his private apartments.

Thomas did not want to share St Peter's shrine even with the Holy Father himself.

His heart thudding, Thomas entered the building.

It was massive, but what caught Thomas' eye was its layout, used as he was to western churches constructed in the form of a cross. Constantine had built the Basilica in a roughly rectangular form, modelling it on the Roman halls of justice. The very eastern wall, where stood the altar over St Peter's tomb, was rounded, but the rest of the Basilica was laid out as an immense hall with four rows of columns supporting the soaring timber roof and dividing the interior into a nave with two aisles to each side.

For long minutes Thomas could not move. His lips moved slowly in prayer, but his mind could not concentrate on the words. His eyes, round and wondrous, roamed the length and height of the Basilica, stopping now and then at a particularly colourful banner or screen, or lingering on the statue of a beloved saint.

Finally, he stared at the altar at the western end of the nave. Even from this distance he could see the exotic twisted columns guarding the altar, covered with a canopy hanging from four of the columns.

Thomas raised a hand, crossed himself, then slowly, and with the utmost reverence, walked down the length of the nave towards the altar. There were a few worshippers within the Basilica kneeling before some of the side shrines, and barely visible in the flickering light of the oil lamps, but there was no one before the altar itself.

Tears slipped down Thomas' cheeks, and his hand grasped the small cross he wore suspended from his neck.

He had walked all his life towards this moment, and he could now hardly believe such was the munificence of God's Grace that he was finally here.

Again Thomas' steps faltered as he reached the altar. He knew that to one side steps led down into a chamber from where he could view through a grille the actual tomb of St Peter, but for now all Thomas wanted to do, all he could do, was to prostrate himself before the altar.

He slumped to his knees, his eyes still raised to the altar, then he dropped his head and hands, and lowered himself until he lay prostrate in a cruciform position before the altar.

It was cold and horribly uncomfortable, but Thomas was filled with such zeal he did not notice.

Holy St Peter, he prayed silently over and over, grant me your humbleness and courage, let my footsteps be guided by yours, let my life be as worthy as yours, let me be of true service to sweet Jesus Christ as you were, let me ignore hunger and pain as you did, let me immerse myself in the true wonder and joy of God. Holy St Peter ...

Hours passed unnoticed, and the Basilica emptied of all save the friar stretched before the altar. Thomas' muscles grew stiff with the cold and the fervour of his thoughts, but he did not notice his discomfort. All Thomas wanted was to be granted St Peter's grace, to be accepted to serve —

Thomas.

Thomas was lost in prayer. He did not hear.

Thomas.

One of Thomas' outstretched fingers twitched slightly, otherwise he showed no outward sign of hearing.

Now the voice grew more insistent, more terrible.

Thomas!

Thomas' entire body jerked, and he rolled onto his back, his eyes blinking in surprise and disorientation.

Thomas!

He jerked again, and rose on one elbow, staring down the nave of the Basilica.

Perhaps a third of the way down, on the left wall of the Basilica, a golden light exuded from one of the side shrines.

Thomas!

Thomas scrambled about until he was on his hands and feet. He lowered his face to the stone floor. "Lord!"

Thomas, come speak with me.

Shaking with fear and wonder, Thomas inched his way across the floor, his breath harsh in his throat, his eyes wide and staring at the stones before him.

Thomas ...

Thomas crept to the entrance of the shrine, daring a quick look.

The shrine consisted merely of a niche in the wall, large enough only for a statue of an angel, arms and wings outstretched.

Thomas supposed that the statue was of some alabaster stone, but now it glowed with a brilliance that made his eyes ache. The face of the statue was terrible, full of cruel righteousness and the power of the Lord.

Thomas averted his eyes in dread.

"Lord!" he said again.

No Thomas. Not the Lord our God, but His servant, Michael.

The archangel Michael ...

"Blessed saint," Thomas whispered, his fingers clawing forward very slightly on the floor.

Blessed Thomas, said the archangel, and Thomas felt a brief warmth on the top of his bowed head, as if the angel had laid his hand there in benediction.

Thomas began to cry.

Do not weep, Thomas, but hark to what I say. There are few men or women these days who can be called of brave heart and true soul. You are one of them.

"I would give my life to serve, blessed Saint Michael!"

I do not think you shall have to go that far, Thomas, for you are of the Beloved.

Of the beloved?

"Blessed saint, I am a poor man with a great sin on my soul. There was a woman who I —"

Think you I know not every deed of your life? Think you that I cannot see into every corner of your soul? The woman used you. She was a whore. What you did was right and caused a great rejoicing among my brethren.

A great weight fell from Thomas' mind. For so long he had laboured under the burden of his sin ... and now to hear from St Michael that it was no sin at all ...

"I thank you," he whispered. He had been right to do as he had. Alice was indeed a whore, for she had betrayed her husband to sate her lustful cravings.

All women are vile. Their flesh leads to temptations. Never forget that it was a woman who betrayed Adam.

"I will never forget it, blessed saint."

You have passed the first test, Thomas. Now comes one much greater.

"Saint Michael?"

Evil roams among your brethren, Thomas.

Thomas shuddered. "Among the fellows of my holy order, Saint Michael?"

It well may, but I speak of the wider community of mankind. For many years now evil incarnate in the form of Satan's imps have walked unhindered, wreaking havoc and despair. The world is altering, Thomas, and turning away from God. You are Beloved of both the Lord God and my brethren, and it is you who shall head His army of righteous anger.

Thomas felt all the disparate elements of his life fall into place. When he'd been closest to despair, unable to see the meaning and course of his life, the Lord had all the while been guiding and training him. He'd thought his life before entering the Order worthless and empty. Now Thomas knew differently.

Exultation filled his soul. He was to be a soldier of Christ ... and the enemy was evil.

"What should I do? I am yours, blessed saint, mind and body and soul!"

Study. Pray. Grow in understanding. In time, and only when the time is right, I will return to give you further guidance.

"But —"

Thomas got no further. Suddenly the glow and warmth was gone, and Thomas found himself alone in St Peter's Basilica before a lifeless statue, its face once more cold and impassive.

He struggled into a sitting position, tears still streaming down his cheeks, his hands clasped before him, staring at the statue of St Michael.

"I am yours!" he whispered. "Yours!"

Aye, came the faintest of whispers, as if from the summit of heaven itself. *You are one of ours indeed.*

II

The Saturday within the Octave of the Annunciation
In the fifty-first year of the reign of Edward III
(27th March 1378)

Thomas told no one of his experience in St Peter's. If Satan's imps — demons — roamed among mankind, then who knew which among his brother friars worked for God, and which for evil? So Thomas remained silent, sinking deeper into his devotions and burying himself in his studies within the library of St Angelo's friary. Here were the ancient books and manuscripts that might cast some light on what the archangel had revealed to him. Here might lie the key to how he could aid the Lord.

He watched and listened, and learned what he could.

His feet healed, and his hands, and somehow that disappointed Thomas, for he would have liked a lingering ache or a stiffness in his joints to remind him of his duty to God, and also, now, to St Michael.

In the year following his ecstatic vision, the archangel did not appear to Thomas again. Thomas was not overly concerned. He knew that the Lord and his captains, the angels, would again approach him when the time was right.

In the meantime, Thomas did all he could to ensure he would be strong and devout enough to serve.

Prior Bertrand observed his new arrival with some concern. He had been instructed by Father Richard Thorseby, the Prior General of the Dominican Order in England, to keep close watch on Brother Thomas Neville. Thorseby, a stern disciplinarian, did not entirely trust Thomas' motives in joining the Order, and doubted his true piety.

Whatever Thomas' motives for joining the Order — and Bertrand agreed with Thorseby that they were dreadful enough for Thomas' fitness for the Order to be suspect — Bertrand could not fault Thomas' piety. The man appeared obsessed with the need to prove himself before God. Every friar was expected to appear in chapel for each of the seven hours of prayer during the day, beginning with Matins in the cold hours before dawn, and ending late at night with Compline. But the Dominican Order, while encouraging piety, also encouraged its members to spend as much (if not more) time studying as praying, and turned a blind eye if a brother skipped two or three of the hours of prayer each day. Dominicans were devoted to God, but they expressed this devotion by turning themselves into teachers and preachers who would combat heresy — deviation in faith — wherever it appeared.

But Thomas never missed prayers. Not only did he observe each prayer hour, he was first in the chapel and last to leave. Sometimes, on arriving for Matins, Bertrand found Thomas stretched out before the altar in the chapel. Bertrand assumed he had been there all night praying for ... well, for whatever it was he needed.

At weekly theological debates held between the brothers of St Angelo's, sometimes including members of other friaries and colleges within Rome, Thomas was always the most vocal and the most passionate in his views. After the debates had officially ended, when other brothers were engaged in relaxing talk and gossip, or wandering the cloisters enjoying the warmth of the sun and the scent of the herbs that bounded the cloister walks, Thomas would seek out those who had opposed his ideas and beliefs and continue the debate for as long as his prey was disposed to stand there and be berated.

Bertrand admitted to himself that he was frightened by Thomas. There was something about the man which made him deeply uneasy.

On occasions, Thomas reminded him of Wynkyn de Worde. That Bertrand did not like. He had fought long and hard to forget Wynkyn de Worde. The man — as sternly pious as Thomas — had frightened Bertrand even more than Thomas (although in his darker moments Bertrand wondered if Thomas would eventually prove even more disagreeable than Wynkyn).

In the years following the great pestilence (and the Lord be praised that it *had* passed!), Bertrand had spent the equivalent of many weeks on his knees seeking forgiveness for his deep relief that Wynkyn had never returned from Nuremberg. He'd heard that the brother had reached Nuremberg safely, but had then failed to return from a journey into the forests north of the city.

Brother Guillaume, now the prior of the Nuremberg friary, had reported to Bertrand that Wynkyn had been consumed with the pestilence when he'd left, and Bertrand could only suppose the man had died forgotten and unshriven on a lonely road somewhere.

No doubt he'd given the pestilence to whatever unlucky wolves had tried to gnaw his bones.

Bertrand spent *many* hours on his knees seeking forgiveness for his uncharitable thoughts regarding Wynkyn de Worde.

He did not know what had happened to Wynkyn's book and, frankly, Bertrand did not care overmuch. Guillaume had not mentioned it, and Bertrand did not inquire. It was not within his friary's walls, and that was all that mattered.

So Bertrand continued to watch Thomas, and to send the Prior General in England regular reports.

He supposed they did not ease Thorseby's mind, and Bertrand did occasionally wonder what would happen to Thomas once the man journeyed back to Oxford to resume a position of Master.

Piety was all very well, but not when taken to obsessive extremes.

Outside the friary, the Romans continued to rejoice in the presence of the pope. Gregory showed no sign of wanting to remove the papal court and curia back to Avignon, and people again were able to attend papal mass within St Peter's Basilica. Every Sunday and Holy Day citizens packed the great nave of the Basilica, their eyes shining with devotion, their hands clutching precious relics and charms. On ordinary days the same citizens packed the atrium of St Peter's, as they did the streets leading to the Basilica, selling badges and holy keepsakes to the pilgrims who flooded Rome. The presence of the pope not only sated the Romans' deep piety, it also filled their purses. Gregory was in his mid-fifties, but appeared hale, and could be expected to live another decade or more. The Romans were ecstatic

The papacy appeared to be once again safely ensconced in Rome, and many a Roman street worker, walker or sweeper could be seen making the occasional obscene gesture in the general direction of France. At night, the Roman people filled their taverns with triumphant talk about the French King John's dilemma. When Gregory had removed himself and his retinue from Avignon, John had lost his influence over the most powerful institution in Europe. Rumour said John was rabid with fury, and plotted constantly to regain his influence over the papacy. Everyone in Rome was aware Gregory had "escaped" back to Rome at a critical juncture in John's war with the English king, Edward III; the French king needed every diplomatic tool in his possession to raise the funds and manpower to repel Edward's inevitable re-invasion of France.

The Roman mob didn't give a whore's tit about the French king's plight — nor the English king's, for that matter. They had their pope back, Rome was once more the heart of Christendom (with all the financial benefits that carried), and they damn well weren't going to let any French prick steal their pope again.

Most of the French cardinals — and they were the vast majority within the College of Cardinals — were vastly irritated by Gregory's apparent desire to remain in Rome (just as they were vastly irritated by, and terrified of, the Roman mob). Beneath the pope, the cardinals were the most powerful men in the Church, and thus in Christendom. They lived and acted as princes, but to ensure their continuing power they had to remain within the papal court at the side of the pope. Thus they were effectively trapped in Rome, although most of them tried to spend as many months of each year back in the civilised pleasures of Avignon as they could.

When in Rome, the cardinals spent hours carefully watching the pope. Was his face tinged just with the merest touch of grey at yesterday's mass? Did his fingers tremble, just slightly, when he carved his meat at the banquet held in honour of the Holy Roman Emperor's son? And how much of his food did he eat, anyway? They bribed the papal physician to learn details of the papal bowel movements and the particular stink of his urine. They frightened the papal chamberlain with threats of eternal damnation to learn if the pope's sheets were stained with effluent in the mornings and, if so, what kind of effluent?

They spent their hours watching the pope's health most carefully ... and most carefully plotting. When the pope succumbed to his inevitable mortality (and, praise be to God, let it be soon!), the cardinals would elect his successor from among their number.

And when that came to pass, they swore on Christ's holy foreskin, they would elect a man who would return them to Avignon and the comforts of glorious French civilisation.

Thomas spent most of his time — when not at prayers — within the library of St Angelo's, as St Michael had instructed. The library was a large stone-vaulted chamber under the chapel; it was cold every day of the year, even during the hot humid Roman summers, but its position and construction meant it was safe from both intruders and fire, and in volatile Rome that was a precious luxury.

Here the records were kept of the Dominican friary stretching back over one hundred years, and before that the records of the Benedictine order that had inhabited the building. The records were kept on great vellum rolls stacked in neat order on racks lining many of the walls.

Desks and shelves stood against the other walls, and in rows across the floor of the chamber. Here sat the several hundred precious books the friary owned: laboriously copied out by hand, the books were wonders of art and of the intellect. Some dated back five hundred years, others were only freshly copied, all were priceless and beloved. They were heavy volumes, an arm's length in height, and half that across and in depth, and not one of them ever left the chest-level shelf or desk that was its particular home. Instead, the reader travelled to each book in turn, moving slowly around the library over the months and years, from desk to desk, and shelf to shelf, carrying with him his own stool, candle (encased in a brass and glass case, lest the dripping wax should fall on the delicate pages being studied) and parchment and pen and ink for when he wished to copy down some particularly illuminating phrase.

Not all brothers were there to read and study. Some three or four were permanently engaged in recopying particularly fragile volumes, or volumes on loan from other friaries and monasteries within Rome or sometimes from further afield within northern Italy. They worked under the one large window in the library, their ink- and paint-stained hands carefully scratching across the ivory blankness of pages, creating works of art with their capital letters and the illustrations of daily life and devotion they placed in the margins of the pages.

Despite the coldness of the stone vault, and despite the presence of a fireplace, no fire ever burned there. The fear of a conflagration, combined with the lesser fear of the daily damage wrought by an overly smoky fire, meant the grate was never laid, and the fire never lit.

Brothers worked wrapped in blankets and their desire to learn.

The activities of the brothers who worked within the library, whether studying or copying, were supervised by an aged brother librarian who had, nonetheless, a keen vision that could spot the dripping pen or candle, or the careless elbow left to rub across a page, from a distance of twenty paces. His hiss of retribution could carry *thirty* paces, and brothers were known to have fallen off their stools in fright if they believed they'd earned the librarian's displeasure.

Not so Thomas.

Thomas worked alone in every sense of that word. He did not speak to any of the other brothers, and he did not appear to notice the constant oppressive presence of the brother librarian.

On the other hand, the librarian had no need to bother Thomas. The man was as rigidly particular about his treatment of the books and records he studied as he was about the attending of his prayers.

Thomas existed within his own shell of piety and obsessiveness, and few people within the friary, or without it for that matter, could penetrate that shell.

Most left him well enough alone.

On the afternoon of the Saturday following the Annunciation, Thomas was, for once, working alone in the library. Most of the other brothers — wide-eyed with curiosity — had accepted an invitation from a neighbouring monastery to view their new statue of St Uncumber, a saint widely worshipped as one who could rid women of their obnoxious husbands. Thomas had not gone. He considered St Uncumber a saint of dubious merits, and believed that marriage was a sanctified union that no woman should seek to dissolve ... by whatever saintly intervention. So Thomas, wrapped in righteousness, stayed behind to continue his studies.

Even the brother librarian had gone. Thomas was, after all, utterly trustworthy when it came to the safety of the manuscripts and records.

In the past weeks Thomas had begun a detailed study of

the records of St Angelo's friary. He had been turning over in his mind the archangel's warning that evil walked unhindered among mankind, and he wondered if perhaps evil had infected some of the brothers within the friary. If so, Thomas hoped that the friary records would cast light on how and when evil had penetrated his fellow brothers. Already Thomas suspected several of his fellows: they were too jovial in refectory, perhaps, or skipped too many prayers, or spoke too wantonly at St Angelo's weekly debates.

Thomas had just unrolled the records for the year 1334 when Daniel, the friary's only novice, burst in the door.

The boy cast his eyes about, obviously looking for someone, but when he realised that the someone consisted only of Thomas, he edged back towards the door.

Too late. The commotion of his entrance had attracted Thomas' attention.

"Daniel! What mean you, creating such noise and distraction within the walls of God's house?"

Daniel's mouth opened and closed uselessly, and he looked frantically for rescue.

There was none.

Thomas left his desk and advanced close enough to grab the boy by the arm. "Well?"

Daniel's eyes were full of tears, but they had been there long before he had burst into the library.

"Brother Thomas ... Brother Thomas ..."

"*Well?*"

Daniel swallowed again. "Brother Thomas. The Holy Father ... the Holy Father ..."

"*What is it, boy?*"

"The Holy Father is dead!"

Thomas' face blanched, but, even though Daniel struggled a little, he did not let the boy go.

"Dead?" Thomas whispered, then he stared narrow-eyed at Daniel. "How do you know this? How can you be sure?"

"The Brother Prior had sent me with messages to the Secretary of the Curia within the Leonine City, Brother.

While I was with him, a Benedictine burst into the chamber and blurted out the news. Then both the secretary and the Benedictine rushed out, forgetting about me. I didn't know what to do, so I ran down to the gates to tell Prior Bertrand. Where is he?"

Thomas ignored Daniel's question, thinking fast. "They let you out the gates of the Leonine City?"

"Yes, although they slammed shut a moment or two after I'd run through. Where is Prior Bertrand, Brother? I *must* tell him!"

"No," Thomas murmured, still thinking. *What were the cardinals up to?* Whether the pope had met a natural or unnatural death was now immaterial. But what the cardinals did would carry the fate of Christendom.

Were they even now meeting in conclave to elect a new and French-loyal pope? Like the Romans, but for different reasons, Thomas despised the French.

Daniel wriggled in Thomas' grip. "Brother. I *must* find Prior Bertrand!"

"No. Prior Bertrand can do nothing — but you and I can."

"Brother?"

"Daniel, the cardinals are even now likely to be meeting to elect another pope, one who will remove the papacy back to Avignon. They have shut the gates of the Leonine City so no word of Gregory's death can reach the ears of the Roman mob. By the time the people discover the death, a new pope will have been installed, and the Romans will not be able to save their papacy."

"But —"

"Daniel. Be as quick as you can — run to the lower marketplace and spread the word that Gregory is dead and that even now the cardinals seek to meet in secret. Do it! *Now!*"

"But —"

"Damn you, boy! Where are your wits? The only means to ensure the cardinals do not deliver the papacy into the French king's hands again is the street mob. Now, run! *Now!*"

He let Daniel go, and the boy dashed out the door.

Thomas was directly behind him, urging him forward. Once they'd reached the street, Thomas paused only long enough to make sure that the boy was heading in the direction of the lower market before he ran, robes bunched about his knees, in the direction of the main market square.

"The pope has died! The pope has died!" he yelled whenever he came across a clump of people.

By the time Thomas reached the main square the news had been shouted ahead of him, and the square was already in furious turmoil.

The people of Rome needed no one to point out to them the implications of an immediate and secret papal election.

Within the half hour a mob ten thousand strong, and growing with each minute, besieged the gates of the Leonine City.

The guards, in dread of their lives, wasted no time in opening the gates.

The cardinals, already gathering in the Hall of Conclave, were not quick enough. Before they had even sat to cast their votes, the mob surged in the doors.

Faced with their imminent murder, the cardinals wisely agreed to defer the election until the saintly corpse of Gregory XI had been interred.

The mob, still surly, gradually dissipated once they were sure the cardinals truly meant what they had said.

Rome settled into an uneasy quiet until the conclave due in two weeks' time. As far as the Romans were concerned, the cardinals either elected a good Italian onto the papal throne . . . or they died.

III

The Octave of the Annunciation
In the fifty-first year of the reign of Edward III
(Thursday 1st April 1378)

Rome waited uneasily for the election of the new pope. The Romans remained restive and distrustful: when they had left the Leonine City on the day of Gregory's death they'd dismantled the gates and carried them away.

No cursed French cardinal was going to lock them out again.

Constantly shifting, murmuring groups of people — peasants in from the surrounding countryside, street traders, prostitutes, foreign pilgrims, elders, out of work mercenaries, lovers, thieves, wives, clerks, washerwomen, schoolmasters and their students — drifted through the precincts of St Peter's.

The threat wasn't even implied. The mob shouted it periodically through the windows of the buildings adjoining St Peter's: *elect a Roman pope, a good Italian, or we'll storm the buildings and kill you.*

The cardinals had caused a block and headsman's axe to be placed in St Peter's itself, a clear response to the mob: *attack us and we'll destroy you.*

There was even a rumour that the cardinals had shifted the treasures of the papal apartments, and of St Peter's itself, to fortified vaults in the Castel St Angelo. Certainly St Peter's glittered with less gold and jewels than it once had.

Rome waited uneasily, the cardinals plotted defiantly, and Gregory's corpse lay stinking before the shrine of St Peter.

Thomas, waiting as anxiously as anyone else, kept himself busy in the library of St Angelo's friary. Gregory's funeral mass would be held in a few days, and a few more days after that the cardinals would meet to elect their new master. Thomas imagined late at night when he lay unsleeping on his hard bunk in his cell, that he could hear the clatter of gold and silver coins being passed from hand to hand atop the Vatican hill where sprawled the Leonine City. The noise of the cardinals passing and accepting bribes, the normal procedure before the election of a pope. He even imagined he could hear the fevered rattle of horses' hooves racing through the night, bearing ambassadors from the kings and emperors of Europe, who themselves bore in tight fists a variety of carefully couched threats and intimidations to ensure that their particular master's man was elected to the Holy Throne.

A bad business indeed, Thomas thought. *The higher clergy should be shining examples of piety and morality to the rest of Christendom. Instead the cardinals had opened their souls to corruption.*

Evil?

Were the cardinals the enemy against whom he would lead the soldiers of Christ?

Thomas tossed and turned, but until the papal election — or until the blessed archangel Michael revealed more — there was nothing to do but wait, and listen, and watch.

And, during those daylight hours not spent in prayer, study the registers of St Angelo's.

St Angelo's had for generations been the centre of the Dominican effort to train the masters and teachers of the growing European universities, and this mission (the reason Thomas himself had been sent to the friary) was reflected in the registers. Thomas found himself curious as he saw the names of now-aged masters he'd studied under at Oxford, and the names of masters famed for their learning who currently taught, or had taught, at the universities of Paris, Bologna, Ferrara and Padua. They had all come to St Angelo's, and Thomas traced their comings and goings: their arrival at the friary as young men, their long years spent moving from cell to chapel, to refectory, to library, to chapel and then back to cell again.

Thomas smiled to himself as his finger carefully traced over the black spidery writing in the registers. He could hear their footsteps as they trod the same corridors he trod every day. He could feel their excitement as they pored over the same books he did, and at night he imagined that he lay in the same cell that some learned and pious Master of Paris or Bologna or Oxford had once reposed in many years previously.

The records showed nothing but the same continuous, comforting pattern of piety and learning, and Thomas thought that was as all Christendom should be. Never changing, but keeping to the ancient and tested ways, the comforting rituals, all under the careful guardianship of the Church, the custodian and interpreter of the word of God.

Only thus could evil be kept at bay.

On this cold April day Thomas came back to the library after Vespers to continue his study until the bells rang for Compline. Few other brothers had come back: the library was too cold this late in the evening.

But Thomas was drawn back, not only by his need to continue his study, but by a compulsion he couldn't name.

There was something in the registers he needed to read. He *knew* it. St Michael had not actually appeared and told him so, but Thomas knew the archangel was guiding his interest.

Thomas had been reading the registers for the 1330s, and, as he pored over the unwieldy parchment rolls under his sputtering lamp, he suddenly realised what had been making him uncomfortable for the past few days.

There was an inconsistency within the registers.

St Angelo's brothers moved through the registers in regular patterns: arriving at the friary, staying months or sometimes years to study, and then departing. During their time at the friary their daily routines never varied: prayers, meals, study.

But there was one friar who did not fit the pattern at all. His name ran through the records like a nagging toothache; he was a part of St Angelo's community, but an unsettling part. For months he would move through the registers as other friars did, not varying his routine from theirs in the slightest manner — although, Thomas noted, he took no part in the weekly debates.

Then, twice a year, he would vanish from the registers for some eight weeks, before his name reappeared within the comfortable routine.

There was no explanation for his absences, and these continuing absences were abnormal. Friars came to St Angelo's, they stayed awhile, then they left. They didn't keep coming and going in such a fashion. If they had business elsewhere, then they travelled to that elsewhere and stayed there. They did not spend years using St Angelo's as some tavern in which to bide their time until they needed to return to their true business.

The first year that Thomas had encountered the friar's unexplained comings and goings he had simply assumed that the friar had some pressing business to attend to in another friary — something that had reluctantly pulled him away. But then the same pattern was repeated the next year, and then the next, and continued in the years after. The friar's departures and returns were consistent: he left the friary in late May of each year and returned in late July, then he left again in early December and returned by the end of January.

Why?

Further, there was another inconsistency. If a friar *did* have to leave the friary, for whatever matter, then he had to seek permission from the prior, and that permission, as the reason for the absence, was recorded. During the 1330s three other brothers had left briefly, and the reasons, along with the prior's permission, had been recorded in the registers.

Not so for this man.

Troubled, Thomas checked back through the records for the 1320s, trying to find when the friar had first arrived ... to his amazement and increasing unease, Thomas discovered that the friar had been moving in and out of St Angelo's all through the 1320s.

All without apparent permission, and always twice each year at the same time.

In late 1327 the incumbent prior had died, and when, five months after the new prior had been elected, this troubling friar had again departed without explanation, there was a record that the new prior had requested an interview with the friar on his return, no doubt to demand an explanation.

And there, at Lammas in 1328, was the record showing the interview had taken place on the friar's return. The only comment on the outcome of this interview was, to Thomas' mind, an outrageous statement that the friar was to be allowed to come and go as he pleased.

No friar came and went as he pleased! His individual interests were always subordinated to those of the Order.

Thomas checked back yet further, scattering rolls of parchment about in such a haphazard manner that, had the brother librarian been present, Thomas surely would have earned an angry hiss.

The friar had arrived at St Angelo's in late 1295.

Scattering more rolls, Thomas searched forward until he found the last reference to the friar.

1348. The man had presumably died in the pestilence which had swept Christendom that year.

Thomas sat back, thinking over what he'd learned.

For some fifty-three years this friar had come and gone from St Angelo's twice yearly with no explanation and no permission from his prior.

During those fifty-three years five priors had died, and each incoming prior — the last being Prior Bertrand in 1345 — had called the friar into their private cell to ask for explanations and, presumably, to mete out discipline.

In all five cases the results of the interview were much the same: the friar was to be allowed to come and go as he pleased, no matter the inconvenience to the friary.

Thomas wondered what threats had been made in those five meetings.

Eventually, after carefully rolling up the parchments and placing them back in their slots, Thomas went to see Prior Bertrand.

He felt both curious and nauseous in equal degrees, and Thomas knew that he'd stumbled upon something of great import.

Prior Bertrand was again sinking down to his knees before the cross in his cell when the tap sounded at the door.

Sighing, Bertrand rose stiffly, one hand on his bed for support. "Come."

Brother Thomas entered, bowing slightly as he caught Bertrand's eye.

"Brother Thomas, what can I do for you this late at night?"

"I have come to ask a favour of you, Brother Prior."

"Yes?"

"I would like to ask about Brother Wynkyn de Worde."

Bertrand stared, unable for the moment to act or speak.

Wynkyn de Worde! He'd prayed never to have that name spoken in his hearing again!

In return, Thomas watched the old man before him with narrowed, speculative eyes.

"Brother Prior? Are you well?"

"Yes ... yes. Ah, Brother Thomas, perhaps you will sit down."

Thomas took the stool, as he had on the night of his arrival, and Bertrand again took the bed. "May I ask, Brother Thomas, why you ask about Brother Wynkyn?"

Thomas hesitated and Bertrand shifted uncomfortably.

"I have been reading through Saint Angelo's registers, Brother Prior, and it appears to me that Brother Wynkyn must have been a considerably disruptive influence to the peace of the friary. I am curious as to why the brother was allowed to continue such behaviour for over fifty years without a single act of discipline from the prior. I —"

"Are you here to examine me, Brother Thomas?"

"Of course not, Brother Prior, but —"

"Are you here to demand explanations of me, Brother Thomas?"

"No! I merely wished to —"

"Do you think that I exist to satisfy your every curiosity, Brother Thomas?"

"Brother Prior, I apologise if I —"

"Your tone carries no nuance of apology or regret, Brother Thomas. I am deeply shocked that you think you have a right to *demand* explanations! Brother Thomas, you are no longer the man you once were! How *dare* you bludgeon your way into my —"

"I did not *bludgeon*!"

"— private devotions to order me to satisfy your curiosity."

"It is not curiosity, Brother Prior," Thomas was now leaning forward on his stool, his eyes angry, "but a desire to understand why such an extraordinary breach of discipline was allowed for so long!"

Bertrand paused. "I think Prior General Thorseby was right to be concerned about you, Thomas. Perhaps you are not suited to the rigorous discipline of the Order after all."

Thomas sat back, shocked and bitter at the threat. About to speak a furious retort, he suddenly caught himself, and bowed his head in contrition.

"I apologise deeply, Brother Prior. My behaviour has been unpardonable. I do beg your forgiveness, and ask of you suitable penance."

Bertrand watched the man carefully. His contrition *did* seem genuine — although it was a trifle hasty — and perhaps it was not surprising that such a man as Thomas should still lapse into the habits of his old life from time to time.

"You must learn more discipline, Brother Thomas."

"Yes, Brother Prior."

"Blessed Gregory's funeral mass is in five days' time. I would that until that day you spend the hours from Prime until Nones in penitential prayer in the chapel. After dinner and until Vespers you will take yourself down to the streets about the marketplace and offer to wash the feet of every whore you can find."

Thomas' head flew back up, his brown eyes once more furious.

Bertrand held his stare.

Thomas finally dropped his gaze. "Forgive me, Brother Prior," he whispered.

"You must learn humility, Brother Thomas."

"I know it, I know it."

"Then learn it!"

Thomas' head and shoulders jerked. "Yes, Brother Prior."

"You will attend Gregory's funeral mass with the rest of our community," the prior continued, "and then you will continue your penance until the day of the conclave."

Thomas stiffened, but did not speak.

"You may leave, Brother Thomas."

Thomas nodded. "Thank you, Brother Prior." He rose, and walked towards the door.

Just as he opened it, Bertrand spoke again. "Brother Thomas?"

Thomas turned back.

"Brother Thomas ... it has been many a year since I spoke of Brother Wynkyn. Now I am an old man, and I should hesitate no longer. Once our new Holy Father is elected, and when you have completed your penance — *and this penance you must complete* — you may seek audience with me, and I will speak to you again. You may go."

Thomas bowed, and closed the door behind him.

Later in the night, when the brothers were in their cells, either sleeping or praying, Bertrand walked quietly down to the library, lifted out all of the friary's records from the

1290s until the time of the pestilence, and carried them one by one up to the deserted kitchens.

There, he threw them on the fire.

He stood and watched until they had burned to ash, then he lifted a poker and stirred the coals about, fearful that a single word should have survived.

Finally, bent and tired, he shuffled back to his own bed.

IV

The hours Thomas spent prone before the altar in chapel were the most blessed he could imagine. The cold of the stone flooring did not perturb him: he did not even notice it. During the set hours of prayer the passing feet of his fellow brothers, as the passing of their eyes, did not bother him: he deserved such humiliation, and he revelled in it. He lay, face pressed against stone, arms extended, and prayed for sweet mercy, for greater humbleness, and for the strength which he would need to be of service to the holy St Michael, messenger of God Himself.

The hours that Thomas spent in the filthy streets of Rome washing the feet of the even filthier whores, were hours spent in hell wiping the stained skin of the Devil's handmaidens.

He dreaded the tolling of the bells for Nones, and the inevitable hand of Prior Bertrand on his shoulder, silently asking him to rise. He would hobble after the prior, wracked with cramps after so many chill hours prone on the chapel floor, praying for God's mercy in order to survive the afternoon.

Today would be his last day of penance: Thomas had

wept when he felt the prior's hand on his shoulder, for he would no longer be allowed to spend so long in silent penitential prayer, but his face had gone as chill and stony as the floor he had recently lain on when he thought of the afternoon's activities before him.

Thomas loathed whores with a vehemence he *knew* he should probably do penance for. To have to bow before them every afternoon and take their outstretched feet between his hands ...

"This will be your last day," Bertrand said unnecessarily as Thomas rose from the refectory table. "Tomorrow the cardinals will meet in conclave ... and the streets will not be safe. Once the election is concluded then I will send for you. You know of what we must speak."

Thomas nodded, and took his leave. He could not think beyond this afternoon, and he wondered if he would be able to bear it.

In the courtyard he lifted a wooden pail and several cloths from a small alcove, then half filled the pail from a large barrel of rainwater standing to one side. He walked to the gate, hesitated, then opened it and walked into the streets of Rome.

If there was one commodity Rome did not lack, it was whores. They catered for pilgrims, traders and the odd diplomat as well as the large number of young men who had yet to take wives. Of course, many husbands numbered among their clientele as well. Some said there were more whores in Rome than wives and, after his previous days in the streets, Thomas did not doubt it.

And, it seemed to him, they all knew he was coming.

The word had quickly spread that a humble friar had been set to do penance washing their feet, and within moments of Thomas leaving the friary there was a crowd of women about him.

Pressing about him.

They rubbed their bodies against Thomas, their hands seeking entrance under his robe. He pushed them roughly away, but they only laughed ... and bared their breasts to him, squeezing them invitingly, and asking if he'd like a taste.

Thomas ignored them.

He walked as far away from the friary as he could, turning two corners, before the crowd became unmanageable, and he stopped.

He lifted his head and looked about him.

It was one of the hardest things he'd ever had to do.

"As penance for my sins," he said softly, "I am to wash the feet of whores until the hour of Vespers. Will one of you step forward, and offer her feet to be washed?"

The women fell silent, as they always did at this point. They were hardened and bitter creatures, used to the abuse and degradation of their profession, and yet this humble friar always rendered them silent with this simple statement.

Not that they had any greater respect for friars than they had for any other men. Too many friars had pushed them up against walls and used them quickly, roughly, for them to think well of any among them.

But this one . . . this one . . .

It was his face, they thought. Not the fact that it was so well made, or so strong, or his eyes so compelling, for they had seen and been used by many handsome clerics in the past.

It was because the set of his muscles and the hardness of his eyes told them he was one of them, in the sense that he was as hard and as bitter as they were.

And this always made them falter.

For a moment.

One stepped forward, young, her face still holding traces of appeal.

"Wash my feet!" she said, and lifted her skirts.

Thomas stepped up and squatted down before her; she giggled nervously as he wrung out a cloth in the water.

Then he held out a hand, his face bowed down, and she lifted a foot and let him take it.

"For a coin I would let you hold a great deal more of my flesh," she said softly, and Thomas whipped up his head and stared at her, his eyes blazing with anger, but at himself, rather than her.

There was a smell about this one, or perhaps it was something in her voice, or the tilt of her cheek, but memories Thomas had long thought forgotten raced out of his past.

Memories from his youth: the laughter and bawdry shared with his two best friends.

The women they had shared, all six sometimes squirming about on the same bed.

The practised moans and squeals from the whores.

Their writhing beneath his body.

Thomas trembled violently, now fighting the rising memory of lust as much as his current anger.

The girl whose foot he still held smiled, and wriggled her hips invitingly. She knew the look in this friar's eyes and had lost any momentary awe she might have had for him.

She leaned forward, her weight on the foot in Thomas' hand, and let the neck of her loose tunic fall away so he could see her firm, pointed breasts.

"I know what you want," she said, watching the direction of his eyes, "and it is yours for the asking."

Thomas raised his eyes to hers, and she felt the pressure on her foot increase slightly.

Her smiled widened. "I want to feel you inside me," she whispered hoarsely, her hips wriggling suggestively. "Now!"

"Slut!"

Thomas' fingers tightened about her foot until she squealed in pain, and then he threw it to one side, twisting her leg badly and causing her to fall heavily in a tangle of swirling skirts.

He scrambled to his feet, ignoring the shouts of the women about him.

Damn all women to the pits of hell!

"Slut!" he spat at her again. "Don't you know your sins will earn you a place in hell for all time? Don't you know that the red-hot pokered Devil himself will take his pleasure with you, time after time through eternity, until you scream and beg for mercy, to no avail? Don't you realise that you and your kind are the slime of Creation? Slime you are and slime you will be, time until end, unless you embrace Christ and beg His forgiveness now. Now! Do you hear me, harlot? Get on your knees and beg Christ's forgiveness now!"

All the whores about him were now screaming and shouting, but the young woman on the ground motioned the other women back with a quick, vicious action, then got to her knees and then to her feet, stumbling a little on her twisted leg.

"I will beg forgiveness from none of your sort, dog!" She spat at him, and Thomas flinched, but made no move to whip the spittle away from his cheek. He was still enraged, and barely holding himself back from taking her neck between his hands and throttling her.

He knew that if he'd had a sword he would have killed her.

"Dog!" she said again, wrenching the top of her tunic closed. "I curse you, Friar Thomas. One day one of my sisters will seize your soul and condemn you to hell for eternity! I damn you with the curse of the whore, Thomas!"

She stepped forward, and struck him with a surprisingly light tap against his cheek.

He raised a hand to strike her back, but stopped, stunned by the lightness of her blow.

"One day," she whispered, her eyes staring into his, "and soon, I pray to the Virgin Mary, a whore will steal your soul ... Nay! You will offer it to her on a platter! You will offer her your eternal damnation in return for her love!"

Now it was Thomas' turn to stand silent, as stunned by the whore as the group had previously been by him.

There had been something in her face and in her voice, in her very bearing, that had rung not only with truth, but with an extraordinary nobility.

The women, still mumbling, started to turn away, two helping their younger companion to hobble down the street.

Thomas watched them go, then shook himself.

Cursed woman!

He grabbed at his pail, lying on its side on the cobbles, and looked back down the street.

Several of the whores, still lingering nearby, turned their backs to him.

Thomas sighed, and rubbed his eyes. What had he been thinking of to let go his self-control so easily? Why had he let his past intrude into his present?

What had he done?

The curse could be disregarded — the simple prating of a wretched woman — but Thomas could not disregard his own actions and words.

He had been a fool. Worse, he had been an arrogant fool. That woman had never wronged him, and her words had only been those of God, testing him.

And Thomas had failed, as he had failed so many times.

Refusing to weep, or show any outward sign of his distress, Thomas collected his rags, hefted the pail, and spent the rest of the afternoon in the almshouse washing the inmates' feet, and speaking to them the words of kindness he should have spoken to the prostitute.

V

Thursday in Passion Week
In the fifty-first year of the reign of Edward III
(8th April 1378)

On the afternoon of 8th April 1378, the feast day of the blessed Callistus, a former pope, and the Thursday within Passion Week, the cardinals met in conclave to elect their new Holy Father before the celebrations of the coming Holy Week.

It was neither a relaxed nor a certain affair.

The cardinals had been appointed by popes who'd lived in Avignon, and all were either Frenchmen themselves — the vast majority — or men closely allied with the French monarchy.

Most, as much as they may have denied it publicly, owed allegiance to the French king before the office of the pope.

What the cardinals *wanted* to do was to elect a man who would remove them from the swamp-ridden and disease-infested ruinous city of Rome back to the culture and civilisation of Avignon.

What they felt *compelled* to do was elect what the murderous Roman mob wanted: a good Italian who would keep the papacy in Rome.

Threats did not sit well with the cardinals. On the other hand, they doubted they could get out of Rome alive if they didn't do what the mob wanted.

It was left to Jean de la Grange, bishop of Amiens, in Rome for the conclave, to suggest a possible way out of the situation. In the days before the conclave, Bishop Grange moved smoothly from chamber to chamber, dropping time after time to his knee to kiss the cardinal's ring held out to his lips, then raising his face to talk earnestly to the man before him.

The cardinals liked what they heard.

Thursday in Passion Week dawned cool and fine, although a yellow fog rising from the swamps beyond Rome's walls lasted until almost Nones when the cardinals were due to meet. Murmuring crowds had thronged the Leonine City since the previous night, sure that if they didn't stake their place well before the election the cardinals would find some way to shut them out. It seemed to the cardinals, peering nervously from their apartments in the palace adjoining St Peter's, that the entire population of Rome was crowded into the streets and the courts surrounding the Basilica.

Their mood was not festive.

The election was to be held in the Hall of Conclave, a great stone hall to the north of St Peter's and adjoining the papal palace. In the hour before Nones, the cardinals moved cautiously through the corridors of the palace towards the hall. They were well guarded with militia, and they wrapped their cardinals' robes tight about themselves and stalked down the corridors, their faces set resolutely to the front, their eyes darting left and right.

The distant murmur of the crowd seemed to swell through the floor beneath their jewelled slippers as much as it did through the window glass.

The cardinals, sixteen in all, filtered into the Hall of Conclave. With luck, the election would not take long. After all, the conclusion had been hammered out in previous days.

Each cardinal moved silently into a curtained-off partition; the voting would take place in seclusion to give the election the aura of secrecy. Within each partition was a chair and a desk. On each desk lay a single sheet of paper and a pen and inkwell.

Each cardinal took his place and, once all were in place and the curtains across each partition closed, a bell tolled from high in the hall's tower.

The election was underway.

Pandemonium broke out.

The crowds outside surged against the stone walls of the hall, beating the walls with their fists, with pikes, clubs, axes, pots and pans, and any other instrument they had found within their homes that they thought might prove to be useful to aid the smooth progression of the election of an Italian to the papal throne.

"Give us an Italian or we'll stick pikes into your well-fed bellies!"

"Give us an Italian or we'll burn the hall down about your ears!"

The cardinals, isolated from each other, as one picked up their pens with shaking hands, dipped them into their inkwells, then hesitated over the sheet of paper.

"Give us an Italian . . ."

Scowls twisted the faces of the cardinals. Damn the unruly mobs! Damn Rome to hell! They'd manage their revenge on this city if it was the last thing they did.

Scowls slowly contorted into thin-lipped grins.

The revenge, as the result of the election, was already planned.

"Give us an Italian!"

Yet still the cardinals hesitated.

Outside, a locksmith, who had been working on the doors leading to the vaults beneath the hall, suddenly yelled in triumph.

The mob surged forward, pikes gripped in white-knuckled hands.

The cardinals slowly leaned towards their papers, their hands shaking as much with hatred of the mob as with fear.

Then, as they still hesitated, they felt the wooden floor beneath their feet shudder, then, horrifically, spears and pikes burst through the floor in eight of the partitions, splintering the floorboards and making seven of the cardinals yell in fright and horror as the weapons narrowly missed their feet.

One of these seven snarled, and, leaping to his feet, shouted through the now broken floorboards, "We'll give you your damned Italian, scum, but you have no idea of what you have done this day!"

Then he yelled throughout the hall: "*Do it!*"

And the cardinals leaned over their papers, each scrawling the same name.

They would see the Romans damned to hell yet!

The mob was almost out of control when the doors of the balcony burst open. A red-robed cardinal strode forth, a paper in his hand.

"Hear this!" he screamed, and the mob growled.

"This day we have elected our most blessed Holy Father —"

The growl deepened.

"The saintly Bartolomo Prignano, Archbishop of Bari, is our new Holy Father, Urban VI!"

The mob quietened, urgent voices whispering throughout its mass. Then a great cheer broke out. "An Italian! An Italian!"

Then the former Archbishop Prignano, the new Urban VI, stepped forward to take the crowd's acclaim. He was a Neopolitan by birth, and enough of an Italian to sate the crowd's anger and suspicion.

He raised his hands, and blessed the crowd, and then Urban said, "The papacy has returned to Rome, beloved countrymen, and it will never leave again! I swear this to you on the name of our beloved Lord, Jesus Christ, and his mother, the Holy Virgin. I swear to you that the papacy will not leave Rome again!"

Behind Urban, five or six of the cardinals shared concerned glances. Wasn't Urban taking his pretence a little too seriously?

VI

Wednesday in Holy Week
In the fifty-first year of the reign of Edward III
(14th April 1378)

Thomas stood against the wall outside the closed door
to Prior Bertrand's cell. His back was straight, his
hands clasped humbly before him, his head bowed.
His back did not touch the stone.

Bertrand had kept him waiting six days since the election
of Urban — claiming the preparations for Easter celebrations
as reason enough — and Thomas was barely keeping under
restraint an impatience that he knew would earn him another
penance if he let it fly.

And that was one thing Thomas did not want. His
previous penance had been more than humiliating, and he
didn't want to see what Bertrand could come up with next.

Since the day the whore had cursed him, Thomas had
spent his time studying, or praying in the chapel and, during
the long dark hours of the night, in his private cell. This
prayer time Thomas spent imploring St Peter for the
patience and humbleness which that saint had so admirably
demonstrated in his struggle to establish Christianity.

Thomas wondered how, if he could not master
humbleness, he could hope to fight the evil that St Michael
told him walked the lands. But he knew that, doubts

notwithstanding, he would have to do his best, so he also prayed to the archangel Michael for guidance, for a sign, for something to show him what to do, how best to fight the evil infiltrating Christendom.

But the archangel had remained silent.

Was it the whore's fault? Thomas tried hard to forgive her, but it was difficult. All his life he'd regarded whores with contempt (although that contempt had never stopped him using them, whispered the voice of his conscience). After his humiliating penance, and the tongue-lashing by the young one, Thomas now loathed whores beyond all measure.

He prayed, but for once that did not bring peace of mind. Suddenly all he could think about was the young girl's breasts, so firm and pointed beneath her tunic. He knew what they would feel like in his hands, and he knew how they would taste under his tongue once he had aroused the sweat of passion in her.

Saint Michael, aid me now! God help me, drive thoughts of this woman from my mind!

Thomas squeezed his eyes shut, his hands now trembling violently as he grasped them tightly together, his body rocking slowly back and forth. He struggled for control, knowing that any moment Bertrand was going to open that door and find Thomas lost in a maddened fit of anger and remembered lust.

Thomas knew he was being watched, knew that the Prior General of England wanted an excuse to throw him from the Order ... and yet still he couldn't bring himself under control ... still he couldn't forget the laughter ... the breasts bared above his head ... still he couldn't forget his humiliation, and his overweening fury ...

"Please ... please, Saint Michael," he whispered between clenched teeth.

Thomas.

Peace flooded Thomas' being, and he almost wept.

Thomas, do not let the thoughts of women control you.

Thomas opened his eyes a fraction. A warm clear light illuminated the dim corridor. He lifted his head slowly.

Five or six feet from him stood a pillar of fire, the form of a man dimly discernible within it. A stern face stared at Thomas from the top of the pillar.

The fire did not sear Thomas, nor did it cause him any fear. He sank to his knees, and clasped his hands in adoration. The archangel had returned.

Women exist only for one reason, Thomas — to bear children. Otherwise they are to be used and discarded with as little thought as the daily sending of excreta on its journey into the cesspool. Use them, but do not let thoughts of them control your life. And never give your soul to one.

"Saint Michael," Thomas whispered. "You are so good to me."

You are a Beloved, Thomas.

"Blessed saint, I have found a name that —"

You have found the name of the man whom you must follow, in body as well as spirit.

"Wynkyn de Worde."

Yes. He worked on behalf of God and His angels until the evil pestilence swallowed him before he could properly accomplish his task.

"And I must take up where he left off?"

You are his successor, although you will grow to be much greater than he.

Thomas' heart swelled with pride. "What must I do?"

Learn all you can about him, learn what he did, and why. Discover what his purpose was, then take that purpose into your own hands. Follow your instincts, for they are the instincts of the angels.

"Can you not tell me what I need to know, blessed angel?"

The archangel's anger seeped across the space towards Thomas.

"Forgive me! I did not think to —"

Learning is nothing unless it is experienced. If I tell you what you need to know then you will not have truly learned. Wynkyn de Worde died before he could train his successor personally, thus the successor, you, had to be bred and must now learn without the aid of the one gone before.

"I will learn, Saint Michael. I give you my oath on it."

You will learn fast, Thomas. Wynkyn de Worde's untimely death was a disaster. For thirty years the minions of Satan have mingled among God's own. Now it is almost too late to prevent the final conflagration.

"Blessed angel, my duties keep me here at the friary. I doubt that —"

The archangel roared, and Thomas cringed in terror.

You work with God's authority! The Church is crippled and useless! Listen only to God's authority, Thomas, not the useless babbling of priests!

"Saint Michael —"

You are God's Beloved, Thomas. You need no other authority than that to work what you must. Already you have allowed Prior Bertrand to deflect you from God's purpose. Do not allow him to do so again.

Thomas began to speak, the questions bubbling to his lips, but the archangel had gone, and Thomas was once more alone in the corridor.

The door opened and there was the sound of a footstep. "Brother Thomas?"

Prior Bertrand.

Thomas unclasped his hands, then slowly rose from his knees and turned to face the prior.

As on the other times Thomas had come to his cell, Bertrand indicated that Thomas should sit on the stool. The prior stood before him, his arms folded and his hands slipped deep into his sleeves.

"Well, Thomas, have you learned humility?"

Thomas, who had been sitting with his own hands folded in his lap and his eyes cast down, now lifted his face.

"I have learned, Prior Bertrand, that I have a greater calling than that which places me under your discipline."

"What?" Truly shocked, Bertrand actually forgot himself enough to rock slightly on his feet.

Thomas held the prior's gaze. "I am Wynkyn de Worde's successor in God's and the angels' eternal fight against evil."

The prior's face completely whitened. "By whose authority?" he whispered.

"By God's authority, and by the authority of the blessed Saint Michael who has blessed me with his presence on several occasions."

Bertrand jerked his eyes away from Thomas, backing up a step or two. He muttered a prayer under his breath, then shook his head frantically as Thomas rose to his feet.

"Tell me what you know of Wynkyn de Worde!" Thomas said.

Bertrand shook his head more vigorously. "No. De Worde is dead. Gone. I do not have to think of him any more."

"Tell me what you know."

"Brother Thomas! You overstep your place! I will not —"

"You *will* tell me," Thomas said in a low voice that was, nevertheless, laced with such venom that Bertrand quivered in fear.

Thomas reached out and seized one of Bertrand's sleeves. The prior flinched, thinking he would be struck, but Thomas only pulled him about and pushed him down on the stool.

"I speak with the archangel Saint Michael's voice," Thomas said. "Tell me what you know of Wynkyn de Worde!"

Bertrand, staring up at Thomas, recognised the power and anger that flooded the man's face. So Wynkyn had also looked when Bertrand had summoned him to an accounting when the prior had first taken his office.

And, as Bertrand had capitulated then, so he capitulated now.

After all, was not St Angelo's dedicated to the archangel St Michael?

Bertrand suddenly understood that he wanted Thomas out of this friary and out of Rome as soon as possible. He was an old, old man, and he'd had enough.

The prior dropped his eyes, and sighed. St Michael's will be done. His face was grey now, rather than pale, and the age-wrinkles in his skin had deepened until they resembled wounds.

"I came to this friary as a young man," Bertrand began,

"perhaps thirty or thirty-two — not much older than you are now — in 1345. I assumed the position of prior, although many, Brother Wynkyn among them, thought me too young for such duties."

Thomas folded his hands and stood straight, regarding Bertrand silently.

Bertrand's mouth twisted, remembering. "Within weeks of my arrival I realised that Brother Wynkyn was ... different. As you have realised, he came and went without asking permission, and he hardly took any part in the life of the friary apart from attending prayers and meals. When he was in the friary he kept to his cell, studying an ancient book he had there."

"Of what was it concerned?"

"I do not know."

"But —"

"Listen, damn you, and keep your questions until I am done!"

Thomas bowed his head.

"Some three weeks after my arrival I summoned Brother Wynkyn to my cell. He sat on this stool and I stood before him. I asked him by what right he ignored his duties within the friary, and by what right he came and went as he pleased.

"He smiled, not a pleasant expression, and he drew a letter from one of his sleeves. 'By this right,' he said, and handed the letter to me."

Bertrand stopped, and he crossed himself with a trembling hand. Thomas remained silent, and waited for Bertrand to continue.

"It was a letter from the holy Boniface of blessed memory —"

Thomas nodded. Boniface had been a great pope until his untimely death in 1303.

"— and it directed the reader to give Brother Wynkyn de Worde every assistance and freedom. It said ... it said that Wynkyn de Worde was the hand of the archangel Saint Michael on earth, and that he worked the will of the angels. It said further that de Worde knew the face of evil, and if de Worde were not allowed his freedom then evil would roam unfettered."

"You did not doubt it."

"No. I could not. All know of Boniface's piety, and of his judgement. He was a great pope, and I believed his words implicitly."

Again Thomas understood, although he did not nod this time. Boniface had been dead some thirty years when Wynkyn had shown Bertrand the pope's letter, but it would have carried the same degree of authority then as it had when it had been newly penned. After Boniface's death, the French King Philip, whom many accused of Boniface's murder (the king had tried an unsuccessful kidnap of the pope, which had prompted a fatal heart attack), had seized control of the papacy via his puppet, Pope Clement, and the popes had retired to Avignon to lead lives of corruption and sin.

Boniface had been the last of the true popes as far as much of Christendom was concerned. If Wynkyn had pulled out a letter from one of the Avignon popes, Bertrand would have been likely to throw it in the fire and laugh in the brother's face.

"And that is all the letter said?" Thomas prompted softly.

"Yes. That was all the letter said. But, combined with the same light in Brother Wynkyn's face that I now see shining from yours, it was enough."

Bertrand heaved himself to his feet and paced slowly back and forth in the confined space between his bed and the door. "After that I let Wynkyn de Worde do as he willed. He was quiet enough, and nothing he did disturbed the peace of the friary. The other brothers left him well enough alone."

"Where did he go when he left the friary?"

"He went to the friary in Nuremberg twice a year for the summer and winter solstices."

Ah! The timing of de Worde's departures and arrivals now made sense. The summer solstice occurred on the Vigil of St John the Baptist in late June, the winter on the night before the Vigil of the Nativity of the Lord Jesus Christ.

"What he did there," Bertrand continued, "I know not, although it had something to do with the evil that was Brother Wynkyn's purpose."

"And the significance of the solstices?"

Bertrand merely shrugged.

Thomas lapsed into thought, pacing slowly before Bertrand hunched miserably on his stool.

"What of this ancient book that Brother Wynkyn consulted? What did it contain?"

"I do not know."

"Does it remain in the friary?"

"No. Wynkyn took it with him on his final journey north."

"In Advent of the first year of pestilence."

"Yes." Bertrand hunched even further on the stool. Why hadn't he destroyed those records earlier?

"And Wynkyn did not return from Nuremberg?"

"No. I presume he died of the pestilence."

"And the book?"

"Wynkyn took it with him encased in an oaken casket. I presume it lies wherever Wynkyn bubbled out his last breath. Either that or it has been stolen."

Thomas stopped his pacing, thinking deeply. In the past hour he'd found a solidity of purpose that had before been only a vague hope and yearning. Now he knew exactly what he had to do.

All thought of whores and naked flesh had fled his mind.

"I must retrace Wynkyn de Worde's last route north," Thomas said, and Bertrand blinked as if he were a prisoner suddenly and most unexpectedly given his freedom.

He would rid himself of this troublesome brother once and for all!

"I must find that casket," Thomas said, "but I will need your aid."

"Ask what you will," said Bertrand, silently wishing that Thomas would just leave.

"I seek an audience with the pope."

"What!"

Thomas looked Bertrand in the eye. "Boniface obviously knew something of what Brother Wynkyn did. What if his secret had also been shared with his successors? I must ask the Holy Father, and perhaps even enlist his aid."

Thomas was prepared to work without it, but the backing of the pope would open many doors for him.

"Sweet Jesu, brother," Bertrand said, "an audience with Urban? But —"

"Can it be arranged?"

Bertrand played with the frayed end of his belt, trying to purchase some time. Arrange an audience with the pope? Lord Christ Saviour! It could mean the end of his career!

"Brother Prior?"

Bertrand gave up, spreading his hands helplessly. "It will take some time, Brother Thomas, and even then it might prove impossible. Urban has only sat his throne some five days ... and some say he may not sit it much longer."

"What do you mean?" Thomas had spent so much time in prayer the past week that he'd not had the time or inclination to listen to gossip.

"You have not heard? Two days after the election, thirteen of the sixteen cardinals put themselves back on the road to Avignon."

"Why?"

"When the cardinals met in conclave they were terrified that if they voted in a non-Roman the mob would slaughter them. Well, we all know that for the truth. But there are rumours of more. They say that the cardinals decided to elect Urban as pope on the clear understanding that he would resign within a month or so when the majority of the cardinals were safely back in Avignon. Once safe, the cardinals will declare the Roman conclave void because of interference from the mob and have a new election."

Thomas fought the urge to swear. The college of cardinals had long had a law that if a papal election came under undue interference then it could be declared null and void.

And Urban's election had indisputably come under "undue interference".

This rumour had the smell of truth.

"That evil walks among us cannot be questioned," Thomas said, "when the cardinals plot such treachery against the Church of Rome!"

"Do you still seek an audience with Urban?"

Thomas nodded. "It will do no harm."

Bertrand folded his hands in resignation. "I will do what I can."

VII

Wednesday in Easter Week
In the fifty-first year of the reign of Edward III
(21st April 1378)

— i —

During the seventy years that the popes had resided in Avignon, the papal palace adjoining St Peter's Basilica had fallen into a state of disrepair. Gregory had not done much to restore it in the year he'd spent in Rome before his death — and many said that that was a clear indication he had not meant to remain permanently in Rome at all — and had only made them habitable.

Thus Urban did not meet petitioners in the great audience hall — half demolished over the past fifty years by Romans seeking foundation stones for their homes — but in a large chapel that ran between St Peter's and the papal palace. It had taken Prior Bertrand a great deal of time and had caused him to call in a great many favours to engineer a place at the Thursday papal audience for himself and Brother Thomas, and even then he did not know if they would get a chance to actually address the pope.

But this was the best he could do, and so, after their noon meal, he and Brother Thomas made their way into the Leonine City.

The gates in the wall by the Castel St Angelo had been restored to their hangings, but were thrown open to the petitioners and pilgrims wending their way towards St Peter's. The rising spring meant that the pilgrimage ways were reopening after the winter hiatus, and both Bertrand and Thomas had to push their way through the crowds thronging the streets leading to the Basilica.

Their robes granted them no favours. Rome was stacked to the rafters with clerics of all shapes, sizes and degrees, and a pair of Dominican friars were inconsequential compared to the hordes of bishops and archbishops, holy hermits, frenzied prophets of doom and wild-eyed nuns in the grip of some holy possession.

Thomas' mouth thinned as he shouldered a way through for himself and the prior. Most of these hermits, prophets and hysterical nuns were but pretenders, their palms held open for coin, their voices shrieking that doom awaited if pilgrims weren't prepared to part with their last groat for a blessing.

"Does the pope not issue orders to rid the streets of such as these?" he muttered as he and Bertrand were momentarily pinned against a brick wall by the pressing throng.

"Rome has always been cursed with such petitioners," Bertrand replied. "Sometimes worse. When Boniface called the great Jubilee several years before he died, Rome was awash with over a million pilgrims ... as with all the charlatans, whores, relic merchants and money lenders the pilgrim trade attracts."

Thomas stared at Bertrand, forgetting for the moment the crowds about them. "A *million* pilgrims? Surely not!"

"'Tis true, my son. Some say the number was even greater."

Thomas shook his head, unable to conceive of a million people. Rome's population was normally about thirty thousand — and that was extraordinary enough in Christendom, where few towns had more than two thousand people. But a *million?*

"Jesu," he whispered, "how was Rome not destroyed amid such a conflagration of people?"

"Rome has survived many things, Thomas. The corruption and madness of Roman emperors, invasions by barbarians and infidels, and the devilish machinations of kings. A squash of pilgrims would not worry it overmuch."

But such a crowd, thought Thomas, *and the sin it must have engendered.*

"Come!" Bertrand said, seizing Thomas' sleeve. "I see a way opening before us!"

They walked as quickly as possible up the steps leading to the entrance into the vast court that lay before St Peter's: they would have to enter the papal presence via the Basilica itself. The steps were as crowded as the streets, and Thomas was appalled to see that the court itself was packed with the stalls of moneylenders and relic merchants.

"How can the pope allow this?" he said, waving a hand at the frenetic activity. "It is like the scene before the Temple of Jerusalem!"

"Money can make even popes tolerant of many evils," said Bertrand, and hurried Thomas forward before the man thought to emulate Christ himself and start to overturn tables. Bertrand just wanted to get this over and done with and, whatever the result of the interview, to then hurry Thomas out of Rome with as much speed as he could.

Bertrand cared not that Thomas spoke with the authority of angels. Wynkyn de Worde had as well, and Bertrand had never stopped counting his blessings that the demented man had not returned from Nuremberg.

St Peter's was relatively quiet after the hustle of the outer court and streets. The nave of the Basilica was crowded with pilgrims and penitents, but it was quiet save for the mumble of prayers, and most knelt in orderly ranks facing the altar of St Peter, or before one of the shrines that lined the aisles.

Bertrand and Thomas genuflected towards St Peter's shrine, then moved up the right-hand aisle towards a small door two-thirds of the way along the north wall of the Basilica. It was well guarded, but Bertrand whispered his name and that of Thomas, and the guards allowed them through.

They found themselves in a small corridor, blessedly quiet after the turbulence of street and court, and Bertrand indicated a door at its end. "Through there. We'll find ourselves at the rear of the chapel. Bow towards the pope, although he probably won't see you, and then come to stand with me to the side. The papal secretaries have your name, and if the pope has time then he will —"

"*If he has time?*"

"Thomas, you are an unimportant man within the hierarchy of the Church. There will be others, many others, and of far more important rank, before you."

"But not of more important mission," Thomas mumbled.

"Do you think yourself Christ?" Bertrand hissed. "Do you think yourself to be announced as the saviour of Christendom?"

"I speak with the voice of —"

"You are still a humble man," Bertrand said. "*Do not forget that!*"

The chamber was packed, but with a far more richly clothed and bejewelled crowd than that which thronged the streets.

Bertrand and Thomas entered silently and bowed to the figure of Urban seated — stiff in his robes and jewels — on the papal throne set on a small dais before the altar of the chapel.

He did not notice their entrance.

The two friars whispered their names to a clerk seated just inside the door, who wrote them down and then passed the paper to a messenger boy who took it to two richly-robed secretaries seated at a table to the pope's left. Bertrand and Thomas then stood with a group of Benedictine monks halfway up the chapel by a shrine dedicated to the Virgin Mary. From this vantage point both men could see and hear well.

There were three cardinals seated on the pope's right. The remaining three, Thomas realised, and wondered why they had stayed when all the others had departed for Avignon. Urban, a bear-like man in his late fifties who wore his robes of office with obvious discomfort, sat fidgeting impatiently while one of the cardinals whispered earnestly to him.

"Ah! Bah!" Urban suddenly pronounced and, leaning back in his chair, spat a gob of phlegm to one side of his chair.

"I give *that* for King John's proposition!" he said, and farted.

The shock in the chapel was palpable. Bodies stiffened and faces blanched.

Grinning, Urban reached for a jewelled goblet of wine on a side table. He downed it in four loud gulps, red wine running down one side of his chin, then slammed the goblet down.

"But, Holy Father," the cardinal said, "the French king has proposed what is only just —"

"What your partners in intrigue have told him is just," Urban said. "I doubt the old man could tell the difference between a woman's breast and a donkey's teat, let alone between what is just and what is not."

The cardinal sat back, glancing at the other two. His fingers drummed on the arm of his chair, then stilled.

"No one doubts that our conclave was under undue influence," he said.

Urban roared and leapt to his feet. "*I will not resign!*" he yelled.

Bertrand leaned towards Thomas and whispered in his ear: "I fear we have arrived at a *most* inopportune moment."

Thomas said nothing, but his face was tight with anger. *The cardinals had elected* this *peasant's arse as pope?*

Urban stepped down from the dais, strode over to a guard, wrenched a spear from the startled man's grasp and stalked back to the three cardinals.

He threw the spear down at the feet of the cardinal who had been speaking to him.

The man's face did not change expression.

"Even if the cardinals point a thousand spears at my throat I will not resign!" Urban shouted. "I am rightful pope, *and I will not resign!*"

"Then we have no choice," the cardinal said, his face impassive. "The cardinals will meet in conclave in Avignon and they will declare the election held here in Rome to be null and void. They will then elect a rightful pope. You are —"

"Don't think that you and your companions here," Urban gestured towards the other two cardinals, "will be joining them. Instead I think you shall spend the next few months in sackcloth in some isolated monastery, living on bread and water and spending the hours of the day in prayer for the salvation of your souls."

And still the expression on the cardinal's face did not alter. "Your orders carry no weight. You can force myself and my colleagues into whatever prison you like, but know that you only stain your soul further by doing so. You are only a parody. A jest."

Urban's fists clenched, and Thomas could see that he was struggling for control. On the one hand, Thomas was furious that the cardinals had, indeed, been plotting to elect another Frenchman to the papal throne; on the other, he was appalled that God's cause should be championed by this pig.

"A parody, my lord cardinal. How many of the princes of Europe will believe *me* a parody? How many would support *another* puppet of the French king taking the papal throne?"

All about the chapel men were turning to their neighbours and whispering furiously.

"Lord Christ Saviour!" Bertrand said softly. "If neither backs down, then both Urban and the rogue cardinals are going to turn this into a European war!"

The impassive cardinal suddenly lost all control. He stood up and made a foul gesture towards Urban.

"There!" he shouted, his face now red. "*That's* the only kind of language you understand, isn't it, you Italian rustic. Let me go or imprison me, I don't care, but your day is over!"

He stared one breath longer in the pope's face, then stalked away.

His two colleagues joined him, their faces stiff with affront.

Urban let them go.

He sat back on his throne and regarded the audience. "Those traitors will tear Europe apart," he said, "and damn their own souls in the doing. I am the true elected pope. A *Roman* pope. If they go ahead with their devil-inspired election, then few but the French will support them."

His face worked, and his hands clenched and unclenched about the armrests of his throne. "Christendom will have two popes," he said, his voice now a near whisper. "What have we done to so earn God's displeasure? What evil stalks among us?"

Thomas stared at the pope, trying to reconcile his disgust at the man's revolting habits with the thought that he might be a true ally he could rely upon. Any pope elected in Avignon would be a tool of the French King ... and that left only Urban who might swing the forces of the Church behind the effort to battle the forces of evil which were even now —

"Ah! Enough of them," Urban said. "What do we have next?"

One of his secretaries handed him a piece of paper.

"What?" Urban yelled as he read. "Some half-crazed friar thinks he speaks for archangel Saint Michael? Heaven aid us all from such dimwitted asses! Where is he? Where? Lord God above, why must I be pestered with such *fools*! If I were to believe every man, woman and child who solemnly swears they've been granted an audience with this saint, or that angel, I'd have to believe half of Christendom sits down to dinner with the Virgin herself!"

Urban crumpled the paper and threw it to one side. "Lord Christ, save me from the addled," he said. "I've too much to do without being bothered with the deranged as well."

Thomas and Bertrand backed unobtrusively away, Thomas cold with anger, Bertrand with shock.

"I had no thought the man would be so ... so ... so ..." Bertrand said as they finally gained the bustling court outside St Peter's.

"So repellent," Thomas finished for him. "He is unworthy to replace the meanest parish priest, let alone act as God's mouthpiece on earth! And yet he is the rightfully elected pope."

"That's your English blood talking," Bertrand said. "All the Frenchmen, Spaniards and Scots in this crowd would agree with the cardinals. Now, let us see if we can return to the friary in one piece."

"No." Thomas pulled away from him. "I shall not return yet. I need to consider what to do."

"Thomas —"

But Thomas was gone, and Bertrand was left to seethe in solitude.

Lord Christ Saviour, but he would be gladdened when he could rid himself of this arrogant priest!

VIII

Wednesday in Easter Week
In the fifty-first year of the reign of Edward III
(21st April 1378)

— ii —

Thomas wandered aimlessly through the crowds, pushed this way and that, trying to sort out his thoughts.

He had taken holy orders because he had wanted to be part of the Church, part of the great institution which spoke with Christ's voice and guided man's footsteps towards salvation.

In doing so, Thomas had hoped to atone for the sins of his past and achieve his own salvation.

But what he'd just witnessed dismayed him, although it confirmed what St Michael had said regarding the Church. How could the Church, as represented by Urban, rally to ward off the evil which the archangel told him walked freely among mankind? And what if the cardinals in Avignon went ahead and elected a new pope? Would Urban resign? No, of course not. He was too ambitious to do that.

That would leave Christendom headed by two popes. Thomas shuddered as he thought through the consequences. Two rival popes, two rival Church organisations, two sets of

Church courts, two hierarchies of clerics ... Sweet Jesu! The Church would be torn in two!

It would become the laughing stock of Europe.

If evil walked the world, then, by all the saints, it had surely taken a stroll through the papal palace in the past few weeks.

Well, there was nothing for it but to proceed without the papal blessing, and without the papal aid and information that he had sought.

"Saint Michael," Thomas whispered into the crowd, "guide my steps, I pray you!"

A hand grabbed his sleeve, and Thomas almost fell over.

He swore — instantly regretting the lapse — and twisted around amid the throng of close-pressed bodies to stare at the man who still had his sleeve in a tight clasp.

"Sweet Jesu, Tom, is that you?"

A man of about thirty-five or six stared at Thomas. He had a deeplylined and tanned face, a knife-scarred chin, bright blue eyes crowded by sun-wrinkles, and fine sandy hair that fell over his forehead.

"Tom? I can hardly tell your face without its black beard."

Thomas gaped at the man. *Was this a guide that Saint Michael had sent?*

"Tom, speak to me ... or are you too proud to pass the time of day with your old friends now?"

"Wat," Thomas finally said. "Wat Tyler."

"Aye, Wat Tyler it is. Lord Jesus, this is no place to talk — a man couldn't even piss in a crowd this thick! Come ... there's a place that I've found ..."

And Thomas found himself being dragged through the crowd and into a side street close to the market — Jesu! Had he wandered out of the Leonine City and back into the heart of Rome without knowing it?

Wat pulled Thomas into a small one-roomed tavern, ill-lit and kept, and almost as crowded as the outside streets. A heavily pregnant and slatternly woman carrying several mugs of ale squeezed her way through the trestle tables and benches, ignoring the obscene remarks and leers that followed her.

"Wat —" Thomas began.

"It's no cathedral, I grant you," Wat said, and pushed Thomas down onto the end of a bench at a crowded table, "but it's the best we can do for the present ... unless you want to invite me back to dine at your friary."

The men about the table gave the priest and his companion only a cursory glance before returning to their drinking and arguing.

Wat squeezed down on to the very end of the bench, forcing Thomas to shuffle along until he was, in turn, squeezed against a sweaty and fat labourer who shot Thomas a sour look before turning back to his companions.

"I am *not* going to talk to you *here*," Thomas said.

"Nowhere else," Wat said. "Christ above, Tom. How many years is it since we've seen each other? And," he lowered his voice slightly, "from what I remember, there was a time you'd have felt at home in a drinking den like this, eh?"

Thomas' mouth tightened, but Wat ignored it, and called to the woman for a couple of ales. She grunted, and disappeared towards a back room.

Wat turned back to Thomas. "But now I see that this warm and companionable room is not good enough. Not for this fine priest. And perhaps I am not good enough, either."

Thomas briefly closed his eyes, and sighed. "Rome is the last place I'd expect to see you. What do you do here?"

There was a time, Wat thought, carefully examining the subtle changes to Thomas' face since he'd last seen it, *when Rome was the last place I'd have thought to meet you, too.*

"I'm here as sergeant of the escort to King Edward's envoy."

Wat finally caught Thomas' interest. "Edward has sent an envoy to Rome? To Urban?"

Wat flipped a coin to the woman who slopped two overfull mugs on the stained table top before them.

"Aye." He grinned, and swallowed a mouthful of the ale. "Edward is skittering about his throne with joy that his rival has lost the papacy back to Rome. He's sent the Archbishop of Canterbury to extend to Urban England's good wishes."

"Edward may not be so joyous for much longer," Thomas said.

"Eh? Why?"

Thomas told Wat about the fear and intimidations that had surrounded Urban's election, the subsequent rogue cardinals' departure for Avignon, and their demand that Urban resign. He relaxed as he talked, falling back into the warmth and trust of a friendship that extended back many years and through many shared dangers.

"I fear," he finally said, turning his untasted mug of ale around in endless damp circles, "that there will be a pope in Avignon, and a pope in Rome ... and a divided Christendom."

Wat shrugged. "It's divided anyway."

"Curse you, Wat! This will mean war!"

Wat looked Thomas directly in the eye. "There will be war in any case. The archbishop is here not only to extend Edward's warm congratulations to Urban, but also to ask Urban's blessing for Edward's new —"

"Sweet Jesu! Edward's going to re-invade France?"

Wat grinned. "*Will* have re-invaded by this time."

Thomas sat back, the mug now still between his hands. Wat looked at him carefully, wondering what memories were scurrying through Thomas' head. Was there regret that he had swapped sword for cross?

"Edward's an old man," Thomas said.

"Edward has stayed at home. You know who would lead such an expedition, Tom."

"Aye," Thomas whispered, his eyes blank, his thoughts a thousand miles away. "The Black Prince."

"And Lancaster."

Thomas' eyes refocused on Wat. "The Duke of Lancaster as well?"

"As all of Lancaster's friends and allies."

Thomas visibly shuddered. "The war can do no good. Edward should accept that he has lost the right to the French throne."

"The war can do no good? You *have* changed, Tom."

Again Thomas' face tightened. "As I said, Wat, Edward is an old man. He should look to the health of his soul, rather than try to win more glory and riches for himself and his sons."

"And I suppose the Black Prince and Lancaster should scurry back home as well, and spend their remaining years on their knees before some altar!"

"Penitence does no one harm, Wat. *You* should look to the health of your own soul. Evil walks abroad."

"And that I cannot disagree with," Wat mumbled, looking away, "for evil has surely stolen *your* soul!"

Furious, Thomas swivelled about on the bench — causing his fat neighbour to curse at the disturbance — and grabbed Wat's shoulder. "I have repented for my sins, Wat, and the Lord God has been merciful enough to grant me forgiveness. Has he done the same for you?"

"Don't preach to me, Tom! Not *you*! You have sold your soul to Rome —"

"I have sold my soul to no one —"

"— when you should remember that you are an Englishman born and bred! What if Edward asked you for allegiance and service ... would you give it to him?"

"I owe my allegiance to no one but God!" Thomas hissed. "I serve a higher Lord than Edward and his pitiful worldly ambitions —"

"I'd give a year's pay to hear you say that to Edward's face," Wat mumbled, the hint of a smile about his face, but Thomas carried on without pause.

"— and any who ride with Edward's captains risk their soul on an unholy cause!"

"You are adept at cloaking yourself in holiness, Thomas, but you cannot forget who and what you once were."

"It is obvious that *you* cannot forget who and what I once was, Wat. How is it you sit here and *dare* speak to me with such familiarity?"

Now Wat's face was tight with fury. "I forget my place, my lord. Forgive me."

Thomas held his stare, then looked away.

Wat took a deep breath, and spoke more moderately, trying to deflect the anger of the past minutes.

"There is a new spiritual adviser at Lancaster's court, Tom. An old friend of yours."

"Yes?"

Wat downed the last of his ale. "Master Wycliffe."

"Wycliffe? But ..."

"Much has happened since you've been gone. Your colleague at Oxford —"

"I hardly knew him. We did not agree on many matters."

And you would agree even less now, Wat thought. "— now has the ear of the Duke of Lancaster and, through him, his father, Edward. Wycliffe says," Wat waved his empty mug to the woman, "that the Church should content itself only with spiritual matters, and not the worldly."

Thomas rubbed his forehead, and did not reply. He and Wycliffe had spent many hours arguing when Thomas had been studying at Oxford, and he did not want to deepen his argument with Wat now over the despicable man.

"Further," Wat continued, "Wycliffe has publicly stated that men who exist in a state of sin should not hold riches or property —"

"The old man has finally said something *sensible*?"

"— and, of all men who exist in sin, Wycliffe holds that the bishops, archbishops and cardinals of the Holy Church are the worst of all."

Thomas raised his eyebrows, not sure that he could disagree with that, either.

"Consequently," Wat continued serenely, handing another coin to the woman who'd bought him more ale, "Master Wycliffe argues that the Church should relinquish most of the worldly riches and land that it holds. After all, is not the Holy Church spiritual rather than worldly? Shouldn't priests be more concerned with the salvation of souls rather than the accumulation of riches?"

Wat grinned wryly at the expression on Tom's face. No doubt the man thought this was all heresy. Well, Wycliffe had many admirers, and many of those among the nobility themselves, who thought that what he said was nothing but sense. If the Church was forced to give up land ... then who but the nobles would benefit?

"And can you imagine what Wycliffe has also said?" Wat said, leaning a little closer to Tom. "Why, he claims that all the masses and the sacraments and the fripperies of the Holy Church are but nothing in the quest for salvation. Instead, so Master Wycliffe claims, salvation can be gleaned from a careful study of the Scriptures without the need for the mediation of a priest. Who needs priests?"

Thomas was so shocked he could do nothing but stare. To point out the corruptions of the Church was one thing, but to suggest no one needed a Church or a priesthood in order to gain salvation was a heresy so vile it *must* have been promulgated by the whisperings of Satan's demons. And here was Wat mouthing such vileness in the very heart of Christendom itself.

"After all," Wat said, wiping away the foam left about his mouth from his draught of ale, "the Church makes itself so rich from the tithes and taxes it takes from the good folk that it would be the last to stand up and say, 'You can do it yourself, if only you could read the Scriptures.' I've heard tell that Wycliffe has his followers translating the Bible from Latin into the King's own English, so as all us plain folk can read it."

Put God into the plain man's hand? "He talks *filth*! He attacks what God Himself has ordained!"

"And yet have you not just told me about the possibility of your beloved Church being headed by two popes? Are you trying to argue that we leave our salvation in the hands of such idiots?"

Thomas was silent.

"Beyond anything else," Wat said softly, intently, "I am an Englishman. I owe allegiance to Edward and his sons before I owe allegiance to a corrupt foreign power that masquerades as the guardian of our souls. I like what Wycliffe says. It makes sense ... his reasoning puts the common man's destiny back into *his* hands rather than leave it in the hands of —"

"You are an unlearned man," Thomas said, and, rising to his feet, stepped over the bench, "but you should know better than to spread the words of a heretic. By doing so you assure yourself a place in hell."

"And you are a self-righteous idiot," Wat said, looking away, "and my place in hell is far from assured."

Thomas stared, then a muscle in his cheek twitched, and he turned and strode out the tavern.

Wat turned his head to watch him go. He snorted. "You may clothe yourself in the robes of a humble friar, m'lad," he said to no one in particular, "but you still walk with the arrogance of a prince!"

Then he laughed shortly. "There may be a space awaiting me in hell," he murmured, "but I have no intention of ever filling it."

After a moment Wat returned to his ale.

"Prior Bertrand. You realise that I must leave."

It was evening, and Thomas had waylaid Bertrand as the brothers filed out after Vespers prayers.

Finally, thought Bertrand, *finally he goes!* He resolved to say a special prayer of thanksgiving to St Michael that evening at Compline. Thomas should have asked permission, but Bertrand was not going to quibble about that small lack of procedure right now.

"You follow Brother Wynkyn's steps?"

"Yes. North to Nuremberg. And then ... then where the archangel Saint Michael's steps guide me."

Bertrand nodded. "I will write a letter of introduction for you." Best to ensure Thomas had all help available in order to speed his steps away from St Angelo's.

Thomas inclined his head. "I thank you, Prior Bertrand."

Bertrand opened his mouth, hesitated, then spoke. "It is said that beneath his rustic exterior, the Holy Father has only the good of the Church at heart."

"Perhaps."

"Thomas ... do not judge any you meet too harshly. We are all only men and women, and are faulted by the burdens of our sins."

Thomas inclined his head again, but did not reply.

Some of us may only be men and women, he thought, *but some of us are otherwise.*

Later, when he was alone in his cell, Bertrand sat at his writing desk in stillness a long, long time.

When the wick in his oil lamp flickered and threatened to go out Bertrand reached for a piece of parchment and, while the lamp lasted, wrote an account of events, and of Thomas' part in them, to the Prior General of England, Richard Thorseby. True, Bertrand was gladdened that Thomas was leaving, but it was best to ensure Thomas never came back at all, and Thorseby would be just the man for that. After all, Thomas hadn't exactly asked for permission to leave the friary, had he? Such disobedience against the rules of the order called for stern disciplinary measures ...

"And I pray to God that I be with You in heaven," Bertrand mumbled as he blotted the ink, "before another emissary of Saint Michael's decides to stay awhile at Saint Angelo's."

IX

Ember Friday in Whitsuntide
In the fifty-first year of the reign of Edward III
(11th June 1378)

Thomas spent the weeks on the road north from Rome in a state of troublesome melancholy, wondering at the future of the word of God in a world which seemed to be slipping ever closer to the blandishments of the Devil. These had been grey weeks of travel. He had been harassed by beggars, pilgrims and wandering pedlars who thought a lone traveller easy prey (even his obvious poverty had not lessened their threatening entreaties), while constant rain and a sweeping chill wind had added physical misery to the spiritual anguish of Thomas' soul. Doubt had consumed him: how could he follow a trail thirty years dead? How could he, one man, rally the forces of God to destroy the evil that spread unhindered throughout Christendom?

Even worse were memories which had ridden untamed through his mind whenever he thought on Wat's news that the Black Prince and John of Gaunt, Duke of Lancaster, were again leading an invasion force into France.

The surge of battle, the scream of horses, and the ring of steel. The feel of the blade as it arced through the air, seeking that weakness in his opponent's armour, and then the joy as he felt it crush through bone and sinew, and the expression of shock, almost wonder, on a man's face as he felt cold death slide deep into his belly.

The glimpse of a sweaty comrade's face, his expression half of fear, half of fierce joy, across the tangled gleam of armour and wild-eyed horses of the battlefield.

The same comrade later that night, lifting a goblet to toast victory.

The brotherhood of arms and of battle.

John of Gaunt — Lancaster — was returning to France, his friends and allies at his back.

Who was with Lancaster? Who? Memories rode not far behind Lancaster's banner.

Thomas cursed Wat daily. Not only had the man spoken heretical words which had disturbed Thomas' soul, the man's very appearance had recalled to Thomas a life and passions he had thought to have forgotten years before. He served God and St Michael now, not the whims of some petty prince, or the dictates of a power-hungry sovereign.

He served God, not the brotherhood he'd left behind.

Man's cause no longer interested him.

On this morning, as Thomas approached Florence, any doubts he may have had vanished along with the cloud and wind. Just after Sext he turned a corner of the road to find Florence lay spread out before him like a saviour.

Thomas halted his mule and stared.

Warm sunshine washed over him, and to either side of the road richly-scented summer flowers bloomed in waving cornfields. But none of this registered in Thomas' mind. He could only stare at the walled metropolis below him. A gleaming city of God, surely, for nothing else could have given it such an aura of light and strength.

He had never seen a city so beautiful. Even Rome paled into insignificance before it. Not only was it larger — Florence was the largest city in the western world — but it was infinitely more colourful, more splendidly built, more *alive*.

Innumerable burnished domes of church and guildhall glittered in the noon sunshine; pale stone towers topped by red terracotta roofs soared from the dark narrow streets towards the light of both sun and God; colourful banners and pennants whipped from windows and parapets; bridges arched gracefully over the winding Arno — the river silver in this light. The tops of fruit trees and the waving tendrils of vines reached from the courtyards of villas and tenement blocks.

Thomas' overwhelming impression was of majesty and light, where his memory of Rome was of decay and chaos and violence.

Surely God was here, where He had been absent in Rome?

Gently Thomas nudged the flanks of his mule, and the patient beast began the descent into the richest and most beautiful municipality in Christendom.

Thomas had thought that his initial impression of Florence might be shattered when he entered the crowded streets, but it was not so.

Where the crowds in Rome had been oppressive, often threatening, here they were lively and inviting.

Where the faces that turned his way in Rome had been surly or suspicious, here they were open and welcoming.

Where the doors of Rome had been closed to strangers and to the always expected violence, here they were open to friend and stranger alike. And it seemed that from every second window, and every third doorway, hung the tapestries and cloths for which Florence was famous — a waterfall of ever-changing colour that rippled and glittered down every street.

Above the voices and footsteps of the streets cascaded a clarion of bells: guild bells, church bells, the bells of the standing watches on the walls and the marching watches on the streets . . . the bells of God.

A tear slipped down Thomas' cheek.

When Thomas rode into the city, he did not immediately seek the friary he knew would give him shelter. It was still high morning, and he could spend the next few hours more profitably seeking out that which he needed than passing platitudes with his brothers in the Order.

Thomas understood now that God needed him on his feet, not his knees.

So Thomas rode his mule slowly through the streets towards the market square. The past weeks on the road from Rome had taught him a valuable lesson: he would travel the quicker if he travelled in a well-escorted train. A lone traveller had to travel slowly and carefully, and not only to avoid the menacements of beggars, for Thomas had heard that the northern Italian roads were troubled by bandits who regularly dispossessed people of their valuables and, if the valuables proved insufficient, often their lives as well.

So Thomas needed to find a well-escorted group which would be travelling in his direction: through the Brenner Pass in the Alps, then north through Innsbruck and Augsberg to Nuremberg. There was only one group likely to be rich enough to afford the escort to travel quickly and safely, and only one group that would be likely to take that route, and Thomas had a good idea of where he'd find it.

Thomas dismounted from his mule and led it the final few hundred yards towards the market square, finally tying the beast to a post beside a wool store that bordered the square itself. The mule was a sorry beast, and Thomas thought that no one would be likely to steal it.

He patted the mule on the shoulder — sorry beast it might be, but it had also been faithful and of good service — and turned to the square. It was large, and lined with some of the most magnificent buildings Thomas had ever seen. There were churches, a cathedral, palaces of the nobles and of prelates and several prominent guildhalls. Colourful stalls had been set up about the square, selling every sort of goods from cloth to nubile Moorish slave girls, and in the centre of the square wove acrobats and jugglers, and a bear-handler with his abject and chained source of income.

The bear-handler was tying his charge to a stake and inviting passers-by to set their dogs to the creature, and to bet on the outcome.

Already a crowd was gathering around him.

Thomas ignored all the activity and set off for the largest of the guildhalls, that of the cloth merchants.

He paused inside the doors, his eyes narrowing. This was worldliness gone rampant! The guildhall rivalled any of the cathedrals Thomas had seen, save that of St Peter's itself: supported by ornamented hammerbeams, its roof soared several hundred feet above his head. Its walls were painted over with scenes from the Scriptures, rich with gilding and studded with gems. Its furnishings were ornate and luxurious.

And Wat thought the *Church* too wealthy?

"Brother?" said a soft voice at his shoulder. "May I be of some assistance?"

Thomas turned around. A middle-aged and grey-haired man dressed in velvets and silks stood there, his well-fed face set into an expression of enquiry.

"Perhaps," Thomas said. "I need to travel north, and fast. I seek any of your number who might be leaving within the next few days."

"You want to travel with a merchant train?"

Thomas wondered if his fixed smile looked too false to this man. "That is what I said."

The man spread his hands. "Surely the Church can afford to share some of the burden of finding a suitable escort for you, brother, if your mission be of such importance?"

"I travel alone, and I need to travel fast. I am sure any of your brothers within the guild would be happy to accept me into their company."

The man raised his eyebrows.

"I would reward them well for their troubles," Thomas said.

"With coin, good brother?"

"With prayers, good man."

The man's face split in a cynical grin. "You shall have to take your proposition to the merchants concerned, brother. It will be their choice or not ... and I am not sure if they are so low on prayers they need to haul along the burden of a friar."

"I will not be a burden!" Thomas snapped, and the man's grin widened.

"Of course not. Well, 'tis not for me to say aye or nay. Take yourself to the Via Ricasoli. There is an inn there, you cannot miss it, and ask for Master Etienne Marcel. He is a Frenchman, a good cloth merchant, and he is leading a party north through the Brenner in two days' time. Perchance he may feel the need of your prayers."

Thomas nodded, and turned away,

"And perchance not," the man added, and Thomas strode out of the guildhall and into the sunshine, the warmth of the day ruined.

He found the inn easily enough — it was the only one on the street — and asked of the innkeeper for Master Etienne Marcel.

The man inclined his head, and motioned Thomas to follow him.

They walked through the unoccupied front room, set out with several trestle tables and benches before a great fireplace, into a narrow hallway leading to a stairwell winding up to a darkened second level. Halfway up Thomas dimly heard laughter, and the clink of pewter — or coin — on a table.

There was only one door at the head of the stairs, and the innkeeper tapped on it gently.

It opened a fraction. The innkeeper spoke softly, briefly, then stood aside and indicated Thomas.

Thomas stared at the dark crack revealed by the open door, but could discern nothing.

The door closed, and he heard fragments of a conversation.

Then the door opened wide, and a well, but not over-dressed young man, with a friendly grin, bright blue eyes and hair so blond it was almost white, stood there, a hand held out in welcome.

"A friar!" he said in poor Latin, "and with a request. Well, brother, enter, if you don't mind our den of sin."

A rebuke sounded behind the young man and he flushed, and moderated the width of his smile. "Well, good brother. Not quite a 'den of sin', perhaps, but a worldly enough place for such as you. Please, enter, with our welcome."

Thomas stepped past the innkeeper, nodding his thanks as he did so, and took the hand the young man still extended. "Brother Thomas Neville," he said, "and I thank you for your welcome."

And then he startled the young man by flashing him a rakish grin before assuming a more sober face as he entered the room.

The young man closed the door behind him.

It was a large and well-lit apartment occupying the entire second storey. Obviously the inn's best. Three glassed windows — this *was* a rich inn — ran along the eastern wall, chests and benches underneath them. At the rear were two curtained-off beds, the curtains tied back to let the day's air and sun dapple across the bed coverings. Travelling caskets and panniers sat at the sides and feet of the beds.

On the wall opposite the windows was an enormous fireplace; room enough for not only the fire, but benches to either side of it. A tripod with a steaming kettle hanging from a chain stood to one side.

But it was the centre of the room which caught Thomas' attention, and which had its attention entirely focused on him. There was a massive table — a proper table rather than a trestle affair — with chairs pulled up about it.

Seated in these chairs were four men, and the young man who had let Thomas in moved past him and sat down to make the number of men five.

All five stared silently at Thomas.

At the head of the table, directly facing him, was a man only a few years older than Thomas, but considerably more careworn. As with the younger man who had met Thomas at the door, he was well, but not ostentatiously dressed: dark green wool tunic and leggings, and a fine linen shirt. There were several gold and garnet rings on his fingers. He had close-cropped greying brown hair, an open face, and dark brown eyes that were lively with intelligence ... and a wariness that Thomas thought was habitual rather than a momentary concern at the unexpected visitor.

"Good friar," the man said. "How may we aid you?"

He spoke in a well-modulated voice, and his Latin was that of an educated man.

Thomas not only inclined his head, he bowed from the waist as well. "Master Marcel. I do thank you for your hospitality in granting me an audience."

For an unknown reason, Thomas felt an instant empathy with the man. This was, indeed, a God-fearing man, and worthy of both trust and respect.

God, or his archangel, Michael, had led him to this city, to this room and to this man.

Marcel nodded, then indicated the other men about the table. "We are a group of merchants, and," he smiled gently at a dark-haired man in his thirties, "one banker, Giulio Marcoaldi, of a most distinguished Florentine family."

Thomas inclined his head at the banker. "Master Marcoaldi."

Marcoaldi similarly inclined his head, but did not speak.

"To my right," Marcel said, indicating an ascetic-looking man of similar age to himself, and as well dressed, "is William Karle, a merchant of Paris."

"Master Karle," Thomas said.

"And beside him is Christoffel Bierman, a wool merchant of Flanders. His son, Johan, is the one who greeted you at the door."

Thomas smiled and greeted the Biermans; the father was an older replica of his fair-haired and cheerful son.

"And I," Marcel said, "am Etienne Marcel, as you have realised. I am a cloth merchant, travelling home to Paris by way of the Nuremberg markets."

"More than a 'cloth merchant'," Bierman said in heavily accented Latin, "for Marcel is also the Provost of Merchants of Paris."

Thomas blinked in surprise. No wonder the man had such an air of authority about him. The Provost of Merchants of

Paris was a comparable position to the Lord Mayor of London. A powerful and influential man, indeed.

And so far from home ... Thomas wondered why he travelled so far afield. Surely his duties as Provost should have kept him in Paris?

"I am Thomas Neville," he said, "and I do thank you for your hospitality."

"Which is not in any manner done with yet," Marcel said. "Will you sit with us? And ease your hunger and thirst?"

Thomas nodded, and sat in the chair Marcel offered. He grasped the mug of ale that Johan handed him, took a mouthful — it was thick and creamy, and of very good quality — and then set it down again.

"You must wonder why I have so imposed myself on you," he said.

Marcel crooked his eyebrows, but said nothing.

"I am travelling north," Thomas continued, "to Nuremberg, where I understand you also travel. I need to get there as fast as I may, and thought to find a group of merchants travelling to Nuremberg as well. I know that the last thing you need is —"

"From where do you come?" Marcoaldi said. "You are not of the Florentine order of Dominicans."

"I have travelled from Rome. Although," Thomas smiled as disarmingly as he could, feeling the weight of Marcel's nationality deeply, "perhaps you can tell by the inflections of my voice that I am —"

"English," said Marcel in a tighter voice than he'd yet used. His eyes narrowed slightly, and he looked intently at Thomas. "Although I did not need to hear your voice to know that. The Neville name is well known throughout many parts of France. Your family's reputation precedes you, friar."

"I am of the family of Christ now," Thomas said softly, holding Marcel's gaze, "not of any worldly family."

Marcel softened his stare, and a corner of his mouth crooked. "Then I would advise you to repeat that as often as you may, Brother Thomas, if you move anywhere near my home country. I hear it rumoured that the English are preparing another invasion into France."

Now his grin widened. "A completely futile exercise, of course. I have no doubt that within weeks King John will send your ... ah ... the English army scurrying home with its tail between its legs. So," he slapped his hands on the table, "you want to move north with us?"

"If I may, Master Marcel. I have little money with which to reward you for —"

"Ah," Marcel waved a hand. "If you come from Rome, then you have much news you can tell us. That will be reward enough for your passage. I hear tell there is trouble in the papal palace."

Thomas' grim face was confirmation enough. "Aye. It will take a while in the telling, though."

"Well, then ..." Marcel turned to look at each of his companions in turn. "Shall we allow this English dog of a friar —" a grin across his face took all insult out of his words "— to travel north with us, then? Eh? Giulio? William? Christoffel? And no need to ask Johan. The boy is agog for a new face to talk to."

At the nods from the other men, Marcel looked back to Thomas. "It is settled! You travel north with us. We leave before dawn in the morning, and we will travel fast. You have a horse?"

"I have a mule which —"

"A mule?" Johan said. "A mule! Good friar, cannot your Order afford even a patient mare to horse you?"

"We are a humble Order, Johan. We have no need of flashy steeds. A mule will do me well enough."

"But it will *not* do us well enough," Marcel said. "You may leave your mule with the Order's friary here in Florence, Brother Thomas, and we will horse you with one of our spares."

"I —"

"I will not accept your protests. I cannot afford to be held back by a stumbling mule. Especially not now," he continued in a lower voice, "that an invasion threatens. I *must* get back to Paris as fast as I can. I *must* ..."

"You *will* take the horse, Brother Thomas," said Marcoaldi, his dark brown eyes studying him intently.

Thomas gave in. "As you wish. I thank you for your assistance."

"Good," Marcel said. "Your mule is outside? Well, I will send one of my men to take it to the friary. It is a goodly walk from here, and perhaps you might better spend the time with us. Johan, tell Pietro to fetch the friar's belongings up here — I doubt he has overmuch with him — then to take the mule to the friary."

"Of course." Johan stood up and left the room.

"And now," Marcel said, "if perhaps you could lead us in prayer, friar?"

Thomas slipped quickly into sleep, warmed by the thick coverlets and drapes of the bed and by the bodies of the two Biermans he shared it with. This was luxury indeed; it had been many years since he'd slept in such comfort.

He sighed and turned over, and slid deeper into his sleep.

He dreamed.

He twisted, and awoke, startled.

Faces surrounded the bed — the Biermans had disappeared — and they were the faces of evil. There were six, perhaps seven, of them: horned, bearded, pig-snouted, and cat-eyed.

And yet, strangely beautiful.

They stared at him, their eyes widening as they realised he was awake.

"Thomas," one said, its voice deep and melodic, "Thomas?"

"Begone!" Thomas cried, wrenching himself into a sitting position, and making the sign of the cross before them. "Begone!"

They did not cringe, nor cry out. Instead their faces grinned slyly.

"We hear you're off to find our Keeper," said one, and it

was a female, for her voice was curiously woman-like. "We do wish you good seeking."

"Thomas," said another, male this time. "Beware of what you think is evil and what you think is good."

"And do beware," said yet another, "of who you think is the hunted, and who the hunter."

They laughed, the sound as soft and as melodic as their voices, and then they reached for him ...

Thomas jerked up from the bed, wide-eyed and sweating, his breath rattling harshly through his throat.

There was nothing untoward in the chamber: the Biermans lay to one side of him, deep in sleep.

In the other bed, Marcel, Karle and Marcoaldi lay still, their breathing slow and deep.

Thomas looked at the window. It was tightly shuttered. He turned his gaze to the door. It was closed, and the fire still burned bright in the hearth, casting enough light around the chamber to show that it was empty apart from himself and his travelling companions.

He swallowed and managed to bring his breathing under control. He lifted a hand, clenched it briefly to stop its trembling, and crossed himself, then sat and bowed his head in prayer for a few minutes, appealing to St Michael and Christ for protection.

He did not close his eyes, but kept them roving about the room, lest the ... the demons should leap out from a shadowed recess.

Finally, after almost an hour of prayer, Thomas lay down. He stared at the ceiling. He did not sleep again that night.

Even though the room appeared empty of all save its legitimate occupiers, Thomas knew that, somehow, he was still being watched.

Somewhere, eyes still gleamed.

GERMANY

"The King comands, and I must to the warres."
"*thers others more enow to end those cares.*"
"but I am one appointed for to goe,
And I dare not for my liffe once say noe."
"*O marry me, and you may stay att home!*
Full 30 wekes you know that I am gone."
"theres time enough; another Father take;
heele loue thee well, and not thy child forsake."

A Jigge (for Margrett)
Medieval English ballad

I

The Vigil of the Feast of St John the Baptist
In the fifty-first year of the reign of Edward III
(Wednesday 23rd June 1378)

— Midsummer's Eve —

Thomas wrapped his cloak tightly about his body, and pulled his hood forward so it cut out as much of the chill wind as possible. It was high summer — Midsummer's Eve — but this far up in the Alps it meant nothing save that the road was not waist-high in snow. He lifted his head and squinted into the mountains.

They were massive, higher than anything Thomas had ever seen. Great craggy peaks, still snow-covered, reared into the afternoon sky, tendrils of mist swirling about their tops.

He shivered. Folklore maintained that mountains and deep forests were the haunt of demons, sprites and unkind elves, and looking at these horrific crags, Thomas could well believe it himself.

And tomorrow, he would have to dare them.

The alpine passes were legendary, and most grown men had been reared on the stories of old men who claimed to have bested them. The great chain of Alps cut Italy, with all her great trading ports and industrial cities, off from northern Europe. Apart from the uncertainties of sea carriage, the only way to get expensive spices and silks from the Far East into northern Europe was via the alpine passes: the Brenner Pass in the western Alps, used by travellers to central and eastern Europe, and the St Gothard and Great St Bernard Pass in the eastern Alps for movement into the west of Europe.

And any who desired travel between the Italian city states and northern Europe also had to use the passes unless, as Thomas had on his journey to Rome, they possessed the courage, or the inclination, to dare the perilous sea voyage.

There were only two periods in the year when the passes were open: high summer and deep winter. Spring and autumn were too dangerous — these were the times of greatest risk from avalanche, when the snow melted, or was only newly laid. In high summer most of the snow had gone; in deep winter it was largely frozen in place.

Now it was high summer, and the passes were safe.

Relatively.

Thomas was under no illusions as to the hazards he and his companions would face in the next few days.

They'd travelled rapidly from Florence — Thomas atop a hefty but swift brown gelding, and desperately trying not to enjoy riding a horse again. Marcel, Karle and Bierman had between them a large consignment of cloths, both Florentine wools and Far Eastern silks and tapestries, to sell in the northern European markets, but they had entrusted most of this cargo to the trusty, though ugly and slow, cog ships that plied the trading route between Venice and the northern cities of the Hanseatic League. The banker Marcoaldi travelled with nothing but a pair of well-braced, locked chests on a packhorse. He never let the chests out of his sight, and had them guarded by six heavily-weaponed and armoured men.

Thomas recognised them instantly as Swiss mercenaries, and thought that Marcoaldi must be wealthy indeed to be able to afford such expensive guards.

Wealthy . . . or extremely anxious.

Apart from Marcoaldi's packhorse and mercenaries, Thomas and the merchants, the train consisted of eight packhorses laden with the merchants' personal effects and small packages of spices to sell in Nuremberg, as well as gifts for their families, and twelve rather rough but apparently reasonably professional German mercenaries who acted as guards for the entire train. The Swiss mercenaries kept themselves to themselves, as Swiss soldiers tended to do, but the Germans were congenial, some fairly well educated, and those not on guard joined Thomas and his companions about the campfire at night when they camped out.

Generally, the merchants and Marcoaldi preferred to find an inn or a monastery guest house to stay in for the night; camping out was all very well, but they vastly favoured the comforts of a mattress above the chill and inflexible comforts of the ground.

And so they had this night. There was a Benedictine monastery at the foot of the Brenner Pass, catering for all manner of travellers, whether traders and merchants, pilgrims, footloose mercenaries, or noble diplomats moving between the Italian cities and the court of the Holy Roman Emperor. The accommodation was better than most monastic houses — Thomas assumed this was because the monastery had been made rich from centuries of patronage by noble pilgrims — and Marcel and his companions were currently enjoying a glass of German wine and sweetmeats in the guest house refectory with their host, the hosteller.

Thomas shook his head, thinking of the accommodation: not only did every guest have his own straw mattress, every guest had his own latrine!

Wealth, indeed.

"Thinking of the difficulties of the Brenner, my friend?" said a soft voice behind him.

Thomas turned around, and grinned. "No, Johan. I was thinking only of the wealth of the monastery below us."

"Aha!" Johan laughed. "I believe you are regretting joining the Dominicans instead of the Benedictines!"

They turned to silently study the mountains soaring before them. Johan and Thomas had become good friends in their journey north through Ferrara to Venice — at which place Marcel, Karle and Bierman had overseen the shipping of their consignments, clucking over its packing and storage in the deep holds of the cogs like mother hens — and then Verona, and from there onto the northern road to the foot of the Alps.

Johan was a likeable lad, a bit too irreligious for Thomas' taste — but then hadn't he been so at the same age? — but well meaning and behaved, traits which Thomas thought had obviously been taught Johan by his serious and moralistic father. Also, Thomas admitted to himself, he was flattered by Johan's attention. The young man admired Thomas' experience in the world, as his deep commitment to the Church, and was slightly in awe of Thomas' family name, which, truth to tell, very occasionally annoyed Thomas.

The Nevilles he had left behind a long, long time ago.

Both Johan and his older companions constantly questioned Thomas about what was going on in Rome; about what he knew of the English plans to invade France.

Thomas was glad to hear that the Frenchmen among the group, Marcel and Karle, were just as concerned to see the papacy remain in Rome as were the others. All were appalled at the idea that the rogue cardinals had returned to Avignon and, for all anyone knew, might have elected a rival pope by this stage.

There were considerably mixed feelings about renewed war between the French and the English. The war, fought because Edward felt he was the rightful claimant to the French throne, had been going on since Edward was eighteen or nineteen. Now he was an old man. Both countries had suffered because of the hostilities, but France had suffered the more. This was a war fought entirely on French soil, although French pirates made life as difficult as possible for villagers who lived along the English south-eastern coast, and the losses of French peasants had been horrendous. Tens of thousands had been killed, and many more were unable to return to lands burned and ravaged by the roving English armies.

There had been a hiatus in hostilities over the past few years, partly because both sides were exhausted, physically and emotionally, and partly because both Edward and the French king, John, had been trying to hammer out a truce.

Evidently, Edward had become impatient and, just as evidently, had managed to raise funds from somewhere for a renewed foreign campaign.

"Not from any of *my* colleagues, I hope," Marcoaldi had remarked darkly one evening when the war was being discussed over their evening meal. When he was a young man, Edward had obtained the funds for his first French campaign by raising a massive loan from the Florentine bankers Bardi and Peruzzi. When it came time to repay the debt, Edward declared he had no intention of ever doing so. Not only were the Bardi and Peruzzi families ruined, so also were many other Florentine families who relied on them.

Edward had not won himself many Italian or banking friends with that action.

Marcoaldi may have been concerned about the financial aspects of a renewed English campaign, but Marcel and Karle were horrified at the thought of what deprivations might await the French people this time.

"And Paris ... *Paris!*" Marcel had remarked. "No doubt the English will again lay siege to it! Thomas, do you have any idea what —"

Thomas had interrupted him at that point, again declaring his allegiance to God rather than to the English king, or even his own family. "I take no part in the war," he said.

And yet ... yet ... hadn't he once been a part of those marauding English armies? Hadn't he himself set the torch time after time to the thatched roofs of peasant homes?

Hadn't he taken sword to husbands ... before wrenching their wives to the ground for his own pleasure?

Thomas stared at the mountains, and wondered if he would ever be able to atone for his sins. The last campaign he had taken part in had been the worst, and the blood and pain and misery caused had, finally, made him pause for thought.

And yet how he still lusted for those days: the fellowship of the battle, the warm companionship of his brothers-in-arms.

"Thomas? Thomas? What's wrong?"

"Ah, I was lost in memories. Forgive me. Johan ... tell me, have you ever been through the Brenner before?"

"Yes. Three times — and once during spring! I swear to God —"

"Johan!"

"Forgive me. I mean, um, I mean it was more dangerous than you can imagine! The last day such a great gust of snow threatened to fall on us that I swear that — sorry — that my father was in fear for his life. You should have been with us then, Thomas, for my father cried out desperately for a priest to take his last confession."

"Well," Thomas said mildly, "I shall with be you on the morrow, should the need arise."

For a moment or two they remained silent, watching the sun set behind one of the taller peaks.

"They are so wondrous," Johan eventually said.

Thomas looked at him, puzzled. "Wondrous? What?"

"The mountains ... their beauty ... their danger ..."

Thomas stared at the mountains, then turned back to Johan.

"That is not 'beauty', Johan. The Alps are vile things, useless accumulations of rock that serve no useful purpose to mankind. Indeed, they hinder mankind's effort to tame this world and make it serve him, as was God's commandment to Adam."

Johan turned an earnest face to Thomas. "But don't they call to you, Thomas? Don't you feel their pull in your blood?"

"Call?"

"Sometimes," Johan said in a low voice, "when I gaze at them, or travel through their passes, I am overcome with an inexpressible yearning."

"A yearning for what, Johan?" Thomas was watching the younger man's face very carefully. Were demons calling to him? Was he in the grip of the evil that St Michael had warned him about?

Johan sighed. "It is so difficult to explain, to put into mere words what I feel. The sight of these majestic peaks —"

Majestic?

"— makes me yearn to leave behind my life as a merchant, and to take to the seas as a roving captain, to explore and discover the world that waits out there," he flung an arm wide, "beyond the known waters and continents —"

"Johan, why feel this way? We have all we need within Christendom, there is no need — and surely no *desire* — to explore the lands of infidels." Thomas laid a firm hand on Johan's chest, forcing the man to meet his eyes. "Johan, better to explore your own soul to ensure your eventual salvation. It is the next world which holds all importance, not this one. This is but a wasteland full of evil, here to tempt us away from our true journey, that of the spirit towards salvation in the next life."

Johan flushed at the reprimand. "I know that, Brother Thomas. Do forgive me. It's just ... it's just that ..." he turned his face back to the mountains, and Thomas could see their peaks reflected in his eyes, "it is just that one day ... one day I wish I could summon the skill and the courage to climb to their very pinnacles and survey the entire world."

Johan looked back to Thomas, and now there was no contrition in his face at all. "Imagine, Thomas, finding the courage within yourself to be able to conquer the greatest peaks in the world."

And with that, he turned and walked back down the road towards the monastery, leaving Thomas to stare, disturbed, after him.

On his own return to the monastery, Thomas was even more disturbed to find that, to a man, the German mercenaries were nowhere to be found. When he inquired as to their whereabouts, Marcel had shrugged, and looked a little nonplussed.

"'Tis Midsummer's Eve, brother. The Germans have gone to join the revels of the villagers in that little hamlet we passed through a mile before the monastery."

At that, Thomas' mouth thinned. Peasants made far too

much of the midsummer solstice, believing that if they didn't mark it with fire festivals and dances, then the sun would not recover from its long slide towards its winter nadir. The Church had long tried to halt the festivals, but with little success. All across Christendom, people walked up hills and to the tops of cliffs, and there rolled down the slopes burning wheels of hay and straw to mark the solstice.

Marcel watched Thomas' face carefully, then said: "Do not judge them too harshly, Thomas. A little colour in their lives, a little fun, is hardly harmful."

"What is *harm*, Marcel, is when they engage in un-Christian rites that allow demons a stronger hold among us."

"Well," Marcel said slowly, "the older and wiser among us are still here, and I have planned a small gathering tonight to give thanks for our continued freedom from the entrapments of evil. I," he hesitated, "and mine always mark Midsummer in this fashion. I will be delighted and grateful if you would lead us in prayer tonight. Come, Thomas, what do you say?"

Thomas sighed, and nodded. "Of course I will. I am sorry, Marcel. Sometimes I think that mankind should all be perfect, and, of course, they are hardly so."

"But there are many good men working within society, brother, trying day by day to bring order to chaos. You must trust in them."

"Yes. You are right."

That night, safe in his clean bed, Thomas dreamed of the mountains overrun with demons scampering across their peaks. He shivered, fearing, then he rejoiced, for behind the mountains appeared the glowing form of the archangel Michael. But, just as he thought St Michael would smite the demons from the mountains, the archangel put a hand to his face, as if afraid, and fled.

Thomas woke screaming, bringing the hosteller, as also Marcel and Karle, running to his side.

The next morning, early, they set out for the Brenner Pass.

II

The Feast of St John the Baptist
In the fifty-first year of the reign of Edward III
(Thursday 24th June 1378)

— Midsummer's Day —

The ascent for the final few miles to the opening of the pass was a sombre one. It was still dark, and cold this high up, but that was not the reason. Thomas was distant and silent, and sat hunched in his saddle as if he thought all the imps of hell were about to descend upon him.

He'd not explained his nightmare of the previous night — even though Marcel and the hosteller had sat by his side until it was time to rise — and in fact had hardly spoken, apart from a few grudging monosyllabic replies, since they'd begun their ride towards the pass.

Thomas was afraid, deeply afraid. If the archangel himself fled before the evil, then what hope had he?

He did not doubt that what he had seen in his dream had been, if not perfect fact, then an accurate representation of the way things lay. All knew that dreams were a window between the world of man and the world of spirits, and dreams were the perfect vehicle by which demons and imps could invade the world of mankind. It was why no woman should ever sleep in a chamber alone, because, faulted with the weakness of Eve, lone women were ever likely to succumb to the blandishments of imps and demons.

In past years Thomas had seen three babies, hideously deformed, that were the obvious results of women who'd allowed (perhaps even begged) the minions of hell to seduce them.

The babies had been killed, the women burned.

But this nightmare was not so easily disposed of. It lingered on the edges of Thomas' mind, making him jump at every shadow, and wince at every glimpse of a looming mountain peak. He could feel the eyes of his companions upon him, and he knew they thought he was scared of the dangerous passage ahead.

True, but not for the reasons they believed. The danger of a footslip on a narrow path did not concern him so much as the thought that the Brenner Pass might hold more evil than he could possibly deal with.

Saint Michael aid me, Saint Michael aid me, he prayed over and over in a silent litany.

But the dream had planted the seeds of doubt in Thomas' mind, and he feared that St Michael might not be strong enough to aid him.

And if the great archangel was afraid and impotent against the evil, then what chance had he?

"Thomas?"

Etienne Marcel, riding close to his side.

"Thomas, do not fear too greatly —"

"You cannot know of what I fear!"

"Thomas." Marcel leaned over and placed a hand on Thomas' arm. "I do know. It is not the heights and the depths and the treacherous ice paths awaiting us which fret at you, but the unknowns. This is ungodly territory, and you and I both know it. Be strong, Thomas. We will prevail."

Thomas looked up, stunned by Marcel's perception ... and equally stunned by the degree of comfort the man had imparted with his words and touch.

Thomas gave a small nod, and briefly laid his own hand over Marcel's. "I thank you. You are truly a man of God."

Marcel's mouth gave a peculiar twist, and then he smiled, lifting his hand away. "I am sent to give you comfort and courage, Thomas. Do not doubt."

Thomas stared at him. God *had* led him to this man. Was Marcel an angel or saint in disguise, sent to guide his steps? Thomas knew better than to question. Better to have faith, and to believe.

He took a deep breath, and threw his hood back. "Shall we chase back the demons of fear between us, Marcel?"

Marcel laughed, glad to see Thomas more himself. "Between us, my friend, we shall make the world a place of our own."

And he kicked his horse forward, leaving Thomas to stare puzzled after him.

They rode until an hour after dawn, when they entered a small encampment at the foot of the pass. There were several wooden huts, and a long building that was obviously a barn. Several team of oxen were waiting outside, yoked to surprisingly narrow carts.

Marcel waved them to dismount. "From here we will go on foot," he said.

Thomas slid to the ground, giving his gelding a grateful rub on his neck, and turned to Johan. "We don't ride?"

Johan shook his head, and tossed the reins of his horse to a rough-dressed and as equally rough-bearded man who'd come up to them. He motioned Thomas to do the same.

"We walk," he said. "It is too dangerous to ride. No, wait. It will be easier for you to see than for me to explain. The guides will blindfold the riding and packhorses and lead them through."

The horses had to be blindfolded? Sweet Jesu, how fearsome was this pass?

Johan walked over to join Marcel, who was haggling with three of the men who were to be their guides through the pass. Thomas looked about him. The elder Bierman had hunched himself into his cloak, staring at the cliffs rising to either side of the opening of the pass; Marcoaldi was standing to one side of Bierman, his hands clenching nervously at his side.

As Thomas watched, Marcoaldi turned and saw him. He almost flinched, then gathered himself and walked over.

His face was death grey, and Thomas reached out, concerned. "Master Marcoaldi, we shall surely be safe. Is this ... is this your first time through the pass?"

Marcoaldi gave a jerky shake of his head. "I've been through once before. Some years ago." He tried to smile, but failed badly, and gave up any pretence of nonchalance. "I went through with my elder brother, Guiseppi. He was my mentor. He taught me all I know about banking. He was also my friend, and my rock through this often frightful existence."

Even more concerned — he'd never seen Marcoaldi demonstrate even the slightest degree of hesitancy — Thomas tightened his hand on the banker's arm reassuringly. "He's dead?"

Marcoaldi did not immediately reply. His eyes had taken on a peculiar look, as if he was staring back into the depths of his soul.

"He died in this pass, Brother Thomas." Marcoaldi drew in a deep, shaky breath. "He slipped on the treacherous footing, and tumbled down a ravine. Thomas," Marcoaldi lifted his eyes to gaze directly into Thomas', "he was terribly injured by the fall, but not killed. We ... we stood at the top of the cliff and listened to him call for hours, until night fell, and the ice moved in. He died alone in that ravine, Thomas. Alone. I could not reach him, and I could not aid or comfort him. He died alone."

"Giulio, he died unshriven? Unconfessed? There was no priest with you?"

Marcoaldi did not reply, but his expression hardened from pain into bitterness.

Thomas shook his head slightly, appalled that Marcoaldi's brother had died unconfessed.

"He must surely have gone to purgatory," Thomas said quietly, almost to himself, then he spoke up. "But do not fear, my friend. Eventually the prayers of you and your family will ensure that he —"

Marcoaldi jerked his arm away from Thomas' hand. "I do not want your pious babbling, priest! Guiseppi died screaming for me, and for his wife. He died alone. *Alone!* None of his family were with him! I care not that he went to the next life priestless, only that he died without those who loved him and could have comforted him!"

"But you should be concerned that —"

"I *know* my brother does not linger in your purgatory, brother. Guiseppi was a loving husband, father and brother. He dealt kindly and generously with all he met. He has gone to a far better place than your *cursed* purgatory!"

And with that Marcoaldi was gone, striding across to where the guides readied the oxen teams.

Thomas watched, grieving. Marcoaldi was lost himself if he did not pay more attention to his spiritual welfare, and if he persisted in his disbelief in purgatory. He was a lost soul, indeed, if he did not take more care.

Perhaps his brother Guiseppi had gone straight to hell if he had not confessed or made suitable penance for a lifetime of luxuriating in the sin of usury. Ah ... these bankers ...

Thomas sighed, and walked away. If a person filled his life with good works, penance for his inevitable sins, and confessed on his death bed, then death should be a joyous affair, and family members should rejoice that their loved one had passed from the vale of pain into an eternity spent with God and his saints.

A death like Guiseppi's, alone, unconfessed, and probably, if he was like his younger brother, unrepentant, was the most miserable imaginable. Thomas hoped that eventually Marcoaldi would see the error of his ways, and spend what time was left to him in repentance and the practice of good works to negate the burden of his sins.

Thomas knew he would have to talk to Marcoaldi again ... but best to leave it until they left the painful memories, and the harsh fears, of the Brenner Pass.

At mid-morning they set off in a single file, led by two of the guides, each leading a team of two oxen yoked to a cart.

Christoffel Bierman and Giulio Marcoaldi sat in the second of the carts, their faces resolutely looking back the way they had come, refusing to look at the chasm that fell away on the left of the trail. One of the guides had offered Thomas a ride in the cart as well, but he had refused, and the guide had walked away, a knowing smirk on his face.

Behind the carts walked Etienne Marcel, Johan Bierman, who had also refused to ride the carts, and Thomas himself. Behind them came more guides walking the blindfolded horses — Thomas could hear them snorting nervously, and occasionally heard the rattle of hooves on the trail as a horse misplaced a step and fought for its footing — and behind them came the guards, grouped in front of and behind Marcoaldi's preciously laden packhorse, and then yet more blindfolded horses and their handlers.

For the first hour the way was not particularly treacherous, nor frightening. The trail wound about the eastern side of the pass, black rock rearing skyward into the cloud-shrouded mountaintops on each man's right hand, and sliding into precipitous, misty depths on his left. There were small patches of snow-melt on the trail itself, but the footing was generally secure, and as long as he kept his eyes ahead, Thomas found he had no trouble.

Save for the black ill-temper of Marcoaldi's gaze as it met his every so often.

Johan kept up a constant chatter, largely to tell Thomas just how difficult and frightening the way would become later in the day.

"And tomorrow," he enthused at one point, "for we must spend tonight camped in the pass, you realise, a man must confront his worst fears, and conquer them, if he is to survive."

"Then I admit I find myself more than slightly puzzled by your cheerfulness, Johan. Surely you regard the approaching dangers with dread?"

"Well, yes, but also with anticipation." Johan threw a hand toward the mountains now emerging from the early morning mist and cloud. "I enjoy the thrill of danger, the race of my blood, and the rush of pride each time I manage to best my fear."

Thomas was about to observe that Johan would be better served if he used this time of mortal danger to look to the health of his soul, but just at that moment he happened to lock eyes with Marcoaldi, and he closed his mouth.

Should he have better spent his time consoling the man's lingering grief at the loss of his brother rather than preaching to him about the dangers of dying unconfessed?

And how could he castigate Johan when he had himself screamed with the joy and thrill of danger in the midst of battle?

But he was not that man now. He was *Brother* Thomas, and one of his duties in life was to guide the souls of the weak towards —

"Thomas," Marcel said, clapping a hand on his shoulder, "you are looking far too grim. There are dangers ahead, certainly, but there is also time enough for a smile and a jest occasionally. Hmm?"

And so Thomas wondered if he was too grim, but then he thought about the mission the archangel Michael had entrusted to him, and that made him even grimmer, and after a moment or two Marcel and John left him alone, and they walked forward silently into the pass.

By late morning Thomas was concentrating far more on keeping his footing than on introspection about the sins of his companions, or his doubts about his own ability to fight evil incarnate. The way had slowly, so imperceptibly that Thomas was hardly aware of it, become so treacherous that he now understood why the passage through the Brenner was regarded with so much fear by most travellers.

The path that clung to the cliff face not only became much narrower, scarcely more than an arm's width — the carts ahead seemed to spend more time with their left wheels hanging over the precipice than on the trail — but it also began to tilt on a frightening angle towards the precipice. Thomas found himself clinging to the rock wall on his right with one hand, while keeping his left splayed out to aid his balance.

Small rivulets of ice-melt running down the cliff face made the going deadly — they not only made the footing slippery, but they had gouged out weaknesses in the path, so that rocks, and occasionally, large sections of footing, suddenly slid away, making men cry out with fear and hug the rock face, pleading to God and whatever saints they could remember to save them.

The horses, even blindfolded, were terrified. Thomas could hear their snorting and whinnies above his own harsh breathing; underlaying the sounds of the horses' fear were the murmured reassurances of the guides. Thomas had wondered previously why the mountain guides had bothered themselves with leading the horses when the task could have been given to the guards in Marcel's train. Now he knew. These rough mountain men were extraordinarily skilled in their manner of reassuring the horses and, without them, most of the animals would surely have been lost.

Thomas could also understand why Bierman and Marcoaldi had chosen to ride in the ox carts. The oxen appeared totally unperturbed by the abyss falling away to their left — at one point where the path had turned right following the line of the cliff face, Thomas had seen the faces of the stolid animals, placidly chewing their cud as if they were strolling through lowland meadow rather than mountain-death trail. The ox carts would surely be as safe — safer — than trusting to one's own security of footing.

Johan appeared hardly concerned, and Thomas wondered at his words that the morrow would be worse than today.

Sweet Jesu! It got worse than this?

As if Johan had guessed his thoughts, the young man turned slightly as he clambered over a deep crack in the path, and grinned at Thomas.

"Brother Thomas! Have you seen that crag to our left?"

Johan turned enough so he could point to it. "I have been studying it this past hour. If a man was strong enough, he could surely climb that south-western face, don't you think? Imagine the view from the top! All of Creation stretched out below —"

Now even Marcel had heard enough. "Silence, Johan! We need all our concentration to keep our feet here, not on some fanciful and totally profitless expedition to the top of a piece of rock!"

Johan flinched as if he'd been struck, and he mumbled something inaudible to which Marcel replied equally inaudibly, and the group continued to struggle onwards.

And so, inch by inch, harsh breath by harsh breath, and sweaty hand clinging to rock after rock, they moved forwards through the day, and through the Brenner Pass.

There was no relief, save for brief rest periods, until mid-afternoon, and by that time Thomas thought his muscles would never manage to unclench themselves from their knots of fear and effort. He had believed himself a relatively courageous man, but this trail . . .

He, as everyone else, let out a sigh of deeply felt relief as the lead ox cart suddenly moved forward far more confidently into a small plateau carved into the side of the cliff.

"We will halt here," Marcel said. "It is the only place where we can camp safely before the end of the pass."

"We don't push on through this evening?" Thomas said.

Marcel gave him an exasperated look. "And you think that you *could* push through another eight or nine hours of what we've just endured?"

Thomas' mouth twisted in a wry grin, and he shook his head. "I thank God I have made it safe this far. You must have needed to travel very fast very badly to dare this pass."

Marcel glanced at Marcoaldi and Bierman climbing unsteadily out of the cart. "We all had pressing business, my friend."

He moved off and Thomas sank down in a relatively dry spot. He leaned his back against the rock of the cliff face and tried to relax his cramped muscles.

Lord God, Wynkyn had done this four times a year? May Saint Michael grant me such courage.

Then he sighed and let his thoughts drift, and, as the guides helped the guards unpack provisions and firewood from the lead cart, drifted into a grateful doze.

They ate about the roaring campfire, talked, ate some more, and then Thomas led the entire group in evening prayers before they retired for as much sleep as they could get on the cold, hard ground. The older men slept in the carts, but Thomas took the blanket offered by one of the guides, and rolled himself up in it, lying down close to the fire. He lay awake a while, cold and uncomfortable, but very gradually he felt himself drifting into sleep, and his last conscious sight was of one of the guards moving among the horses, making sure their hobbles and tethers were secure.

He woke sometime so deep in the night that the fire had burned down into glowing coals. There was complete stillness in the camp — not even the horses moved or snuffled.

He blinked, not otherwise moving, and wondered if this was a dream. The night had such an ethereal quality . . .

Something moved to one side, and Thomas lazily turned his head.

And then stared wildly as a shadow leaped out from under the rock face and thudded down on his body.

Thomas opened his mouth, although he was so winded — and so agonised — by the weight of the creature atop him that he did not think he could —

"Make a sound, you black-robed abomination, and I will gut you here and now!"

Thomas stilled, his mouth still open, and stared at the face only a few handspans above his.

It was incomparably vile, if only because the creature had thought to assume the face of an angel, but had been unable to accomplish the unearthly beauty of one of the heavenly creatures. The face was vaguely manlike, although the eyes were much larger and were such a pale blue they almost glowed in the fading firelight. Its chin was more pointed than a man's, and its forehead far broader and higher. Its skin was perfection: pale, creamy, flawless.

But there the beauty ended. At the hairline, among the tight silvery curls, curled the horns of a mountain goat, and when the creature smiled, it revealed tiny, pointed teeth.

"You see only what you want to see," it hissed, and then shifted its weight slightly. Thomas groaned, for one of the creature's — *the demon's!* — clawed feet was digging into his belly, and another cut through both blanket and robes and pinned his right upper arm so agonisingly to the rocky ground that Thomas thought it might be broken.

"Uncomfortable, friar?" the demon said, and laughed softly. "Waiting for an angel to save you? Well, where is your blessed archangel now, priest? *Where?*"

"Get you gone, you hound from hell!" Thomas whispered, and the creature lifted its head and tilted its face to the moon, shaking with silent laughter.

As it did so, its features blurred slightly, as if the demon only wore a pretty mask to tease Thomas.

Thomas realised that something truly frightful writhed under that facade.

Suddenly the demon dropped its head so close that its lips touched Thomas' forehead. "Your God and all your bright collection of saints and angels will not help you now, priest. It is just you and I —"

Thomas fought back equal amounts of nausea and fear, and managed to speak. "In the name of the Father, and the —"

The demon lifted the clawed hand holding down Thomas' right arm and slammed it over Thomas' throat, making him gag mid-sentence. He twisted his head from side to side, desperately trying to breathe.

"*I ordered you not to speak!*" the demon said.

Thomas managed to lift his right arm — Lord God, the pain! — and grabbed at the clawed fingers over his throat, but the demon was the size and weight of a pony, and he could not shift it. Instead, he felt the demon shift its weight so that more of it bore down on the leg on Thomas' belly, and he almost passed out from the torment.

The demon snarled, and shifted its weight again, easing the pressure on both Thomas' neck and belly.

"I know what you are doing," the demon said. "*We all know!* You think to take Wynkyn's burden on your shoulders, you think to take his place. You pitiful creature! We have been free too long now to submit again to the seductive songs of the *Keeper* —"

"Who are you?" Thomas croaked. "Who?"

"Who? Who?" The demon hissed with laughter again. "I, as mine, are your future, Thomas. One day you will embrace us, and throw your *God* —" he spoke the word as the most foulest of curses "— onto the dungheap that He deserves!"

"I will never betray my God!"

The demon's mouth slid open in a wide grin. "Ah, Thomas, but will you be able to recognise the manner of temptation we will place in your way?"

"*I will never betray my God!*"

"You think to hunt us down, Thomas," the demon said, very softly now, "but one day ... one day ... you will embrace us."

Suddenly the demon lifted its head, and stared across the rock plateau as if something, or someone, had caught its attention.

It blinked, and cocked its head, its horns catching a shimmer of moonlight.

Then it looked back at Thomas. "You think to lead the armies of righteousness against us, Thomas. You think to be God's General. Well, one day, one wicked black day, you will crucify righteousness for the sake of evil!"

Then the fingers still about Thomas' neck tightened to impossible cruelties, and Thomas blacked out.

"Thomas? Thomas? Good brother, only a friar used to the hard couches of his priesthood could possibly sleep so well on this stony ground!"

Thomas opened his eyes, felt the hand on his shoulder, then jerked up into a sitting position, making Marcel reel backwards onto his haunches.

"My God, brother, do you always wake this anxious? It must be the shock of hearing the bells for Matins in the middle of every night!"

Marcel was trying to make a jest of Thomas' reaction, but Thomas was in no mood for jests. He got to his feet, wincing at the pain in his arm and belly, his eyes skittering about the campsite.

"Thomas?" Marcel half reached out a hand, then thought better of it.

Some of the others, including the two Biermans and several of the German guards had stopped what they were doing to watch Thomas.

Everything seemed usual; there was nothing to indicate what had happened to him last night.

Thomas looked back to Marcel, who was staring at him with a concerned face.

"Thomas ... Thomas, what is wrong?"

Thomas took a deep breath and calmed himself. "A demon haunted this camp last night, Marcel."

"*What?*"

"It taunted me with failure, and told me I would betray my God."

"Lord Christ Saviour, Thomas! Are you certain? This was not a dream?"

Thomas tore back his right sleeve and exposed his upper arm. "Is *this* a dream?"

Marcel looked at Thomas' arm, then gasped in shock. It was covered in blue and black bruises, etched here and there with deep abrasions.

He crossed himself. "A demon? Lord Christ save me! Save me!"

He closed his eyes, steadied himself, then hesitantly took Thomas' hand. "You beat him off with the strength of your faith. This *is* ungodly territory, but you were strong, and you prevailed. You are a good man, Thomas. A good man."

Thomas let Marcel's words and touch comfort him, but he knew that the demon had been in no danger from Thomas. It had left of its own accord, or obeying whatever had called to it, rather than being beaten back by the strength of Thomas' will ... but, as Marcel's grip tightened slightly, Thomas persuaded himself that the demon had known its cause was hopeless, and so left him alone.

"And your neck," Marcel said softly. "You have been ill-used indeed, brother. Come, one of the guides has some skill in healing, and has some pouches of salves that ease the worst of rock sprains and bruises."

Thomas smiled slightly to thank Marcel for his concern. "And let us hope that they ease demon strains and burns, my friend."

Marcel took Thomas over to one of the guards, leaving him sitting on a rock as the guard rummaged about in a pack for his salves.

Thomas saw Marcel walk over to his companions, and lean down to speak to Marcoaldi who was still wrapped up in his blankets on the ground. Unheard words passed between them, and then Thomas saw Marcel harangue Marcoaldi angrily. Thomas frowned, wondering what the banker had done to earn Marcel's ire, when the guide drew back his sleeve to inspect the abrasions and bruises.

The man laughed, his tongue running about his thick lips, and he looked slyly at Thomas. "I hope she was worth the sport," he said, and made an obscene gesture with one of his hands "and that your loving left her unable to walk for the next three days."

He roared with laughter, and Thomas, furious, pulled himself out of the man's grip and stalked away.

Peasant!

Marcel kept close to him for the day's nightmare journey through the last part of the pass. The trail was not appreciably narrower or steeper, but what made this section so dangerous were the constant waterfalls that roared down the cliff making the footing so treacherous that the guides insisted that everyone be roped together. It saved Thomas' life on three occasions.

Once he fell so badly he slipped entirely over the edge of the path, leaving Marcel and one of the guides to haul him back to safety.

When he finally stood on his feet again, shivering with terror, he looked up to see Marcoaldi staring at him with eyes filled with bitterness and grief, and perhaps a little regret that Thomas had not also fallen to a lonely and unshriven death. The banker seemed unwell, as if he had caught an ague from his night spent on the cold ground.

But perhaps he was only discomforted because Marcel had so berated him for some unknown misdeed.

When Thomas finally began to move along the trail again, his hands and legs uncomfortably wobbly, he forced himself to look over the edge.

The precipice fell away with no slope at all, but occasionally a rock or two jutted out from the rock face; on these rocks hung bleached bones, sometimes held together by a strip of skin or tendon.

Thomas leaned back, shut his eyes briefly, and fought to forget what he'd seen.

All the men made it safely through the pass, but four of the horses had, in that final horrific stretch, fallen screaming to their deaths. Gratefully, Thomas' own mount was safe, but he found himself hoping ungraciously that one of the doomed horses had been the pack animal carrying Marcoaldi's precious chests. But it was not so, and once on relatively flat ground the banker was reunited with his chests and also, it appeared, with his good temper, for he greeted Thomas cheerfully as the friar walked past.

"And now," Marcel said as they bid the guides farewell and remounted their horses, "Nuremberg."

III

Vigil of the Feast of St Swithin
In the fifty-first year of the reign of Edward III
(Wednesday 14th July 1378)

For over two weeks they rode north from the Brenner Pass, making the best speed they could. The mood of the group had changed since the passage through the Brenner. Outwardly as cheerful as it had been previously, there was nevertheless a sombre undertone to the banter of the day's rides and the evening discussions about the campfire or tavern table. Marcel and Karle appeared preoccupied with their need to travel as fast as possible. While this suited Thomas, it nevertheless added a degree of tenseness to both travel and relations within the group.

Marcoaldi, though, had reverted to his charming, friendly self, and the Biermans were as genial as ever, although Johan actually seemed subdued now that he'd left the mountains behind him.

Thomas had no more visitations, whether of dream or actuality. He prayed constantly to St Michael, as well as to Christ and the Holy Virgin, seeking guidance in his journey ahead, spending many hours of each night on his knees, or prostrate on the ground or inn floor.

From the Brenner the group travelled almost directly north through Innsbruck and Augsberg. This was the road that Wynkyn de Worde would also have travelled, but Thomas found no clues on the road, nor in the faces and words of those they passed.

All he felt was a pressing urgency within him to arrive at Nuremberg, and this Thomas believed was the work of the archangel on his soul, driving him forward to find Wynkyn's secret and the secret to negating the evil that now walked abroad.

Sweet Jesu, how could it be defeated, when already demons walked with such impunity among God's chosen? Saint Michael, grant me strength, I pray you.

Sometimes, when such thoughts ran through Thomas' mind, he would turn and see Marcel watching him, as if the man knew his doubts. Marcel would nod, his face grave but comforting, and Thomas would take heart.

Perhaps the archangel had chosen to walk in mortal disguise to aid him, for Thomas found Marcel a continual comfort.

On the Vigil of the Feast of St Swithin, nearing mid-July, they rode weary and sore from the pace Marcel had set into a small town, Carlsberg, a day's ride from Nuremberg. Here Marcel called a halt.

"There is an inn here that I know well," he said. "The innkeeper is a good man, and hospitable, and we shall spend a comfortable night before we reach Nuremberg on the morrow."

The others merely nodded, and followed Marcel into the bustling courtyard of a substantial inn. Here porters and grooms busied themselves with the arrivals' horses and packs, and the men stretched stiff limbs, and pulled gloves from hands as Marcel led the way into the inn itself.

It was a large establishment, roomy, clean and warm, and the innkeeper hurried to greet Marcel. They passed some words, brief and mumbled, and Marcel turned to the others.

"There is a messenger waiting here for me," he said, his face creased with worry. "Please, sit down before the fire. I will return shortly."

The innkeeper, a thin man with an innocuously round, red face, waved them towards benches set before a fire, promising ale and bread within moments.

They all sat, except William Karle, whose eyes followed Marcel as the merchant entered a small side room.

"Forgive me," Karle said, and hurried after Marcel.

Johan raised eyebrows at his father.

Bierman shrugged, then smiled and accepted the frothing mug of ale a serving girl had brought over. "Ah, every day these past few weeks I have cursed Marcel for his uncompromising pace, but for this ale I could forgive him anything! No wonder he rushed so!"

Thomas smiled at the girl as she handed him a mug, and then turned back to the Flemish merchant, ignoring the sudden flush in the girl's cheeks at his smile.

"There has been far more to Marcel's haste than a desire to reach the amenities of this inn, Master Bierman," Thomas said, and took a sip of his ale. "And now he has rushed out to meet with this messenger, and Karle with him, as if his salvation depended on it. Do trading matters always generate such disquietude?"

"It is perhaps more than trading matters, brother," Marcoaldi answered for Bierman. "Marcel is the Provost of Paris, and as such has more to concern him than the price he might get for his bolts of Florentine silks. And," Marcoaldi looked directly at Thomas, "with an English invasion threatening, and perhaps even at the gates of Paris itself, Marcel might well be desperate with worry. The fate of his fellow citizens concerns him deeply."

Thomas felt an edge of hostility to Marcoaldi's voice. "I am not responsible for the actions of the English, Master Marcoaldi."

The banker grinned. "Of course not. But you can understand Marcel's worry, can you not?"

Thomas inclined his head, and was about to say more, when Marcel strode over to them.

If he'd appeared concerned previously, now he was patently agitated.

"Events have moved faster than I could have imagined," he said, glancing at Thomas. "The Black Prince and the Duke of Lancaster have indeed landed a massive invasion force in Gascony, and even now march north. King John prepares to meet them — his vassals are mobilising to join with the king at Orleans."

"And Paris?" Marcoaldi said.

"Is in a bad state." Marcel had lifted his eyes, and was now staring at a blank space on the wall above the fireplace mantle. "John has levied extraordinary taxes to pay for his campaign ... and he is stripping Paris of all defences in order to meet the English in the south. My friends," he looked back down, and put one hand on Thomas' shoulder and the other on Bierman's, "I must leave ... within the hour. I wait only for fresh horses to be readied, and to have a meal."

"You're not going to Nuremberg?" Bierman said.

"No. I cannot. My friend, may I ask you to deal with my business there. It is much to ask, but you know what needs to be done, and I cannot —"

"Of course," Bierman said. "Your interests shall be well served."

Marcel nodded his thanks, spoke quickly to Marcoaldi, and then turned to Thomas.

"Thomas," he said softly. "We must talk. Will you join me in the kitchen as I eat?"

Thomas sat at the board table in the kitchen and watched as Marcel ate several hurried mouthfuls of food: Karle, who was also leaving with Marcel, had ladled some vegetables and grain thickened with gravy into a trencher of bread and had hurried out to the stables to oversee the packing of the fresh horses.

Marcel swallowed, took a gulp of ale, wiped his mouth with the back of his hand, and looked at Thomas sitting with expressionless face opposite him.

"My friend," Marcel said, "I need badly to talk with you, and had hoped to do it in Nuremberg before we went our different ways. Now ..."

He waved a hand helplessly, and gulped another mouthful of food. "Now there is no time, and there is a great deal that I must say to you.

"Thomas, you have never told me the reason you needed so desperately — no, do not protest, for I have observed your desperation clearly enough — to get to Nuremberg. I most certainly do not think it to be any ordinary mission. Particularly after your experience in the Brenner."

He fell silent, and stared at Thomas.

Thomas shifted uncomfortably. He was loathe to speak plainly, and yet he felt he deserved to give Marcel some explanation, for his hospitality and friendship, if nothing else.

But, if Marcel was indeed a mortal incarnation of St Michael, or of some other angel or saint sent to guide him, then there was every reason he *should* speak.

"Etienne ..." Thomas leaned forward on his arms on the tabletop. He sighed, his eyes downcast.

Marcel waited, sopping up gravies with his bread, and not shifting his eyes from Thomas' face.

"Etienne ... I travel north, even further than Nuremberg, I believe, on the gravest of missions. Many years ago, during the time of the pestilence —"

Marcel nodded. He knew the time of the pestilence very well.

"— a friar from the Saint Angelo friary in Rome departed north to Nuremberg. He carried with him a book which I *must* find."

"A book of what? Tithes the good folk of Rome have neglected to pay? A record of the words Saint Peter himself uttered during his martyrdom?"

For the first time Thomas lifted his face and stared directly at Marcel. The older man was watching him carefully, his brown eyes narrowed in thought, although whether speculative or fearful, Thomas could not tell.

"It is a book of a certain Wynkyn de Worde —"

Something flittered across Marcel's face, and Thomas understood then that Marcel knew very well of what he spoke.

"He was a friar of my Order," Thomas continued, "who managed ... ah!" Thomas shook his head in frustration. "Who managed somehow to hold in check evil incarnate — demons — with which Satan would corrupt God's work on this earth. Now that de Worde is gone evil incarnate walks unhindered. Demons threaten all of Christendom."

"And you are to set this to rights?"

Thomas was relieved to see that Marcel had not disbelieved him.

"I am to try and contain the evil again, Etienne. I am Wynkyn de Worde's successor."

Marcel sat back, and pushed his plate away. His face was blank, but Thomas thought it was a careful expression designed to hide inner tumult. "And on whose orders do you do this, Thomas? Your prior's? The Holy Father's?"

"Neither." Again Thomas hesitated, then decided if he had trusted Marcel with this much, then he could trust him with the rest. "The archangel Saint Michael appeared to me, and said to me that evil incarnate walked abroad, and that I was to head God's army of righteousness in order to challenge and contain the evil."

Marcel stared at Thomas, his expression one of absolute wonder and fear combined. "The archangel Saint Michael appeared to you?" he whispered.

"Aye."

"Sweet merciful Mother of God!" Marcel said, and crossed himself. "*It has begun!*"

Thomas frowned. "What has begun?"

"The final battle between good and evil, Thomas. Judgement is nigh."

His words chilled Thomas, the more because he could not disbelieve them.

"I doubt myself," Thomas said. "How can I be strong enough to persevere against the forces of evil? How can I —"

"Hush," Marcel said and, leaning over the table, took Thomas' arm in his firm grip. He stared Thomas directly in the eye. "*You are not alone!* There are many who will help you and enable you to be strong. Many who you might not immediately suspect to be your allies."

"You are one. I have suspected it these past weeks."

Marcel smiled gently, and let Thomas go. "Aye. I am one. And — if all truth be told between us — your arrival at my inn in Florence was not totally unexpected."

"How could you have known? Did Prior Bertrand —"

"I doubt that your Prior Bertrand has been of great assistance to you, Thomas. Nor the greater hierarchy of your — *our* — Church. You will tread a solitary path for a while to come, until I can rally greater numbers to your aid."

"But you have not told me how you suspected my arrival in Florence."

Marcel grinned. "We have a mutual friend, Thomas. Wat Tyler."

"You know Wat? How?"

"Wat is an old soldier, Thomas, and he has fought his way about much of Europe. I met him first years ago and, since then, he has proved most useful to me."

Thomas grunted. No doubt Wat would sell his soul to the Devil himself if the price was agreeable enough: that he should have sold it to the Provost of Paris in return for a bit of information now and again was not surprising. But . . .

"I'd said nothing to Wat about travelling north," Thomas said. "Nothing."

"Wat is an observant man. I have no doubt that he talked to many people while he was in Rome. Besides," Marcel grinned again, "Wat observed you leaving Rome. Indeed, he was on the road behind you for several days, long enough to know your general direction."

"Then why didn't he make himself known!"

Now Marcel's eyes were a good deal more careful. "Perhaps he thought his company might not be welcome. My friend, you do not have so many allies who will aid you that you can discard them for unwelcome familiarities."

Sweet Jesu, Thomas thought, *how much does this man know?*

"And so now," Marcel said. "You go to Nuremberg. And once there? And *from* there?"

Thomas shrugged a little helplessly. "All I know is that Wynkyn de Worde travelled to the friary in Nuremberg. I hope that the prior there can give me more information. And, if God is good, perhaps the prior will even have the book that I seek."

An indefinable expression played across Marcel's face, but Thomas did not see it.

"And if I should need to travel *from* Nuremberg," Thomas said, "then ... then ... well, then I do not know where my travels will take me."

Now it was Marcel's turn to grunt. He leaned back, and drained the dregs of his mug. "You cannot see past Nuremberg, can you? Well ... I do not think you will get much aid from your Church, or your Order. I doubt that you actually waited to receive your Prior General's permission to leave Saint Angelo's ... did you?"

Thomas' eyes widened. He hadn't thought of his Prior General, by whose grace he'd been given permission to travel to St Angelo's in the first instance. "I'm sure Father Thorseby will understand."

Marcel contented himself with a cynical look.

"I am *sure* that Father Thorseby will understand."

"Thomas, the Church is not going to unbend itself to forgive the transgressions of a friar scurrying about Europe on celestine orders! Sweet Jesu, Thomas, they're just as likely to set the Inquisition on you as wish you well on your way!"

"If I have to die to —"

"Oh, save me! You'll do no one any good — save evil incarnate itself — by martyring yourself on top of a bundle of burning wood, Thomas. Be sensible!"

Thomas retreated into silence, studying the back of one of his hands.

"Then at least accept the offer of aid from your friends. Thomas. Keep the brown gelding. He's grown attached to you, although why, I cannot know!"

Thomas' mouth quirked at the affectionate exasperation in Marcel's voice, but he did not look up.

There was a small thump on the table, and Thomas looked up to see Marcel had placed a small purse there.

"Gold, Thomas," Marcel said. "Not a great deal, but enough to see you out of trouble should you encounter it."

"I don't —"

"Every man needs a little gold at his waist, Thomas, whether priest or merchant. Take it. Think of it as my donation to the Church in order to save my soul.

"And if ever you travel through France, Thomas, then seek me out. I will do what I can for you. Here — something else for you."

Marcel slid a ring across the table. "It is a seal that I use as part of my duties as provost. If ever you are in Paris, and in need of me, give that to any guildsman. He will bring you to me."

Thomas pocketed the ring and purse, finally meeting Marcel's eyes. "I thank you, Etienne. You are right, I cannot afford to disdain the aid of true friends."

"Humph." But Marcel grinned, and Thomas returned it.

"And now," Thomas said, "what has caused you so much concern that you must rush from us tonight?"

"It is as I said. The threatening war has caused the ordinary people of Paris, together with those in the surrounding countryside, great distress. Taxes have risen until many starve in order to pay, and the city militia are being directed south to join King John's armed forces in order to repel the English. Paris is unprotected, and its people alarmed."

"You must hate the English," Thomas said softly.

"Nay. Not the English. More, we hate our own nobles and king for draining us of our livelihood and the food from our tables. The years of war have exhausted us, and exhausted our trust in those who should protect us."

"But you owe allegiance to your nobles and king, Marcel!"

"We owe them nothing when their taxes starve us, and when they do not protect us!"

Thomas sat back, disturbed by Marcel's attitude. "And when you get back to Paris, Marcel? What then?"

"Then I will do what is necessary in order to alleviate the people's suffering."

"Even to encouraging discontent that might destroy the ordained order ... *God's* ordained order?"

"I will destroy that order myself, Thomas, if I see one child starve on the streets because we have been abandoned by those who should preserve us!"

Thomas was silent a long moment before he spoke again. "You speak rashly," he finally said.

"Aye. I do. It is my hot temper and my concern for family and friends that makes me speak thus. Forgive me, Thomas. I *was* rash."

Thomas nodded, accepting the apology although his mind remained deeply disturbed. For a few minutes they spoke of minor things until Karle came in and told Marcel that the horses were ready.

"I must leave," Marcel said, and, standing, walked about the table to embrace Thomas. "Never forget that I will help if I can. Good luck, my friend. Go with God."

"Go with God," Thomas whispered, and then Marcel and Karle were gone, and the night was filled with the sounds of horses' hooves rattling over the courtyard cobbles.

That night, Thomas had a bed and a room to himself for the first time in many weeks, but he slept only fitfully. Every time he slipped into sleep he dreamed of merchants wearing crowns and wielding sceptres.

IV

The Feast of St Swithin
In the fifty-first year of the reign of Edward III
(Thursday 15th July 1378)

— i —

Nuremberg was one of the richest trading cities in northern Europe, boasting several powerful trading and merchant guilds and associations and a host of wealthy craft guilds. The buildings, especially the cathedral and castle, were magnificent, the streets bustling, the voices cheerful, and yet Thomas found it a depressing city, perhaps because of the drizzling rain and chill wind, and perhaps more so because he missed the company of Etienne Marcel.

He had risen early that morning, spending an hour or more in prayer before the others rose and broke their fast with a hasty meal, all riding out just as dawn broke.

Everyone was keen to get to Nuremberg. The Biermans because of the wealth they expected to make for themselves — and Marcel — in the markets; Marcoaldi because he could finally dispose of whatever it was he'd so carefully guarded in his chests; Thomas for his own reasons; and the guards, both Swiss and German, because this was where they would receive their final pay and go home, or on to their next employment.

Thomas said goodbye to his companions of the past

weeks once inside the main gate of the city. He knew the location of the friary and it would take him nowhere near the main square that the others were heading for. Their goodbyes were hasty, and Johan Bierman was the only one who genuinely appeared to regret the loss of Thomas' company.

"Be careful of goblins," Johan said with a grin.

Thomas jumped slightly, then took the remark as a jest, and replied in kind. "And you be wary of your admiration for mountains," he said, "for otherwise they will be the death of you."

And for the others there were nods, the briefest of polite words, and that was it.

Despite his depression, Thomas felt an immense relief as he once again set out on his own.

The Dominican friary was set against the eastern wall of the city, a small establishment for such a wealthy city, and Thomas wondered if it had ever managed to recover from the ravages of the pestilence thirty years previously. Many communities, whether those of the Church, or of secular society, had been so decimated by the pestilence they had never recovered from its horrors.

"Pray God there is someone here who remembers Wynkyn," he muttered as he tied his horse to a ring set in a side wall of the friary's courtyard.

A young friar, his earnest face marked by the scars of boyhood acne, walked from a door and greeted Thomas.

"Well met, brother. May we offer you the hospitality of the friary?"

Thomas thanked him, then asked if he might, first, speak with the prior. "If he is not at his prayers."

"Oh, no," the young friar said with a smile. "Prior Guillaume will be more than glad to welcome a visitor."

"Pray tell me, is Prior Guillaume an old man?"

"Oh, very," said the friar, and Thomas wondered if, being so young himself, the friar thought of all men past thirty as "old".

But Prior Guillaume was indeed old — ancient, Thomas thought, and hoped that he not only had been here during the time of the pestilence, but could remember if Wynkyn had passed through.

Guillaume was very fat — his head wobbled continuously atop four or five chins — but surprisingly agile for his bulk, and apparently very pleased to greet a visitor.

"Brother ... Thomas?" he asked, his Latin well modulated and with not a trace of any accent that Thomas could discern. "What brings you to our humble friary? And from whence have you come? Please, do sit down. Brother Gerhardt will fetch some water — no, not to worry, it is perfectly clear and untainted — for you to refresh yourself. So ...?"

Guillaume sat down on a well-reinforced bench and looked inquiringly at Thomas.

"My home friary is in the north of England, Prior Guillaume —"

"Ah, a splendid country!"

"— but I have come from Saint Angelo's friary in Rome."

Guillaume stopped breathing for several heartbeats. His skin went a horrible waxy grey shade, and his cheeks quivered.

"Ah, so," he finally said, and wiped his upper lip with his hand. "Prior Bertrand has finally sent for news of Brother Wynkyn."

That was not strictly correct, but it served Thomas' purposes well enough, so he merely nodded.

Guillaume heaved a great sigh. "Well, I shall tell you what I know, and then you shall be on your way."

No hospitality here, thought Thomas. Not when the visitor is connected with Wynkyn de Worde.

"Wynkyn left us at the height of the pestilence," Guillaume said, "and carrying the pestilence himself. No doubt he died of it not overlong after he left here."

"And he went ...?"

Guillaume shrugged slightly, his neck disappearing as his shoulders rose. "He went north on the road to Bamberg,

Brother Thomas. I do not know precisely where, or even if, he left it."

"But surely —"

"Brother Wynkyn was a secretive man," Guillaume said, "and he kept his secrets well. All I know is that he went north, as he did whenever he came to our friary, but this time he never returned. As I said, he would have succumbed to the pestilence he carried not many days after leaving us. He was a sick, sick man."

Thomas shifted in frustration. "There must be something more you can tell me, Prior Guillaume."

Guillaume opened his mouth to rebuke Thomas, when he did, indeed, remember something. "He once mentioned the village of Asterladen. It is perhaps a day's journey on the road north. I am sorry, brother, but that is the best I can do. Will you be leaving immediately?"

"Shortly. There is one other thing. Wynkyn had with him a casket —"

"Ah!" Guillaume threw his hands up in the air. "That cursed casket! It caused me much misery. I should have burned it."

"You did not, surely!"

"Nay. But I should have." Guillaume heaved a great sigh, his fingers kneading deep into flesh where they rested on his thighs. "Wynkyn asked me, that if he did not return, which he did not —"

"Yes, yes."

"Be patient, man, I am reporting as best I may. Well, Wynkyn said that if he did not return then I was to return the casket to his home friary. Sweet saints above! It took me months, and much gold," he looked at Thomas significantly, but Thomas ignored the hint, "to find a merchant who would take it for me. The Lord alone knows whether or not it ever arrived."

Thomas shook his head, worried and disappointed beyond measure. "It did not come back to Saint Angelo's —"

"To his home friary, man! Have you not understood a word of what I've said?"

"But Saint Angelo's —"

"Saint Angelo's was not Brother Wynkyn's home friary. Like you, he was an Englishman — do you all have such inexcusable manners? — and his home friary was on the edge of Bramham Moor. You must know of it. It is, I believe, in the north of your country."

Thomas stared gape-mouthed at the obese prior. Wynkyn de Worde was English, and he came from Bramham Moor?

"Ah, yes, yes, I have heard of it, but I have never been there ... Wynkyn is not an English name, surely ... he was English? And the casket went back to England?"

Guillaume stood up just as Brother Gerhardt came in with a pitcher of water and a beaker.

Guillaume waved him away again.

"I'm sure you will need to be on your way," he said to Thomas. "Now."

"But —"

"There is nothing more I can tell you, Brother Thomas. Your answers lie back in England. I wish you a good day, and a good journey."

Thomas finally managed to rise, and he stiffly inclined his head in Guillaume's direction.

"I do thank you for your hospitality," he said. "You have been most gracious."

Guillaume flushed. "You must understand, brother, that the name Wynkyn de Worde brings nothing but bad memories with it. It is a blessed thing that he has gone. I hope he did not die unshriven."

"It is the worst possible thing that he is gone," Thomas said, barely keeping his anger under control, "for without him the world descends ever deeper into ungodly chaos. I wish you good day, Brother Prior."

And with that he was gone.

V

The Feast of St Swithin
In the fifty-first year of the reign of Edward III
(Thursday 15th July 1378)

— ii —

Thomas paused in Nuremberg only long enough to purchase some food and a flask of watered wine in the market before he left the city by the northern gate.

He was furious at Guillaume, but most of his fury was displaced deep frustration at discovering that the book he so badly wanted to read had been dispatched to *England*. And that thirty years ago! The Lord Saviour only knew what had happened to the casket and its contents on its perilous journey across a Christendom ripped apart by the chaotic aftermath of the pestilence.

Thomas should have stayed the night in Nuremberg. He knew that. His horse was tired, and needed a feed and a rub down. *He* was tired and needed a feed and a place where he could collect his thoughts enough so he could pray in peace.

But anger and disappointment drove him forward. He would see if anyone in this village of Asterladen knew of Wynkyn de Worde and where the mysterious friar had gone in his journeys north of Nuremberg, but Thomas seriously doubted he would find much information lurking about the village. Thirty years had passed, most of the people who would have known of Wynkyn would be dead, and those that had been alive during the Christmastide that year would have been too young to know the location of the friar's secretive hole in the woods.

A day and a night, that is all he would waste on Asterladen, and then he must needs begin the long and difficult journey home to England.

So great was his frustration Thomas found himself wishing that he was safe back in St Angelo's friary, studying its generally innocuous registers, and that St Michael had found someone else to lead God's armies against the invasion of evil.

"The trail is too old," he muttered. "What can be done?"

And so Thomas rode on.

This time of year the road that wound north was busy with carts piled high with hay, or fruits, or broodily grumbling calves or pigs, heading for the markets and stomachs of Nuremberg. Pedlars jangled by, their carts packed with bright pots, cooking utensils, and ribbons and fripperies for goodwives to waste their hard-earned coin on. There were innumerable pilgrims, travelling in bands that were sometimes small, sometimes huge. Thomas counted four-score in one gaily chatting band that passed him late in the evening.

And there were soldiers. Stragglers, rather than coherent units, and probably mercenaries moving south to look for work. Thomas had no doubt that when they heard of the impending war between the French and English forces they would head west with alacrity, intent on selling their skills to the highest bidder.

Among the carts of merchandise, pedlars, pilgrims and soldiers straggled the occasional peasant, perhaps wandering down to Nuremberg in the hope of picking up work somewhere. Since the pestilence, there were very few people who could find no work, but there were always some: the sick or crippled, those lingering on the borderlands of insanity, and the sheer malingerers who preferred a life drifting from employment to employment rather than settling down to establish a godly life for themselves.

Of all the travellers, Thomas hated the beggars the most. They were society's pests — skulkers who had lost even the art of malingering — who no longer even wished to pretend an interest in work. Most had a missing limb, generally a foot, and they hobbled past on crutches, or rumbled by on ill-made, hand-propelled carts.

It was easier, Thomas realised, to hack off a foot than a hand.

Besides, a beggar did better with two hands with which to beseech alms.

Dusk drew in faster than Thomas had anticipated, and he realised that he'd left Nuremberg so late that he didn't have a chance of reaching Asterladen before full night. He pulled his gelding to a halt and looked about.

The road was empty. Everyone else, even the malingerers and the beggars, had found shelter for the night.

Thomas swivelled in his saddle and looked behind him, then stood in the stirrups, peering as far as he could down the road.

There was no habitation in sight, not even a shepherd's croft, let alone a village or inn.

He sat down in the saddle again, and his gelding heaved a great sigh, and shifted his weight wearily from one hind leg to the other.

"Ah," Thomas said, "I have been so lost in my own troubles that I have forgot yours, my friend."

He patted the horse's neck, then dismounted, and the gelding swung his head about and butted Thomas in the chest in gratitude.

Thomas' mouth twisted. His horse needed rest and feed, and so did he, and if he hadn't been so lost in anger and frustration he wouldn't have departed Nuremberg so precipitously without making sure he knew where he could have found both on the northern road.

Now both he and his mount were stranded on a deserted road with no aid in sight.

"Well, a night of roadside grasses for you," Thomas said, taking up the horse's reins and leading him forward, "and a meal of fallen acorns, if I'm lucky, for me. Come on, there must be a sheltered spot nearby."

He walked the horse along the road for a few more minutes until the deepening dark made further travel impossible. Just off the road to his left was a stand of beech trees, and Thomas supposed it would have to provide the both of them with enough shelter for the night.

He gave the reins a slight tug, and the horse obediently turned off the road, slipping a little down the loose earth on the embankment, and landing with a surprised snort on soft grass. Thomas led him into the stand of trees, unbuckled the girth and slipped the saddle off, then the bridle, using the reins to hobble him so he wouldn't wander too far during the night.

He gave the horse's rump a slap, and the gelding wandered off a few paces, then dropped his head to graze.

Thomas drew his cloak close about him — despite being high summer the night would be a chill one — and picked out a solid beech under which he could sit and lean against.

What was he going to do?

Thomas had few doubts that he would discover little at Asterladen, and without a local guide there would be no means by which he could find where Wynkyn de Worde had gone. If he tried to find it by luck, then Thomas knew he'd be spending the rest of his life wandering about the sprawling forests of Germany; Wynkyn had protected his secret well, and would surely have ensured that casual eyes would pass straight over any turnoff or pathway.

And after Asterladen?

England.

A thousand miles away, and a murderous war to negotiate to get there.

Thomas couldn't resist a grin. Here he was with, to be sure, the few gold coins that Etienne Marcel had given him, but very little else. His robes of a friar would do little to protect him against felons or brigands, or the rampages of disbanded and unpaid soldiers. Meanwhile, he had unfriendly territory to traverse and, more importantly for the moment, an empty stomach to endure.

Whatever he'd said to the horse about acorns, the last thing Thomas felt like now was crawling about the earth like a mad Nebuchadnezzar looking for nuts.

He smiled again, more genuinely this time, watching his horse snuffling about happily beneath a tree a few paces away. Well, tomorrow he would set out early for Asterladen, beg a meal (*would it be better if he hacked off a foot tonight in order to win more sympathy?*), and then hope that some tired old peasant could wake up enough from his doze before a fire to recall *something* about an ill-tempered old friar who had once passed his way.

And then, Thomas suddenly, stunningly, realised he was actually a little happy. He hadn't realised how much he had missed the roving life, living from hand to mouth, surviving the daily surprises that foreign territories were likely to throw at him, being alert and quick enough to swing about and stick a murderous bandit who'd leaped out from beneath a tree before the bandit had time to stick him.

Thomas slumped down a little further against the tree, wrapping himself more securely in his robe.

In the morning he would cut himself a stout stave from a young tree. That would afford him almost as much protection as a sword.

Happy, warm, and with something to keep him occupied when he woke in the morning, Thomas slipped into sleep.

He woke deep into the night, wondering what had roused him. He heard the soft sounds of the horse, but did not think that that was what had woken him: the gelding was some way distant, searching the banks of a small creek for young grass.

If not the horse, then what?

Thomas was cold, and horribly stiff, and he found it difficult to move. He twisted his head about slowly, trying to spy out anything else unusual. At this distance from habitation it could be anything, from prowling cats to something far more sinister.

Night was an untamed landscape, and the abode of demons.

Thomas suddenly remembered the horror of the demon visitation the night spent in the Brenner Pass, and he jerked fully awake, scrambling into a sitting position and staring wildly about.

He heard the horse give a snort of startlement, and then shift as quickly as his hobble allowed.

Thomas got to his feet, cursing both his left leg, which had gone numb and would hardly hold him, and his stupidity in not having the foresight to cut himself a stave before he had gone to sleep.

He leaned against the trunk of the beech with one hand, rubbing and kneading at his treacherous left leg with his other hand, and looked about.

There, the horse, standing rigid and wild-eyed, staring at a spot some thirty paces away.

There stood a massive oak tree, and from the massive trunk of this oak emanated a silvery glow.

Imps? Fairies? Elves?

Worse?

Thomas finally managed to get some feeling back into his leg, and he hobbled forward a few paces, looking for something he could use as a weapon.

The horse gave another sudden snort, and Thomas looked up again.

A huge, razor-tusked boar had emerged from behind the oak and was walking stiff-legged, head down, towards Thomas.

It was glowing with a strange, ethereal light.

Thomas stared, his fear freezing him into immobility. Ordinary wild boars were the most dangerous creatures of the untamed landscape.

A demon-boar was infinitely more hazardous.

Thomas, the boar whispered, and it swung its head threateningly to and fro.

Thomas backed up until he was trapped by the trunk of the beech tree.

Thomas.

Thomas' hands groped about the trunk behind him, desperately hoping that he might find a loose branch ... something ... that he might use as a weapon.

Thomas, you go to a bad place. Beware.

And then the apparition was gone, and Thomas was left shaking and sweating and wondering if the boar had been St Michael or some demonic phantasm sent to confuse him.

He sat awake for many hours, until finally, in the cold pre-dawn, he fell into a deep slumber.

VI

The Friday before the fifth Sunday after Trinity
In the fifty-first year of the reign of Edward III
(16th July 1378)

— i —

Thomas woke with a start.

Something warm and damp was running over his face, and he flailed out with a hand, cursing.

His horse gave a snort of disgust, and backed away, and Thomas finally managed to unglue his eyes.

It had only been his gelding. Lonely perhaps, and wanting his human companion's company.

Slowly Thomas got to his feet, apologising to the horse with a few soft words.

What had happened last night?

He remembered waking, and seeing the ethereal boar.

What was it the boar had said ... danger? Well, there was danger everywhere, and the boar, whatever or whoever it had been, had told him nothing he was not already aware of.

Thomas shook his head, trying to clear it of his remaining sleep fuddlement. Of what came after he remembered nothing; it was if he had fallen directly back into deep sleep.

"Beware," Thomas muttered as he brushed dead leaves

away from his cloak. "Beware of what? Asterladen? Wynkyn's hidey-hole?"

His stomach growled, and Thomas sighed, rubbing his face to try and wake himself up a little more. He needed food, and a warm fire to eat it by, and a good husbandman who would rub his horse down for him.

Groaning at the remaining stiffness in his limbs and back, Thomas retrieved the bridle and saddle, and whistled the horse over.

Asterladen, as it turned out, was only a morning's ride away, and Thomas was there by noon after being given directions by a friendly pedlar he had encountered just after setting out. It was a large village a mile off the road. Some thirty well-kept stone houses, their steep roofs tiled with slate, sat about a grass square where young boys herded grazing geese, and girls sat on three-legged stools to milk placid, fat sheep.

A husbandman, his smock and leggings marked with the labour of his morning's ploughing, walked out of the nearest house, his face curious, if not particularly welcoming.

"Good morning to you," Thomas said in Latin, and then realised his mistake as the husbandman's face creased in ignorance.

Thomas repressed a sigh. He was so used to dealing with people who, with some education behind them, could converse in the universal language of Latin, that he now had to think hard in order to find some words which this peasant could understand.

"Good morning, man," he tried again, this time in heavily accentuated German.

Thank God he'd spent some time talking with Marcel's German guards in their journey north.

In reply the man merely nodded, his eyes narrowing in suspicion.

"Ah, I wonder if ..." Thomas thought hard, trying to remember the words and phrases, "if I might trouble you for a small meal and something to drink."

"Be off!" the man yelled, his face now openly aggressive.

"We'll have none of your begging kind here! Your masters are rich enough to feed you, go beg at *their* feet!"

Thomas wondered if he should offer the man some coin, but was loath to do it for two reasons. One, all Christians were obligated to feed and shelter clerics who wandered by, and, secondly, Thomas didn't want this man — or any of his neighbours — to know he carried a purse of gold hanging at his belt.

"I ask in Christ's name," Thomas tried again, but was interrupted by the man who took two strides forward, and waved a hand threateningly.

"Be off with you! We've enough troubles without having to feed your kind as well."

Lord Christ! Thomas had heard stories of the depth of German resentment to the taxes and dues exacted by the Church, but to this hour hadn't ever realised its depth.

"Then I shall seek sustenance elsewhere," Thomas said. "But I wonder if I might trouble you to inquire —'

"Begone!" The man grabbed his horse's bridle, and attempted to pull the gelding's head about.

Thomas had endured enough. He reached down, seized in his turn the man's arm, and gave it a mighty wrench.

The man's hand dropped away from the bridle and he let out a howl of pain.

Out of the corner of his eyes Thomas saw several other men running, and he silently cursed. *What had he done!* He'd never get any information out of —

"Ernst," a woman's voice said, "he is only a friar, needing a moment of warmth and some gruel. He shall not eat us out of house and field, I am sure."

Then, stunningly, the woman spoke in skilful Latin. "Good friar, I regret my neighbour Ernst's hasty actions and words. Will you be so kind as to sup with myself and my husband?"

Thomas finally looked away from Ernst, standing well back and rubbing his arm and growling softly with the several other men who were now grouped at his shoulder, and down at the woman who'd walked up to his horse's near side.

She was thirty-ish, with a broad pink-cheeked friendly

face, curious eyes the same shade as her dark brown hair, and a five-month belly rounding out her apron. A year-old infant was slung across her back in a cloth, and a toddling boy clung to one of her hands.

"You speak wondrous Latin, good wife," Thomas said. "How did you learn such?"

"Ah," the woman said, and smiled, revealing surprisingly good teeth for a peasant woman. "I have led a charmed life, and have been privileged to learn of many things. My name is Odile, and my husband is Conrad. Please, will you grace our home? It is humble, but we have warmth, a place for you to sit, and an extra plate for you to eat from."

"I do thank you, Odile. But ... I do not want to turn your neighbours against you."

"Ah," Odile said, and, turning slightly, waved the surly group of men away. "They will bear no grudge against me or mine for this single act of hospitality."

She spied an eight-year-old boy standing curiously to one side. "Wolfram! Come, attend to the friar's horse."

Wolfram wandered up, and shyly took the reins from Thomas, who had dismounted when the men had walked away.

"He is my eldest," Odile said, "and an honest lad. He will take good care of your mount."

Her good humour had infected Thomas — *Saint Michael must have set this good woman in his path!* — and he returned her smile.

"I am indeed hungry, Mistress Odile, and would eat a blanket if you boiled it for me."

She burst out laughing, and —

— *and for an instant Thomas thought he saw another woman's face superimposed over Odile's ... a younger woman, with a shining cloud of bronze-coloured hair and infinitely sad, dark eyes* —

— took Thomas' arm with a little too much familiarity, but Thomas was still so startled by the momentary impression of seeing another woman's face he did not object.

Odile led him to a house set back a little further than the

others, and a little larger. She noted the expression on Thomas' face when he saw the house.

"This was my parents' house, and when my Conrad took me to wife, he built this room here, see? And added the attic and side barn. We live well."

And then again she turned and smiled, and said: "I have lived a charmed life."

And then they were inside.

It was a typical peasant's home, in spite of being slightly more spacious. There was no chimney, and the smoke from a central hearth drifted out a small window set to one side.

Most of it. The rest drifted about the interior, giving everything a slightly dingy appearance.

There was a tripod set above the fire, a pot suspended from it. It gave off such a delicious aroma that Thomas' mouth instantly watered. Bread from the village oven lay wrapped in a cloth to one side, a bowl of beans by it.

There were several stools and two benches about the fire, a large, curtained bed at one end of the room, and at the other end were several chests, set against the wall, which had pegs for the family's few spare clothes. A variety of farm implements — rakes, shears, a scythe and a sickle — leaned against the wall by the door, and scattered about the rest of the room were the accoutrements of peasant life: a spindle, baskets and pails, torn nets waiting to be mended, some leather tackle, storage pots, and around and about all scurried chickens, a goose, and two cats chasing a mouse.

Odile sent the toddler she'd held with her other hand towards the fire, where the boy obediently scrambled atop a stool and sat watching his mother, who lifted the infant from her back and put him in a crib.

She turned and grinned at Thomas, her hand splayed across her swollen belly. "A girl, I pray," she said, and then made a face. "A girl would be useful about the house, for the boys will be no use when they're old enough to work alongside Conrad in the fields. Not that I was happy, mind, to find myself breeding again so soon after the little one's birth. But Conrad does demand his rights ..."

Thomas sat down hurriedly on the stool Odile indicated, hoping she wasn't going to go into too much more detail about Conrad's lusts when her husband himself came in.

He was a huge man, all muscle and dark beard, and he grunted in Thomas' direction as Odile explained his presence. He sat down on the stool next to Thomas', belched, then picked at his teeth with a thumbnail.

"Odile's led a charmed life," he said in thick German by way of conversation, then lapsed into silence as he stared into the fire.

Thomas tried to find something to say, then realised Conrad didn't expect a reply.

And so he, too, contented himself with staring into the fire as Odile prepared a simple meal.

As she started to slop portions into large hollowed-out sections of bread, her son Wolfram came back in.

"Horse is rubbed," he said, averting his eyes. "And eating."

"I do thank you," Thomas said, and risked slipping a small coin from his purse to hand to the boy.

"Oh, no, no need for that," Odile said. "Please, put away your coin! We've no need for payment. Why —"

"I know, I know," Thomas said. "You've lived a charmed life."

Odile grinned happily, and handed Thomas a wooden spoon and a bread trencher filled with a thick vegetable and grain broth.

He wolfed the broth down, making no pretence to manners. It was very, very good, strongly flavoured with herbs the way only a peasant woman could do it, and as tender as if it had been simmering the entire day.

As soon as he'd spooned out the last mouthful, Odile was at his shoulder, her ladle brimming, and filled his trencher to the top again.

Thomas nodded his thanks, and resumed his dinner.

When all had eaten — the bread trenchers as well as the

broth — Odile put away their spoons after giving them a cursory wipe with a corner of her apron, then sat down herself, her infant son in her arms. The baby was whimpering, and Odile unselfconsciously pulled down her blouse to expose a full, dark red-nippled breast.

The baby didn't instantly respond, and Odile cooed and sang to him, encouraging him to suckle.

Thomas stared; he couldn't help himself. He found himself wanting to reach out and cup Odile's breast in his hand: it looked so smooth, so warm ... so full ...

The baby twisted his head, and latched on to the nipple, and the spell was broken.

Odile looked up as Thomas averted his eyes and her mouth lifted, as if at a secret thought.

"You've come about Wynkyn de Worde," she said, and Thomas stared back at her again.

"How —"

"We've always known someone would come a-looking for him," she said. "Strange, horrible man that he was."

"You're too young to have known him."

"Aye. I was but an infant in my mother's arms the night Wynkyn passed through for the final time. My parents told me all I know."

"Do you know where he went?"

"Oh, aye. But it is best to show you, rather than try to explain."

And Odile lifted her head from her infant and smiled at Thomas, but again the face of the strange, beautiful woman hovered over hers, and the woman wore the face of dread.

Thomas' eyes filled with tears, although he did not know whether at the momentary vision, or with gratefulness that Odile should know what he needed.

"We shall go when my babe has finished his suck," she said.

VII

The Friday before the fifth Sunday after Trinity
In the fifty-first year of the reign of Edward III
(16th July 1378)

— ii —

"My mother and father told me much about that night before Yuletide," Odile said, leading Thomas through the village green to a small track that led into the forests. Neither husband nor child accompanied them.

"How did your village know Brother Wynkyn?"

"Asterladen fed him whenever he came through," Odile said, branching off the main track onto one overgrown with shrubs and wild grasses. "He paid us well."

"And you know of the place where he ... worked?"

"I know of it, as did my elder brother and sister. No one else. We found it when playing as children. There was a pile of bones there ... my brother said it must have been Brother Wynkyn. There was a cross about his neck. Further on there is a place, a strange place, which my brother told me was where the friar came twice a year."

"And your brother ... where is he now?"

"I am the only one of my family left," Odile said.

"Your brother and sister died?"

"Nay. Both left to work at crafts in Nuremberg."

Odile stopped and turned back to Thomas. "I have never seen either again. I do not know if they live or not."

She was obviously upset, and without thinking, Thomas gathered her to him, patting her back clumsily.

Her pregnant belly pressed firmly into his, and he thought he felt her child squirm.

He blinked, surprised, for it was a rather pleasant sensation.

Odile smiled awkwardly, and extracted herself from Thomas' arms. "No doubt they now have families of their own," she said. "As I have."

And with that Odile turned and led Thomas deeper into the trees.

They walked into ever thickening forest, and eventually Thomas took the lead, pushing aside low-hanging branches and scrubby bushes so Odile could pass easily. He worried for her, for the woman appeared unsure, and occasionally she clasped at her belly, as if reassuring, or seeking reassurance. Thomas had suggested she go back, but Odile had shaken her head, wide-eyed, and refused.

She would be well, she said, once they had reached the path leading to the gorge.

A gorge? Is that where she was leading him?

He turned to question Odile further, but all she did was smile very gently, and say: "It is a strange place to which I take you, but quiet, and very peaceful."

Thomas nodded, and would have turned to resume their progress when Odile spoke again.

"My parents, as many of the older folk within the village, say that the gorge harbours demons, but I do not believe the tales. Neither I, nor my brother or sister have ever been troubled."

"And you know not why Brother Wynkyn came twice yearly to the gorge?"

She tipped her head on her side, almost flirtatiously. "Why? Well, now, Brother Thomas, perhaps he went to the gorge to reflect, or perhaps even to talk to his God, for that surely is the kind of place it is."

Odile pushed past Thomas, her pregnant belly bumping

his arm as she went. "I will lead from here," she said. "The way is clearer now."

They walked for perhaps another half an hour before the track left the trees and opened out into the beginnings of a valley.

Odile called over her shoulde,. "We're almost there!"

Thomas peered ahead. The valley was narrow — sheer cliffs rose either side of a floor no wider than ten or fifteen paces. Odile was right, it was more a gorge.

"Where does the gorge lead?" he asked.

Ahead Odile shrugged her shoulders, and Thomas couldn't help noticing the way her dress rode up over her buttocks as she did so.

"Nowhere," she said, twisting about slightly as she walked so he could hear. "It ends in a rock wall."

There was a skittering sound to Thomas' left, almost as if a light foot had inadvertently slipped on leaf litter, and he jerked his eyes toward the sound.

There was nothing but a thin scattering of trees and the soft dappling of late-afternoon shadows over the ground.

He looked forward again.

Odile was now standing facing him, a peculiar light in her eyes.

"He was there," she said, and pointed to one side of the track.

Thomas squatted down, but there was nothing to see. "Where are his bones now?"

She didn't reply, and after a moment Thomas turned to look at her.

Odile was grinning broadly, as if at a private jest. "My brother and sister and I took the bones and buried them," she said. "We thought it was neater."

"You thought it was *neater*?"

"They were jumbled all over the place, as if wild beasts — or worse — had scattered them."

Thomas stood up. "And there was nothing but bones ... and the cross?"

"Aye. There was nothing else. The bones were picked clean and bleached by their years in the sun."

"What became of the cross?"

"My brother said it would do well enough to finance his apprenticeship in Nuremberg."

Thomas bit back a bitter reply. Odile's brother had taken the cross and sold it ... did they have no idea that —

"It was doing the dead friar no good," Odile said, watching Thomas carefully, "and had not done well by him. It were best it be put to some other use."

"What do you mean 'not done well by him'?"

"It hadn't saved him, had it? It was useless gold. My brother took it and gave it back some use."

Odile's brother was obviously not a particularly devout man, Thomas thought.

Now Odile was looking towards the gorge. "All I know is that the friar called this place the Cleft," she said.

Thomas turned and regarded the gorge as well. "The Cleft," he murmured.

What was it about this place that made it so important?

Odile took his hand in hers. "Come," she said. "There is no danger."

And so, hand in hand — and Thomas not even wondering that he held the hand of a woman — they walked into the Cleft.

It was a strange and utterly eerie place. Odile had called it peaceful, but Thomas found that every nerve in his body jangled the further they walked in.

Strange misshapen boulders lay strewn everywhere, their edges blurred, as if they had melted and run in some demonic furnace.

Small shrubs struggled out of dry, cracked earth, and blackened trees stood outlined against the sky. The entire gorge seemed arid and sterile.

What was it about this gorge?

"There's been a fire through here," Thomas said, letting Odile's hand go and walking forward a few paces.

"Oh, aye, there's been a fire or two through here," Odile said, and at the tone of her voice, Thomas turned and looked.

Odile was smiling at him ... and she was also pulling her loose-necked dress down over her shoulders and breasts.

"This is a place of fires," she said, and the dress dropped to the ground.

Underneath her dress Odile wore no underclothes. She stood there, still smiling, her head tilted to one side, one hand gently rubbing her protruding belly in circles.

Thomas knew he should look away, but he couldn't not look at her. Her naked body fascinated him, and aroused him in a manner he'd never felt before.

She was well-formed with the strong legs and arms of all peasant women. Her skin was white, marked here and there with pale freckles.

Her breasts were large and stretched tight with milk, and her belly was so rounded it formed an invitation all of itself.

Thomas' breath caught in his throat.

Odile stood there like an ancient goddess of fertility, her pregnant belly making her more desirable than had it been flat and virginal, and Thomas recalled the pleasant sensation he'd felt when she'd pressed against him in the forest.

"Odile," Thomas managed to whisper.

There was no thought in his head of fleeing, or even of castigating her for her blatant display.

All he could do was stare and lust for her as he had never lusted for any other woman.

He did not feel any shame or guilt. Had not St Michael himself said that women were to be used, and then discarded?

Well, here stood Odile, her face wanton with the lusts of a whore ... and whores Thomas understood very, very well. They were to be used, and not to be thought of again.

Odile walked over to Thomas, and lifted one of his hands to her breasts.

"Tom," she whispered, and pressed herself against him.

Hatred consumed him. Thus had another woman, her belly as swollen with child as Odile's, once pressed herself against him, thinking to use him, to manipulate him, thinking to destroy his life.

Bitch!

He had been right to do as he had then, and as he would now. There would be no guilt, not ever again.

"Bitch," he whispered, and pushed her to the ground.

Odile fell heavily, but she laughed, and rolled immediately to her back, lifting and spreading her legs.

All clefts led to hell. Thomas knew that. One woman's cleft had led him to his own personal hell ... but that was gone now. St Michael said God had forgiven him, and this woman rolling like a harlot on the ground was only there to be used, and then to be discarded ...

Thomas fumbled with his robe, lifting it above his waist, then tore at his underclothes. Within a heartbeat he was kneeling on the ground before Odile, and then atop her, driven to a distraction of desire by her soft laugh, and even softer hands against his flesh.

There was no thought in his head for soft caresses, nor for any words of reassurance or affection.

All he wanted to do — *now, now, now* — was to drive himself inside her, and feel her softness and warmth wrap itself about him.

In his eagerness he pushed her a little way along the hard earth, and Odile gave a grunt of discomfort. But Thomas paid her no heed. He cursed, forcing her legs further apart with an impatient hand, and —

— *the face of the younger woman again floated above that of Odile. She was frightened, close to tears, although she bit her lip and tried hard to keep them at bay.*

She was so beautiful —

— the face vanished, and there was only Odile, laughing and encouraging him, teasing him about the amount of time he was taking to enter her.

Thomas groaned and, lifting his hips, thrust himself with all the force he could into —

— Lord God, she was a virgin! He heard his own cry of surprise, and heard her whimper with the pain of his penetration.

But he would not stop, not now, and so —

— he thrust even harder, and now he was inside her, and her pregnant belly pressed against his, and they were both writhing and moaning, impatient to sate their lust, and —

— again the face of the dark-eyed woman floated over Odile's. Her bronze-coloured hair was spread in thick waves across the linen cloth of the pillow. It was such stunning hair, ripples of gold running through it like the first fingers of fire through a velvet cloak left puddled too close to a hearth.

Ripples of gold, like a molten crown encircling her head.

She was staring straight into his eyes, shocked beyond even the pain of her deflowering.

"Meg," said the man atop her. "What is wrong?"

"Meg," Thomas muttered, his eyes shut now, lost in his vision, and Odile wrapped arms and legs about him, rocking him back and forward in his maniacal mating, and he murmured, "Meg, Meg, sweet, sweet Meg."

Odile laughed in triumph.

"My lord," she whispered. "Forgive me. For a moment I had thought you beardless."

And tonsured, like a monk, but this she did not say.

She touched the man's face, wonderingly.

"I think you must drink your wine a little more watered from now on, my dear," said the man.

And then he grunted, and thrust so deep within the woman that she cried out in pain, and then he cried out too, thrust once more, and was still.

Thomas collapsed across Odile's body, spent.

She ran her hand through the thickness of his black hair, marvelling at the nakedness of his tonsure, and then trailed her hand down his face, turning it towards her.

His eyes flickered, and then opened.

"Thomas," she whispered.

He blinked, a slow smile forming on his lips, his thoughts still disordered in post-coital abandonment. "Alice?"

Odile lifted her hand, then struck him a light blow on his cheek. "You will live a charmed life, my dear," she said.

Thomas stared, then his eyes widened in total disbelief at the situation he found himself in, and he jumped to his feet, fumbling with his robe to cover himself.

"Whore," he said, his voice flat.

Odile did not move from the ground. Instead, she lolled yet more provocatively, laughing at him.

"Priests are always the best," she said. "So impatient, so frantic!"

"Cover yourself," he said.

"Why?" Odile said. "Does not the sight of a woman's body inflame you, Tom? Or is it my belly? Ah, yes, the last time a woman came to you with her belly so swollen you burned her, did you not, Tom? Ah, poor Alice. Poor sweet Alice."

So stunned and horrified he did not truly realise what he was doing, Thomas leaned down and grabbed Odile's hair, hauling her from the ground.

"Witch!" he cried, and shook her so violently she cried out in pain.

"One day," she said, jerking the words out with hatred, "you will hand your soul to a woman on a platter, and you will offer her earth's eternal damnation in return for her love!"

Thomas was now beyond reason. Fear such as he had never known before coursed through him. *She had known about Alice! She was a sorceress!* His hand tightened in her hair, and he drew his other hand back, clenching it into a fist, meaning to break her loathsome face apart.

"Stop," a surprisingly calm voice said. "You shall harm no more women."

Thomas jerked his eyes towards the voice ... and let Odile go so suddenly she dropped to the ground with a surprised grunt. She rolled over, grabbed her dress, and ran for safety.

Thomas was hardly aware of her departure.

Instead, his eyes were glued to the demon standing some five paces away, between himself and the mouth of the gorge.

VIII

The Friday before the fifth Sunday after Trinity
In the fifty-first year of the reign of Edward III
(16th July 1378)

— iii —

As was the creature who had tormented him in the Brenner Pass, so was this one beautiful, but incomparably vile in the beauty.

"You think to emulate the loveliness of those you loathe," Thomas said, trying to keep the fear from his face. *Lord God, why had he allowed himself to be trapped in this manner?*

"You mean the angels?" the demon said, and walked forwards a few steps. Its creamy skin glowed with an unearthly radiance, and its huge eyes shone impossibly blue.

Now that one stood before him Thomas could see that it was slightly taller than a man, and more heavily muscled, although its entire carriage was one of elegance rather than ungainliness. Its hips were narrow, its legs well formed, and thick silvery hair, similar to that which covered its head, tufted above its genitals.

The demon smiled, revealing two perfect rows of tiny pointed teeth. "I have no choice but to emulate the angels, Tom."

"We *all* have choice," Thomas said. "God has given us choice. We can choose either the road to redemption, or the road to —"

"Stop being so tiresome!" the demon said. "Of course we all have choice, and I and my kin have chosen as best we can."

The creature walked forward another two steps — it was now only three or four paces from Thomas — its movements exquisitely graceful.

The demon laughed softly at Thomas' reaction. "Must we hobble and lurch to satisfy your preconceptions, priest? Why can we not have some goodness within our natures and bodies?"

Thomas almost backed away, then realised there was no escape for him in this blind gorge.

He was trapped.

"You are *evil*!" he said.

"Ah, has the pretty angel told you that?" the creature said.

Thomas held his tongue. His terror had dissipated, and he felt only anger and a remaining burning humiliation at the way Odile had managed to tempt him.

How had she known about Alice?

"We know all about you," the demon said, and then smiled at the expression on Thomas' face. "No, Odile was no demon — do not think you have wasted yourself inside one of *our* bodies! — but merely a beloved woman."

"She is a whore and a sorceress."

The demon shrugged, then lifted one of its hands — its long fingers were tipped with sharp talons — and studied it carefully. "You do seem to attract them, don't you, Tom?"

Suddenly it lifted its eyes back to Thomas. "No. Do not think you can overpower me. You can't. Stay where you are, and listen."

The demon waved its hand about the gorge. "Like many of my kind I come back here every so often. To remember, and to swear that never again will I, or any of my kind, be trapped."

"What is this place?"

The demon laughed, genuinely amused. "You don't think I will tell you, do you? Well, I will! The Cleft is the gateway to hell, Thomas, the only one to be found on this dear, sweet earth ... and Wynkyn de Worde was the only one who knew how to open it and close it at his leisure."

"The book ..."

"Yes. His nasty little book of incantations. And you think to call *us* witches and sorcerers! Wynkyn de Worde was the last in a long, long line of human sorcerers who worked God's will on earth, Tom."

The demon's brow wrinkled, as if he were thinking. "Sorcerer ... nay, that is too kind a word for him! Wynkyn was a disposer of rubbish, Tom. He swept up the angels' errors.

"And now God and Saint Michael have chosen you to succeed him. No, no need to look so frightened, Tom. We have no intention of harming you. After all," the demon laughed, "better the devil you know than the devil you don't!"

"All evil will fail. It must."

"Evil incarnate walks unhindered among mankind ... isn't that what Saint Michael has told you? Well," the demon's face and voice hardened, "you do not know the nature of evil, Tom. You have not even started to learn."

"I will destroy you and your kind!"

"With what, Tom? Ah, yes, of course, how very silly of me! With Wynkyn's book, of course."

The demon stopped, grinning at the expression on Tom's face. "Yes, we know of the book, but you must be of good cheer, for we cannot harm it, nor even open it."

"Why tell me that?"

The demon hesitated, thinking. Finally it raised its eyes to Thomas'. "Believe it or not, Tom, we mean you no harm. Indeed, we wish you well, for you may one day be of great benefit to us."

"What? What do you mean?"

The demon shook its head. "There is a long road ahead of you, Tom, and no one, not even Saint Michael, can see all its twists and turns. The archangel told you that you must learn yourself, and for once I agree with the cursed angel. He cannot teach you, as I cannot. But just remember, Tom, that we're *all* watching you."

The demon turned, as if to go.

"Wait!" Thomas said. "Why bring me here today? Why tempt me with Odile?"

The demon stopped, and turned its face slightly so it could speak to Thomas over its shoulder.

"To mate you with your test. Now another woman is pregnant with your child. Don't you realise, Tom? Don't you? The fate of the world will twist and turn on the outcome of Tom's test. Choose one way and God will triumph, choose another and we will overrun earth and turn it to *our* will."

And then the demon walked away.

Thomas blinked, and the demon was still walking away, his gait smooth and elegant, and then Thomas blinked again and the demon had vanished and he was alone in the Cleft.

Alone, but for the memory of the vision which had sprung before his eyes while he sated his lust on Odile. The vision of the beautiful, sad woman into whom he had somehow — through some demonic sorcery — spent his essence.

A test? A woman? How could that be? Beautiful or not they were all whores, to be used and then discarded. A woman was no "test", even if, even if what the demon said was true, and she had conceived.

Thomas brushed off the remaining smudges of dirt on his robe and walked to the mouth of the Cleft.

There was no sign of Odile or the demon, but there was his brown gelding tied to a sapling ash, saddled and waiting.

There was a bag of food tied to the cantle of the saddle.

Thomas walked slowly over, not sure if the horse was an apparition or reality, but the beast gave a soft whicker as Thomas neared, and shook his head and mane as if to hurry him up.

Thomas gave his neck a pat, then looked at the bag of

food. He laid a hand on it, hesitated, then wrenched it off the saddle and threw it away.

He didn't need the aid and succour of demons, or of whore-witches.

He glanced about, then sighed, undid the horse's reins and mounted. There was no point staying here. There was nothing to be discovered in this rocky gorge, this Cleft. Wynkyn de Worde had left no clue, and if the demons reappeared they would only feed him falsities.

Best to be on his way.

To England, and to Wynkyn de Worde's ever-mysterious book.

Thomas turned the horse's head to the path, and gave him a gentle nudge in his flanks.

Best to move while there were a few hours left of daylight.

They had a long way to go.

Far away, the man and woman lay in silence for a long time, staring at the ceiling of the canopied bed. Outside the gently moving walls of the tent came the quiet, yet somehow urgent, sounds of an army encampment.

"I did not know you were a maiden," the man said finally.

"I did not know how to tell you, my lord."

He rolled over slightly, resting his head on a hand. "Why did your husband not touch you? Was he one who preferred the harder caress of men?"

She shook her head slightly. "He was too ill. We were wed when I was sixteen, and he twenty-five, but he was weak even then. He would sigh, and roll away."

He stared at her, wondering what she expected of him. "What we have just done is no sin," he said. "We are both widowed, and free to choose as we will. But, Margaret," his voice hardened, "do not think that I will marry you. I cannot do that. You know it."

"And if I bear a child?"

"Do you think to trap me?"

"No, my lord! I ... I ..."

"If there is a child, there will be no reason it could not be your husband's. He is only recently dead. Do you understand me?"

"Perfectly, my lord."

"We have a contract, you and I. You lend me your body for my easements, and I will aid you to return to your home. There will be nothing more. I have sons enough, I do not need bastard ones."

"I understand you, my lord."

"Good." He rolled away and got out of bed. He was lithe and battle-hardened, and his chest and arms bore the scars of many engagements. He spoke softly, and his valet stepped forward from a darkened corner with wash clothes and clothing.

He turned and regarded Margaret as the valet fussed about him. "I will return after dusk. Be ready for me."

She did not reply, and neither did she attempt to slide the bed covers over her breasts as the valet slid surreptitious glances her way. She was a whore now, and need not hide herself from any man.

FRANCE

"itt is to farr for Pegg to goe with mee."
"*I will goe with thee, my loue, both night and day,*
and I will beare thy sword like lakyney; Lead the way!"
"but we must ride, and will you follow then amongst a troope of vs thats armed men?"
"*Ile beare thy Lance, and grinde thy stirrup too,*
Ile rub thy horsse, and more then that Ile doo."

A Jigge (for Margrett)
Medieval English ballad

I

The Feast of the Nativity of the Blessed Virgin Mary
In the fifty-first year of the Reign of Edward III
(Wednesday 8th September 1378)

From the Cleft Thomas rode north-west through golden
fields where red and green clad peasants wielded
scythes and through small villages where boys herded
geese and old women spat down wells. After several days'
journey he arrived in the town of Bamberg. From there
Thomas followed a small river west, arriving in Frankfurt
during the last week in July. He stayed at a small Dominican
friary in the city for five days, knowing that both he and his
horse needed time to rest. He spoke only rarely to the
brothers there, and they let him be. He was a quiet guest,
and did not disturb the peace of the friary, and so he was
welcomed and left to his own devices. Unlike his time in St
Angelo's friary, where he'd spent so many hours of the day
stretched out before the chapel altar, Thomas stayed in his
own cell in Frankfurt, preferring to pray in solitude.

Praying, and thinking.

Evil was loose in Christendom, and it took the form of
Satan's imps, demons, who had determined to make
Christendom their own by turning mankind's allegiance
away from God. The evil had grown infinitely worse in the

years since Wynkyn de Worde had died, years when no incantations had been spoken to open the gates to Hell and push the demons back from whence they'd come.

Now Thomas, Beloved of God, was here to take Wynkyn de Worde's place and restore goodness to Christendom.

All he needed was de Worde's book.

But was it safe? The demons *knew* of its existence, but had not the demon also said that they could not open it, or harm it?

Could he trust a demon's words?

And why had the demon been so forthcoming with him? Not only had the demon told Thomas that he and his kind knew of the book, but he had also informed Thomas that the friar would face a test upon which mankind's fate would be determined: "*Choose one way and God will triumph, choose another and we will overrun earth and turn it to our will.*"

And this test was to be a woman? Thomas couldn't help but laugh every time he thought about it. He knew precisely what the test would be, for had not the whores in Rome, and then Odile, made it plain? One day he would be tempted to hand his soul to a woman on a platter and, if he did so, then God and the angels and all hope for mankind would be lost.

But that was so ridiculous! Only the most pitiful of men would fail *that* test! No wonder St Michael and God had chosen him to shoulder the burden that de Worde had put down, for Thomas had already shown that he was well capable of turning his back on any woman.

God would be triumphant, not the demons ... but in the meantime what mischief were they up to?

There was one thing that particularly unsettled Thomas. He was beginning to suspect that the demons could shape-shift at will. Certainly the two he'd met had assumed appearances other than their own vile and lumped forms. He also realised that the demons had him under close observation, for they knew his plans and movements. Possibly he had even conversed with demons on one or more occasions ... but he had not known it. What if the demons could blend in with mankind? Would he know demon from true believer?

Who could he ever trust?

Thomas cast his mind back over the past few months of travel. Who? Marcoaldi for certain. Thomas remembered the man's bitterness, and apparent hatred of not only the clergy but God Himself. Yes, it must have been Marcoaldi who had shape-shifted into a different form in order to torment him in the Brenner Pass.

Who else in that party? *Lord Christ Saviour, it could have been anyone!*

Marcel? Thomas had seen him arguing vehemently with Marcoaldi the morning after Thomas had been injured by the demon. He seemed so godly ...

"I must be careful," Thomas murmured to himself several times a day, "and trust no one."

And certainly not the woman — this "Meg" — he'd seen in the vision when he had lain with Odile. Ha! *She* was the one the demons hoped to tempt him with.

Well, she was beautiful, but she was a harlot (was she not lying with a man at the same time as he lay with Odile?) and as worthless as most women. She was a whore and a witch, and Odile's sister in nature, if not in blood. She would not tempt him.

Thomas knew the trap the demons had set for him — *and for them to be so confident they would actually tell him!* — and he knew he could avoid it.

Thomas prayed constantly to St Michael for guidance, but the archangel did not reappear or speak to him in any manner. This did not perturb Thomas, for the archangel had made it plain that Thomas must find his own way in order to learn.

Thomas was content enough, even though he had so far yet to travel. He took each day at a time, and he watched the actions and listened to the words of those about him with closer than normal attention.

There was no one he could trust.

When he left Frankfurt, Thomas chartered a small riverboat on the Rhine to take him south-west to Strasbourg, from where he could ride directly west for Paris.

As silent as he had been in the Frankfurt friary, Thomas said very little to the boatman as they sailed down the river, sitting in the prow of the boat holding the reins of his ever-patient horse, his eyes sliding over castle upon castle that rose bleak and threatening on the cliff tops at every turn of the river.

The Rhine was the major transport system of Europe, and hundreds of barges and ships, small and large, plied their way up and down its length. Their captains and passengers called greetings to Thomas, but the friar ignored them, and left it to the boatman to greet the passing barges and ships in turn.

The boatman was glad to see the back of him, and would not have protested even had Thomas neglected to pay him.

But Thomas was careful to pay his way, and, before he mounted his horse, gave the boatman coin from his purse.

He rode directly through Strasbourg. Cities were merging one into the other now, and the walls and crowded streets of one might as well have been the walls and crowded streets of the last.

Thomas kept an eye out for demons amid the scurrying townsfolk, but he never saw one. They knew he was paying attention now, and they were being cautious.

From Strasbourg it was a direct westerly route through the outer regions of France towards Paris. There Thomas hoped to be able to sit and rest awhile. Talk with Etienne Marcel, who might — or might not — be able to ease his soul, before continuing his relentless journey west, west, west …

Just after the first week in September, on the Nativity of the Blessed Virgin, Thomas found himself in the province of Lorraine. It was late afternoon, and time to find somewhere to shelter for the night. Thunderclouds were billowing in from the north-west, and Thomas knew it would be a night when demons roamed.

He needed to find shelter.

As dusk approached and Thomas despaired of finding suitable accommodation, a village loomed up out of the greyness. A well-dressed peasant stood by one of the first houses — it almost appeared as if he'd been waiting — and greeted Thomas kindly enough.

"I thank you for your greeting, good man," Thomas said in excellent French; like all English nobles he was as fluent in French as in English. "Can you tell me where I am? I thought to be in Saint Urbain before the night, but ..."

The man laughed good-naturedly. "Ah, my friend, you still have several days, ride ahead of you to reach Saint Urbain. You are in the village of Domremy."

He held up a hand, and Thomas took it.

"My name is Jacques d'Arc," the man said, and Thomas smiled, for the man's touch imparted more comfort than he'd felt in weeks.

"And," Jacques d'Arc added, "my daughter Jeannette told me this morning that you would arrive with the setting sun. Will you sup with us, sir?"

Domremy was a small and humble village, and d'Arc's home was similarly humble, a small cottage that was nonetheless well maintained and clean. There was a pile of hay and a pail of water to one side of the cottage. D'Arc tied Thomas' gelding to a post close by and indicated that a boy, already hurrying out of the twilight, would attend to him.

Inside the one-roomed home a fire crackled cheerfully, a pot of frothy grain gruel bubbling below a tripod. D'Arc's wife turned from the fire as they entered, and d'Arc introduced her as Zabillet.

But Thomas quickly turned to the fifteen- or sixteen-year-old girl who emerged from one of the dim corners. She was a typical peasant girl, dressed in rough and patched clothes, not overly tall, her thick body and limbs well muscled and sturdy from her hours of labouring to aid her mother in the house and her father in the field. Her thick, dark brown hair was cut in a ragged line just above her shoulders, and her face was as rough and as plain-featured as the cottage itself.

But it was her brown eyes which caught Thomas' attention. They were so peaceful and composed, and so knowledgeable, that Thomas wondered at the soul which inhabited this peasant body.

What was she?

"This is my second daughter, and fourth child," d'Arc said, and Thomas switched his eyes back to the father, wondering now at the very slight tone of puzzlement in the man's voice. "Her name is Jeannette."

D'Arc blinked as he looked at his daughter, and Thomas realised that, like himself, d'Arc was puzzled by the girl's composure and sense of purpose.

Jeannette was not the usual adolescent peasant girl, the one moment giggly and shy, the next brash and ill-mannered, thinking only of the next day's labour or of which village boy she could seduce into her bed and subsequently into a betrothal.

"Your father said you knew I was coming, Jeannette," Thomas said.

She nodded slightly, and smiled, but did not speak, turning instead to help her mother with the supper as her elder sister and two brothers came in from their evening chores.

The meal was largely eaten in silence, but Thomas did not feel uncomfortable. Instead, the d'Arc family, as their home, exuded an embracing comfortableness, even though Jeannette was so patently unusual.

Finally d'Arc spoke a little of himself and his family. He was not a native of Domremy, coming to live in the village from Ceffonds in Champagne in order to wed Zabillet. Nevertheless, d'Arc was a man of some importance in Domremy, being the doyen, or sergeant, of the village, a position which ranked only behind those of the mayor and sheriff. Nevertheless, Thomas knew that d'Arc's position was a difficult one, because as the doyen, the man would be responsible for the collection of taxes.

As Zabillet collected the platters and spoons, aided by both her daughters this time, d'Arc poured Thomas a large mug of ale, and leaned back in his chair, the only one in the cottage — everyone else sat on stools or benches — and sighed.

"These are not propitious times, Brother Thomas," d'Arc said.

Zabillet, shy and ill at ease with the Dominican where Jeannette was not, placed a platter of apples and goat's cheese on a stool between the two men, then bustled her daughters off to a corner of the cottage where all three busied themselves in mending. The two boys had gone back outside, presumably, Thomas thought, to bed down whatever animals the family owned.

"I have heard that there is war about," Thomas said, hoping d'Arc had news of the English, while at the same time praying that his French did not betray his English origins.

D'Arc grunted. "Worse than just 'about'," he said. "Rumours consume the country. A week ago a pedlar came through, saying that King John was driving his army towards a place called Poitiers."

D'Arc sounded uncertain about the name, and Thomas nodded to encourage him to continue. No doubt d'Arc had never heard of Poitiers, a town far to the south-west, let alone visited it.

"Well," d'Arc continued, "John drives his army hard for Poitiers, and the English bastard dark prince from hell drives his army as hard. It is said there will be a great battle."

D'Arc turned his head slightly and spat into the fire. "The Devil take the English! I hope King John spits each one of them on good French pikes!"

Thomas fought the urge to sigh. The English king, Edward, should forget his pretensions to the French throne and concentrate instead on building a good and godly kingdom at home.

Worse than Edward's wayward lust for the French throne was the fact that the war would make things difficult for

Thomas. More than anything else Thomas wanted to get to Wynkyn de Worde's book before the demons forgot their fear of it and snatched it from under his nose. Any distraction, whether a half day wait for a ferry, or the threat of bloody war raged across his path, was equally unwelcome.

"At least you should not need to fear the effects of the war this far north," Thomas said.

"Bah! Already taxes have risen threefold so that John can pay for his army. Brother Thomas —"

D'Arc leaned forward and looked Thomas in the eye.

"— *I* am the one charged with the responsibility of collecting taxes. And yet these taxes have now become so weighty that I fear I will be destroying my neighbours' lives by seizing their hard-earned grain, or wool, or wine!"

"And I fear for my husband," Zabillet put in softly, almost apologetically, from her corner, "for our neighbours now regard the taxes with such loathing, they look at my Jacques with eyes of hatred."

Thomas glanced her way, and was disconcerted to see Jeannette staring at him, making no pretence of attending to the holes in the worn stocking she held in her hands.

Her mouth curved in a small, knowing smile, then she bowed her head and resumed her mending.

"Ah," d'Arc said, his voice more moderate now, "but you have your own troubles, do you not?"

Thomas' breath caught. *What? Was d'Arc a demon to know of his troubles?*

"As the English are at war with our king," d'Arc continued, "so our beloved Church now divides itself into two armies."

Thomas frowned, thinking for the first time that he should have made more effort before now to acquaint himself with the latest news. "What do you mean?"

"You haven't heard?" d'Arc said. "Brother Thomas, where have you *been*?"

Thomas shrugged helplessly, wishing the man would get on with it.

"Travelling, Jacques, travelling. *What is happening?*" Thomas asked.

D'Arc stared incredulously at his wife, then back to Thomas. "You know of Urban's election in Rome?"

Thomas nodded. "I was there for it. What —"

"Then you know that some cardinals were unhappy —"

"Sweet Jesu! They haven't —"

"The cardinals are in Avignon, and there they have elected a new man to the Holy Throne. A good Frenchman," Thomas noted well the satisfaction on d'Arc's face, "who has taken the name of Clement."

"But has Urban resigned?"

D'Arc laughed dryly. "No. He has excommunicated Clement as an impostor, and Clement has excommunicated Urban as a rogue and a fool. Each now surrounds himself with cardinals, or creates new cardinals if he can't find enough to fill his court, and threatens war on the other."

The amusement faded from d'Arc's face. "It is a disaster, my friend. For the Church, and for every good soul in Christendom."

Thomas shook his head, not knowing how to comment. Even though he had expected trouble from the rogue cardinals who had departed for Avignon, now that he'd actually heard the results of their trouble-making he was horrified.

Sweet Jesu, is this the work of the demons?

If they'd wanted to divide Christendom and turn it in upon itself, they couldn't have done better. The Germans and English would back Urban, while the Spaniards and French would support the new pope, Clement. Europe would splinter into various alliances, some supporting the Roman pope, others the French pope. Still other groups would denounce both, and agitate for the election of a third, impartial pope.

And the forces of evil would revel in Christendom's disunity.

"Jesus Lord Saviour!" Thomas finally whimpered.

He had to find Wynkyn's casket ... he had to!

"Will you lead us in prayer, Brother Thomas?" Zabillet said, as she rose and gathered her daughters about her. "Evil descends about us, and I am afraid."

He slept that night in the small lean-to barn adjoining the d'Arc cottage. The family had little spare bedding, and Thomas was content enough to wrap himself in his cloak and an ancient and well-patched blanket in the soft and sweet new meadow hay stacked up from the village's recent haying.

"Slept" was a poor word to describe Thomas' tossings and turnings. He drifted in and out of sleep, ever slipping into oblivion only to jerk awake within a few minutes from a dream of nameless evil striding across a darkened world.

Finally he gave up even the attempt at sleep, and sat wrapped in his cloak and blanket, staring through a chink in the rough plank wall at the darkness outside and wondering if wickedness and gloom were indeed about to consume all of mankind.

"Brother Thomas?"

Thomas jumped, surprised and frightened. He twisted about — there was a short, thick figure standing in the doorway.

"Do not fear, Thomas," said a girl's voice, and Thomas' heart slowed down, for he recognised it as Jeannette's.

"What do you here?" Thomas said, curious but also more than a little suspicious. No young girl should be wandering about at night, and especially not to talk alone with a cleric.

What did she want? Was she another Odile?

"I am here to comfort you," Jeannette said, and Thomas' suspicions deepened.

She walked in through the doorway, pulling the door closed behind her, and Thomas' eyes narrowed. "Who are you?" he said.

What would d'Arc think if he knew his young daughter was whiling away the night hours alone with a priest in his barn?

Jeannette sat down at Thomas' feet, pulling a little hay about her for warmth.

"I am Jeannette," she said, "and I am your sister in Christ."

She paused, and in the faint light Thomas could see the gleam of her eyes as she regarded him.

"The archangel Saint Michael sent me," she said, and Thomas went stiff in shock.

Jeannette reached out and took one of his hands between her own. "Do not fear. Please. Evil is truly about us, but we will prevail."

Thomas' eyes tightened even more in suspicion. "Saint Michael has spoken to you?" he said.

She sighed sweetly.

"For the past year. He comes to me often, as do Saint Catherine and Saint Margaret." Jeanette paused, and one of her hands touched him comfortingly. "He is a comfort, but when he speaks of the Enemy —"

Thomas knew she spoke of Satan ... peasant folk often referred to him as the Enemy.

"— then I am afraid."

Thomas leaned forward, and patted her shoulder with his free hand. "Do not fear, Jeannette. God and Saint Michael have sent me to fight the evil that —"

"But I must fight, too!" Jeannette cried, and pulled away from Thomas' touch. "God has also spoken to me through Saint Michael's voice, and he has told me what to do!"

Thomas' initial shock was rapidly being replaced with anger. *How could Saint Michael have spoken to this ignorant peasant girl as well as he?* "He has told you of Wynkyn de Worde?"

"Who? No, he has told me that my steps will be different to yours. I will not travel as far or on such a deadly mission."

She paused, and Thomas had the impression that she was momentarily consumed with an infinite sadness.

"Although," Jeannette finally continued, "my mission shall be deadly enough. Thomas, evil stalks this precious land in the guise of an English soldier, and evil must be destroyed. The English must be pushed out of France!"

Thomas was unsettled by the girl's attack on the English. Was this merely the French in the girl talking? The English were the invaders, and thus they must necessarily be representations of evil?

"Evil walks everywhere, Jeannette, and we must fight it wherever we meet it. Sometimes it may walk in the guise of an English soldier, true, but oft times it might walk in the habit of a local pedlar, or —"

"There is no greater evil than the English king," Jeannette said softly, but with such conviction that it disturbed Thomas.

As much as he didn't want to, he had to believe that the archangel Michael had also spoken to this girl. Jeannette glowed with such a peace and such a presence that Thomas knew her to be heaven-blessed. Nevertheless, her peasant ignorances and bigotries obviously still undermined her judgement, and Thomas wondered if she would be as useful as St Michael believed.

A war needed strong men to fight it, men of God, not unlearned peasant girls.

And how many others had the archangel spoken to? Was Thomas to lead God's armies against the demons ... or did Saint Michael merely mean him to be a captain among many captains?

"The English king speaks with the voice of evil," Jeannette said. She had let go of Thomas' hand now, and was sitting back a little, her voice taking on the singsong quality of repetition — or of such firm belief that nothing would ever sway it. "He is foul beyond knowing. His armies must be defeated and he must be burned so that his depravity cannot infect —"

"Edward is an old man," Thomas said, his voice hard, "and unlikely to infect anyone with anything. Besides, it is not Edward who leads the English armies, but his son, Edward the Black Prince."

"Edward?" Jeannette said. "Edward? I do not speak of Edward, either father or son, but of the young king. The blithe young man."

Thomas' earlier suspicions of the girl's ignorance were now confirmed. "My dear child, the English king is Edward, and his son is Edward, and when the elder Edward dies then so the younger Edward will succeed him. Neither man is in the bloom of first youth ... and certainly not 'blithe'. There will be no 'young' king. Not for many years to come."

"You do not believe me," Jeannette said, drawing even further back. "And yet what I have said was spoken to me by Saint Michael himself."

"Dearest Jeannette, I do not doubt for a moment that the blessed archangel Michael has spoken to you, but perhaps you have misunderstood him. It might be better if you prayed for enlightenment and guidance. Would you like me to help you? "

Jeannette was silent, but Thomas could feel the weight of her stare.

"Jeannette, what can you hope to do in this fight against evil? You are a peasant and a girl, and your role can only ever be a small one. You should be content with your lot, and not dream of grandness."

"I —"

Jeannette was interrupted by the opening of the barn door. She gave a small squeak of surprise, then she slipped forward onto her knees and clasped her hands before her. "Blessed saint!"

Thomas stared, wondering what she could see in this dark that he could not.

A shadow beyond the door moved, and then revealed the form of a crouch-backed man leaning heavily on a staff.

Thomas gave a sigh of relief. Not d'Arc, then, come to accuse him of fornicating with his daughter.

And surely not the archangel, either, whatever the ignorant peasant girl beside him thought.

Sweet Jesu, she must spend her time praying to the shadows of the crows that whirl overhead on a sun-filled day! And he had thought to believe that she actually —

The shadowy man stepped fully into the barn, and thumped his staff on the earthen floor.

Instantly the small barn was filled with a light so wondrous that Thomas almost fell in his haste to slip to his knees besides Jeannette.

The outward figure of a hunched, bowed aged man straightened into that of a man in the prime of his mind and body, and his face was now suffused with such power and anger that Thomas knew that it could be only one being.

"Saint Michael," he whispered, and prostrated himself on the floor, gladdened beyond measure that St Michael had again appeared, but even so, irritated that he must share this experience with this peasant girl.

Beside him Jeannette likewise fell to the floor, stretching out her hands so that she lightly grasped the saint about his ankles.

Thomas wondered that she dared, and then further wondered at the regard in which St Michael must hold her, if he allowed such a simple peasant girl to take such familiarities with his heavenly flesh.

Ah, my children, as one of you is my left hand, so the other is my right hand. Together, you shall work my will on earth.

He leaned forward, stretching out both hands — the staff mysteriously gone — and placed one on each of their heads.

Warmth and comfort and hope radiated out from his touch, and tears welled in Thomas' eyes. He was grateful beyond reasoning that the archangel spoke to him with such warmth and love.

And, as hands, then must you both work in tandem, whether in strength of faith, or in potency of action, for if one falls, then surely shall the other. Do not resent each other, nor strive to outdo each other in my favour. You are both equally loved and favoured.

His hands lifted slightly and, as they did, so both Thomas and Jeannette rose until they knelt upright before the angel, staring with bright zealous eyes at his shining form.

"I don't understand," Thomas said. "I thought that I was to be the one to —"

Beware of pride, Thomas! You have your role to play, as does Jeannette. Thomas, when truth is spoken to you, then you must listen. Jeannette spoke truly when she said that evil stalks in the form of the English king. To England you must go, Thomas, not only to retrieve de Worde's book, but also to destroy the many demons that have permeated the English court.

Thomas lowered his forehead to the dirt, almost loathing Jeannette for witnessing his humiliation.

Your paths shall be different, and they will never be what you expect. Thomas, you will fight for God from within the English camp, for they have been befouled beyond knowing. You must stop them. Find the cancer within, and destroy it.

"Blessed Saint Michael, the demons have spoken to me, and they too know of de Worde's book. What if they manage to destroy it?"

Again St Michael reached out his hand, but now he cupped Thomas' chin in it.

The pressure of his fingers was gentle, and loving. *The demons will never — can never — destroy that casket and its contents. It exists to be found, and to be used by the forces of God and goodness. It is a tabernacle, Thomas. They may hide it, but it cannot be destroyed by the many-fingered hates of the demons.*

Yet again tears welled in Thomas' eyes. This time they slipped past his eyelids, and slid down his cheeks.

Fight for me, Thomas, the archangel whispered, and then turned his face towards Jeannette.

Ah, most beautiful girl. You have such an unusual path before you, and you will see many unusual things. Walk in God's love always.

Remember — now the archangel addressed them both — *your paths will appear strange to you, and sometimes hateful, but do not hesitate. I, as God in all His Majesty, and as the saints and angels, and as the entire Hosts of Heaven, depend on you. Be true. Trust, however strange the way ahead.*

He leaned forward, and touched his lips to each of their brows in benediction.

Go in peace and the love of God.

Then he was gone, and there was nothing left in that barn but the peaceful breathing of Jeannette and Thomas.

II

Octave of the Nativity of the Virgin
In the fifty-first year of the Reign of Edward III
(Wednesday 15th September 1378)

The English and French armies had been skirmishing for days with relatively few casualties and no result. On the eighth day after the Nativity of the Virgin, Edward, Prince of Wales, known as the Black Prince, led his army of some four thousand knights and men-at-arms, one thousand armed sergeants and two thousand archers (both longbowmen and crossbowmen) into the fields outside the town of Poitiers.

The French army, led by King John II, numbered some fifty thousand.

Before the battle commenced, the French Cardinal Périgord approached King John and pleaded that he might be allowed to go to the Black Prince with a proposition.

"What is it?" asked King John.

"My very dear lord," said the cardinal, "you have here the cream of your kingdom's nobility pitted against a mere handful of the English. If you could overcome them without a fight by accepting their surrender, it would redound to your honour more than if you risked this large and splendid army in battle. I therefore beg you humbly, in the name of God, to let me ride over to the Prince and persuade him of the great peril he is in."

"I agree," said King John, shifting slightly to ease the cursed pressure of his bladder, "but do not be too long about it."

The cardinal was not too long about it at all, for the Black Prince merely laughed in his face and said that the only surrender he was interested in was King John's.

Périgord bowed his head, accepting the Prince's bravado, and rode to inform his king of the Black Prince's response.

King John smiled, anticipating the triumph when he would put the tip of his sword to the English ass-prince's throat. And the comfort when he could finally divest himself of his piss-stained suit of armour. At his age he couldn't go longer than an hour without needing to relieve his bladder, and he'd been so long in plate already he'd had to let the cursed urine trickle down his left leg on several occasions.

His skin itched damnably.

Piss-stained armour notwithstanding, within two hours John led his army of fifty thousand into blood-drenched horror.

Late that evening, even as the victors were wearily cutting the throats of the injured, and screaming, enemy trapped in the bloodied mud of the battlefield, an English clerk and frustrated poet called Geoffrey le Baker sat down and composed an entry for the campaign diary he would eventually turn into a chronicle. After describing the initial manoeuvring of the respective sides, le Baker continued:

As King John moved his forces forward, Prince Edward looked about him and surveyed his position. He saw that a hill near his army was completely encircled by fences and ditches, and its slopes almost entirely covered by pasture land thick with shrubbery, vineyards and fields of growing crops.

Edward decided to make his stand in the hillside fields, but to reach the hill his army had to cross a river in a deep marshy valley. His troops found a narrow ford and crossed the river with their carts. Then they moved through the fences and ditches and seized the hill, their movements hidden by the undergrowth.

On realising that Prince Edward's standard had disappeared, King John assumed the prince had fled. The French advanced towards the hill, believing they were chasing retreating Englishmen. Suddenly the leading French pikemen were attacked by well-equipped English knights, who successfully parried the thrusts of their enemy's pikes.

As more French advanced on the hill the battle raged in a fearful conflict of lances, swords and axes. High on the mound of the hill, the English archers and crossbowmen rained down their arrows and bolts on the French, who had reached, or were approaching, the ditches.

All did not go well for the prince's forces, however, for many of his archers had lagged behind his main force, and were trapped in the marshes.

These men the French cavalry trampled beneath their horses' hooves.

The fury of the carnage wore on. Both French and English sounded their fanfares, the wail of trumpets, horns and pipes echoing from the stony valley wall through the forests of Poitou until it seemed the very moutains moaned and the clouds shrieked. To the accompaniment of this horrible music, golden armour glittered and twisted, and burnished steel spears thrust like lightning bolts, shattering anything that lay in their path. The English crossbowmen made a night of the day, showering the French with a thick cloud of bolts, and this fatal downpour was further thickened with the arrows of the archers.

Madly the prince's forces hurtled on
Against the dense-packed shields, to seek a way
To pierce their enemies' armour and to strike
The hearts beneath the breastplate's firm protection.

Now Edward, Prince of Wales, strode into battle, hacking his way through the enemy lines and leaving ruin and death in his path:

> Savagely circling
> His sword on all sides
> Strikes his foes
> Crushes them down.
> Thus drops each man
> On whom its blow falls.

The French lines faltered and grew ragged, and Edward turned his fearsome advance upon King John and his retinue. The French standard bearers faltered, and then fell. Some were trampled beneath the feet of man and horses, their bowels ruptured and spurting their contents upon the earth; others were impaled to the ground by English spears; still others had their arms struck from their bodies. Of those who fell, some drowned in the soaking blood about them, while others screamed and wailed as they were crushed beneath the weight of those who fell atop them.

The shrieks of the dying joined the fearful clatter of the battle, and the blood of peasant and noble alike mingled in a single flow that fed the now scarlet fish of nearby streams.

And so the Black Prince, the wild boar of Cornwall, he who loves only the paths that flow with blood, hacked his joyous way towards King John's position. He and his forces broke through the French defences and, with the noble savageness of the lion, crushed the proud, spared the humble, and accepted King John's surrender.

Geoffrey put down his quill, carefully set his pages to one side, then rested his face on his arms on the desk and wept. It was the first battle he had seen, and such was the horror and the bloodshed, the stench of ruptured bowels and the screams of the dying, that Geoffrey did not think his soul would ever recover.

She waited long into the night, pacing back and forth before her lover's tent, pale with fear and sickened by the shrieks that still floated above the battlefield.

The Black Prince had won, she knew that, but at what cost? Who among his knights had fallen?

Who had fallen? What if one of the screams she had heard had been *his*?

At last, finally, long after the bells of Compline had rung out from a distant church, she heard the sound of hooves and men's voices as groups of the Black Prince's force filtered back into camp.

Her fear grew. Where was he?

What if he had died? What would happen then?

At last heavy hooves thudded towards the tent. A black destrier loomed out of the night, close followed by others bearing her lord's squires and valet.

"My lord!" she cried, and hastened to his side.

He waved her away. He was exhausted, and knew that if he fell from his horse he would crush her beneath the weight of his armour.

"Be still, Margaret," he said. "Let my squires aid me to the ground."

She stood to one side as the squires dismounted wearily to aid their lord, so consumed with fear that she thought she might faint, wanting to ask if *he* had also lived through the horror, but not daring to, knowing she had no right to ask.

He finally managed the ground, two squires to either side helping him walk.

"You're wounded!" Margaret said, fluttering about the group of men as they entered the tent.

"A scratch," he said. "For the Lord's sake, Margaret, let me be! My squires can bathe me and staunch the bleeding."

Margaret's face crumpled, and she stood back as the squires undid the buckles of her lord's armour, gently lifting each piece away from his body.

Beneath the armour his tunic was grey with sweat, and, in places, stiff with blood caused as much by the chafing of the armour itself as by sword or axe wounds.

The squires unlaced the tunic, folding it away from their lord's body while the valet brought warm water and wash cloths.

Useless and unwanted, Margaret stood in the shadows of the canopied bed, silent tears streaming down her face.

Was he alive? She would die if she did not know —

A footstep sounded outside the tent, and a man entered. He was young, much younger than Margaret's lover, and somewhat taller, with fine fair hair — now matted with sweat — and piercing light grey eyes.

Under normal circumstances he was an exceptionally handsome man; now he looked ashen and exhausted.

Margaret's lover turned at his entrance, and made as if to rise.

"My lord!" he said.

"Peace, Ralph," the newcomer said, and waved him down. "I have merely come to see that you are well, and well attended to."

"Ah," the older man said, "my squires have all survived, and are fit enough to serve me still, as you can see. And when they tire, Margaret is always here."

At her mention, the young lord turned his head to look at Margaret, although he had been keenly aware of her presence since the instant he'd entered the tent.

"My lady," he said, and inclined his head very slightly.

Tears still coursed down Margaret's cheeks, but now they were tears of sheer relief rather than fear. She curtsied deeply.

"My lord, I am heartily glad to see you well."

"It has been a bad day, Margaret, and we must pray that it will be the last we shall see for the present time. Many of our men have died, and many more lie screaming under the surgeons' knives."

She rose, her gaze locking into his. "But you have won the day, my lord, and you live."

And that is all I live for, she thought, knowing that he also knew it.

The older man moaned as his valet pressed the wash cloth too firmly against an abrasion, and both Margaret and the young lord turned their eyes back to him.

"I must leave," said the younger man. "My father will ride in soon."

"I thank you heartily for your concern," said the older man, and the younger nodded, and walked to the entrance of the tent.

Margaret mumbled some excuse to her uncaring lord and still-busy squires, then hastened after him.

When they were outside, and the tent flap shut behind them, they embraced briefly, fiercely, and then as quickly stood apart lest any see them.

"Hal," she said, "I am with child."

He drew in a sharp breath. "Then it has begun," he said. "We are committed."

III

The Thursday before the Feast of St Michael
In the fifty-first year of the Reign of Edward III
(23rd September 1378)

The day was burning, almost as if Satan had opened the gates of hell to allow a little of his devilish heat through to torment the poor souls of Christendom. Thomas rode through a shimmering landscape of corn-stubbled fields and rising dust. His horse was bathed in sweat, and Thomas was in no better condition. He had thrown off his black cloak and rode in his white tunic, its sleeves rolled up. Every so often Thomas tugged his robe's neckline down as much as possible to let air (the hot, hot air) circulate between the thick wool cloth and his slick, scratchy skin.

Although it was early autumn, the hot day was not unusual. This was the time of year when pests thrived in the summer's lingering heat and on the wastage of the harvest; grubs writhed through dunghills, rats scrambled through thatch, and fleas and ticks and mites bit deep on the flesh of man and beast alike.

This was the time of year for disease and pestilence, the time of annual fear, and Thomas had been regarded with both suspicion and eagerness in the villages he'd passed through these past weeks; peasants kept their distance, but needed his news. Had he witnessed corpses by the sides of the roads? Had he seen any freshly-dug graves? And had he delivered last rites to men or women with the swelling foul evidence of pestilence in their armpits or groins?

To these questions Thomas always answered no. Sometimes the peasants grudgingly gave him food (handed to him at arm's length lest he unwittingly carried contagion about his person); less often they gave him shelter.

As Thomas travelled west from Domremy he avoided other travellers, preferring to journey in solitude. He could purchase supplies in small town markets with what remained of Marcel's gold, and the nights were warm and pleasant and conducive to sleeping rolled in a blanket under the stars.

Thomas did not mind being left largely to his own thoughts. He knew the path ahead would be hard — and oft times confusing, according to the blessed St Michael — but he trusted in God and in the archangel. He, as Jeannette, would manage to drive out the filth of demonic contagion from Christendom and restore it to godliness and goodness. Thomas knew that he would without doubt become a soldier of God in this crusade, a General of either Church or secular army, but he sometimes wondered at the part Jeannette would play. The conscience of a king perhaps? Whispering encouragement and godly reassurances so that some glorious knight could ride to Thomas' assistance ... what else could a mere peasant girl do but become a blessed nun?

Thomas' way was now clear, if thorny. Find the blessed tabernacle of Wynkyn de Worde. Use its contents to destroy the demons. Thomas was well aware that the demons would attempt to destroy him in turn, but for that Thomas was prepared. He knew how they intended to use him — tempt him with this witch-woman Meg, for Christ's sake! — and he knew how he could counter their plans.

A sword through her belly, a single stroke, killing both her and the wicked issue she had conceived through her demonic sorcery.

Thomas smiled, contented.

By mid-afternoon the heat had become extreme. Some distance ahead of Thomas rode a company of fifty or sixty horsemen, soldiers, by the glimmer of weapons, and with at least one knight in their company. Both heat and the dust thrown up by the horsemen caused Thomas to pull his gelding back to an ambling walk; best to let the horsemen get further ahead. He supposed they were riding to join King John's campaign against the English — but on this hot, dreamy day the battles between English and French seemed very, very far away.

Everything about this day was dreamlike: the heat shimmer across the fields, the dust billowing gently across the road ahead of him, the stillness ... the consuming silence ...

In the end it was the stillness and silence that alerted Thomas to danger.

It was hot, yes, but the fields should still have had men and women working in them. There was threshing to be done, and hay to be carted, and the grape harvest to get in, and the pigs to drive to pasture to fatten for the annual autumn slaughter. And yet there was nothing.

The fields were empty; what hovels Thomas could see in the distance appeared deserted, the road was similarly empty save for the company of horsemen in the distance, and Thomas himself.

As with the fields, the road should have been busy. This was the time of year when goods and grain were moved towards the great autumn markets and fairs ... and in riding across north-eastern France towards Paris Thomas was travelling the busiest land trading route in Europe. Sweet Jesu! There should have been pedlars, merchants, pilgrims, beggars, cripples and the flotsam and jetsam of society at every bend of the road!

And yet there was nothing but silence and stillness.

Even the woods in the near distance to Thomas' left were still.

Not even birdsong.

Thomas sat up straighter, pushing the reluctant gelding into a fast walk. He looked to right and left.

Nothing.

He twisted about in the saddle — but there was no one behind him.

Thomas could see a considerable distance about him: the road was empty, the fields offered no hiding place for brigands ... but he could not help the tingle of fear up his spine.

Something was very, very wrong.

Where was everybody?

Thomas pulled the gelding to a halt and stood up in the stirrups, peering ahead.

The company of soldiers had, apparently, spurred into a gallop towards some far distant trouble, for there was no sign of them ahead, just the lingering dust of their passing.

But ... but there was something ... something else ... Thomas wrinkled his nose, then sniffed.

"Sweet Jesu!" he muttered, then thumped back into the saddle and dug his heels into the flanks of his mount.

He had smelt that odour once before in his life, and the cause then had been so appalling that he'd hoped never to smell it again.

It was the tainted scent of roasting human flesh.

The gelding snorted, then broke into a gallop.

Within minutes Thomas caught sight of a village ahead. It appeared as any other village he'd passed through: a collection of timbered and thatched cottages grouped about a communal green, a stream and a pond, a scattering of geese, chickens and pigs, and, just beyond the village, a small hill with a stone church halfway up its rise, a fortified manor house on its crest. And yet, as Thomas rode closer, he saw that it was very much *not* as other villages he'd passed through.

The village green was thronged with soldiers, presumably those Thomas had been ambling behind for the past half day. They were dismounted, among them a tall and solidly-built knight dressed in a chain mail hauberk and with an unvisored globular basinet on his head. Both his arms and legs were protected with white plate armour that sent shafts of sunlight glinting in every direction as he turned this way and that.

His sword was drawn, and he was gesturing angrily to his soldiers who, as Thomas rode closer, commenced a frantic search of the village buildings.

There were no peasants to be seen ... and Thomas quickly realised why.

In the centre of the green was an open fire, and over this fire was a large spit, and still gently rotating on this spit was the blackened corpse of a man.

To one side was a group of huddled bodies, although Thomas could not yet discern whether they were villagers or others.

The knight turned, several soldiers leaping to his aid, as Thomas rode into the green.

When the knight saw Thomas' robe, he waved his soldiers away and lowered his sword, striding towards Thomas with undisguised relief across his face.

"Brother!" he cried, and his voice betrayed that emotions other than relief were raging within him: horror, disgust, and anger beyond reasoning.

Thomas did not look at him, nor could he speak.

He could only stare at the sickening scene before him.

It was not so much the corpse roasting on the spit — now close, Thomas could see it was a man — but the huddle of corpses to one side.

Women and children. The two adult women were naked, their legs lying sprawled uncomfortably apart, blood and semen staining their inner thighs.

Each had been stuck through their bellies with stakes.

With them were the bodies of three small girls — none over the age of eight. The two eldest had been violated in the same manner as the women; they had died through the haemorrhages caused by their brutal rapes.

The youngest child, probably only two or three, was lying partially huddled beneath the still form of one of her older sisters.

The children still wore fragments of their clothes and it was obvious that these were not peasant children, but of noble blood.

"Brother," the knight whispered, and Thomas felt a hand on his thigh. "Brother?"

Thomas dragged his eyes away from the carnage and back to the knight.

The man had tears streaming down his swarthy face, and his face worked with emotion. He had to struggle to speak, and he needed to swallow in order to get his words out.

"Brother ... Brother, please, they need your care."

Slowly Thomas dismounted, his eyes moving between roasting corpse — God! but someone had sliced some of the flesh off his buttocks! — the bodies of the women and children, and the knight.

"How?" Thomas said once he was finally off his horse. "Who? *Why?*"

The knight shook his head, and held out a hand in either uncertainty or supplication. He did not speak.

Thomas walked hesitantly towards the man on the spit. He reached out a trembling hand and grabbed the handle of the spit, stopping it dead.

Sweet Jesu! The spit had been driven through his anus up through his body to emerge from his throat!

Thomas sent a swift prayer to all the saints in heaven that the man had already been dead when his murderers had commenced hammering the spit through. But somehow, considering the brutality of this scene, he thought the man had more probably been alive ... at least for the initial part of the spitting.

"His name is Sir Hugh Lescolopier," said the knight, who had stepped up behind Thomas. "And that," he pointed to the first of the women, "is his wife Marie, and there his sister Beatrice, and these his three daughters. This is Hugh's land. His manor house stands beyond the common fields."

Thomas did not look at the house in the distance. He could not look past the corpses before him.

"But who could do such a thing?" Thomas said.

The knight spat on the ground. "Who? *Who?* His vile peasants, bastard dogs all, did this! Can you *see* what they have done? Look! Look! They have sliced Hugh's meat from his body and forced it into Marie's mouth even as they were forcing themselves into her body! Can you see? *Can you see?*"

Thomas stepped closer to the women, and saw a piece of blackened flesh protruding from Marie's mouth.

He crossed himself, closing his eyes briefly, and murmured a prayer.

The knight moved to his side, and when he spoke his voice was flat with hatred and grief. "I am Gilles de Noyes," he said, "and Marie was my sister."

Thomas turned and stared at the man. De Noyes was staring down at his sister, and there was revenge and grief mixed in equal amounts there.

He introduced himself to de Noyes, and added, "God will have his vengeance on her murderer."

"Not before *I* have *my* vengeance!" de Noyes said, and would have said more, but just then there was the faintest movement on the ground before him.

Thomas jerked his hand away from de Noyes' arm and stared wild-eyed at the bodies, half expecting the brutalised Marie to twist about on her stake and point a cold dead finger to where her rapist-murderers hid.

But it was not Marie, nor the Lady Beatrice.

It was a rat, chewing on the leg of the smallest girl.

Without thinking, de Noyes leaned down and pulled her from the pile of bodies, swatting violently at the rat, which scurried off.

"Is she alive?" Thomas asked. He hoped not. It would be far better if she were dead.

"Nay," de Noyes mumbled. "She could not have survived what has been done to her." He lifted his head, and stared at Thomas with a face so ravaged by horror he looked an old man. "She has been violated as have the others!"

"Sweet Jesu!" Thomas tried to peer about de Noyes' arms, but the man had the dead girl folded so tight Thomas could barely see her.

"Gilles, my friend, perhaps we could —"

"Do not touch her! Ah, Thomas, I am sorry, but I remember holding this girl in my arms last Christmastide. She had barely begun to walk then, and she laughed and giggled as if she had no care in the world. Why this, Thomas? Why this?"

Thomas gestured impotently. "God's will —"

"Then I say fuck to God's will!" de Noyes yelled. "How can *God* will such as *this*? Eh? Tell me that, friar!"

Then, before Thomas could respond, there came a shout from behind one of the cottages, and several of de Noyes' soldiers emerged dragging with them a middle-aged man.

De Noyes roasted him as Lescolopier had been roasted. He even used the same stake that Lescolopier had been spitted on, although he had the man tied to it with chains rather than driving it through his body; de Noyes wanted the man alive to feel the full enjoyment of the fire. De Noyes personally worked the spit, turning the peasant over the bright flames that one of his soldiers had built, until the man had screamed out the hiding place of the other villagers.

Then de Noyes simply walked away, leaving the man screaming as his flesh blistered and burned, calling to his side his company of soldiers.

Thomas stood to one side the entire time, silent, holding the girl's corpse in his arms. De Noyes had finally handed her to him at the prospect at being able to torture one of her rapists.

Finally, in the absence of de Noyes and the soldiers, and to the accompaniment of the screams of the man roasting alive above the fire, Thomas calmly walked over to the corpses of the women, the other children and the blackened corpse of Lescolopier, and, shifting the tiny corpse into the crook of his left arm, knelt to begin the ancient ritual of the last rites.

The Lescolopiers would be heaven bound, even as their murderers would undoubtedly roast in hell.

If de Noyes didn't give them a roasting in this life first.

De Noyes and his soldiers returned at sunset. With them, bound and either cursing or screaming, were some nine men and three women.

The rest, de Noyes informed Thomas, had managed to flee before he'd found their hiding place.

"Attend to the bodies of the innocent first," Thomas murmured as the weary de Noyes dismounted. "I have already given them the last rites, and we can bury them in the churchyard tomorrow."

De Noyes nodded. "I do give you my thanks for your presence and aid, Brother," he said. "Without you their souls would surely have been in purgatory."

"Surely there must be a priest close by?" Thomas suddenly realised he hadn't thought about the priest who, in normal circumstances, would surely have lived in the house close by the church.

De Noyes shook his head, almost too weary to speak. "Later," he said. "When we have time to sit and eat. Did you give the girl her rites as well as the others?"

"Yes. Gilles, she will be heaven bound, surely."

De Noyes nodded. "You will say the funeral mass for them in the morning."

Once the bodies of Lescolopier, his wife and children, and the Lady Beatrice had been washed and wrapped in the fresh linens one of the soldiers had fetched from the manor house (along with the steward and two serving boys who had remained hiding in the house's buttery during the terror), de Noyes turned his attention to the peasant men and women.

He asked them the reasons for their brutality.

None replied, staring at de Noyes with faces stony with rebellion in the flickering torchlight.

De Noyes asked them again.

Still there was no reply.

De Noyes sighed, and nodded to his sergeant.

The three women were, for the moment, hauled to one side, screaming abuse as they watched their menfolk being stripped and tied to stakes de Noyes had caused his soldiers to erect in the green.

As soon as the peasants were secured, de Noyes drew his sword, walked up to a man picked at random, and sliced off his genitals, tossing them on to the still burning fire with its still turning spit of now dead and over-roasted meat.

Whilst the wounded man screamed and sobbed, twisting about the stake as blood pooled at his feet, de Noyes again asked the line the reason why they had attacked and killed Lescolopier and his family.

Again, no reply.

And again de Noyes strode to one of the tied men. This time he contented himself with grabbing the man's genitals in his hand, and raising his sword, again he asked, *Why?*

"Because," the man hissed between teeth clenched in pain and fear and resentment, "he was unreasonable, and too zealous in collecting his taxes. He made our lives miserable, and he deserved to die miserably."

"As do you," de Noyes said, and the sword dropped.

The man's eyes popped, and his entire body went rigid as de Noyes turned away and tossed the now severed genitals on the fire.

Then de Noyes turned aside to a pile of metal bolts one of his soldiers had gathered.

Beside the pile of bolts lay a mess of dog excrement.

De Noyes leaned down, took a hammer, then a bolt, and carefully coated the shaft of the bolt with dog shit.

Then he walked back to the line of staked men, and hammered the bolt into the belly of the first man.

He smiled as the man shrieked and sobbed, and turned back to the bolts and dog shit.

To the side Thomas watched unblinking. De Noyes was ensuring the men a painful and lingering death. The bolt shaft itself would not kill instantly, but, rather, the men would die over the next hours and days as the poison shafted into their bellies took hold.

Their deaths would not be pleasant, but then, neither had Lescolopier and his family enjoyed agreeable deaths.

As de Noyes walked away from the last screaming man, he nodded to the men holding the women.

They shouted, laughing, and dragged the women to the ground, tearing their clothes from their bodies as they did so.

There were three women and over sixty men, and Thomas understood that the women's deaths would not be either quick or painless.

Thomas and de Noyes sat under an apple tree in an orchard that had been planted just below the stone and timber manor house. Below them rose the church and cemetery, and below this still further lay the village. The orchard was a good place to rest and eat, far enough from the village green that the sounds of the dying men and the brutalised women were faint and unbothersome, and airy enough on this hot night for comfort.

Neither Thomas nor de Noyes had wanted to rest in the close and stifling manor house.

Across the small fire they had built (more to keep the insects away than for warmth), De Noyes watched Thomas with a drawn and haggard face. He'd taken off his basinet and mail, and sat clothed only in a linen tunic and leggings.

His sword he kept close by.

Neither of the men had eaten.

Thomas finally introduced himself, too tired and wrought to care if de Noyes took instant offence at his English name.

But de Noyes only shrugged. "Why travel westwards, Brother Thomas?"

"I need to reach my home friary," Thomas said. It was not strictly true, but it was close enough.

Again de Noyes shrugged. "For your aid and comfort here, brother, I wish you Godspeed ... but I doubt you will manage your journey without some misadventure."

"Have you heard news, Gilles?"

"Oh, aye." De Noyes glanced over to the village green. "Did you know King John was riding south to meet the English?"

"Yes. Towards Poitiers, I believe."

De Noyes nodded. "There has been a great and bloody battle at that place." He gestured tiredly towards the green. "In part, this is a result of it."

"A battle? What news?"

De Noyes grimaced, and in the firelight his eyes glinted.

"Your Black Prince —"

"I am of God, not of England."

"Whatever. The Black Prince, may his blood stain French soil, led his forces to a mighty victory. Many thousands of the flower of French knighthood died in the fields outside Poitiers."

"Sweet Jesu!"

"And that is not the worst of it." Suddenly de Noyes' face appeared to collapse in upon itself, as if death's fists had seized hold in his bowels. "The Black Prince has captured King John, and holds him to ransom."

Thomas was too shocked to speak. The English had the French King! But that would mean the war was all but over ... unless ...

"And the Dauphin?" Thomas said, referring to Prince Charles, the grandson and heir of King John. "Is he ...?"

"He is in Paris, Thomas. That is all I know. I was riding to join him ... there are still good men left alive after Poitiers, and there are many knights and lords of the north of France who had not joined King John's force. *Mon Dieu*, Thomas. John had fifty thousand men with him. Who thought he would have needed a *hundred* thousand to defeat the English?"

Was there any army which could withstand the Black Prince? Thomas wondered.

"And they would join with Charles?" he asked. The Dauphin was only a young man, perhaps three or four years younger than Thomas, and had not had any battle experience, let alone success.

And, besides, who knew if the madness that had afflicted his father also lurked within him? Few people had seen John's son, Louis, in the past ten years. Not since his extraordinary encounter with a peacock in the courtyard of the Louvre. It was said that John kept his son locked away in a remote castle.

Officially Louis was dead.

Unofficially, all knew he was alive ... if raving mad. For the past eight years, on Louis' nameday, Edward III had solicitously sent a cartload of peacock feathers to the French court for "the Crown Prince's adornment and comfort".

His gestures hadn't helped the cause of peace, and Thomas was sure that if the outcome of Poitiers had been reversed, the Black Prince would have been sent back to his father with every single one of those eight years' worth of peacock feathers stuffed inside his throat.

De Noyes shot Thomas an unreadable look. "It is join with Charles, or accept Edward as our king."

Then his face creased in worry. "Charles has worse news to deal with than the capture of his grandfather."

"Yes?"

"His mother, Isabeau de Bavière, has set about a rumour that she is not sure *who* Charles' father is ... there is her husband, Louis, true, but there was also the Duke of Orleans, and the Master of Hawks, and an unnamed man at Palm Sunday celebrations that she dimly remembers."

Thomas laughed shortly. "Isabeau has always been the opportunist. No doubt she hopes the Black Prince will pay her well for her tale of random fornications."

"Whatever, her slur has cast doubts in many men's minds. Has God withdrawn his favour from the royal house? Louis is demented, and his son ... well, *has* he a son? *Is* there a direct heir to the throne should John succumb to his age?"

De Noyes shook his head, and fiddled with a twig he'd picked up. "The only way we can hope to repel the English is by a strong and decisive leader. And Charles ... well, he is all we have."

"Where are the English now?"

"They won the day, but they were badly scarred. I hear that the Black Prince has his forces ensconced in Chauvigny.

But the rumours ..." he waved his hand helplessly about the scene below, "the rumours swear that the Black Prince is advancing on Paris and will overrun the north within a month. France is terrified ... and the rural folk are angry that the nobles don't seem to be able to protect them. Violence is spreading as peasants take the law into their own hands, trying to grab what they can while they can, and, as has happened here, venting on the innocent their years of frustration at the high taxes John has had to impose to fight the English."

De Noyes paused, gathering his thoughts. "I do not believe their grievances. They have just suddenly thought that here was the opportunity — their lords slain or captured in the bloody field of Poitiers — and so they seized upon it. I, as many of my fellows in these parts, have spent the past few days riding about the countryside, trying to impart order. If there is no priest here, then he has either fled, or been murdered. I hadn't thought it too serious ... not until this afternoon."

"There is evil about," Thomas murmured. "I have come from the east, from Lorraine, and yet I have seen no violence there, or on my passage west."

"No. This is the furthest east it has spread. Most of the trouble is in the regions closest to Paris. The city itself is in turmoil, and —"

"Paris is in turmoil?" Thomas said.

"The entire world is in turmoil," de Noyes said quietly, and to that Thomas had nothing much at all to add.

That night he dreamed.

He dreamed that he ran through an ancient dead forest with the tiny girl in his arms. She was not dead now, but screamed with the thin animal wail of terrified children.

Behind Thomas thundered something so horrible that Thomas knew that both he and the girl would die if it caught up with him.

He wanted, more than anything else in the world, to be able to save the girl from the beast.

And even in the midst of the dream he reflected on the strangeness of this feeling. The girl was, after all, but a girl-child, and not of much use at all. Even as young as she was, she had tempted the lusts of men, and thus must bear the sin of Eve.

Was she worth this rush through the forest to save her?

But he ran anyway. He ran for what seemed like hours, days, weeks, he ran until the breath tore raggedly through his throat, and until he begged brokenly for mercy for the girl.

He thought he had finally won mercy for her when he believed the horror behind him had lost pace and interest, but just as he slowed himself, he caught his foot in an exposed tree root, and he tripped.

He thudded painfully to the ground, rolling into a ball as he did so to protect the still-screaming child in his arms.

Suddenly the malevolent horror was upon them, and Thomas turned and stared at the murder that was about to descend on him.

It was the archangel St Michael.

"Time she went to hell," said the archangel, and reached down flaming arms for the girl.

Thomas screamed, but the archangel was too strong, and tore her from Thomas' arms.

He screamed and screamed, struggling to his feet, but it was too late.

The archangel had gone, the girl with him.

All that was left was Alice, standing before him, her body afire, a hand held out in supplication.

"Why did you let our child die?" she asked.

IV

The Friday before the Feast of St Michael
In the fifty-first year of the Reign of Edward III
(24th September 1378)

"Brother Thomas? Brother Thomas?"

Thomas rolled over, and groaned. His head felt as if a hive of angry bees had colonised it during the night.

"It is day, Brother Thomas, and the Office of the Dead waits to be performed."

Thomas opened his eyes, blinking against the light.

De Noyes stood over him, fully mailed, helmeted and weaponed, his hands on his hips. "Brother Thomas?"

Thomas groaned once more, and rolled onto his hands and knees, shaking his head free of the worst of the bees. His nightmare must have been sent by the demons.

De Noyes grasped Thomas by an arm and helped him to rise, handing him a flask of watered wine. "Drink."

Thomas accepted the flask gratefully and slaked his thirst. He blinked, rubbed his eyes, and looked about.

He was still in the orchard, now bathed in gentle dawn light. He shifted, and stilled. In the churchyard below were arrayed five bodies sewn into shrouds. The smallest of them had been placed atop one of the adults: the dead girl, held and comforted by an equally dead mother.

For an instant Thomas' mind was consumed by the image of Alice on fire, her hand held out, pleading for their child.

"We did not know if you needed them in the church," de Noyes said.

Thomas dragged his eyes away from the girl's shrouded corpse. "Take them inside," he said, "and place them before the altar."

And without further word he started down the hill.

Thomas managed, somehow, to get through the Office of the Dead. The ritual itself was familiar enough to him — saints knew how many funeral masses he'd attended in his lifetime! — but as a friar attached to a scholarly order, Thomas had not had much experience in actually conducting the funeral mass.

Nevertheless, for the sake of these five poor souls, he coped.

The village church was relatively plain. There were several poorly executed paintings on the walls — variously depicting Adam and Eve's expulsion from the Garden of Eden, the flood, Noah's Ark, and the Day of Judgement — two exquisitely embroidered hangings behind the altar (doubtless the handiwork of Marie Lescolopier or her sister-in-law, Beatrice), and an enamelled and jewelled cross on the altar itself. There were two carved pews for Sir Hugh and his family, and rushes strewn over the floor for everyone else.

Of the resident priest there was no sign. As Thomas prepared himself for the funeral mass Gilles de Noyes had murmured that there was blood found in the priest's quarters. Thomas had no doubt that the priest's corpse lay dismembered in some dark corner of the village or surrounding fields.

Thomas could do nothing for the priest; unless his corpse could be found the poor man's soul would linger in purgatory. Even if it *could* be found, Thomas knew there would be little hope for the priest's soul if he'd died without absolution or without time to say final prayers.

For the sake of the Lescolopier family, Thomas hoped they had had time and the opportunity to murmur a quick prayer before their torturous deaths.

And the tiny girl? Had she the wit and composure to say her prayers before her rape and murder? Was she damned, or saved? Was he now wasting his time trying to say the Office of the Dead over her body?

"Brother Thomas?"

Thomas dragged his thoughts back to the matter at hand, realising his voice had stumbled to a halt mid-prayer, and he nodded to de Noyes, moving smoothly back into the ritual.

Apart from de Noyes, there were only ten soldiers in attendance. All other soldiers were out scouring the countryside for more peasants, and as for the peasants they'd brought back for justice the previous evening, they were all now rotting in hell, their earthly corpses flung to the crows in the fallow field.

Thomas raised his hand in a final benediction, and de Noyes motioned to the soldiers.

They moved forward quickly and gathered up the shrouded corpses. Shallow graves had been dug in the cemetery: de Noyes could waste no time trying to dig out a vault within the church itself.

As Thomas shrugged off the chasuble he'd donned for the funeral mass, de Noyes stepped up.

"You will continue on your way?"

"Yes. I must get to Paris."

"I thought you said you were on your way to your home friary in England. There are many roads leading to the French coast that will not take you through Paris."

"There is someone I must see there."

"Then you are a fool! There is *no one* that you could need to see so badly you would risk your life so carelessly. Paris is in open revolt, man! You do *not* need to —"

"Listen to me, de Noyes! You have seen what has happened here. Murder so foul that it can only have been instigated by the minions of the Devil himself! Yes?"

De Noyes was silent, staring at Thomas with eyes sharp with anger and grief.

"This village has been touched by evil," Thomas continued, speaking low but forcefully. "Foul evil that has spilled out from the gates of hell and into Christendom. I have seen it, and spoken with it. The final battle between good and evil is about to be played out in our lifetime, Gilles."

Now de Noyes' eyes widened.

"Do you doubt what I say?" Thomas said. "How *can* you? Evil walked into this village and whispered in the peasants' idiot minds. Nothing else can explain the defilement of the Lescolopiers. Nothing else can explain the foulness of their murders, or the troubles spreading about France now. Gilles, demons walk among mankind —"

"And you think to stop them?" There was little respect in de Noyes' voice. "You did not stop my sister's murder."

"I —"

There was a shout and then the distant sound of horses' hooves and Thomas and de Noyes hurried outside.

A party some twenty strong had ridden through the village common and, following the pointing fingers of de Noyes' men, now approached the church.

De Noyes stared, then jerked in his breath in astonishment. "Sweet Jesu!"

Thomas glanced at de Noyes, then back at the riders now drawing their mounts to a halt before the church. Most of the riders were men-at-arms or richly-clothed servants, and all appeared to be grouped about two riders just behind the leading four men-at-arms.

"My prince!" de Noyes said, and dropped to a knee.

Thomas looked carefully at the two whom everyone else protected and deferred to. One was a woman, barely out of girlhood, thin and pale and with dark hair that had been disarranged by the ride and the tug of the hood of her blue cloak.

The other was a man of some twenty-four or five years, as dark-haired and pale-faced as the woman, but far more obviously discomposed. He looked between de Noyes and

Thomas, then relaxed slightly as he realised they posed no threat.

"Who are you?" he asked in a thin, cracking voice.

"Gilles de Noyes, your grace, of the lordship of Maronesse, and your humble and obedient servant."

"De Noyes? Maronesse?" The young man fidgeted and looked from side to side uncertainly.

The young woman leaned close to him, and said something in a low voice.

Her eyes did not leave de Noyes and Thomas.

"Ah," the man said. "Maronesse is just south of Montmirail, is it not?"

"Yes, your grace."

The man turned his head towards Thomas, visibly less curious about him. He was, after all, only a priest.

Thomas did not introduce himself immediately. He well knew this man, although he'd not seen him for at least eight years. Prince Charles, Dauphin of France and heir to the French throne.

Thomas had never seen any man apparently less ready to shoulder the responsibilities his grandfather's capture thrust upon him than the Dauphin. His eyes were fearful, his entire demeanour unsure, and he did not seem capable even of giving coherent directions regarding the use of a privy, let alone the ordering of a nation.

And what was he doing here?

"My name is Thomas, your grace," he said. "Of the Order of Preachers."

"Well, I can see *that*." Charles frowned a little. "Your face seems familiar."

"All priests look much the same, my lord."

"Well, perhaps that is so. De Noyes," Charles turned back to the knight, "how many men do you have at your disposal?"

"I have sixty sergeants with me, but, given a week or more, can call to my back some eighteen knights and over a hundred men-at-arms. They are yours, your grace!"

"Ahem. Yes, well ..."

"I find it strange that you should be riding east, your grace," Thomas said. "Surely Paris would be safer?"

Charles' face flushed, and several of his men-at-arms made as if to ride forward, but it was the woman who spoke.

"Paris is in open revolt," she said in a clear voice. "I and my brother have been forced to flee."

The Princess Catherine, Charles' younger sister. Thomas had never seen her before.

"Name your destination," de Noyes said, "and I will join you there within ten days with all the knights and men-at-arms I can muster!"

"Ah ... um ..." Charles said, and suddenly Thomas understood very clearly what had happened.

For whatever reason, and through whatever means, Paris had risen in revolt, and Charles had thought only of an escape, not of a destination.

Why east? Probably because the Dauphin had been closest to the eastern gate of Paris when he'd decided to flee, or perhaps the eastern gate had been the only one open.

"We ride to la Roche-Guyon," Catherine said. "There my brother will raise the force necessary to retake Paris and repel the bastard English."

It was a shame, Thomas thought, *that she had been born the woman and Charles the man. Catherine displayed far more spirit and determination than her brother.*

De Noyes nodded. "It is a strong castle, your grace. And a good site from which to launch your campaign."

Charles looked distinctly unhappy, and Thomas realised that the *last* thing the man wanted was to launch a campaign against anyone at any time.

Sweet Jesu, Thomas thought, *the Black Prince has won here and now!*

"Then we thank you, good sir," Catherine said, and smiled sweetly at de Noyes. "If you know the names and situations of those that might join us, perhaps you could use some of your men to send to them immediately?"

"It is done, my lady," de Noyes said, bowing to Catherine, then turning to one of his sergeants standing close by and issuing urgent, low orders.

Catherine looked back to Thomas. "Good friar, from where do you hail? Your intonation is strange, and I cannot immediately place it."

"I am come from Rome, my lady."

She smiled, but it did not reach her eyes. "You are English."

An instant stillness fell about them as the attention of the Dauphin's escort focused entirely on Thomas.

"I was born in England, my lady, but I am of the —"

"No man ever escapes his blood," Catherine said, and, stunningly, her face twisted in hatred and she spat at Thomas' feet. "I find you vile!"

De Noyes moved away from his sergeant and looked uncertainly between Catherine and Thomas.

"The friar has done good service here, my lady," he said. "There has been a wretched murder done in this village. The lord, Sir Hugh Lescolopier, his wife — and *my* sister — Marie, their children and his sister Beatrice had been ravished, tortured and murdered. Brother Thomas performed the last rites and, just now, a funeral mass. Without him . . ."

"Without the English there would be no uprisings and no murder," Catherine said, her eyes still on Thomas. "Your kind are eating our country and its people alive, sirrah."

Thomas did not reply, for there was nothing he could say.

Catherine opened her mouth to speak again, but just as she did so her face paled even further and she swayed alarmingly on her horse.

One of the men-at-arms steadied her, and Charles, surprising himself, managed to take the initiative.

"We must rest," he said to de Noyes, "for we have ridden over two days without stop. Is the manor house habitable?"

"Yes, your grace."

As Charles moved to give the order to ride up the hill, de Noyes turned and spoke quickly and quietly to Thomas.

"If you value your life, brother, I would hasten your departure. Once the Princess Catherine recovers ..."

Thomas nodded and, as the Dauphin's party rode away, turned and walked toward his own horse.

He would be more than glad to leave this place of death.

Charles and his sister rested twenty-four hours in the Lescolopier manor house before they resumed their ride south-east to the cliff-top fortification of la Roche-Guyon. When they left, de Noyes rode with them.

At dusk on the first day back on the road they came upon an extraordinary sight.

A young peasant man stood in the centre of the roadway, holding a mule so that their path was blocked.

One of the escort rode forwards, intending to strike them away.

But before his raised fist could descend, the peasant spoke up.

"You are Charles, grandson of John," said the peasant, and both Charles and Catherine were astounded to hear a girl's voice from the man's clothing.

"And you are beloved of God," the girl continued. "I am here to lead you to victory."

Catherine would have laughed aloud, but Charles leaned forward eagerly. "Who are you?" he said.

"My name is Jeannette d'Arc," she said.

Catherine's mouth twisted grimly. The man-at-arms should have struck her before she spoke!

"Well, Joan of Arc," Catherine said, "you speak out of turn, I think. Be on your way, and we will disregard the matter."

Joan turned surprisingly calm and steady eyes to the princess. "You have been misled," she said, "if you think your current station in life is your correct one. You are not where you should be."

Catherine reeled back in her saddle, more frightened and angry than she had ever been in her entire life. *Witch!*

Joan switched her gaze to Charles who, unlike his sister, regarded her with rapture.

"I am beloved of God?" he said.

"Yes. I am here to lead you to a victory against the devils from beyond the narrow seas."

Charles laughed, a little too loudly, and thumped his saddle with a clenched fist. He turned to his sister. "Well, what think you of that, Catherine?"

But Catherine could say nothing, only stare at the girl-woman before them.

"You go to la Roche-Guyon," Joan said. "That is a good place to begin."

And so saying, she turned, climbed on her mule, and led the royal party deeper into France, Catherine's sharp eyes on her back the entire way.

V

**The Vigil of the Feast of St Michael
In the fifty-first year of the Reign of Edward III
(Tuesday 28th September 1378)**

— i —

Thomas knew that the most sensible thing would be to avoid Paris completely ... but he wanted to see for himself what was happening there.

And what part Etienne Marcel played in the revolt.

Thomas had no doubt now that the troubles in Paris, as in the surrounding countryside, were part of the evil spread by the demons, and he knew he could not ride away from them.

It was always better to know your foe intimately than to spend your time guessing from a safe distance.

Signs of trouble increased the closer Thomas rode to Paris: manors burning, gangs of peasants roaming lanes and by-ways (they stayed off the main road as there were still many bands of men-at-arms riding east, presumably to join up with the Dauphin), and crops and livestock standing unattended in fields. Thomas was not troubled himself, and he assumed that as a poor travelling friar the rebels would have no interest in him.

Within a day of Paris Thomas encountered large groups of men and women fleeing the city with whatever of their goods they could manage to stuff into carts. They were pale and silent, refusing to answer Thomas' questions.

His concerns grew, but so too did his resolve. Paris held answers to questions he needed answered, and he could no more avoid Paris than he could his own conscience.

By the Vigil of Michaelmas Thomas was within a few hours of the city. He could see it dimly ahead, a grey haze on the horizon.

Distance haze, or smoke?

Thomas slid a hand into a pocket of his robe and fingered the seal ring Marcel had given him. God only knew if it could still afford him protection ... or if it might, in fact, call more harm on his head.

He no longer trusted Marcel.

Thomas had seen Paris once before, some ten years ago. Then it had been a vibrant community of noise, commerce, bells and colourful banners, if also narrow streets so bestrewn with animal dung that passage through them was both difficult and odoriferous.

As he drew his horse to a halt some half a mile out, Thomas saw that the city had been heavily fortified. At least it was not on fire as he had first thought. The walls, once somewhat neglected, had been patched and strengthened. Guards and archers stalked their heights. Wooden towers that Thomas could not remember previously now rose from key points along the walls, and he could see that they bristled with the machinery and weapons to repel sieges. Thomas' eyes narrowed. This was not the result of a hasty rebellion, but of years of planning.

He remembered his last conversation with Marcel: the hatred and resentment the provost had revealed towards the established authorities ... the ambition behind that resentment.

"God help you, Etienne," Thomas whispered, "if somehow you are involved in this."

Because if Marcel *was* behind this revolt — a revolt

that struck at the heart of God's established hierarchy on earth — it meant that he must be a subordinate to Satan, if not a demon himself.

Thomas clucked to his horse, and the creature moved forward. His head was high, his ears pricked, and Thomas realised that the horse knew that his home stable was nigh.

He *was* Marcel's horse, after all.

Thomas managed to approach the north-eastern gate, the Porte Babette, without any difficulty, but he was stopped some twenty paces out by a surly group of armed townsmen.

Rebels.

"Are you truly a priest?" a burly and heavily bearded man asked, a tanner by trade from the smell that lifted off him like a noxious miasma. "Or a spy of the cursed Prince Charles, or even of the devil-damned English?"

"If I spy," Thomas remarked mildly, "then I spy only on God's behalf."

He leaned forward over his saddle, ignoring the man's repellent smell. "Should I suspect you, my good man, of working for those forces ranged against God and all his saints in heaven?"

Thomas' tone had harshened as he spoke, and the tanner stepped back, a lifetime's fear of Dominican inquisitors taking automatic hold.

"These are difficult times," said another man, better dressed and spoken. He stepped past the tanner, and looked Thomas in the eye. "I am Jean Daumier, a Master of the Wool Merchant's Guild, and I speak with the authority of those now in control of Paris. What do you here, brother friar? What business do you have that you demand entrance to our city?"

Thomas sat back in the saddle, his eyes never leaving Daumier's face, and slipped a hand into the pocket of his robes.

Instantly men's faces and bodies stiffened.

"I have no weapon," Thomas said, and slowly withdrew his hand. "Merely this."

And he held out his hand, palm facing upwards. In its centre sat Marcel's seal.

Daumier's eyes widened when he saw it. "Where did you get that!" he said, his voice betraying anger and outrage.

"I was given it by the man I wish to see," Thomas said. "The provost, Etienne Marcel ... if he still lives amid this Godforsaken revolt."

Daumier's face still reflected suspicion, but he waved the armed men around him back a few steps. "I will take responsibility for him," he said, and took the ring from Thomas' hand. "But beware, brother, if you come in ill will. These are terrible days, and tempers are short. Be careful. Now get down from your horse. One of my comrades here will see to his safety and care. We must needs use our feet to get to our destination."

Daumier led Thomas through the gate — just in time, for steps to close it against the night (and likely attack) were already underway — and led him, not down the main thoroughfare leading to the central districts of Paris, but down a narrow winding street that followed the inner line of the city walls.

Daumier set a brisk pace, and Thomas had to work to keep up with him in the dim light of the street.

"I have heard only glimmers of news of Paris," Thomas said. "What has happened here?"

"The people have claimed their rights," Daumier said, somewhat unhelpfully.

"Yes, but I need to know what has actually —"

Daumier stopped abruptly and swung about to face Thomas. "If you seek Marcel then you *must* know what has happened!" he said.

"All I know is that Marcel befriended me some months ago," Thomas replied. "I need to speak with him about some matters we discussed then. In the meantime —"

"There is no 'meantime' for you, priest!" Daumier said. "You have skinned the ordinary man as much as the lords have! Your tithes and taxes, as well as your harsh screams of hell-fire awaiting sinners, have only added to the burden imposed by the king's taxes and demands. Well, the Parisians, at least, have had enough! No longer do we listen to the pratings of lord or priest."

And with that he swung about and stalked off into the deepening dusk.

Deeply alarmed by, and even more suspicious of, the man's extraordinary statements, Thomas hurried after him.

Daumier eventually led him through five or six twisting streets to a fortified house set against the city's northern wall. Here Daumier spoke to the several guards outside the front door, showing them Marcel's seal ring, before the guards stepped aside and allowed Daumier and Thomas passage inside.

The house was richly appointed: Italian tapestries and eastern silks hung from walls, while deep wool carpets — also eastern, by their exotic patterning — were scattered across the floors. Intricately carved chairs and chests stood in the hall.

Daumier gave Thomas no time for a close inspection of the furnishings, leading him straight to a closed set of double doors. Without further ado, he opened one of the doors, spoke quickly and quietly to a guard on the other side, and then stood back to allow Thomas through.

"The ring," Thomas said as he drew level with Daumier.

With a grimace, Daumier handed it back to him, and then walked away without a word.

Thomas entered the room.

There were several guards directly inside the door — who pointedly laid hands on the swords at their sides as Thomas passed them — but Thomas had eyes only for the two men seated at a table set before a roaring fire.

They rose, silent with question, as Thomas entered.

One was Marcel, his face lined with care and lack of sleep.

But Thomas ignored him. He could only stare at Marcel's

companion, a darkly handsome man in his thirties dressed in rich velvets and brocades.

The man stared briefly at Thomas, then grinned easily.

"Why, if it isn't Lord Thomas Neville," he said, "all dressed up in the garb of a damned Dominican friar, and with his pate all a-shaved! What do you here, Tom?"

And then the notorious Philip the Bad, King of Navarre, Count of Evreux, and cousin to the French king, stepped forward and embraced Thomas.

VI

Compline on the Vigil of the Feast of St Michael
In the fifty-first year of the reign of Edward III
(night Tuesday 28th September 1378)

— ii —

"No, wait!" Philip cried, leaning back a little, although he still kept Thomas' shoulders in a tight grip. The king's face was alive with mischief.

"Say nothing!" he continued. "I can guess why you're here. Why, you damn Englishman, you have come to spy on us, have you not? Capture our goodwill and then lead us straight into the heart of the Black Prince's camp? Ha! Tom, you cannot fool this fine fellow!"

"Marcel!" Philip turned so he could see Marcel, who had risen from his chair, completely shocked. "Marcel? You know this man? Ah," Philip turned back to Thomas, who appeared only marginally less shocked than Marcel, "Tom, my friend, it is too many years since we have hunted the boar together."

"Philip ... your grace, what do *you* here?"

Philip continued to grin happily at Thomas. "You do not know?"

Thomas looked over at Marcel, then back to Philip. "I ..."

"If I know Thomas," Marcel said, regaining his composure,

"he has been locked away on some obscure Church business and has completely failed to note the doings of the world beyond the door. Thomas, come, sit down. I am as pleased to see you as his grace obviously is. Although," Marcel sank down into his chair as both Philip and Thomas took their seats, "I had no idea that you knew the King of Navarre."

A servant glided out of the shadows with a goblet, which he set down beside Thomas' right hand.

Philip waved him away, and poured Thomas a measure of wine himself. "If you know Thomas, Marcel, then you must know he is a Neville."

"Of course," Marcel said, making a small gesture of self-deprecation. "I should have known that as you are of similar age and station you must have shared —"

"Many youthful adventures," Philip said, and laughed good-naturedly. "Tom spent much time with my family when he was a youth and learning the arts of the knight. Ha! But look at you now!"

All merriment left the king's face, and when he spoke again his voice was serious. "A damn priest. I heard rumour you'd joined a monkery, Tom, but I had given it little credit. I am ... dismayed ... to see you thus."

"We must each follow our own hearts," Thomas said.

"But to give up your heritage, Tom ... and your lands! What on earth possessed you?"

"The Holy Spirit —"

"No! Save me. I do not want to hear priestly prattle from *your* mouth."

Philip sighed, fiddled with his goblet, then looked at Marcel. "And you, my rebellious friend —"

Thomas looked sharply at Marcel.

"— where did you make Tom's acquaintance?"

"Brother Thomas joined my company as we travelled the Brenner Pass, your grace. We were both going to Nuremberg, although I had to break my journey short and hurry homewards when I heard news of the ... troubles."

"Ah, yes, the 'troubles'," Philip said and leaned forward, sloshing more wine into his goblet. "The troubles ..."

"I have been," Thomas said quietly, "too deep in my own problems the past weeks and months to be much aware of the outside world. Such news as I have heard has largely passed me by untouched. But, as I entered France, and travelled westwards, I have heard of — and seen — great miseries. King John," Thomas risked a glance at Philip, "has met with disaster at Poitiers, I believe."

Philip said nothing, but took a deeper swallow of wine, and grinned.

"As a result," Thomas continued, "I hear there has been disturbance in Paris. The Dauphin has been ejected, and now gathers men to the east —"

"What?" Philip and Marcel exclaimed together.

"*What do you know?*" Philip said, once more leaning forward, his goblet now pushed to one side. His black eyes were intense, but with what emotion Thomas could not guess.

Marcel sat back a little, allowing Philip precedence, although the provost was clearly as desperate to hear Thomas' news as was the king.

"I need to know what has happened here first," Thomas said, "or else I may not be able to explain coherently my own news."

Philip's mouth curled; it was not a pleasant expression. "What you mean is that you need to know where Provost Marcel and I stand so that you may tailor your news accordingly.

"Marcel," he waved a languid hand at the provost, "tell the friar what you've been up to."

Marcel looked down at his hands resting on the top of the table for a moment, then raised his eyes to Thomas' face. "The war with the English has sent Paris spiralling into chaos, Thomas. King John, as you have heard, has fought a disastrous campaign —"

"The scabby senile old man couldn't have won a battle with a three-legged kitten," Philip said, almost under his breath.

"— and has been captured as a result. The Black Prince

has demanded a huge ransom, as well as a winter truce that would see most of France under English control."

"Where are the English?" Thomas said.

"Still south," Marcel replied. "The Black Prince has moved his force into Chauvigny, where he waits like a spider for his next meal. Whatever, for the moment we have greater troubles than the English."

"What greater trouble can there be than the *English*?" Philip said, smiling once more.

Marcel took a deep breath. "If your grace will allow me to finish ..."

Philip waved a hand again, and Marcel turned back to Thomas. "The Dauphin summoned the Estates General —"

"The representative assembly?" Thomas said. "But that hasn't been summoned in decades."

"Nay. But Charles needed it. Desperately." A vein began to flicker in Marcel's neck, and his hands clawed into fists on the table. "In order to raise the ransom, Charles needed to levy taxes — such taxes as you cannot believe! — on the citizens of Paris and the surrounding provinces. This war between our king and yours, Thomas, has caused us such great misery for the past years that you cannot begin to imagine. Now, Charles proposes taxes that would cripple most honest people!"

"And so the Estates General refused to grant the taxes." Thomas sincerely doubted that Charles had *proposed* much at all — undoubtedly he'd been mouthing the thoughts and phrases of some poor advisers.

"The Estates General did not have much say in the matter." Marcel paused. "*I* would not allow such taxes."

"What do you say?"

"The Parisians had had enough, Thomas," Marcel said. "All they wanted was some man to stand up for them, to lead them —"

"And you were there," Thomas said, remembering the conversation he'd had with Marcel on that final night they spent together in Germany.

"There was a spontaneous uprising," Marcel said,

"which, if someone had not given it direction, would have caused massive bloodshed."

"And ...?"

"And so, on behalf of the people of Paris, and of France, I set before Prince Charles demands that needed to be met before we could allow ourselves to be taxed one more sou."

"And the demands?"

"That power be passed from the hands of the king into the hands of the people," Marcel said.

Thomas stared at the provost, almost unable to believe what he had heard. This went beyond rebellion ... this was a heresy against the ordained order.

"The people are not the ones to make demands on the king," Thomas said quietly, holding Marcel's stare. "Kings are ordained of God, and the only office which has the authority to chastise kings is the papacy."

Philip chuckled, and Marcel sneered.

"*Which* papacy?" Marcel said. "It appears that in these days of suffering we can pick and choose. Kings have abandoned the common people, and the Church is in disarray! It was time we took matters into our own hands."

Thomas said nothing, and so Marcel continued. "I headed a deputation to the Louvre, and we set our demands before the Dauphin. He refused to listen to me. There was a ... small altercation."

Philip laughed softly again. "What he means, my dear Tom, is that Marcel's 'deputation' got slightly out of control, seized two of Charles' marshals, and tore them apart on the spot.

"Of course," Philip leaned back in his chair, and rested his elegant silk-hosed legs on the table, "*I* should not be the one to mouth complaints. At the time, the Dauphin had me incarcerated in a dungeon for some imagined wrong. Marcel, once he'd managed to keep the mob back from the Dauphin, had me set free."

"Ah," Thomas said, finally understanding. "And so now you are allies against the Dauphin." He wondered if Marcel knew what kind of ally Philip could be.

"His grace and I have struck a bargain," Marcel said. "He supports my and my fellows' bid for a representative say in government, and we support him as rightful claimant to the French throne."

Now it was Thomas' turn to burst out laughing. "The French throne has more 'rightful claimants' than a dog has fleas! You cannot hope to succeed!"

"And we will not," Philip said, "if you do not tell us what you know."

"It is not much," Thomas said. "Charles has, as you say, fled Paris. He gathers troops, to the east somewhere, although I do not know the precise location. Forces rush to join him. When he has an adequate complement, I have no doubt that he —" *or, more likely, his sister* "— will lay siege to Paris."

Philip and Marcel looked at each other, and Thomas watched the both of them.

France is tearing itself apart, he thought. *All the Black Prince need do is give them time enough to complete their own murder and the path to the throne of France will be his father's for the taking.*

"I need to leave," Philip said. "Now."

Marcel nodded, rising. "I will have horses and an escort for you within a few minutes. Wait here." He spoke briefly to one of the guards at the door, then left.

Thomas and Philip waited until he had gone, and then Thomas looked directly at Philip.

"What *are* you doing, Philip?"

Philip did not evade his eyes. "I am going to leave this Godforsaken city," he said, "and I am going to ride to my estates to the west. I have men there, waiting. I will raise an army."

"And then?"

"And then ..." Philip smiled, utterly malevolent, "I will have to make up my mind *who* to support, won't I?"

"You cannot think to support Marcel! What he advocates is treason to both man and God."

Philip rose, scraping back his chair. "You know me well enough, Tom. *You* tell me who I will support."

"Whoever promises you the most," Thomas said bitterly.

Philip gave him a small, cold smile, then stalked out of the room.

Thomas sat for a few minutes, staring into the fire, then he, too, rose and walked to the door. He knew now that Marcel was undoubtedly demon-corrupted, if not demon himself, and he had confirmed the method of the demonic assault of Christendom: through their evil, both subtle and direct, the demons meant to launch an attack on the traditional and God-given hierarchy of society. They would attack the Church, and they would attack the right of the nobles to govern society, and they would persuade the common man that he had a right to his own destiny. Sweet Jesu! It was a nightmare! The commonality were simple folk, who needed the love and direction of the higher orders of priests and nobles. God's order on earth would collapse if common men were allowed freedom of choice! Ah, it was best he leave now, before Paris disintegrated into flames around him. He could prevent more damage the quicker he found Wynkyn de Worde's casket, and threw the secrets it contained against the demons.

As he went to pass the guards, two stepped forward and grabbed Thomas by the upper arms.

"What —"

"The provost's order, brother. For your own protection," said one guard.

The other grinned, his eyes malicious. "Paris is a dangerous place these days. We wouldn't want you to come to any harm ... would we?"

VII

The Feast of St Michael
In the fifty-first year of the reign of Edward III
(Wednesday 29th September 1378)

— Michaelmas —

It was a surprisingly good Michaelmas at la Roche-Guyon, and the Dauphin Charles was in surprisingly good humour, considering that the English controlled the entire south of France, they held his grandfather (as well as much of the flower of French nobility) for ransom, and he had fled Paris not a week before in fear of his life.

All this was due to the peasant girl, Joan of Arc.

She had said little on the day and a half's ride it took to reach the castle of la Roche-Guyon, save that she worked God's and the angels' will and that all would be well in due course. De Noyes, as well as Catherine and most of their escort, regarded her with some suspicion.

Who could not be suspicious of a girl who dressed as a man?

And what peasant girl claimed to have the knowledge to lead France to a victory against the English?

Catherine, in the few minutes she had alone with de Noyes at dusk on the day Joan had joined them, whispered the word "witch" at least four times, and further claimed that she was probably a harlot who wanted to seduce Charles for her own gain.

De Noyes, although he thought his princess might have gone too far in her assumptions, nonetheless had his own reservations about the girl.

Mon Dieu, she wasn't even beautiful! No knight could be inspired to perform valorous deeds on the battlefield by a stumpy, brown-faced, thick-waisted girl!

Charles, however, was fully prepared to be enraptured. He had prayed for a sign from God that all was not lost, and here it was, albeit in the slightly unglamorous form of Joan.

They arrived at la Roche-Guyon at dusk on the evening of the Feast of St Michael, their mounts wearily plodding the steep roadway up the chalk cliff to the citadel. La Roche-Guyon was an ancient castle with a great round keep soaring above its walls, dominating the curve of the River Seine far below. It would be a safe and convenient site for Charles to rally the remnants of the French nobility and army about him ... if he had the nerve and the skills to do it.

By Compline that evening Charles, Catherine and de Noyes had eaten and rested, and Charles called the girl, Joan of Arc, before him.

He leaned forward in his chair, his face eager, as Joan sank to her knees before him.

She had not washed, nor set aside her travel-stained clothing since her arrival, and Catherine's mouth curled very slightly in distaste as she noted the stains about the girl's face and body.

No doubt the witch thinks it gives her an air of hermetical mysticism, she thought.

"How may I know that what you say is true?" Charles asked. "You said that you have been sent by God so that I may achieve a victory against ... what did you call them? Ah, yes, the 'devils from beyond the narrow seas'."

"Sire," Joan said, and Charles' heart soared at the title. He *was* "sire", wasn't he, if his grandfather lay impotent in an English dungeon?

"Sire," Joan said, "if I tell you things so secret that you

and God are alone privy to them, will you believe that I am sent by God?"

"Assuredly," said Charles, leaning even further forward, his face flushed. "Continue."

"Do you remember," Joan said, "that on the night of the Feast of Saint Maurice, just a week past now, you sat in the chapel of the Louvre and prayed to God?"

"Aye, I remember," Charles said, and turned to his sister. "Catherine, I *was* there! You remember ... you had to run to the chapel to fetch me so that we could flee!"

Catherine said nothing, and Charles turned his attention back to Joan.

"Yes?" he said.

"You prayed to God that if you were indeed bastard-bred then He should take the realm from you."

Charles sat back in the chair, pale and trembling. "It is true," he whispered. "That is what I prayed."

"Then I am here to tell you," Joan said, "on behalf of God, that you *are* the true heir to the throne, and that your mother speaks nothing but lies."

"And *you* are nothing but a witch!" Catherine said, standing from her own chair. "Who are you to speak on behalf of God?"

Joan turned her face to Catherine, and something in it made the older girl take a half step back and sink down into her chair.

"I speak the word of Saint Michael, who deigns to appear to me," Joan said, holding Catherine's gaze. "I am a poor and unworthy peasant girl, but I am no witch, nor harlot, nor," her eyes hardened, "am I a bastard born of cold lust, unloved by my father."

De Noyes and Charles frowned at this last remark, not knowing the sense of it, but Catherine cowered in her seat, again terrified by the girl.

She is *sent by God!* Catherine thought. *Merciful Jesus, how am I to protect myself against her?*

Joan turned her regard back to Charles. "Many will come to la Roche-Guyon to join you," she said, "but you must not tarry long here. When you have a suitable force behind you, return to the fields outside Paris. There you will meet a man who can aid you."

"Who?" Charles said.

"His name," said Joan, "is Philip, and even though he has a serpent's tongue, you can mould him to your advantage."

Later that night, when the entire citadel slept save for the guards atop the walls, Catherine sat alone by the window in her chamber, staring at the silvery river winding far below.

She shivered in her thin nightgown, and wrapped her arms about herself.

Joan was dangerous beyond compare ... and none had suspected her, nor thought the angels might send one such as her.

She could ruin everything ... everything ...

Catherine tried to hold back her tears, but such was her despair they escaped anyway.

How could she warn of Joan ... how could she warn the man she loved so desperately, and he her?

There was no communication between them. Not now. Not under these circumstances. And, dear Jesus, it might be years before she saw him again.

Catherine did not know how she would survive if her brother fell under the witch's spell and allowed himself to become God's instrument on earth.

She did not know how any of them would survive that.

Finally, her despair grew too great to bear quietly, and she leaned against the cold stone of la Roche-Guyon and broke into loud, wracking sobs.

VIII

The Thursday before the Eighteenth
Sunday after Trinity
In the fifty-first year of the reign of Edward III
(14th October 1378)

There were only so many things a man could do to keep himself occupied in a room no larger than the meanest monkish cell — furnished only with a stool and sleeping pallet — and during the past two weeks Thomas had done them all a dozen times each day. He had prayed, meditated, listened, thought and, most of all, angrily paced the confines of the room.

He'd been such a fool! Ever since his experience at the Cleft, Thomas had known there was good reason to be suspicious of Marcel. So what had he done? Walked straight into the man's den. Now here he was, confined and useless, and the demons outside in the street could work their will unrestrained.

Perhaps even now they were crawling over de Worde's casket, trying to find their way in.

Dear God, but he was useless until he could find that casket.

Did the demons mean to keep him here, trapped, until it was time for this "test" they had taunted him with?

When he wasn't pacing, Thomas prayed, but he found

little relief in prayer. St Michael had aided him all he could. It was up to *Thomas* to act and to find his way, and he knew he couldn't rely on being saved by the archangel every time he misjudged.

How could he lead the battle to send the demons back to hell if he couldn't manage to escape a simple prison cell?

Finally, after over two weeks of frustration and self-recrimination, footsteps approached his door, and Thomas heard the bolt being slid back.

He turned to face the door.

There was a murmur of conversation on the other side, then the door swung open.

Marcel entered. His face was drawn and exhausted, the skin a sickly grey, and his clothes were crumpled and stained here and there with the mud of the streets.

Thomas stared boldly, unblinking, not willing to be the first to speak.

"Put on your cloak," Marcel said, "and come."

Thomas made no move, nor did he shift his regard away from Marcel.

Marcel sighed, almost inaudibly, and his eyes drifted past Thomas and focused on some distant object through the tiny window.

"I would like," he said, "to speak of who I am."

Thomas' eyes narrowed.

Marcel's gaze refocused on Thomas. "*And* of what I do. Come. Please."

Marcel turned and walked out the door. Thomas slung his cloak about his shoulders and followed.

For a long time they did not speak.

Thomas had been kept in a room of the fortified house that Daumier had led him to that night two weeks ago, and now Marcel led him up through a maze of corridors, through the front door, and then into the narrow, twisting street beyond.

There were people about — this was a normal working day — but the mood was grim, almost sullen. There were not the voices and laughter that Thomas normally associated with a busy market and craft city, but only a subdued gloom that emanated from the people moving along the street.

Several greeted Marcel respectfully enough, but Thomas noticed that occasionally a face would turn to the walls, and then the sky, as if the person expected some kind of retribution, whether earthly or heavenly, to fall upon him or her within the next instant.

Suddenly Thomas recognised the atmosphere. It was that of the penitent, crawling helplessly (and hopelessly) towards his confessor.

This city was preparing for death.

"Marcel?" he said, but the provost had walked out onto the street and was now moving westwards, and Thomas hurried after him.

They walked swiftly, moving from the narrow, winding streets close to the walls into the wider and straighter main thoroughfares of the city. Here people thronged, making pretence at conducting daily business and trade, but everywhere was the same sense of apprehensive waiting.

"It has all gone wrong for you, hasn't it?" Thomas said as they eventually swung into the Grande Rue and headed towards the Seine, the hunched grey shape of Notre Dame rising into the grey low-slung clouds ahead.

"Thomas," Marcel began, his pace slowing amid the commerce and traffic of the Grande Rue, "I have tried my best, but I fear I have failed."

Thomas said nothing, knowing that Marcel had to unload his conscience without prompting if his repentance was to be a true and honest one.

Marcel nodded and smiled at a carter who greeted him with a wave, then resumed. "I grew to manhood in this city, and have loved it, and its people, with all my being."

Thomas nodded, acknowledging Marcel's beginning. *His first mistake. He should have loved* God *with all his being*.

"Paris is a city of light," Marcel said, slowing a little as he sidestepped a heap of dung piled outside the front door of a stone-fronted house, "its brightness fuelled by the honest hearts of its citizens. To them I have devoted my entire life."

Again Thomas nodded, knowing. *It was to God that you should have —*

"You tiresome priest," Marcel said mildly. "I know your thoughts. I am not confessing, only showing you the road ahead."

Thomas stopped and turned to the provost, halting him with a hand on the sleeve of his heavy coat. "Marcel —"

"No. I would speak, and I would have you hear me out." Marcel pulled his sleeve from Thomas' grasp. "You do not yet understand the basic difference between us, my friend. You devote your life to God, and God's work. I devote — have devoted — my life to the people of my city, and," Marcel's eyes hardened and his mouth lifted slightly as he spoke his heresy, "to wresting them from God's overly protective hand."

"That is sacrilege — but then, what could I expect from *you?*"

Marcel laughed, low and bitter. "Sacrilege? Nay. Not in my eyes, nor in the eyes of those who love me and for whom I work. But in your eyes ... well, yes, doubtless I am," he smiled very slightly, "a true imp from hell. Will you come with me this day, or do you fear what I might show you?"

"Nothing you show me could shake me, or my faith."

"Perhaps not what *I* show you," Marcel said, resuming his stride down the thoroughfare, "but I can make a start."

Angered, puzzled and appalled in equal amounts, Thomas again hurried after him, pushing roughly past the Parisians who crowded the small open square the Grande Rue had opened into. It was almost noon, and the markets and associated commerces and crafts around the sides of the square were at their peak.

Bells sounded, and Thomas glanced upwards. A magnificent guildhall, the wool merchant's guild, according to the signs attached to walls and hanging from balconies, rose to his right. It was decked with gilded spires as — *more* — ostentatious than any cathedral's, and in its tower sat a fat-faced clock, its hands marking the midday. As Thomas stared, figures painted in scarlets and golds ran out on cunning rails from the right-hand base of the clock, raising hammers and axes and staging a mock battle before sliding back into an all but hidden door on the left side of the clock.

At the same time the bells of Notre Dame sounded, yet — and even accounting for the fact that the great cathedral was still some distance away — Thomas had the uncomfortable feeling that the bells of the guildhall almost completely obliterated the cathedral bells.

Indeed, the people in the square raised their eyes and exclaimed at the bells — but they looked to the guildhall, not Notre Dame.

They worshipped at the house of Mammon, not the house of God?

Thomas dropped his eyes, and saw that Marcel was watching him with a horrible intense *knowingness* in his eyes.

"See these people," Marcel said, letting the crowds swirl about himself and Thomas. A husband and wife, two small children grasped firmly by their hands, passed close by, and Marcel smiled and nodded at them. "They are honest people who pain and love and suffer as all people on this earth do. All they want is the chance to make their lives bearable —"

"They hunger for the wrong thing," Thomas said, not willing to allow Marcel to indulge in his own prating. "This life is not important, nor worthwhile. Instead, they should concentrate on the next life and of achieving their salvation therein, not on the worldly distractions of this wasteland of a world."

"You are a sad man," Marcel said, "and deluded. Why is this life not worthwhile? Why are their lives," his hand swept out, embracing the entire crowded square, "not important?"

"We are all sinners and this life is but a temptation to sin further. Can you call that worthwhile?"

"Can you not see how blind you are?" Marcel said. "Can you not see how beautiful this world and this life is?"

"All I see is ignorance and sin."

"Then I pity you," Marcel said, and walked into the

crowd, disappearing behind a swirl of red and green-cloaked shoulders and peaked hoods.

Furious, Thomas pushed through the throng after him. "What have you done?" he shouted.

"I have done my best," Marcel said over his shoulder, continuing to walk briskly.

Thomas cursed, and followed him.

He'd thought Marcel was leading him towards the guildhall, but the provost abruptly turned into a tiny alley just to the side of the hall, leading Thomas to a small shop set under the overhang of the dwelling above.

Marcel stopped by the doorway, waited for Thomas to catch up, then knocked and entered, holding the door open for Thomas to follow.

Grateful to be, at the least, out of the press of the market crowds outside, Thomas looked about.

A man dressed in a leather apron stood behind a table strewn with tools. He was in mid-life, his fair hair thinning, his beard streaked with grey, his face worn and tired.

He was holding a small chisel in one hand, a mallet in the other. On the table before him there was a roughly hewn, curved board covered in chalk lines to guide the carpenter's hand and eye. To one side of the table were planks and carved bits of wood ... Thomas realised with a small jolt that they were pieces of choir stalls, beautifully worked and carved.

To the other side of the table, staring at Thomas with frightened eyes, was the carpenter's wife, and a small boy-child of about seven years clutching at her side, as frightened as his mother.

"What is wrong?" the carpenter said, his eyes darting between Marcel and Thomas. "Has my work been found wanting?"

"Nay, Raymond," said Marcel, smiling reassuringly at Raymond's wife and tousling the boy's hair before looking back to the carpenter. "Who could find your work wanting?"

The fear did not leave Raymond's eyes. "Then why is *he* here? Perhaps I have carved an inaccuracy into one of the stalls. Carelessly misrepresented one of the saints, or perhaps one of the Church Fathers? Brother," Raymond dropped his tools and held out his hands to Thomas, "none of it has been intentional. I have not meant to represent any heretical idea with my carvings! I —"

"Peace, Raymond," Marcel said. "Brother Thomas has heard only of the precision and beauty of your work, and has come to praise, not condemn."

Marcel turned to regard Thomas, his eyes wide and disingenuous. "Isn't that so, brother?"

Thomas glared at Marcel, but softened his expression as he moved over to examine some of the boards that had been completed.

The carving was exquisite, the figures and representations flowing across and through the grain of the wood almost as if God had placed them there, not the skill of the carpenter.

But then, wasn't that the truth? These carvings were truly the work of God, rather than of the carpenter, who was himself only a tool of the Master Craftsman.

Marcel's mouth twisted slightly, bitterly, cynically. "Raymond has, at the behest of the archbishop, been working on improvements to the choir stalls in Notre Dame for the past eight months."

At the tone of Marcel's voice, Thomas turned away from the woodwork and looked back to the provost. "His work is wondrous, and will surely add to his store of good works so that —"

"So that when Raymond dies," Marcel finished for him, "and appears before the angels of judgement, his eight months spent working on these carvings, and on nothing else, *and with no payment*, will undoubtedly weigh heavily in his favour. Of course, it doesn't help at the moment, when Raymond is not allowed to work on any other project that might actually earn him the coin with which to feed his family."

"I am not complaining," Raymond said anxiously.

"Of course you are not," Marcel said. "You are merely doing what the Church has told you is necessary for the good of your soul. Meanwhile, you would starve if not for the beneficence of the carpenters' guild, which provides your family a small stipend to see them through their hardship. Raymond's plight has not," Marcel turned to Thomas with flat, cold eyes, "bothered the archbishop of Paris, who resides comfortably in his palace, with his seventy-nine servants, gold platter, jewelled fingers and bevy of seductive-eyed teenage 'housekeepers'. Fear of the next life, Thomas, is an excellent way of obtaining free services in this one . . . is it not?"

Thomas did not reply. He was furious, but he would not give Marcel the satisfaction of a shouting match here in the carpenter's poor shop.

"Raymond," Marcel said, dipping his head at the carpenter. "Gissette. I wish you a good day."

And he led the way back into the street.

Thomas strode out, banged the door closed behind him, and opened his mouth to speak.

Marcel's fist closed in the front of Thomas' robe, and the next instant Thomas found himself pushed back up against the door with Marcel's equally furious face not a finger span's from his.

"Is that *fair*, priest? Is that *right*? Do you think it is *acceptable* that *your* Church can demand that it be fit and proper for Raymond and Gissette and their children to starve for the future benefit of their *damn* souls? And if the Church doesn't demand free work for a nebulous future benefit in heaven, then the nobles or the king or some self-righteous local lord demand taxes and dues that mean starvation and misery. Ah!"

Marcel wheeled away, and Thomas straightened his robe and followed him.

"I —" Thomas began.

"Wait," Marcel said. "There is a place we can talk."

And he led a silently fuming Thomas into the glittering guildhall.

Marcel showed Thomas into a quiet room off the main public space of the guildhall. The room was well furnished, and richly appointed, and Marcel noted Thomas' disapproval.

"What I advocate," Marcel said, "and what I have fought for here in Paris, is a levelling out of the social order."

"The social order was established by God," Thomas said, refusing the chair that Marcel indicated, and folding his hands inside the black sleeves of his outer robe.

Marcel shrugged and sat down, meeting Thomas' eyes easily as the brother continued to stand over him.

"And yet you have just witnessed how unfair that is," Marcel said. "The majority of people slave for the nobles and the priests in conditions that are beyond the pitiful. They are taxed beyond reason, and yet they are told that they must be grateful. Nevertheless, the priests tell us that most of us will enjoy an eternity in hell for our repulsive sins, and the nobles fight ambitious wars among themselves instead of providing protection to the good folk they promised it to. And always ... the taxes, the taxes. I have had enough, and many among the ordinary ranks of people have had enough. We have minds and souls of our own, and we demand the rights that are due to us as individuals."

"Individuals mean *nothing*!" Thomas said, fighting to keep his voice even. "Everyone exists for the good of the whole, and everyone —"

"Everyone exists to keep the nobles and the clerics well fed and housed," Marcel said. "Nothing else. For too many centuries you have fed off our toil for nothing but misery in return."

"What you suggest will bring order crashing down about our ears. There will be no society — nothing but *chaos*! But that is what you want, isn't it? Chaos would suit your plans perfectly."

"I plan for the betterment of society, yes. I plan to give every man and woman a larger say in their own lives, yes. I plan to hand dignity out on street corners, yes. I plan to give *all* men the right to determine their own paths in life, yes. Do you call that 'chaos'?"

"I call that *evil*."

"I think, Thomas," Marcel said, his expression bland, "that you and I differ on what our perception of evil is."

Thomas took a step back, his face pale. "On my way to Paris I passed through a small village. The lord and his wife had been slaughtered, the lord roasted alive, his wife violated by many men as they forced her husband's flesh down her throat."

Marcel's expression did not alter.

"Worse," Thomas continued, his voice lower now, and harsh, "their three daughters had also been violated. Even their youngest, a girl of only two or three years, had been raped. *Is that what you call justice?*"

"There have been many regrettable —"

"Regrettable? You claim to want to create a 'better' life in 'this beautiful world', but instead you have spread such horror as can hardly be contemplated. That little girl —"

"What happened to that little girl is but a reflection of the indignities and violations heaped on the peasants! I do *not* condone their actions, but I understand their cause. Your innocent little girl is but one victim of thousands among the poor city folk and rural peasants who die from starvation each year because the Church has taxed the flesh from their bones and their lords have forgotten to protect them and their fields from the damned, *cursed* English."

Now Marcel was standing, shouting so violently that his cheeks flushed and his eyes started from his face. He raised a hand and waved a shaking finger in Thomas' face. "How can you even *pretend* to know of the struggles and horrors of the poor in society? You have been of the elite and the privileged all your life, whether nobleman or priest! You know *nothing* of misery, Thomas! *Nothing!*"

"The Church —"

"Is but an engorged instrument of privilege, dispensing fear and terror in order to keep people in their place. Damn you, Thomas. You protect an institution that says to the starving carpenter and his wife grovelling amid the wood shavings, 'Rejoice, for surely your current hunger increases your chances of salvation in the next life'!"

Thomas fought back his fury, and tried to speak in a level voice. "I know what you are, Marcel, and I *know* what you plan! You and your kind plan to make this earth yours, destroying God in the process. You —"

"Do I want to destroy God? If he gets in the way, yes. Do I and my kind want to make the earth ours? Yes. But, Tom, haven't you ever paused to consider what a wondrous life it might be if we did manage to oust God and make the earth ours?

"Who are the 'demons', priest, when you and yours preach that it is better to suffer misery than to yearn for a better and more just life?"

"You will fail," Thomas said. "You must. Righteousness will prevail and mankind will beat back the evil that afflicts it."

"I pity you," Marcel said softly, moving to a chest set by a wall. He lifted the lid, and took a rolled parchment from the chest. Then he straightened and regarded Thomas again.

"But, yes, you are right," he said. "*I* will undoubtedly fail, but my cause? Justness and fairness? I think it will not." He walked over to a table, undoing the thong binding the parchment.

Thomas smiled, his face cold and full of his own self-righteousness. "Philip has betrayed you, hasn't he?"

Marcel glanced at him, then unrolled the parchment across the top of the table with a flick of his wrist. He stabbed a finger down. "See here?"

Thomas hesitated, then walked over. Marcel had unrolled a map of Paris and its immediate environs, and his finger now indicated a spot just beyond the eastern wall and above the Seine, where it flowed into the city.

"Three days ago the Dauphin encamped a force in these fields."

Thomas looked to Marcel's face, and smiled slowly, knowingly. Catherine had done well. "How large?"

"Roughly fifteen thousand — knights as well as foot soldiers and archers."

Thomas' smile broadened, although it did not warm his cold eyes. "Philip?"

Marcel did not look at him. Instead he moved his finger to a point just beyond the western wall of Paris, and slightly south of where the Seine exited the city on its journey towards the coast.

"And here is poor Marcel," said Thomas softly, tapping the city itself. "Caught in between."

"I need you to act as an emissary," Marcel said. "To Philip. You and he have been well acquainted since childhood, and he will allow you an audience."

"And what would you have me say to him?"

Now Marcel straightened and looked Thomas in the eye. "I would have you remind him of our agreement. He helps the people of Paris, allowing us a representative assembly and a say in the governing and taxing of this realm, and we help him to the throne."

"You would displace the true king, *and* his heir to the throne?"

"If it aids our cause, yes."

"You justify everything, every misery, for personal gain, don't you?"

"For the gain of my people, for whom I speak, yes," Marcel said quietly. "Will you go?"

"Oh, aye," Thomas said. "I will go."

"Do I have your word that you will say to him what I have asked?"

Thomas hesitated, only slightly. "Yes."

Marcel nodded, and his face was very sad and very tired as he turned away.

When Thomas had gone, Marcel fetched ink, quill and parchment, and scribbled a hasty letter:

Beloved lady and sister, greetings. This will, I believe, be the last time I can write you. Events have moved swiftly. The friar has been and has now left to consult with Philip. Philip will doubtless send him south with an offer to the

Black Prince ... I do not expect either the friar or Philip to come to my aid. I find it hard to use words to describe my feelings. Gladness that it is, as we all knew it would soon be, finally over. Sadness that I have not achieved the greatest of victories — some measure of freedom for my fellow citizens of Paris. Nevertheless, I believe I have sowed in this fairest of cities a seed that will, one day, ripen into such wondrous fruit that all Europe — all mankind! — will stop and admire its beauty.

But that day is far into the future, and for now there is only myself, and my two brothers and sister. Lady, know that, as I cannot use your name in this letter, lest it fall into the wrong hands, I cannot write to either of our cherished brothers. If circumstances permit, pass this letter into their hands and make sure they know of my news concerning the friar. Oh, how proud I am of all of you! And how greatly I love you all! You shall have wondrous futures. I hope and pray they will be the best possible.

The friar now comes your way. Be prepared, for he is of stubborn mind and even worse faith, but rejoice, for he is vulnerable where we need him to be weak. You know to what I refer — our fairy brother planned well, and the execution was perfect.

Beloved sister, I embrace you now for the last time. Go with love, and into love,

IX

The Friday before the Eighteenth Sunday after Trinity
In the fifty-first year of the reign of Edward III
(15th October 1378)

The square, high-peaked tent was dyed scarlet and gilded about its edges; tasselled and beribboned banners and pennants fluttered from its corners and peak. Its interior sheltered a very large and ornate mirror that had been cast in the east and then encased in a jewelled and gilded frame in Constantinople before being shipped westwards.

It was very, very expensive.

Philip thought it framed his glory perfectly. When he was king of all France — finally reuniting the kingdoms of France and Navarre — he would surround himself with such objects.

When he was King of France . . .

Philip smiled at his reflection, turning this way and that. He lifted his hands, pausing briefly to admire the glint of gold and turquoise of their rings, then ran them down the rich embroidered red velvet of his coat armour. He tapped it lightly with the fingers of his right hand, enjoying the dull thud that sounded from the metal breastplate beneath.

Then Philip frowned at his reflection, and, after a moment's consideration, undid the top three buttons of the coat, revealing not only a shine of steel breastplate, but also the exquisitely worked coat lining of gold silk.

"Your grace."

Philip turned and took the sword belt his manservant held out, and fastened it about his hips. Save for his basinet (and that Philip was not yet ready to don, and may not have to, if circumstances were favourable), he was arrayed for war in full battle armour ... but he was not about to enter a physical fray. This armour, the jewellery he wore about his person, and the haughty confidence of his face were to be worn for the purpose of diplomatic combat, a war of words rather than of swords.

The manservant made another slight noise behind him, and, slightly irritated this time, Philip turned once more from his reflection and took the sword the man held out, sliding it impatiently into its scabbard.

"Is everything in readiness?"

"Yes, your grace."

"My escort?"

"Mounted and waiting, sire."

Philip sighed, and fiddled with the hilt of his sword, suddenly unwilling to rush. He must not let his self-confidence work in his disfavour. Charles would be difficult to deal with ... but ...

"But at least I have something with which to bargain," Philip muttered, "and at last he needs something from me so badly is he prepared to talk to achieve it."

"Sire?"

"Nothing!" Philip snapped, and waved the man away. "Leave me be!"

His expression quietened once the man had gone, and he stared at his reflection with eyes unfocused.

His entire life had been moving to this point. Navarre was not enough for him ... Philip knew that with the right combination of circumstance and cunning, he could also have the French throne.

Now the circumstance was right, and he need only add his cunning. John — despicable, senile old man — was in the hands of the English (who were never going to let him go, whatever ransom demands they mouthed), and his grandson Charles was so unsure and indecisive he could undoubtedly be induced to fall upon his own sword at some point.

Of course the peacock king, Louis, could be disregarded completely.

Once John, Louis and Charles were disposed of, Phillip would be next in line to the throne. The irritating fact that King Edward of England also happened to be a close blood cousin to John could be disregarded. The French would never accept an English king.

Philip smiled, cold and feral.

The French throne was his. So long as he kept a cool head, and was prepared to sway whichever way the wind dictated.

There was a movement, and then a heavy swish as the tent flap was pushed back, and one of the outside guards poked an uncertain head in.

"Sire, I —"

"What is it?"

"There is an emissary from the provost of Paris, your grace. A friar by the look of him —"

Philip burst out laughing. Marcel had sent Black Tom to argue on his behalf?

Well ... Marcel must know he was dead.

"He is outside?"

"Yes, your grace."

Philip smoothed down the velvet where it had crumpled a little over a line of bolts in his breastplate. "Bring him in."

"Thomas!" Philip said as the friar entered. "My friend! I am so glad you escaped."

Thomas gave Philip a cynical look, then bowed in courtly fashion. "Your grace looks very ... very ..."

"Flamboyant is the word you seek, Tom. No need to hesitate."

Thomas walked a little further into the centre of the tent. Philip had truly set himself up in style: a bed, complete with tapestried hangings, stood to one side; a brass brazier glowed in another corner. Intricately carved cedar chests, draped with as intricately embroidered cloths and linens, were scattered about, and rich wool and silken rugs covered the floor so that not a single degrading speck of dirt, nor blade of grass, might touch the boots of Philip the Bad.

"You have done well for yourself," Thomas said. "When I was escorted through your camp I made a rough estimate of the number of fighting men you have here. What? Several thousand knights? And some five or six thousand pikemen and archers?"

"Twenty-eight hundred knights," Philip said, "as many men-at-arms, and *eight* thousand pikemen and archers."

"And yet you were released from Charles' gaol a bare two weeks ago. Nevertheless, either John or Charles have had you incarcerated so many times for so many imagined — or not — plots against their lives, that you must have had good practice in recovering your strength on release."

Philip moved, quite gracefully considering the armour he wore, to a chest and picked up a jug and goblet. "Wine?"

"I thank you. I have had a trying two weeks myself under the care of Marcel."

Philip handed Thomas a goblet, and poured one for himself. "And now Marcel has sent you to plead for him."

Thomas drank some of the wine, rolling it about his mouth a little, enjoying its mellowness. Philip lived very well indeed. "Marcel," he finally said, "has sent me to *remind* you —"

Philip snorted into his goblet, then drained it in a single, abrupt movement.

"— of the agreement you and he reached."

"Yes, yes, yes. I aid him and his rabble and he gives me the throne."

Thomas said nothing, waiting.

"Of course," Philip said, a smile slowly forming, "no prince considers an agreement made with a murderer and traitor binding, does he?"

Now Thomas smiled, too, and drained his own wine. "And so what will you do?"

"I will do what I must."

"And let me see if I can guess what it is you *must* do. On my way through your lines I saw an escort ready and waiting for your presence. It was richly furbished, and not only with your colours and livery ... but with —"

"With those of my *dear* cousin Charles! How observant you are."

"You ride to deal with him."

"To a point. I ride to suggest that we unite for the moment against our twin enemies — Marcel and his rabble, and the English."

"Ah. I think I understand. Between you, Paris will fall — I hear tell that Charles has a considerable force beyond the city's eastern wall, and Paris cannot hope to withstand both of you. Then, once Paris is under control —"

"Then I will review the situation," Philip said. "As any good prince would."

Thomas laughed softly. "As any good and *ambitious* prince would. But I am glad, Philip, that you mean to put Marcel down. He ..." Thomas hesitated, his face clouding over, and Philip's eyes narrowed as he watched him, "he frightened me with his vision of the uneducated and ill-bred masses rising against their betters. There is good in order, and our order is good. You, the princes and the barons, protect those who till the soil on your behalf, and we, the priests and monks, nurture and protect their souls. To think that —'

"There is no point trying to lecture me on the subject, Tom. I am a complete convert to the all-consuming power of prince and priest. But I can see that you remain concerned."

"It is not only Marcel. Philip, there is a great evil abroad, and Marcel represents only a small part of it. There was a soldier I spoke to in Rome, and there is a renegade priest in England, both of whom spoke of the same thing: the questioning of the order of society — an order ordained by God! Sweet Jesu, Philip, do they think to destroy the hand that feeds and nurtures them?"

"I thought," Philip muttered, turning away, "that it was the hands of the uncultured masses who fed *us*. But —" he turned back to Thomas, "— to return to more important matters. It is good that you are here, for you can do me a great service."

Thomas raised his eyebrows.

"I go to ally myself with the sweet boy, Charles, but ..."

"But you think there may be more worthwhile allies in the offing."

"Aye. I was mightily impressed that the Black Prince managed to defeat John's fifty thousand. Now he holds King John, and France, hostage. The Dauphin cannot, or will not, ever pay the ransom or accept the conditions that the Prince asks."

"What are they exactly?"

Philip grinned. "Your Prince of Wales has balls, Tom. He shall make a great king one day. Of *England*, of course. Well, as to his terms. First Charles must pay a ransom of 700,000 English pounds —"

"Sweet Jesu! No king on earth commands a treasury that large!"

"— but, before the Black Prince hands the doddering idiot back to his grandson, Charles and John must *both* be signatories to a peace treaty that recognises the Black Prince as John's heir, not Charles! Thus, 700,000 pounds the richer, the Black Prince will succeed to the French throne once John dies. Which shall not be too long, considering how John looked and acted the last time I saw him."

"And Charles?"

"Charles gets his life, some pretty title and is exiled to the far south where he lives out his life in useless luxury."

Thomas thought about it. Charles might actually agree to the terms without too much persuasion. He didn't look much like a man with the backbone to fight the Black Prince for the throne.

But then, with Catherine there ... and he *was* apparently prepared to fight for Paris.

Philip watched Thomas carefully, knowing the pattern of his thoughts.

"Yes," he said quietly, "Charles has shown *some* enterprise in managing to return to the walls of Paris with a few men at his back —"

"And that is his sister's doing, to my mind, rather than Charles'."

"Aha!" Philip's eyebrows raised, considering this new piece of information. *Catherine rides with Charles? Yes, he could work with her nicely.*

"Whatever," Philip continued, "the situation has grown interesting since Poitiers, and I do not want to close the door on any possibility. I should like you to convey to the Black Prince —"

"Why would the Black Prince even want to *think* about negotiating with you? He and his army have just murdered the flower of French knighthood in the fields of Poitiers. Perhaps he is marching north even as we speak, and might not be many days away. Prince Edward is far more likely to want to ride straight over you than to negotiate with you."

"Ah, a great victory Prince Edward may indeed have won, but those of his men still on their feet must be exhausted ... and winter is even closer to Paris than he is. I doubt the Black Prince has shifted out of Chauvigny, and most likely will not ride for Paris until next spring when he has rebuilt his force and the weather will be kinder. And in that time, who knows what kind of force Catherine ... ah, I mean Charles ... will command? Edward would do well to consider my offer."

"And that is?"

"Why, that I ally with him, of course, to ensure that Charles accepts his terms and hands over the cash and the throne! I can bring fresh troops to his cause, as also a large part of France. The Black Prince controls the south, I control the west, and between us we can squeeze Charles into a whimpering agreement to the Black Prince's terms."

Thomas bowed very slightly. "You are a true friend to the English indeed, Philip. But — and you know how I do hate to bring this up — there must be a price you demand."

"I am sure that the Black Prince and I can come to some

mutual agreement over some of the rich southern provinces. I have always had a penchant for the vineyards of Gascony,, for example."

Thomas regarded Philip carefully. He believed none of this. Not only was Philip's offer to the Black Prince too good to be trusted, but Philip was undoubtedly aware that the Black Prince would never give up any of the rich southern provinces which the English had held since Eleanor of Aquitaine had brought them as dowry into her marriage with Henry II.

"And yet," Thomas said, "if I do as you ask and deliver this offer to the Black Prince, I must also advise him that when I left you, you were fitting yourself out in suitable gaudery to meet with Charles himself. How should the Black Prince regard that?"

"I only parley with Charles in regard to putting Marcel out of his misery, Tom. Once Paris is back under control, then I may not be so willing to sup with the Dauphin." Philip's face was innocent-eyed and apparently candid, but Thomas was not fooled.

"You aspire to the French throne yourself, my friend. Why conspire with the Black Prince in order to hand it to the English?"

Philip shrugged. "You read too much into my offer. I merely ask you to carry a message, Tom. You did it for Marcel, why not for me? Besides, I am sure you cannot wait to return to your homeland — with all this battle and shining armour about you must be uncomfortable indeed. I cannot believe but that you must, somewhere, somehow, yearn for what once was."

"I am a priest now," Thomas said. "I yearn only to do God's work here on earth."

Philip shot him a glance heavy with cynicism, then his expression cleared, and his face assumed a genuinely puzzled expression. "You and I are soul mates, Thomas. And blood brothers — surely you have not forgot that pact we made as boys in the meadows of my father's estates? I ... I cannot understand why you have thrown away your entire heritage for ..." Philip walked over to Thomas and plucked at his robe, "for *this*!"

"I came to regret my sins —"

"Bah! You became frightened!"

Thomas' face closed over, and he pulled away from the king. "May I rely on you providing an escort to the English lines?"

"Believe it or not, Tom," Philip said softly, "if you asked me, you could rely on me for your life."

Later that day Philip stood before Charles, his face wreathed in disbelief. He'd known Charles ever since he'd been an infant, and had long ago decided the man had a craven soul and would be of no use to anyone.

But here the Dauphin stood, his entire bearing radiating assurance and authority, and speaking of a girl who had come to him with the word of God.

Philip would have laughed, save he could see by the face of Catherine — whom he had also known all her life and, subsequently, knew her intelligence and courage — that this story had more than the ring of truth about it.

God had picked *Charles* in this battle?

Philip hastily revised his plans, and smiled and bowed to Charles. "Perhaps we can come to some arrangement," he said, and Charles returned his cousin's smile and nodded.

X

Twentieth Sunday after Trinity
In the fifty-first year of the reign of Edward III
(31st October 1378)

— i —

The road south from Philip's encampment in the fields outside Paris towards Chauvigny two hundred miles distant was fraught with danger. Tens of thousands of peasants were on the road fleeing north towards some hoped for sanctuary in order to escape a feared English drive towards Paris. They were frightened, noisy, and dangerous: many had eaten little for days, even weeks, and they took every opportunity they could to steal and grab anything that looked vaguely edible, or anything that might be bartered for food. Philip had given Thomas an escort of thirty soldiers, but that was only barely enough to keep the hungry and angry bands of peasants at bay.

Thomas wondered what Philip and Charles would do with them once they arrived at Paris.

Worse than the peasants were the soldiers. When the Black Prince's army had defeated the French at Poitiers, those foot soldiers — pikemen, archers, and ordinary soldiers — who had survived the vengeful blades of the English fled into the surrounding countryside. Now many of them were moving north, not only to escape the English, but also, Thomas supposed, to seek pay from the Dauphin Charles. King John had, it seemed, forgotten in the heat and frustration of his capture to pay out wages due to his soldiers and the mercenaries he'd hired from abroad.

Now these men — German and Swiss mercenaries among the Frenchmen — were creating as much havoc and misery as the approaching English army. They stole, burned, raped and killed, moving through the countryside like a swarming cloud of vermin. Several of their bands attacked Thomas and his escort, but Philip's soldiers were good, and battle hardened, and managed to beat them back.

Between the hungry and angry peasants, and the hungry, angry and unpaid soldiers, the journey south was perilous and uncertain. Thomas and his escort sought shelter each night where they could — an inn, the burned-out shell of a peasant's hovel or barn, the tangled, worm-ridden detritus of a wood felled in an ancient storm — many of them spending the greater part of the night awake and alert lest they be attacked, suspecting every creeping shadow of intending murder, jumping at every twitter of a field mouse that had somehow escaped the jaws of marauding refugees.

Day was somehow even worse, spent creeping down sunken laneways off the main roads, sitting tense in saddles, eyes darting from tree to tumbledown wall, wondering what each one hid. Thomas could not rely on his Dominican habit to save him: most of the refugees they came in contact with, whether peasant or soldier, spat at him as readily as they spat at Philip's soldiers. They loathed the sun for rising each morning, and hated and blamed everyone in any form of authority for their misery.

You didn't save us. You couldn't stop the English. Why then should we respect you?

By the time they drew within twenty miles of Chauvigny, two weeks after they'd left Philip's camp, it was not only hungry peasants and marauding soldiers who ate at their assurance. They heard rumours of rogue bands of Englishmen roaming above Chauvigny, looting what they could.

Some eighteen miles north of Chauvigny, just after Thomas and his escort had passed through a tiny, burned-out village, they came upon a solitary traveller on the road moving towards them.

Even a single man, and even one as patently exhausted and wounded as this one — he hobbled on crutches, one foot heavily wrapped in bandages reeking of old blood and new infection — caused Philip's soldiers to bunch in tight about Thomas, and ready hands on swords.

In these grim days, no one was to be trusted.

But the man fell to his knees as the horsemen approached, crying softly, involuntarily, as his foot hit a sharp rock.

"Brother!" he called, reaching out with one hand. "Brother, a blessing, I beg you!"

Thomas waved the soldiers back, and reined his horse (still Marcel's trusty brown gelding) in beside the man. He lifted his right hand in benediction and sketched the sign of the cross over the man's head, murmuring a blessing.

"Thank you, brother," the man said, lifting his tear-streaked face. "Thank you!"

"Where do you come from?" Thomas said.

The man sniffed, and wiped the back of a hand under his nose. "From a small village just south of Chatellerault, Father. Chatellerault is —"

"I know where it is. What news can you tell me? Where are the English? What is their condition?"

"What is their condition? Brother, you may as well ask me for the condition of all mankind. There is nothing but evil behind me: the ambition of the devilish English, their ravagings, their murders, their hate. The countryside is afire, whether from the torches of the English dogs, or of good Frenchmen who do not want their hearths and stores to fall into the hands of the English. A pall of smoke lies over the land, fear seeps into every crack. I lived through the great pestilence, brother, and yet then I did not know half the despair I do now."

"How were you injured?"

"I hid in a haystack. Fresh, sweet hay that I had scythed

from my own land. The English dogs came through, and they thrust long spikes into the hay, seeking honest French blood. The spike that pierced my foot also tore out my wife's throat. When the English saw the blood seeping through the hay they laughed, and set it afire. I barely escaped. I was the only one from my village who escaped alive."

"And the English? Do they remain in Chauvigny?"

"Yes, brother, although they ravage the land far about for their food and sustenance. I pray to God every hour I still live that the pestilence returns and wipes all English life from French soil."

Thomas nodded his thanks, then wheeled his horse away. The man did not have long to live — already the grey streaks of poison had spread as far as his neck and lower face — and would soon escape this miserable life.

By late afternoon they were within a few miles of Chauvigny. The castle town rose in the distance, a crowded collection of keeps and towers and ramparts. It was an ancient fortification, which consisted of not one, but five castles — all built at different times. Now, after generations of alterations and additions, the castles were so interlaced by connecting walls and twisting streets and courtyards they formed one virtually impregnable fortress.

Surrounded by rich farming lands, swathes of woodland and the gentle sweep of the Vienne River, Chauvigny sat on a hill overlooking the countryside — it was one of the most beautiful and magnificent fortifications in France. Even from this distance, Thomas could see the flags and pennants fluttering atop the towers and walls. Despite all his protestations over the past weeks that his loyalty belonged to God rather than to the English, Thomas could not help a rush of excitement and anticipation. That walled fortress held so many friends ... so many memories ...

Thomas shivered, and looked about. The fine weather and splendid view would not last — already an autumnal evening fog was sweeping in from the river.

Thomas turned his horse to face his escort. "Go home now," he said, the indistinct forms of men and horses looming out of the fog like underwater rocks seen through several feet of murky stream. "I cannot guarantee your safety — nor mine, for that matter," he added with a low, mirthless laugh. "You can do no more for me. Go back to your lord, with my thanks. I wish you safe journey."

There were quick glances exchanged among those soldiers whose faces Thomas could make out, then one, the sergeant, nodded, and saluted. "Go in peace, brother," he said.

"Peace?" Thomas said. "I doubt any of us will ever find that again."

But he, too, raised a hand and managed a half smile, and then he turned his horse's head for Chauvigny, and the names and faces of his youth.

Behind him Thomas thought he heard the sound of hoof fall, and perhaps even the jingle of a bit in a horse's mouth, but then there was silence, and the feeling that Philip's escort had never been anything more than a insubstantial dream.

There was only him, his horse, and the fog.

He rode for what may have been an hour, perhaps two, but no longer. Night had not yet closed in, for there was still some dim, reflected light within the fog, but it could not be far off.

There was not much else to see.

Very occasionally the fog rolled and lifted enough for Thomas to glimpse the rough stubbled earth of autumn fields waiting for their November ploughing and sowing of the winter crops.

Somehow, Thomas did not think much ploughing or sowing would get done this autumn — and that meant that the misery and starvation would continue well into next year, and even beyond.

Evil indeed.

Dusk closed in about him, and Thomas shivered, and pulled his hood close about his face. Surely he should have reached the fortress by now? Where were the English? Was there anything alive in this cursed mist?

Were demons even now creeping upon him, ready to leap and impale him with their fangs, or, worse, their lies?

Thomas twisted about in the saddle, but he could see nothing except several trees — their twisted branches bare of leaves — looming off to his left.

He turned about to stare to his right. Nothing there save more trees. He must have wandered into one of the patches of woodland close to Chauvigny.

Lord Christ Saviour, aid me!

There were crackling sounds in the fallen leaves, then a low laugh — or was it a hiss? — that came from Thomas knew not what direction.

His heart thudded in his breast, and he pulled his horse to a halt, staring impotently through the clinging, obscuring droplets of the fog.

Now even his horse was tense. Thomas could feel the beast's muscles bunching beneath the saddle, and he shortened the reins, tightening his hold upon them, speaking to the horse in low, reassuring tones.

There, another movement in the fog to his left: a shadow, darting behind a tree. It was humped and misshapen, but Thomas did not know if that was because it belonged to a devilish creature, or because of the distorting effects of the fog.

The horse whinnied, and tried to shy.

Thomas jerked him back under control, then pushed him forward at a fast walk. There was no point standing still here for whatever blade or shaft was pointed at his back.

The woods closed in, as did Thomas' sense that he was surrounded on all sides. He thought to call out, then didn't, because he thought it might reveal the extent of his own fear.

No, no, God and St Michael rode with him, surely.

Surely.

Thomas suddenly remembered what day it was. All Saints Eve, yes, but All Souls Eve in popular custom, a night when the souls of the dead stirred and walked once more over the land.

What was in the fog about him?

Suddenly a glow blossomed somewhere before him. Thomas slowed his horse, then kicked him forward again, his heart now leaping so violently he thought it might escape through his mouth.

Sweet Jesu, he didn't even have a sword with which to defend himself!

The glow dimmed, then resolved itself into five or six pinpoints of light about a small clearing.

Torches, set in the trees.

Thomas halted the horse at the edge of the clearing. The light from the torches only added to the obscurity of the fog: light glistened off the droplets within the mist, giving everything an eerie yellow and rose glow, as if creation itself was afire.

Then why so cold, why so damp?

Thomas swallowed, gathered his courage, and finally spoke. "I am Thomas Neville, brother of the Order of Preachers, come from Philip, King of Navarre and Count of Evreux, with a message for the Black Prince, Edward, Prince of Wales."

Nothing.

Thomas looked about him, his eyes staring, feeling sweat trickle down his back and pool underneath his buttocks. Should he speak again? Surely there were men behind these trees to hear him! Surely —

There was a movement directly across the clearing, and Thomas tensed.

A horseman appeared; a knight in full battle array, wearing a great helm with its visor down. His destrier was massive, a grey stallion that dipped its head and pawed the ground as his rider pulled him to a halt, the beast's snowy mane falling down over the mirrored steel of his faceplate.

But Thomas had eyes for no one but the rider. His heraldic badges were clearly displayed on shield, helm and the hangings over the stallion's armour, and even though the visor covered his face, Thomas well knew who he was.

Henry of Bolingbroke, son of John of Gaunt and Blanche of the Duchy of Lancaster, eldest grandson of Edward III, and prince of the realm, if not quite heir to the throne.

"Hal!" Thomas whispered.

There was just the slightest movement of Bolingbroke's helm, then the prince reined his stallion about and disappeared into the fog.

After a heartbeat's hesitation, Thomas followed him.

XI

Twentieth Sunday after Trinity
In the fifty-first year of the reign of Edward III
(31st October 1378)

— ii —

Bolingbroke led Thomas through the woods along a path so obscure and ill-defined Thomas thought either Hal or his horse must have fairy sight to be able to discern it. Within a few minutes, however, the path broadened, then began to rise. The woodlands and fog fell away.

Chauvigny appeared directly before them, bathed in moonlight.

There were several small camps of foot soldiers and pikemen outside the outer walls of the fortress, and Bolingbroke lead Thomas through them towards the main gates.

Soon Thomas realised the reason for the outside camps. The English had built great lines of trenches filled with spikes beyond the walls in case of attack. These soldiers were here to man them ... and also to show friends the passage through.

As Bolingbroke and Thomas rode through, a man would occasionally call out to Bolingbroke, and one or two ran up and touched the shoulder of his war horse, speaking quick words to the prince before turning respectfully back to allow him passage.

There were no frowns, no sullen resentful faces turning slowly away.

Hal is as popular as ever, Thomas thought. *It would take a disaster such as England had not yet endured to make the commons turn their hearts away from fair prince Hal.*

Thomas studied what he could see of Bolingbroke ahead. It had been many, many years since he had seen Hal. Had their friendship managed to weather both time *and* the distance Thomas' habit now put between them? Thomas had heard that Hal cursed and raged when he learned of Thomas' decision to join the Dominican Order.

Why, Thomas was not sure. Was it because Hal felt he'd lost a friend to the Church? Was it because Hal felt Thomas had rejected him in favour of holy vows?

They had grown up together, spending long summers playing with wooden swords in the tilting yards, longer summer nights exploring the sweet passions of burgeoning manhood. They had planned grand futures for themselves. Hal that he would somehow succeed his grandfather to the throne of England, even though he was only the son of King Edward's fourth son; Thomas that he would lead a glittering crusade back to the Holy Land, pushing the Arabs back into the desert wastes where they belonged, and wiping all trace of their presence from the holy stones of Jerusalem for eternity.

But then, five years ago, Thomas had turned away from his heritage, and his friendship and future with Hal, and entered the Church, and Hal had been left to face his future alone.

Was there a friendship left?

Eventually, in full cold night, Bolingbroke led Thomas through the gates and into the narrow, twisting streets of Chauvigny, where they immediately dismounted. The horses would be stabled in the lower quarters of the fortress, and

Bolingbroke and Thomas would have to complete the journey into the heart of Chauvigny on foot. Thomas looked above him as a squire hastened to lift Bolingbroke's helm from his head, and remove the clumsier pieces of armour from his body. Flags and standards fluttered from the walls, each denoting a particular prince, or baron, or count, or any one of countless other ranks among the nobility. His breath caught in his throat — the full flower of English aristocracy was here! There the standard of John of Gaunt, Duke of Lancaster and King of Castile, Hal's father. There the standard of the Black Prince. There the standard of Thomas of Woodstock, Duke of Gloucester and youngest brother of Edward the Black Prince and John of Gaunt. There ... there the standard of the Earl of Northumberland — was Hotspur here as well? And there the standard of Baron Raby fluttering cheekily on the tent next to that of Northumberland, his greatest rival for power in the north of England.

Thomas grinned slowly to himself. Raby was no doubt spending his non-fighting time plotting against Northumberland, as Northumberland was doubtless similarly spending his spare time. Were they even now in their respective chambers within the fortress, sharpening their blades, their eyes fanatical with hatred and ambition?

Bolingbroke mumbled his thanks to the squire who had aided him, and Thomas turned to study the prince.

Hal Bolingbroke stood in a shaft of moonlight, looking for all the world like one of the fabled fairy-folk. The moon turned his fair hair a glittering silver gilt, and made his light grey eyes colourless and unreadable. Since Thomas had last seen him, Hal's handsome boyish features had hardened into those of a man. There were faint lines of care about his eyes, and more running from his straight nose to his mouth, and the strength of his unbearded jawline revealed a certain pitilessness that made Thomas wonder what tragedies Hal had endured over the past five or six years.

"Well, Tom," Bolingbroke said in a quiet voice. "Have you come to take our confession? Perhaps deal us our penances? Or mayhap you have grown tired of your scratchy black robe and yearn once more for the caress of metal."

"It is good to see you once more, Hal," Thomas said.

Then he bowed deeply in Bolingbroke's direction. "My lord, it *is* good to see you again. The years between us have been too long."

"Indeed," Bolingbroke said softly, "but it was not *I* who walked away."

Thomas winced, and would have spoken, but Bolingbroke turned his back and walked towards the dark mouth of a narrow street between two soaring buildings.

"This way, Neville," he called back over his shoulder. "My uncle awaits your news of our distant cousin, Philip."

Thomas jerked in surprise. *Had the Black Prince and Hal known of Thomas' approach, and the reason for it, before he'd announced it in the clearing?*

The he shrugged. No doubt the roads had been thronged with as many English spies as refugees, and the livery of his escort had been unmistakable.

A soldier behind Thomas gave him a none-too-gentle shove in the back, and Thomas paused long enough to give him a hard stare before he followed Hal.

They walked high and deep into the heart of the fortress, the street wide enough only for the passage of one person: it was no wonder they had had to leave their horses below.

As well as being narrow, the way was steep, more a stairway than a paved street. Any flat section was never more than three or four paces long before yet more steps that twisted and turned between the walls of the buildings above them.

Bolingbroke strode lightly ahead of Thomas, and Thomas wondered at the man's fitness. The way was steep, Hal still wore the greater weight of his armour, and yet he sprang ahead as if he carried nothing more than a linen loin wrap on his body.

On the other hand, Thomas was panting within moments of the ascent. Five years of prayer did nothing for the strength and suppleness of muscle.

Eventually Bolingbroke led Thomas into a small courtyard before the main entrance of one of the castles. The door was heavily guarded, but the men stepped back without a word as Bolingbroke and Thomas neared.

As soon as they were inside the entrance hall, Bolingbroke stopped and waited as Thomas caught his breath. Then, without a word, he led him into a spacious chamber to one side of the main hall.

The chamber was richly appointed. To one side sat a good-sized and well-furred canopied bed, a fire crackled in the hearth set against an outside wall, intricately carved benches and chests were set about, and embroidered heavy tapestries were set against the walls to hold back the draughts. Gilt and silver goblets and platters sat on a small table set to one side; someone had just concluded a meal. Despite the warmth and comfort of the chamber, it contained a strange atmosphere, a tension that Thomas couldn't immediately place. Then he was given no time for thought, for a lithe middle-aged man with thinning grey hair rose from a table strewn with maps and reports, walking to stand a few paces in front of Thomas.

Thomas bowed — if he hadn't been a cleric he would have gone down on one knee. "My lord prince," he said. "I greet you well, and trust I find you in favourable health."

In that instant, as Thomas straightened and looked into Edward, the Black Prince's face, he knew he'd said the wrong thing.

Edward was patently *not* well. His skin was stretched tight and pale over his prominent nose and cheekbones; his forehead was as wan as a shroud; his brown eyes reflected a deep weariness. Nothing could have shocked Thomas more. Edward was all of fifty-five or six, true, but he had been in rude health all his life. What miasma was this that had dug its fingers into his bones?

The Black Prince stood with his feet slightly apart, his arms folded. He wore a shirt of chain mail over a deep blue tunic, but otherwise wore no other armour or weapons.

"Thomas Neville," he said, and, belying his appearance, his voice was as strong as Thomas remembered it. "Here you stand before us, with, I believe, messages from the King of Navarre?"

At that moment Thomas realised what was wrong with the atmosphere. It was chill and antagonistic, and had Thomas still been a knight, and weaponed, he would have instinctively reached for his sword at that point.

The antagonism was clearly directed at him.

"How nice that you could drag yourself away from your divine mission to save the world from evil for this errand," Edward continued.

Now utterly shocked, Thomas could do nothing but stare silently at the Black Prince's face.

The prince stared back at him.

Thomas jerked his eyes about the rest of the chamber. Bolingbroke stood slightly back and to the right, between the Black Prince and Thomas. His hand was on the hilt of his sword. There was another man far back in the shadows — a knight, for Thomas could see the glint of steel — but neither his face nor insignia were discernible. Several guards stood about, within easy striking distance of Thomas, and clearly ready to do so at the first sign of aggression on Thomas' part.

Silence.

Thomas dragged his eyes back to the Black Prince. "My lord prince, I regret to find you unwell —"

"A passing flux only. What does Philip have to say?"

"Uh, he says, to be plain —"

"I would appreciate that."

"He says that he offers to ally with you against the Dauphin. Philip will bring substantial troops to your cause, as a substantial part of France. Between you, he says, you can force Charles to accept the terms of ransom and treaty."

There was a guffaw of laughter from the shadowy figure at the back of the tent. "Philip was ever the jester!"

Thomas recognised the voice instantly, and peered towards the figure, but the Black Prince spoke again, and Thomas jerked his eyes back to him.

"And the price?" Edward said. "Philip always has a price."

"Gascony."

At that even Edward smiled, and as he did so much of the sickness lifted from his face.

"I thank you for Philip's offer," he said, unfolding his arms and walking back behind the table. "I shall, after consultation with my commanders, take it under due consideration."

"I have much other information, my lord prince, apart from what Philip has offered. I have —"

"Yes, yes," Edward said. "But not now."

He picked up a parchment from one corner of the table, and unfolded it as if it contained a sliver of pestilence.

"Brother Thomas Neville, friar of the Order of Preachers," he began in a such a cold formal tone that it sent chills down Thomas' spine. "I have here an order from Richard Thorseby, Prior General of England, to hold and contain the said Brother Thomas Neville until he can safely be transported back to England to face disciplinary proceedings against him in the court of —"

"What?" Thomas said. "You have no right to arrest me!"

The Black Prince threw down the parchment. "I have every right!" he shouted, making Thomas flinch. "You have abandoned your post without permission and have apparently run amok over Europe on some deranged quest on behalf of, for sweet Jesu's sake, the blessed Saint Michael himself. You have disobeyed your superior! By God, Tom, if you had done this to me *I would have gutted you and strung you up for the crows to eat!*"

He stared at Thomas, then spoke again, lower now, but in a voice quivering with anger and outrage. "You have disgraced your family, and brought the Neville name into disrepute. Damn you, Tom, you were raised better than this. *How dare you abandon your post for this fanciful pilgrimage?*"

Thomas could not speak. He was completely shocked, not only at the sudden turn of events (*Thorseby wanted him placed in custody?*) but also at the Prior General's knowledge of his visions of St Michael.

Had Prior Bertrand sent reports back to Thorseby?

"I —" he began.

"You will *not* speak," said Edward, "because anything you say at this moment will only serve to anger me more. I am handing you over into the custody of your uncle, Baron Ralph Neville of Raby. You *will* accept this custody. He will keep you confined until I can bring myself to talk with you again about what you have seen in the northern provinces."

And Edward turned his back on Thomas.

Baron Raby stepped forth from the shadows, a small mirthless smile on his face. His strong features, brown eyes and waving black hair were an older copy of Thomas' own, although the twenty years he had on his nephew had wrought deep lines about his eyes and forehead.

"I only gave you leave to enter holy orders, Thomas," Raby said, "because I believed you were truly committed to God and because I hoped the Order would curb your impetuous nature. I was wrong. You have disgraced our entire family. Come."

Without waiting for an answer, Raby brushed past Thomas and walked out of the chamber.

Thomas stared at Bolingbroke — his face was as implacable as Edward's and Raby's had been — then silently turned and followed his uncle outside.

What had gone so wrong?

Raby led him silently through the corridors of the castle into an apartment set in the walls overlooking the inner courtyard.

Once he reached his chamber he entered without a word, and Thomas followed him.

The chamber was smaller than that of the Black Prince's, but as comfortably appointed. There was a bed standing against the back wall, deep pink and scarlet hangings falling down about it, and as Raby and Thomas entered a figure moved out from its shadow.

She caught Thomas' eye instantly, and if the previous events had shocked him, nothing horrified him more than the sight of her.

She had bronze-coloured hair, strangely accentuated with strands of gold, tumbling loose and heavy over one shoulder. Her face was beautiful, as if it was that of a saint. Bright black eyes stared at him with as much horror — so it seemed to him then — as he regarded her.

"Sweet Meg," he whispered.

She took a step back, one hand instinctively resting protectively over her belly, and lifted the other to her face, stifling a soft cry.

XII

Twentieth Sunday after Trinity
In the fifty-first year of the reign of Edward III
(31st October 1378)

— iii —

Raby looked at Thomas, surprised at his words, then at the woman.

"You know the Lady Rivers?" Raby said to Thomas.

"No, no, I mistook her for another."

Despite his smooth answer, Thomas could hardly believe his eyes. Here she was! The woman the demons had said would steal his soul ... no, no, they had not said that, but it was clear enough that this *was* the woman, this the bait, this the body he had seeded when he'd lain with Odile.

This was his failure ... this *Christendom's* failure. But only if he allowed her to steal his soul.

"The Lady Margaret Rivers," Raby was saying, and Thomas concentrated on his voice only with the greatest effort, "has had some difficulties —"

Thomas managed to look back at this "Lady Rivers", and suppressed a sarcastic laugh at the mixture of seeming innocence and consternation on her face.

"She lost her husband to the wasting sickness when they were in Bordeaux —"

Wasting due to sorcery, no doubt, Thomas thought, and hoped the witch could hear his thoughts.

"— with no means to return to her home, nor even to eat. I happened upon her by chance —"

There was no "chance" in this meeting, uncle.

"— I took pity on her, and since that day the Lady Margaret has been travelling with my retinue. Soon, I hope to enable her the means to return to England."

"She has been 'travelling with your retinue'?" Thomas said, looking back at his uncle.

Raby regarded him with eyes as coldly steady as Thomas' own. "She has been a comforting companion," he said softly.

Thomas turned back to Lady Rivers, still standing as if mortified by this exchange. "Then I am sorry, Lady Rivers. I did not mistake you when first I entered. You *are* a whore, after all."

There was a momentary, shocked stillness, then Raby hit him.

Raby was a great deal older than Thomas, but he was a lifelong warrior, lean and strong, and as tall as his nephew. His blow sent Thomas sprawling across the timber floor.

Margaret Rivers gave another low cry — still she had not said a word — and reeled back as if she had been the one hit.

"Get up," Raby said.

Thomas raised himself on one elbow, stunned by the blow, and stopped, slowly shaking his head back and forth. Both his nose and mouth were bloody.

"*Get up!*" Raby shouted and, leaning down, grabbed hold of Thomas' robe and hauled him to his feet.

Thomas wrenched himself out of Raby's hands, and wiped the blood away from his mouth. "Am I to be punished for speaking truth?" he said.

"Am I then a whore also?" Raby seethed. "Margaret and I are way beyond the age of consent, and we are both widowed. Where is the sin in that?"

"Saint Paul said that lust is to be confined to the marriage bed, and that —"

"I give not a damn what Saint Paul said! The cursed man probably lusted after every woman who walked past him!"

"Please, I beg you ..."

Both men turned and glared furiously at Margaret, and she backed even further away, wishing she could snatch back her words.

Raby whipped back to face Thomas. "You spent your youth disobeying your parents, you spent your young manhood disobeying me, and now you disobey your Prior General. You have *ruined* our family name! I care not for whatever visions your impetuousness has created for you! Ah! I am too angry to speak with you now. You will spend the night in my squire's quarters ... and you *will* spend the night there, Tom, be sure of that. I will not have you escaping off into the night. *Will!*"

A tall young man with short curly brown hair and a ruddy complexion walked from an inner door. "My lord?"

"I told you we were expecting my nephew. Well, here he is. He will spend the night in your chamber — I am sure you can find him a pallet — and you will bring him to me in the morning to break his fast at my table. Will, ensure he *is* at my table in the morning. I am under an obligation to the Black Prince to hold him securely."

Will shot Thomas a look of utter disrespect, then bowed his head courteously to his master. "He will be at your table in the morning, my lord. Brother Thomas? You will come with me."

Thomas hesitated, furious, but not knowing how to express it. Finally he contented himself with directing a look of utter malice towards Margaret, then he stalked over to the corridor doorway and walked through.

Will followed him, pausing at the entrance to look back to Raby. "My lord, should I ask your valet to attend you?"

"Nay, Will. The Lady Margaret shall attend me well enough."

Will nodded, then was gone.

Raby stared at the closed door, then turned to Margaret. She had by now backed up against the far wall of the chamber, and was almost hidden in the shadows cast by the bed hangings.

"Meggie," he said, and held out his hand.

She stared at him. How could a man of war, so frighteningly angry one moment, display such tenderness the next?

"Meggie," he said again.

"How can a man be full of such anger?" she said so softly that Raby almost did not catch her words.

"Tom has ever been full of anger. Meggie, Meggie, do not stand there in the shadows. Come."

Hesitantly she walked towards him and took his hand.

"Good girl." Raby bent down and kissed her on the mouth. "Now, will you attend me? I will crush my fingers if I attempt these buckles on my own!"

She half smiled at his attempt at humour, and lifted her small hands to the sleeveless stiffened leather coat he wore over his tunic. It was buckled tightly down each side, and Raby sighed with relief when it finally lifted off, grabbing it out of Margaret's hands as she almost dropped it, surprised by its weight.

"I would give half my estates if I had the chance to recline all day in your dainty linens, my dear," he said, running the fingers of one hand over the soft grey material stretched tight over her breasts.

He frowned slightly at this reminder of her pregnancy.

"My lord would look quite the fool if he were to don my gowns," Margaret said, then froze, staring into his face, certain she had offended him. "My lord, I did not mean —"

"No matter, girl. Here, ah, take my boots — such pinchers!"

Margaret took his boots, as well his leggings and underclothes, and averted her head as he wandered naked about the warm chamber, sipping a goblet of wine.

She had been married ten years to her Roger, and had never in that time seen a man naked. Well, Raby certainly seemed intent of divesting her of whatever girlish modesty she still retained.

She bent over a chest, folding away Raby's clothes, when she heard him walk up behind her, and felt his fingers at the fastenings of her own gown.

"I have thought of you all day," he whispered, now sliding a hand inside her gown, rubbing her waist and belly. "Hungered for you all day."

She trembled, and he turned her about, pulling her against him for a kiss that did, indeed, demonstrate his hunger.

"To bed," he said.

They lay a long time, naked, not speaking. Raby was content to lie thus, running a gentle hand over her body, marvelling at its whiteness and slenderness.

As yet her pregnancy had not marred the smooth planes of her belly.

He sighed, holding his lust for her in check: it would be the sweeter when finally sated if he lingered a while yet.

"Have I displeased you?" she whispered.

"No." He laid a finger on her mouth to prevent further speech, then continued to caress her body. He could still hardly believe her husband had not once thought to lie with her during ten years of marriage. Who would want to deny himself this? And Margaret had said he had not even glanced at her body, let alone caressed it. The man had been an unnatural!

His face went expressionless as he cupped a breast. She tensed slightly; her breasts were tender now, and she was always afraid he would hurt her. Raby trailed a finger over a blue vein winding away from her nipple, and then traced it down over her waist to her belly.

"Does the sickness still trouble you?"

"It has passed in recent days, my lord."

"Ah. Good." He hesitated, now running his hand more firmly over her thighs and buttocks: he would not contain himself much longer. "Margaret ..."

"My lord, I know that you will not wed me —"

"I *cannot* wed you, Margaret. Our stations are too far apart."

She began to weep, knowing the truth of what he said. He needed a new wife — his first had died a year previously birthing their eleventh child — but he would marry estates and nobleness, not some landless widow of an unimportant country knight.

Raby shifted irritably. How many times had they had this conversation? He had an image of her when her belly was as round and bulky as a kettle drum, waddling into court, and weeping and wailing and begging him to make an honest women of her. Damn it! She had agreed to spread her legs for him; what did she expect would come of it? Virgin or not, she was a grown woman!

"Margaret! Stop your tears! I will ensure you and your," and Margaret drew back at the emphasis on the "your", "child will be well cared for. But I will not, ever, claim this child as mine."

Margaret blinked away her tears. *No*, she thought, *for you did indeed not father this child, although its father was in this chamber this night. But how can I say that to you?*

"I will not be a trouble to you," she said, and Raby relaxed.

"Good." He rolled her flat on her back, moving closer himself. She ate of his food, and basked in the warmth and shelter he provided. Now she must pay her dues.

She quivered slightly as he entered her. In the past few months she had become used to the sensations of loving, and no longer feared her time in Raby's bed. "Your nephew is a very strange man," she whispered, and received no reply save for a grunt.

Margaret ran her hands softly down his back, smiling into the darkened chamber. Poor Thomas. He had thought he had only the demons to battle. Now he has his Church as well.

Raby cried out and clutched at her, relieving his lust at last, and Margaret whispered soothing and loving words into his ear. Margaret truly cared for Raby, and she prayed that the tenderness and concern that he exhibited (try as he may to hide it) might also present itself in his nephew.

If Thomas was beyond caring, if he was beyond loving, then she and hers could have no hope at all.

Raby rolled off her, heaved a great sigh, kissed her cheek, and gathered her into his arms. Margaret snuggled close to him, resting her cheek against his warm chest, letting the beat of his heart soothe her.

Her time with Raby would not last long, and Margaret wanted to savour the warmth and comfort of the man while she still could.

XIII

Prime on the Feast of All Saints
In the fifty-first year of the reign of Edward III
(daybreak Monday 1st November 1378)

— All Hallows Day —

— i —

Thomas sat awake through the night, wondering, fretting, fuming, and frustrated beyond measure.

After he'd spoken to a guard in the corridor, Will had led Thomas to a small chamber some thirty paces distant from Raby's accommodation. Will sat Thomas on the pallet a guard brought with the clear warning that if Thomas were to leave, he would get a blade through his gut for his presumption.

To make his point, Will had opened the door to reveal three guards outside: battle-scarred, hard-eyed men, who stood with their hands close by their swords, to prove the truth of Will's words.

A prisoner ... of his own countrymen!

And of the Prior General.

And here he was, confined by common soldiers.

Him! A Neville. A Dominican friar. An intimate of St Michael!

And so Thomas sat awake on his pallet and fumed until well into the early hours of the morning when he finally managed to laugh at himself. *Lord forgive my pride*, he prayed. It was no wonder both the Black Prince (and King Edward, for all he knew) and his uncle were furious at him. It was no wonder that the Prior General wanted him hauled back to England in chains.

He had, after all, left the friary in Rome without permission. He had wandered through half of Europe without permission. And he had talked of strange visitations by St Michael and even stranger missions.

Who could possibly believe him?

And especially, Thomas thought further, sobering completely, after the misadventures and misdalliances of his youth and early manhood.

It was no wonder, either, that his uncle and the Black Prince were so angry with him. The English throne and high nobles depended on the goodwill of the Church, and to offend the leader of one of the most powerful orders within the Church — and one that could call the Inquisition down upon their heads! — was a sin almost without parallel.

He took a deep breath. God had sent this predicament to test his mettle and strength of purpose.

He would not fail. Circumstances seemed against him, true, but he could turn them to his favour. The Prior General wanted him back in England? That was good, because that was where Thomas needed to go to find Wynkyn's casket, and if the Prior General was angry enough, it would mean that he would be sent all the faster.

Once he was in England Thomas would decide how best to deal with the Prior General's anger.

For the moment he needed to regain the confidence of his uncle, as of the Black Prince.

And then ... there was *her*. The witch's appearance in his uncle's bed had been a stunning shock, and yet not a surprise. It only confirmed in his mind the lengths to which the demons would go in order to achieve their ends.

He had thought once to kill her, but now he realised that

that would only serve to further alienate his uncle. It would also mean that he might not know the shape and name of the next temptation the demons sent his way. No, as that damned imp had said back at the Cleft, better the devil you know than the one you don't. The demons thought they would tempt Thomas through Margaret. Thomas knew they damn well couldn't.

No, better that she remain alive.

Whatever, he would keep her under close watch ... perhaps even learn from her more details of the demonic conspiracy to wrest control of this world from God and the Church. Every warrior, whether dressed in armour or holy robes, knew that the enemy understood was the enemy defeated.

If he was to keep her under close watch, if he was to study her, then, again, he would need his uncle's goodwill.

Thomas sighed, and shifted. He had not made a good start.

Thomas noticed that Will was still awake, regarding him from beneath the blankets of his bed. Doubtless he had witnessed a fine display of emotions roiling across Thomas' face in the past hours.

"I have been a fool, Will," Thomas said softly.

"Oh, aye, that you have."

"Will you talk with me awhile? It has been a long night and there yet remains much of it to be endured. Come, Will, I have been away from my home many years, and have much news to catch up on. Tell me, when did my Lady Raby die?"

"A year ago now," Will said, a little reluctantly, and even more reluctantly sat up, pulling his blanket about his shoulders.

"No doubt from exhaustion," Thomas said, smiling, then crossed himself and sobered. "God take her soul, but ... sweet Jesu! Raby kept her permanently breeding."

Disarmed by the charm Thomas could exhibit when needed, Will's mouth twitched, and he relaxed slightly. "Raby's castle rattles with the footsteps of his brood. He has uncommon luck. How many other men can boast eleven children?"

"Aye." In this world, most children died before the age of five, succumbing to either disease or the frightful rigours of childbirth. Raby had been blessed indeed.

Thomas grinned. "Eleven children! 'Twas no wonder I joined the Church, Will. I gave up hope of inheriting his estates after the birth of his fourth son!"

Will laughed outright, and within minutes the two men were chatting as if they had been bed companions all their lives.

Raby's face was hard when Thomas entered his chamber just after dawn.

Thomas glanced quickly about. The witch was nowhere to be seen.

"She is not here," Raby said. "She has gone to attend Gloucester's wife."

"I spoke harshly to her last night," Thomas said. "I would that I may find the opportunity to take those words back."

"You cannot throw stones," Raby said. "Not you."

For one horrible moment Thomas thought Raby referred to the fact he had lain with Odile in the woods outside Nuremberg, then realised his uncle referred to Alice ... and to the incident which Thomas had entered the Church to try to atone for.

Thomas looked away, not wanting his uncle to see his lack of remorse for what he'd done to Alice. And why should he be remorseful? Hadn't St Michael said he was forgiven? In fact, hadn't the archangel said he'd done the right thing?

Raby stared at him, then indicated the table. Some well-watered wine sat in a rock-crystal ewer, and a platter held some bread and fruit. "Sit down and eat."

Thomas sat down and fiddled with a loaf of bread, breaking off a piece to then break the piece into a score of crumbly fragments.

"What can I do to make amends?" he said finally, raising

his eyes to Raby, who bit into an apple as he stared at his nephew.

"Not only with the Lady Rivers," Thomas hastened on, "but with you, and the Black Prince. I have darkened the Neville name with my actions, and deeply angered the prince."

Raby raised his eyebrows. It was not quite "Thomas" to be the penitent. He chewed his mouthful of fruit, and did not answer.

"I am under your command, and that of the Black Prince," Thomas said, "until you can hand me into the command of the Prior General."

"Enough, Tom," Raby said, swallowing his mouthful with a gulp. "I cannot bear the contrition!"

He sighed and put down the half-eaten apple. "You have been recently in Paris, and talked with Philip. And the Dauphin?"

"Aye, although I met — and only briefly — with the Dauphin some days to the east of Paris."

"Ah, well, whatever you can tell us will doubtless be more than we know. Tom, we are all but blind here. Should we deal with Philip — and who trusts him? — or with Charles? Should we risk war-weary men and the winter snows and make a push into Paris to force Charles' hand? Or should we wait out the winter here ... and risk Charles raising a force to confront us with in the spring? God knows that the lands of France have far greater resources than England. On the other hand, some think we should simply repair back to England with King John in tow and continue the negotiations from there ..."

Thomas nodded, smiling to himself as Raby's voice trailed off. It was obvious which choice Raby did not want the Black Prince to take.

Raby leaned over the table. "We need all the intelligence we can gather, and you can go some way to restoring a measure of goodwill towards yourself by adding to our store of knowledge."

"Yet you knew I was on my way, and that I bore a message from Philip. You knew I had left the Saint Angelo friary in Rome, and that I have, um, experienced visions. I know that the prior of Saint Angelo's must have sent word to Thorseby, and that the Prior General then asked the Black Prince in a letter to take me into custody. But how did you know I was on my way from Philip?"

"Because half of France knew," Raby growled, then leaned back in his chair. "Because Bolingbroke has his spies, and one of them passed on information that you had spoken with Philip and were heading towards us. It took no great leap of imagination to realise that Philip would take the opportunity to confuse us with some offer of alliance."

Raby stood up. "Ah! None of us can decide what to do sitting about tables eating apples. Come. I cannot stand all this idleness. Let me show you my new war horse — as fine a destrier as ever I saw — and as I do, I can tell you of our magnificent victory over John."

Raby's face brightened. "Whatever else, we still have the French king! If we get hungry enough … why, perhaps we can eat him!"

Thomas laughed, and stood up. "I am not to be kept under close guard? I do not need the sword at my neck?"

Raby paused, considering Thomas. "Do you give me your word you will not escape?"

"You have it."

"Then you have your freedom of the fortress. Come on, nephew, I want to see if your eye for horseflesh is as good as once it was."

XIV

The Feast of All Saints
In the fifty-first year of the Reign of Edward III
(Monday 1st November 1378)

— All Hallows Day —

— ii —

Raby led Thomas down towards the stables, but
deviated on the way to show his nephew the retinue he
had personally contributed to the Black Prince's
campaign. Raby had brought twenty-five knights (each with
at least three horses, and a retinue of the knights' own
valets, pages and squires), forty-six men-at-arms (who had
two horses and one valet each), sixty mounted longbowmen
(with only one horse each, and they fought on foot rather
than on their horse, and with fifteen valets shared amongst
them), and almost eighty foot soldiers to the Black Prince's
side, and he was well pleased with his contribution. Raby
was particularly proud of his longbowmen. They were
veterans of Edward III's wars with the ever-troublesome
Scots, and they were good, very good. Raby liked to boast
that each of them had brought down at least two score of
French mounted men during Poitiers.

Most of these men were lolling about in their quarters,

some cleaning or restringing their bows, some cleaning their swords and oiling them against the encroaching dampness of winter (the archers being equipped with swords and daggers as well as bows). Several were having their hair cut (it was a requirement that all longbowmen keep their hair razored close to their head, so that it could not get caught in the strings of their bows), a dozen were fletching new arrows, and others tidied the rooms — the English were not so much concerned with neatness as with the inevitable sickness that struck down any fortress that was not kept spotlessly clean. The bows of the archers were hung neatly in rows of racks, arrows stowed in chests (each archer had at least sixty arrows in his personal sheaf), and what few personal possessions each man had were rolled into neat bundles by their sleeping pallets.

When Raby finally led Thomas into the horse stables, Thomas saw that the equine accommodations were as clean as those of the men. The stables had been divided into quarters that housed different breeds — the equine hierarchy was almost as rigid as the human social hierarchy. The knights' destriers, powerful and strongly built creatures, were kept slightly apart from the lesser horses of the men-at-arms and archers. The destriers were also kept slightly apart from each other, for all were highly-strung stallions, bred as fighting machines as well as a means of locomotion, and most spent the greater part of their time looking for something, or someone, to strike at with hooves or teeth. Grooms scrambled about the horses, grooming, muck-raking, feeding and keeping a respectable distance from the teeth and rear hooves of the destriers.

An army encampment, thought Thomas, *was as busy and self-important as any bustling market town.*

He sniffed the air: there was the sweet smell of newly baked bread wafting over and above the sweet warm odour of the stables, and he swore he could scent the heavily spiced tang of roasting meat.

Raby saw him, and smiled. "It is a feast day, Tom. There will be a banquet this night. Grovel hard enough at the Black Prince's feet and you may well get yourself invited."

"A banquet is well enough for the lords, uncle, but surely this smell must drive the soldiers mad with hunger."

"Chauvigny was well stocked by the French, Tom. After the battle at Poitiers the garrison here fled without destroying a single crust. Everyone shall feast well tonight ... and for months to come, should Edward decide to stay. Besides, Lancaster has negotiated a deal with the mayors of the neighbouring towns. They supply us what we need ... and we forbear attacking them."

Thomas grunted. The Duke of Lancaster was nothing if not a supreme negotiator. He had negotiated two marriages, both of which had brought him a fortune in land and income. His first marriage to Blanche had brought him the duchy of Lancaster; his second to Constance had brought him the kingdom of Castile. Between his wives and his own astute purchases and deals, Lancaster was now the richest and most powerful man in England — his wealth outstripped even that of his father, Edward III. Consequently, Lancaster had to demonstrate even further his diplomatic skills in walking the tightrope between those who suspected him of trying to gain the throne for himself, and who thus worked night and day for his downfall, and those who curried his favour. Getting a bit of bread and meat out of a mayor scared witless by the outstanding success of an enemy army would have been nothing.

"Ah, here!" Raby said, stopping by the stall of a great black stallion. "Is he not magnificent?"

Thomas stopped, awed by the beast. He was at least eighteen hands high, his black hide rippling with muscle and health, his eyes wide and intelligent — and more than a little bellicose.

Both Raby and Thomas stood just out of biting range.

"He is Spanish," Raby said, and Thomas' admiration soared. Every knight prized Spanish war horses above all others: they were worth a fortune. No ordinary knight could ever possibly afford one, and Thomas suspected that even Raby, with his numerous castles and estates, would have been hard pressed to find the money for him.

Raby grinned as he watched Thomas' face. "He didn't cost me a single penny," he said. "Although I did get a nasty gash on my left shoulder for my troubles."

"Ah," Thomas said, understanding. "He is part of your spoils of war. And the man who rode him?"

"Is waiting dejectedly for his family to come up with the ransom I have demanded. Sweet Jesu, Tom, the number of counts, barons and sundry dukes we captured — England will be the richer by far for this war!"

"Hmm." Tom dared a closer inspection of the destrier, keeping an eye on the whites of the beast's eyes and the flash of his teeth as he did so. Every nobleman went to war with two purposes. Firstly, the desire to actually win the war, and secondly, and far more importantly, the desire to capture for ransom as many knights of the opposing force as he could: family fortunes could be made (and lost) on the battlefield. If the Black Prince ever managed to extract from the Dauphin a ransom for King John, England would be awash in gold coin for decades to come. Raby had obviously done well for himself, but at that Thomas was not surprised. His uncle was an outstanding warrior, backed by a well-trained and battle-hardened retinue. No doubt every one of his men would be going home the richer for Poitiers.

Thomas stroked his hand down the flank of the destrier, soothing the stallion's ill-temper with quiet words.

"I do hope," a voice said behind him, "that you can soothe Prior General Thorseby as easily as you do that destrier."

Thomas turned quietly, careful not to startle the stallion and earn himself a sharp hoof in the belly for his troubles.

"My lords," he said, and bowed.

Edward, the Black Prince, and his brother the Duke of Lancaster, John of Gaunt, had joined Raby. No doubt both had been visiting their own destriers and checking their comfort; the bond between rider and war horse was of vital importance, and no knight ever ignored the wellbeing of his mount, nor neglected to visit him at least once a day.

Both the Black Prince and Lancaster regarded Thomas thoughtfully. He'd shown such promise as a lad, and had come from such good blood, that to lose him to the Church, of all things, had been a blow.

And now, to have him bolt from his adopted stable and gallop about Europe like an out-of-control and untrained war horse was more than just an extreme embarrassment.

"I can understand," Lancaster said, "a man's desire to take holy orders. But, in doing so, he is supposed to give up his own will for the will of God, as expressed through the Church. He is *not* supposed to embark on actions that violate every trust that has been placed in him."

Thomas again bowed, lower this time. Lancaster's quiet words had hurt where the Black Prince's shouts had only angered. He straightened, looking the Duke in the eye. Lancaster was tall, the tallest of all Edward's sons, a lean and spare man with deep grooves running down either side of his nose and fanning out from the corners of his eyes. His hair, once a rich brown, had now faded into a lacklustre drabness. Lancaster was showing the weight of his cares, although he did not appear ill, as was his older brother.

"I have been foolish in the extreme," Thomas said, his eyes unflinching as he addressed both the Black Prince and Lancaster, "and have proved an embarrassment to my family and to the crown of England. Sirs, I beg your goodwill, and place myself entirely under your care until you can present me to the blessed Prior General." Thomas bowed his head, and folded his hands before him. "My contrition is true, good sirs."

The Black Prince and Lancaster exchanged brief glances. Like Raby earlier, they did not entirely trust Thomas' words, and his now humble mien. It just wasn't "Thomas" at all ... at least not the Thomas they had known.

On the other hand, both were seasoned warriors, courtiers and diplomats. If Thomas was prepared to give his word that he would place himself under their command, then ...

"I am yours to command," Thomas said, precisely on cue. He had, after all, been brought up in the same surroundings, and according to the same rules of conduct, as had the two princes standing before him now.

"And *will* you be commanded?" Lancaster said.

Thomas looked him in the eye. "Aye, my lord. As far as my clerical habit permits."

Lancaster's mouth, as the Black Prince's, twitched in a wry smile. But it was good enough. Thomas would not, as a cleric under holy orders, give his allegiance to them before his allegiance to the Church.

Lancaster's eyes roamed over Thomas. "You do not fit that robe well, Tom. I preferred you in helm and armour. And I fancy that you look slightly the fool with your pate shaved in that manner."

"I am a priest before I am a man, my lord."

"Aye, well … my brother tells me you have talked with the pretty King of Navarre. Will you now talk to us of him, and his offer?"

"Gladly, my lord."

The four men turned away from Raby's new acquisition, both princes and Thomas making suitably admiring remarks about the destrier — to Raby's obvious pleasure — and walked into the stable courtyard to a small group of fruit trees whose leafless branches twisted black against the clear sky.

"Philip says that he will ally himself with you to —"

"Aye, aye," the Black Prince said. "I am sure that he has promised to lay his life before me so that I might finally succeed to the French throne. No doubt he has also promised me Charles' head and balls on a platter."

"He did not put it quite like that," Thomas said, and received for his troubles an irritated glance from the Black Prince.

They spoke a little about Charles, and Thomas told them what he could of his meeting with the man outside Paris, and the fact that he was going to la Roche-Guyon in the hopes of raising some troops.

The princes and Raby listened, but Thomas had little intelligence regarding the Dauphin, and Charles was only doing what any prince could be expected to do … although that, in itself, was out of character for the Dauphin.

Whatever, the Black Prince responded to news of Charles as he almost always did, with a dismissive shrug.

"We are, perhaps, more interested in the state of the northern provinces and of Paris," he said to Thomas. "What can you tell us?"

Thomas related what he had seen of the peasants' bloody uprising against their lords as well as what he knew of Marcel and the revolt. He carefully explained Marcel's stand on winning rights and dignities for the common men and women.

Now all three men stared at him, eyes wide with horror at Marcel's ideas more than at Thomas' description of the horrors meted out to the Lescolopier family.

"But that —" Raby said.

"Would result in utter chaos," Lancaster finished for him. "What can they mean ... the right to determine their own paths in life?"

He shook his head slightly, unable to come to terms with the concept. "All men are born into their positions in life: some born noble, some free, some bonded, some unfree. It is the way of things, and *cannot* be changed. To clamber up and down the hierarchy, looking for a more comfortable place than the one you were born into ... sweet Jesu! What if everyone thought they could move out of their appointed places? We would have carpenters wanting to be kings."

And presumably no kings wanting to be carpenters, Thomas thought, but realised it might be prudent to leave that thought unspoken.

"It will not come to that," he said. "Philip and Charles are both as appalled as are you. Paris will not long hold out in its bid for freedom."

"I have heard reports that Philip and Charles have forces encamped beyond Paris' walls," the Black Prince said, looking up through the branches of the fruit trees as if he expected retribution to drop down suddenly from heaven. But the sky shone a soft, calm blue, the only cloud a flock of barn swallows winging their way south for the winter.

"Aye," Thomas said. "I believe they will ally to attack together."

"And then find something to argue over and attack each other," Lancaster said, "or whatever suits Philip's ambitions."

He walked away a few paces, his hands clasped behind his back, thinking. "Thomas," he said eventually, turning back, "is all northern France seething with resentment?"

"Much of the north is in disarray," Thomas replied. "The people hurt with the taxes they must pay in order to finance the war against you, and seethe with resentment that their nobles cannot protect them. The northern provinces are stacks of kindling, waiting for someone to throw a match."

"And added to that," the Black Prince said, "the two highest nobles, Philip and Charles, are at each other's throats." He would have said more, but Lancaster caught his eye, and Edward swallowed his words.

Instead he turned to Thomas. "You have acted the part of a fool," he said, "and I doubt the depth of your contrition. But I still respect your word. If we allow you the freedom of the fortress, will you not disabuse our trust and bolt off on whatever angelic mission you believe yourself engaged in?"

"You have my word," Thomas said, once again bowing slightly to the two princes. "But, my lords, I do desire to return to England as soon as I can, so that I may also make my peace with the Prior General. Is it possible that —"

"Yes, yes," the Black Prince said, waving a hand. "Whenever it suits us. I am most certainly not going to leap and dance at the whims of the Prior General. Perhaps he should wait a while."

"My lord, it *may* be best that you send me back as soon as —'

"I will send you back when I damn well choose!" the Black Prince said. "And for the moment you may yet be of some use to me."

"As you wish, my lord." Thomas bowed again, and, while he was determined in his mind to get back to England, he also fully realised that the worst thing he could do now was to further antagonise the Black Prince ... or Lancaster and Raby, for that matter. Any one of them could incarcerate him in a some dank gaol indefinitely, and if that happened, then no one could have any chance against the demons.

What demons walked in disguise within the English camp? The archangel had said that the English camp was particularly infected ... but which faces about him were those of true Christian men, and which of demons? *Who were they?*

"Very good, Thomas," the Black Prince said, then smiled. "Has your uncle told you of this evening's banquet?"

Margaret sat at the open window of Gloucester's apartment, a half-stitched linen under-tunic in her small hands. Directly below flowed the waters of the Vienne, and even though they were so high, Margaret sometimes fancied she could see the flashing shadows of fish deep within it. Beside her sat Eleanor, Duchess of Gloucester, wife of Thomas of Woodstock, the youngest surviving brother of the Black Prince and John of Gaunt. Gloucester himself was nowhere to be seen, and Eleanor had merely shrugged when Margaret hesitantly asked after him. He was off doing what all men of war did when cooling their heels in a fortress, apparently, and Margaret did not want to ask further what that might be.

Eleanor was of an age with Margaret, about twenty-five or six, a tall, elegant woman with shining golden hair, her chief glory. Today she sat uncomfortably, her huge belly protruding before her. Eleanor was too tired to even sew, and she had in her hands a beautifully illuminated book of hours — her husband, Thomas, was a patron of the arts, and had an extensive library. Every so often she would read a page, reciting the prayers under her breath. Eleanor, like any careful woman approaching the dangers of childbirth, was preparing herself for death.

The duchess was almost to term with this her fourth child, and Margaret did not envy her giving birth in this forbidding fortress. Her presence here was not in itself unusual. Many noble wives accompanied their husbands on campaign — King Edward's wife, Philippa, had given birth to eight of her children while following her husband about Europe on his eternal quest for more land and glory — but Margaret hoped that she herself would be in a far more comfortable environment when the time for her confinement came.

Where? she thought. *I have no home save with Roger's parents ... and what if they should discover that this child is not Roger's, but a bastard born of their daughter-in-law's whoring?*

Besides, Margaret did not get on well with Sir Egdon and Lady Jacquetta Rivers. They had never approved of their son's choice of wife, and no doubt would blame her for the fact that he had died abroad while on one of his ceaseless pilgrimages to shrines, seeking a divine miracle for his affliction.

Eleanor regarded Margaret as surreptitiously as the other woman did her. Eleanor suspected the woman was breeding — she'd had enough pregnancies of her own to recognise the symptoms in another woman — and now she wondered how best to broach the delicate subject.

In the end, Eleanor decided she so outranked the Lady Rivers that she need not be delicate at all. Besides, her back ached and her feet hurt, and she was in no mood for niceties.

"It must be a great gladness to you, Lady Margaret," she said smoothly, keeping her eyes on the open page of the book of hours, "to know that even though your husband is now with God, you still have his child growing in your belly."

Margaret's fingers stilled, then she shakily threaded her needle into the linen and sat back, looking at Eleanor.

"It is an increasing sadness with me," Margaret said, "that the child will be born fatherless."

Eleanor smiled at her, coldly. Born without a father indeed! Well, Baron Raby would certainly never name it as his own.

"Perhaps," she said, "you hope that Baron Raby will provide for the child's future."

Margaret dropped her eyes and did not reply.

Eleanor sighed, suddenly sick of speaking in such delicate niceties. "I can understand why you went to Raby's bed," she said, and Margaret jerked her eyes back at the duchess, her cheeks reddening, "but you cannot think that he will wed you himself."

"He has made that plain enough to me —"

"You cannot even hope," Eleanor said. She bit her lip, wondering how much she should say. Margaret's sensibilities did not concern her at all, but this was a highly sensitive matter ...

"I have heard," Eleanor said, her voice very, very careful, "that Raby already has another marriage planned."

Margaret's eyes widened, and Eleanor could see that the woman had indeed hoped that Raby would wed her. "He has said nothing!"

"He may not think it concerns you."

Furious, both with this haughty woman before her and with Raby, Margaret looked away, pretending an interest in a group of archers at target practice in a field beyond the river.

"High nobles have been known to prefer a mistress before a wife," she said.

Eleanor knew well to whom Margaret referred. Lancaster had kept a mistress, Katherine Swynford, through three decades, and gave her two children along with his heart. But Lancaster's arrangement with Katherine was something Margaret could not hope for with Raby, especially since Eleanor had heard ... ah! She hated keeping secrets, but was too afraid of both Lancaster's and Raby's anger to inform Margaret just how hopeless her position truly was.

"My advice, Lady Margaret," Eleanor said, "is to seek another marriage as soon as possible. Raby will speak for you, and his is a powerful voice. There are many knights who would be glad enough for your hand ... even big with another man's child."

And especially if she was big with child to a nobleman rich enough to provide the penniless widow with a large dowry to go with her hand. And Raby would be generous when it came to handing Margaret on to another man. Margaret did not yet realise how desperate Raby would be to save both himself and his future bride the embarrassment of being faced with a hysterical woman flaunting her belly at court and demanding recompense.

"All my life," Margaret said softly, resuming her stitching, "I have been handed from man to man to suit another man's purposes. It would be nice, perhaps, for once to choose my own mate."

"No woman ever chooses her own mate," Eleanor said briskly. "We must take who our parents or lord picks for us. It is our duty."

Well enough for you to say, Margaret thought. *Gloucester is a handsome and courtly man who is unfailingly kind and generous to you.*

"Ah, Margaret . . ." Eleanor leaned over awkwardly, and patted Margaret's hand. "No one can say, especially not to us, sitting here heavy with child, that a woman's lot is not to suffer."

Margaret let herself be comforted, and smiled disarmingly, changing the subject and engaging Eleanor in a spirited discussion about the relative merits of Flemish cloth over Florentine.

But her thoughts lingered on both childbirth and Raby's supposed secret marriage negotiations. Eleanor would have been shocked to know that Margaret did not intend to "suffer" through childbirth at all — not if she were allowed enough seclusion — and that she knew all about Raby's secretive courting. Indeed, Raby's growing concern that Margaret might create a serious disturbance and threaten his marriage negotiations suited her own purposes admirably.

It was, in the end, the one guaranteed way to enable her to obtain the mate of her choice after all.

XV

Compline on the Feast of All Saints
In the fifty-first year of the Reign of Edward III
(night Monday 1st November 1378)

— All Hallows Day —

— iii —

The night was clear, cold and windless, threatening a deep frost in the morning. Throughout Chauvigny men bedded themselves and their horses down for the night, piling straw not only about the legs and flanks of their mounts, but about their own sleeping places as well. Wood, mercifully plentiful in the ancient forests standing about Chauvigny, was stacked close to hand so that a man might only lift an arm from his blankets to toss more on the fire. Despite the cold, the men were generally in a good mood. Earlier, cooks and servants had passed about bread trenchers filled to the brim with hot, spiced meat swimming in gravy, together with a mug of rich honeyed wine for each man. It was a feast day, after all.

To the west of Chauvigny spread a great forest. Many of its oaks and beeches were over a thousand years old — great gnarled trees, their trunks and limbs twisted by millennia of storms and hardship. The Black Prince was so confident of his hold on central and southern France that he felt able to hold his All Saints banquet in a grove deep inside the forest. During the afternoon the grove had been cleared of its twigs and rocks and tangled dry autumn grasses; now the ground lay smooth and elegant under a layer of mats and rugs. In the ring of gnarled trees about the grove were set torches, their flickering light supplemented by torches atop spikes taller than a man that had been placed between the trees. About the outer circle of the grove were set braziers, glowing warm and comforting; in the centre of the grove, in the rectangular space created by lines of trestle tables, were three roaring fires.

Here, in this ancient, natural space, man challenged winter with a blazing exultation of light and warmth.

The trestle tables and their accompanying benches had been positioned as they would be in any noble hall. At the top of the grove (where, it must be noted, the torches and braziers were grouped more thickly) stood the High Table, where the mightiest and most powerful of men would sit. Here, and only here, had the benches been replaced with carved wooden chairs and, in the centre, three wondrously carved thrones. Then, spreading down each side of the grove, were the two long arms of tables, finally joined in the dim distance by a table placed to close up the rectangle. The High Table was strewn with magnificent cloths: the finest linens, tapestries, and even, here and there, the glimmer of silks. The two long side tables were set with clean and sturdy linens, the foot table was set with a coarser cloth, but one that, like all the other tables, still had dried summer flowers and greenery threaded along its edges.

The lesser tables were set with fine plate, goblets, lidded cups and pewter spoons; the High Table was set with jewelled gold plate and spoons that glittered like fire in the torchlight. Before the three thrones sat a magnificent gold salt cellar fashioned in the shape of the Tower of London. No doubt it would serve to remind King John of his captive status as well as display the wealth and power of the Black Prince.

Serving tables were set at regular intervals behind the

rectangle of main tables. On these were set pitchers and ewers filled with the finest Gascon wines, as well as cider and perry, a potent fermented pear juice. They were also piled high with neat stacks of linen napkins, washing bowls and pitchers of the sweetest water so that all the guests could wash their hands before, during and after their meal.

This was a feast over which a Prince of Wales would preside and at which a king would be guest of honour.

Thomas stood with a group of ranking nobles a few paces behind the right-hand arm of the rectangle of tables; his place would be close indeed to the High Table, and he wondered at the honour accorded him. About the grove, either standing a few paces behind the tables, or in the first line of trees, were the banquet guests.

All were silent. Waiting.

Among them snuffled a score of greyhounds, as well as other hunting dogs. The property of either the Black Prince, Lancaster or Gloucester, they had been let loose for the evening to enjoy the feast along with their masters. In truth, the greatest of these hounds would be ranked higher in the social hierarchy than some of the lesser knights who would attend the feast, and would be deferred to as such. If a hound chose to defecate on the hem of a lowly knight's robe, then that knight would not so much as grimace, but accept the soiling of his attire with good grace.

Thomas also noticed several of the Black Prince's hawks sitting hooded and quiet just behind the first trees. They, too, were here to participate and enjoy.

Despite the general aura of warmth and barely restrained cheer, Thomas was uneasy. He sensed something *else* waiting within the trees, beyond the flickering light of torch and brazier. Demons? It was night, their natural landscape through which they could escape their burdensome human forms and scamper with ease. Thomas shifted, his unease growing. Why hold the banquet in this grove? At night. Was not the Black Prince aware the night was the haunt of all manner of imps and sprites ... even if he was not aware of the extra evil which had escaped from the Cleft outside Asterladen?

Thomas slid his hands inside his voluminous sleeves and rubbed his forearms up and down. Should he tell the prince about the demons? Would the Black Prince even believe him?

But how was Edward to be on his guard against such insidious evil if he did not understand its true nature?

And how was Thomas going to be able to continue his journey to England if he didn't confide in the prince?

"Tom," said a voice just behind him, "you look as if you have an ague. Why jump up and down like that? Are you cold?"

Thomas turned. It was Bolingbroke ... Hal.

The man's face was wary, and not entirely friendly. But, if wary, then at least Hal indicated he was prepared to be civil, and even to listen to what Thomas had to say.

How much of our once strong friendship remains? Thomas wondered.

"I am impatient for the feast to begin," Thomas said with a disarming smile. "Poor friars do not often sit down to such richness."

For a moment Hal said nothing, his hard grey eyes studying Thomas intently, and Thomas remembered Hal's comment after they'd dismounted inside Chauvigny: *it was not I who walked away.*

"How is it," Hal finally said, softly, "that you chose such a life, Tom? You did not even consult with me about your decision. You walked off the tourneying field one summer's afternoon, smiled at me, said you would drink me under the table at that evening's feast for a change, and you ... walked ... away. I never saw you again — not until you rode into the woods the night before last. Why? Why?"

Thomas was stunned at Hal's apparent pain. He had never realised, or even thought, about the grief he might cause Hal by not talking to him about his compulsion to take holy orders.

But then, the compulsion had come upon him somewhat

suddenly, hadn't it? In fact, the compulsion had overcome him the instant he'd walked back into his chamber to let his squire and valet divest him of his armour to find the tidings awaiting him ... tidings of the Lady Alice.

Those tidings had, in an instant, altered his life. War and the challenge of man against man no longer interested him.

Instead, it seemed as if God had leaned down from heaven and said, *Your life must be spent in atonement, spent in My servitude, My Church.*

"I'm sorry," Thomas said, although he was not sure if he was apologising to Hal, or the still-present ghost of Alice.

"You *know* why I entered the Church," he continued. "You heard as well ..."

"Did you think it would do Alice and her children any good to have you praying night and day for God to forgive your sins?" Hal said. The other nobles standing about them had now retreated several paces to give the illusion of privacy. Nevertheless, their backs and shoulders were still, listening. "Curse you, Tom, what good did that do *Alice*? Or her children? Damn you, Tom, *she had three children*!"

Thomas blinked, astonished at Hal's emotion. What was Alice or her children to him?

Hal jerked his eyes away, and heaved a sigh. "Ah! It is all gone now, Tom. Alice is gone, her children are gone, our youth is gone ... *you* are gone."

"What do you mean?"

"What stands before me now is not Tom who once was my friend," Hal said. "What stands here is a man hiding behind his clerical robes and vows. A farce of a man. A man who uses piousness to blame others for his own lack of judgement and mercy."

"Hal ... Hal ... you cannot understand what I have seen these past months, what I have learned. If I seem overly pious —"

Hal turned his face away.

"— then that is merely a reflection of the gravity of my task. Hal, we have both taken different paths. Can you not accept that?"

Again Hal considered, lowering his head and studying the ground beneath his feet. He scuffed some dirt into a small pile with his left boot, then raised his head and looked Thomas in the eye.

"I accept your right to take a different path, Tom," he said. "Every man, every woman, has that right. It's just that I think you took the wrong one for the man that you are. The man that I *know* is in there." He tapped Thomas gently on his chest.

There was a slight rustling sound in the near distance, then a jangle of bells, and a clarion of horns.

Hal glanced to the rear of the grove, then looked back at Thomas, a gentle smile softening his face. "Can we be friends for this one evening, Tom? Can you forget that you wear your robes for just this one banquet? I would have my friend back ... I would have his friendship to ease the soreness of my heart."

Thomas opened his mouth to protest that he could not set aside who and what he was, that his vows to the Church and to God could not so easily be "forgotten" for the sake of a banquet friendship ... but then he saw the pleading in Hal's eyes.

He held out his hand. "A deal, then, my friend ... and in return you can tell me the wonders and glory of Poitiers. Every time I think to ask my uncle we are interrupted either by women or by *your* father and uncle!"

Hal gripped Thomas' hand and arm fiercely. "A deal!"

The clarion sounded again, and both turned to watch the procession into the grove: Edward the Black Prince, with King John of France at his side. Both were relaxed and laughing softly as they shared some jest. Behind them walked John of Gaunt, Lancaster somehow managing to look far more regal in his loneliness than the two in company who preceded him. Behind Lancaster came Gloucester and his wife; she leaned heavily on his arm, and yet, even so, and even with her belly protruding, Eleanor conveyed nothing but grace and elegance. Completing the procession was Ralph, Baron of Raby.

Thomas was pleased to see that the witch was not at his

side, although he knew her lowly rank would never have allowed her to sit at High Table.

The group walked to the table, servants hastening to settle them into their chairs. Edward took the central throne, King John the one to his right. On Edward's left was a more ordinary chair, although even so it was commodious and delicately carved, and this Eleanor of Gloucester took. As she was the only woman to be seated at the High Table, and as the most highly ranked woman in the encampment, she would act as hostess for the evening. To King John's right sat Lancaster, also in a throne, as befitted his rank as King of Castile; to *his* right sat Raby, in an ordinary chair, and Gloucester, at the opposite end of the High Table, took the final place.

As they sat, so the assembled nobles walked forward from the shadows, laughing and cheering, and took their places along the benches.

Hal sat next to Thomas at the first table that stretched down from the right of the High Table. Thomas was well aware of the singular honour of having Bolingbroke sit next to him (Hal would not have been out of place at High Table), as well as being placed so near to the princes and kings at the head of the gathering.

Thomas glanced at the High Table, where servants were moving forward to pour water over the guests' hands and proffer linen napkins to wipe them dry. He wondered at his uncle's presence there (as a baron, he was high nobility, but was he high enough to share meat with princes and kings?), then settled back to enjoy himself.

Perhaps Hal was right. It would do him no harm to take delight in the feast … and surely the light was too thick, and the mood too joyous, for demons or imps to risk scurrying out of the night.

A servant spoke in his ear, and Thomas smiled, and turned slightly to wash his hands in the bowl the man held.

As the guests finished the ritual washing of hands, servants hastened forth to pour wine into cups and goblets, water into small bowls set by each place to wipe greasy fingers in between courses, and to set down the dishes for the first course of the evening: boar's meat coated with a thick, grainy mustard, eels in a spicy sauce, several varieties of fish, and delicate pastry pies. Each guest used his or her personal knife — everyone carried them dangling from belts — to lift food from each dish and place it on their bread trencher. As in any noble gathering, each guest observed decorous table manners: no one touched their food with their right hand, they helped themselves to only small portions, the sweetest delicacies were always offered to one's neighbour, and everyone used their napkin to wipe their fingers, not the tablecloth. As with manners, so with conversation: it was kept polite and as muted as possible considering the amount of wine flowing. Every care was taken not to disturb their neighbours' talk.

Hal chatted, slowly at first, but gathering in vivacity. He talked of men whom Thomas had known all his life, and of their women, who were more shadowy figures.

"I saw Northumberland's standard when first I rode into Chauvigny," Thomas said as Hal used his knife to lift a small portion of salt from the pewter cellar before him and place it on his trencher. "Where is the Earl ... and ..."

"Is Hotspur here?" Hal finished for him, chewing heartily. "Not tonight. Neither Northumberland nor his son are here, although they are not far. Our rear has been harried by a few ragtail elements of the French army, and Edward sent Northumberland and Hotspur back to clear them out."

He laughed. "Poor Hotspur — he will be furious to learn he has missed out on such a feast."

"How is Hotspur?" Henry Percy, son of Northumberland, had earned his nickname as a youth, pushing his destrier to extremes of bravery (or foolishness, depending on one's viewpoint) in any engagement.

"As you can surely imagine," Hal said, "*he* has not changed overmuch in the passing years."

"How surprising," Thomas remarked, selecting some boar's meat for himself. "I felt sure he had an inner vocation for the nunnery."

Hal paused, stared at Thomas, then burst out laughing. "Well said, my friend! But, of course, Hotspur *has* a vocation for the nunnery. I cannot think of the number of nuns he has wooed away from their vows to Christ!"

Thomas had to smile — he had, after all, begun the jest — but he felt some discomfiture at Hal's irreligious comment, as with the irreverent attitude that lay behind it. Too many people laughed at clerics in these days ... too many people took clerics' vows lightly ... too many *clerics* took their vows lightly!

Sweet Jesu, the demons had enjoyed thirty years to seduce people with their devilish ideas. How was he going to turn back the tide?

"I struck a nerve, it seems," Hal said, his tone lower now as he watched Thomas carefully. "I do apologise, Tom."

"Well," Tom said, twisting his mouth into the semblance of a grin, "you can do just penance by describing to me the wondrous battle of Poitiers. Hmm?"

"Gladly, Tom! Ah," Hal leaned back, his eyes alight, wiping his greasy fingers on his napkin, "Poitiers ... such a great victory. Tom," he leaned forward again, now talking earnestly, "our force was but small, and the French outnumbered us three to one ..."

Hal continued to describe the battle, the largest he'd ever been in, waving his hands about in excitement as he did so.

"It was a carnage, Tom," he finished, "conducted under the warm blue skies and to the accompaniment of hundreds of horns, flutes and pipes."

Thomas nodded, draining his goblet of wine. *Once I also would have revelled in the thrill of the battle, the victory of the slaughter, and the happiness of captured richness ... but no longer. I have grown beyond that.*

"Ah, Tom," Hal said, gesturing to a servant to pour Thomas some more wine. "Rolling out of a cold pallet to say Matins prayers in the dark hours of a winter's morning does not quite compare, does it?"

"We all have made our choices," Thomas said, instantly regretting the piousness of the tone he'd used.

"And yet there are still choices to be made, my friend," Hal said in a soft tone that was, stunningly, full of love.

Thomas stared at him, meaning to ask of what he meant, but just then a squire stepped up to Hal and whispered in his ear.

Hal turned back to Thomas. "Will you excuse me, Tom? It seems that Gloucester needs me to settle a dispute he has with Raby about the number of hairs in a horse's tail." He paused, grinning. "Methinks the wine is taking hold."

And then he was gone.

Thomas stared a moment at the space on the bench, and then leaned on the table, not interested in talking to the men either side of him and knowing that they, in their turn, would have nothing to say to him. Not for the first time in the past few years, Thomas was grateful for the distance his clerical robes put between him and other men.

Servants set the next course on the table. Yet more fish — grilled, baked, roasted, minced — chicken, roasted swan, baked porpoise and jellied sparrows, accompanied by sugary pink sweets in the form of noblemen and their ladies.

Thomas sighed, picked up one of the sugary noblemen, and absently chewed. His eyes roamed up and down the tables, his thoughts drifting, wanting Hal to come back.

Then his eyes stopped, and the half-eaten sugar confection paused halfway to his mouth.

There, at the far table, sat the witch. She was grouped with several other minor ladies, most of them ladies attending the noblewomen in camp, others, like Margaret, whores to the noblemen. She sat demure, eyes downcast, wearing the same simple grey gown he'd seen on her the night he'd arrived. Her hair was bound in a long plait now, woven in and out with what appeared to be, at this distance, late daisies.

As he watched, she lifted a morsel to her lips, tasted it, then put it down, turning her beautiful face aside.

So intent was Thomas upon the Lady Margaret Rivers he did not notice that two others watched her with similarly wary eyes. John of Gaunt, Duke of Lancaster, and Baron

Raby both sat silent, staring down the length of the tables towards her.

Eventually Lancaster turned his head and said something to Raby.

Raby replied, shaking his head and gesturing emphatically, then both men relaxed, and laughed.

Just then, musicians and mummers entered the space between the tables and there was cheering and laughter, and the entertainment began in earnest.

Many hours later, close to dawn, when the feast was over and weary-eyed servants moved slowly between the tables clearing away the remains, Thomas stood in the gloom under one of the great knotted oak trees. Most of the torches had burned themselves out many hours previously, and now only a few flickered erratically to light the servants' labours. He leaned against the tree trunk, his arms folded, his face calm and peaceful under the black hood of his cloak.

Hal had not returned to his side, and Thomas had spent the remaining hours of the feast — no one could leave until the royal party departed — drinking too much wine and overindulging himself on the sugar confectioneries and spiced meats. Sometimes he had listened to the conversations of those about him — sometimes they had, dutifully, and badly, tried to include him — and sometimes he had glanced towards the witch, but mostly he had simply sat, thinking about his position and fretting at the delays he continually faced in reaching England ... in reaching Wynkyn de Worde's book of secrets.

Finally, however, he had succumbed to the lethargy of the wine, and had simply let his thoughts drift until, eventually, he'd realised that not only had the royal party left, but so had the majority of the other guests.

The witch was nowhere to be seen.

Not wanting to go to bed so befuddled with wine — a more comfortable bed in his own chamber, now that he was back in some form of favour — Thomas had gone for a brisk walk along a nearby forest path. The trees were not thick, and the night well moonlit, and he felt no danger. Now, his head far clearer than it had been, he stood watching the servants stumble about in the grove, his mind reciting prayers — surely it must be Matins by now — his eyes largely unfocused, his body relaxed.

"Father, forgive me —"

Thomas jerked into full awareness, and turned about.

She stood there, her hands demurely folded before her, her head bowed.

"What do you here?" Thomas said.

Margaret lifted her head and stared at him with wide dark eyes from under the rough brown wool of her hood; she had donned a cloak against the descending morning frosts.

"I could not rest," she said. "I needed to talk to you."

"And what did you tell Raby when you climbed out of his bed? That you were off to find his nephew for some added comfort?"

"He has spent the night drinking with the Black Prince and King John. He has not needed me."

"Then what do you here?" Thomas repeated, his entire body tense.

"My lord ... Thomas —"

"You may address me as Brother Thomas, as is fit and proper."

Her eyes flashed. "You called me a whore, Thomas. I can hardly be the one to think of the 'fit and proper', can I?"

"Say your piece, then, and go."

"I was married when I was sixteen," she began, and Thomas moved irritably. "No, wait, I must say this —"

"I have no time for —"

"You must have time, Thomas, when it was your face that I saw, your body I felt, the night I lost my virginity!"

Thomas reeled back. "You are a witch!"

"No more than you."

Thomas stared at her.

"I had nothing to do with that night!" she said urgently, weaving forward a little as if she wanted to touch him, and then thinking better of it. "I thought I lay with Raby, and then . . . then . . ."

She stopped, apparently distressed, and turned her eyes away. Thomas, watching her closely, thought she was either a fine performer, or was, indeed, entirely innocent.

When Margaret looked back at him, her eyes were filled with tears. "I am not a willing whore, Thomas. I was the dutiful wife for the ten years of my marriage. I followed my husband from shrine to shrine, from Jerusalem to Santiago, from Canterbury to Rome, always seeking — and never receiving — divine aid for his wasting sickness. He died in Bordeaux a little over four months ago. We had no money left. I was destitute. My plight came to Raby's attention, and he offered me a solution. Share his bed, and he would see me safe home to England. He had no reason to think I was still a maid.

"Thomas, I fought with my conscience, but I was tired, and hungry, and frightened. Raby was kind to me — you know what a personable man he is! And . . . and, truth to tell, I was tired of remaining a maid for six-and-twenty years. I wanted to become a woman."

"You let your lusts overcome you."

She breathed deeply, her face pale, her eyes so large and black. Thomas wondered not that Raby had used every means possible to win her to his bed.

Something flitted across her face. Anger, perhaps, or resentment. "I let my lusts overcome me, yes . . . as did you."

"What? I —"

"I was not the only one who spent the afternoon of Saint Kenelmus' Day fornicating! As I lay with Raby, so you must also have lain with a woman!"

"Witch!"

"Not I! Not I! I am as innocent as you, Thomas." She paused, letting the meaning of her words sink in. "As innocent as you."

For a few minutes there was silence, each staring at the other.

"Are you with child?" Thomas finally asked.

She hesitated, then nodded.

"It is a child of sorcery. No doubt it will be born deformed and humped, and with the horns of a devil."

Margaret winced, and turned her head away before Thomas could see that he had truly hurt her. She hugged her arms tight about her chest, wishing that someone, somewhere, would claim her and might love her.

"You mean to use this child against me."

"I —"

"Another woman thought to use a child against me once ... she thought she could manipulate me with her swelling belly. She did not accomplish her purpose. Neither will you."

Margaret turned back to him. "I will never use this child against you!" Sweet Jesu, were all the Neville men in Christendom going to line up and accuse her of trying to trap them with this child?

"Then you mean me harm," Thomas said, his voice flat.

"Nay. I do not ... although I do not expect you to believe me." In a gesture of uncertainty, or perhaps even impotence, Margaret lifted her hands and ran them back through the burnished thickness of her hair, tipping her hood off her head with the movement.

The moonlight washed over her face, clothing her already lovely features with yet more beauty.

"I have been told," Thomas said quietly, his eyes steady on her face, "by those you undoubtedly know, of the fate that awaits me should I fail in my resolve. Evil will snatch my soul, and mankind will fail ... but only if I offer my soul to a woman."

Margaret surprised him by laughing harshly. "Then what do you fear, Thomas? Me? I do not want your soul! Besides, you must *offer* your soul, is that not so? It is not to be snatched, nor to be stolen, but must be offered. Thus," her smile stretched, and became a grimace, "you are only in danger of failing should you allow your mortal weaknesses to overcome you."

Her smile faded. "I am no danger to you, Thomas, unless you permit me to become a danger."

She reached out, and touched his face so fleetingly he did not have time to draw back. "I am only a danger if you allow yourself to love … and I do not think there is much chance of that, do you?"

And before Thomas could find the words to answer, Margaret turned and walked back into the night.

XVI

Matins of All Souls Day
In the fifty-first year of the reign of Edward III
(pre-dawn Tuesday 2nd November 1378)

— i —

Contrary to Margaret's words, Ralph, Baron Raby, was not spending the remaining hours of the night drinking and carousing with the Black Prince and King John.

After the royalty and high nobles had left the feast there had been, true, an hour spent in gentle conversation soothed by even gentler wine in the Black Prince's chamber, but then King John, aged and slightly intoxicated, had retired to his own section of the castle for his bed and the warm and smooth wench who awaited him there.

Raby, the Black Prince and Lancaster had courteously wished him a sweet night's rest, and then settled back into their chairs, refilling their goblets with some watered wine. A short space of time after King John had retired, Bolingbroke and Gloucester joined them.

All men were sober, and clear of eye and mind.

"Do we negotiate with Philip?" the Black Prince said. He was pacing slowly back and forth, one hand fiddling with his short beard, the other twirling an empty goblet around. His colour was better than it had been for days, and Edward thought he might finally be leaving behind the flux he'd caught after Poitiers.

"I am uncertain about even negotiating," Lancaster said, watching his elder brother carefully, "and we certainly go no further. We do *not* deal. Sweet Jesu, man! Philip would have no qualms about selling the Virgin Mary as a cheap whore for the Devil if the occasion — and price — presented itself!"

"He could be of some use," Edward said slowly. "Brother ... what options do we have? Poitiers did not win us a kingdom, only the rich southern provinces. To gain the throne we need to advance on Paris ... but our men are so war-weary that we risk total defeat if we do it on our own. With Philip we might just manage a complete victory before winter closes in. Without him we must perforce wait out the winter ... and give the French enough time to raise another army to meet us in the springtime."

Lancaster grunted, and looked away.

"Does Philip ask too much for his aid?" Bolingbroke said, looking between his father and the Black Prince. "Gascony, for whatever help he can give us? *Is he worth that?*"

"*I* say we push forward *now*," Lancaster said, now leaning forward in his chair, his eyes bright, "and leave Philip for the Devil. We have the advantage ... the French are in disarray, and yet the longer we leave them be the more chances they will have to regroup."

"Our men are too tired, John," the Black Prince said, finally stopping his pacing and regarding Lancaster with a steady eye. "We lost a goodly proportion of our archers at Poitiers, and you know how our battle success depends on them."

"Bah!" Lancaster said. "When have you ever been the cautionary one? I say," he thumped the arms of his chair, "we push forward *now* and *without* Philip's aid. We could have the French throne for our father, and eventually for *you*, Edward, within two months."

Edward shook his head slowly. Move forward on their own? It would be folly! "We risk meeting Philip and Charles combined, John. We would not survive it."

"I do *not* want to negotiate an alliance with Philip," Lancaster said, his brow furrowing over narrowed eyes. "I do not want to owe that cur anything, and I do *not* want to depend on him. Hal," he swept his eyes towards his son, "what say you?"

Hal looked between his father and uncle carefully. Both men spoke sense ... but which sense made the better battle plan? Alliance with Philip, push forward now without him, or wait out the winter to regain strength ... only to risk the French regaining theirs as well?

"Do we want Philip as an ally," he asked, "or as an enemy? If we negotiate with him, then at the least we stay his own hand for a few weeks or months. If we refuse to negotiate, he becomes an instant foe, and as likely to ally himself with Charles."

"And while we 'negotiate' with him," Lancaster said, "it is just as likely that Philip will also be negotiating with Charles. Gloucester, Raby, why so quiet? Give us your thoughts?"

Raby glanced at Gloucester for permission to speak first, then he sat forward, his fingers tapping against the arms of his chair. "Philip is dangerous. Whatever we do. I knew him as a lad — the Lord Saviour alone knows how many summers he spent with me, and how many Tom spent with him — and I did not trust him then. I most certainly do not now. What think I? I think Philip will do anything he can to ensure *he* gains the French throne. My lord," he inclined his head toward the Black Prince, "I do not think he means to aid you, but to hinder you in every way he can."

Gloucester nodded. "Lancaster and Raby both speak sense, Edward. Philip is dangerous ... but do we cut our own throats by pretending to deal with him, or by brushing his offer aside and marching directly on Paris ourselves? Such an action will almost certainly throw Philip into an alliance with Charles ... and that means we will face a strong force to take Paris."

Edward sighed tiredly and sat down. "We could always winter here, wait for spring —"

"And thus give both Philip and Charles the time to strengthen their hand against us," Lancaster said, "whether together or separately."

"We must not forget King John," Bolingbroke said. "How can we best use John?"

Lancaster laughed dryly, and poured himself some more of the watered wine. "I cannot believe either Charles or Philip will pay a single gold piece for the return of their king. I think we did them a service when we captured him."

"Perhaps Tom can aid us in this decision," Raby said, more than carefully. "He has spoken with Philip, and has seen with his own eyes the situation in the north."

There was silence.

"But can we trust Tom?" Lancaster said quietly, his eyes riveted on Raby's face.

He switched his gaze to Bolingbroke. "You were once his best friend, Hal. What say you? Does Tom speak with the voice of the Church ... or with a voice that remains allied with our own interests?"

Bolingbroke took his time to answer.

"Tom has changed," he said eventually, studying intently the rug between his booted feet. "He is not the man he was ... or perhaps he has hidden that man so deep he cannot find him again. Tom ... Tom was once a man of passion, warmth, a hearty laugh, of pride and impetuosity, it must be said, and yet a man of gentleness. I cannot see that man now. All I see is a cathedral —"

"What do you mean?" Lancaster said.

"He is nothing but a great stone edifice. Cold and heartless, mouthing the litany of the Church, and over-draped with hangings and banners that mean nothing. And as with all great stone edifices, Tom is hiding something ... a powerful secret buried deep within his vaults."

"He fled Rome too suddenly," the Black Prince said, now sitting down in a chair close to the brazier. "And has wandered through half of Europe. Why? It was not a mission that the Church sent him on ... the fact that the

Prior General has ordered him back to make full account of his action demonstrates that the hierarchy of both the Order and the Church is gravely displeased with him."

"And these apparent visions of Saint Michael," Gloucester put in, his face closed and moody. "I trust no man who has visions. The Lord Saviour alone knows whether he speaks honest truth ... or whatever phantasms his visions have placed in his mind. Perhaps he has spent too long fasting —"

"Tom tells us nothing," Lancaster said. "And he certainly has told us nothing about what he has been up to. What does he hide? Why did he bolt from Rome and the discipline of the Order? I like it not."

"Who knows his mind?" Bolingbroke said. "But he certainly has a secret. Uncle ... father, I think it is important we keep an eye on Tom. I would not willingly hand him over to the Prior General until *we* find out what veiled mystery he carries within him."

Lancaster grunted again. "All I want to know is whether Tom can be trusted to tell us the truth of Philip's plans, and the truth of what he has observed in the north. Saint Michael can be damned if he can't tell us what Philip and Charles plan."

Bolingbroke smiled at his father's blasphemy. "I don't know if Tom can be completely trusted, father. But what I *do* know is that it would be a poor thing indeed if we handed him back to Thoreseby before we know the secret he carries locked away in the stone vaults of his mind."

The Black Prince gestured impatiently. "So we will keep Tom with us for a while. He eats little enough. Bolingbroke, Raby, I entrust you both with *ensuring* he remains with us. You have also been his closest companions — find out the mystery that lurks within him. But for now? Well, for now we might as well question him a little more closely."

"Whatever," Lancaster said, "you will need to speak your decision about Philip's offer within the next few weeks, Edward. If we move from Chauvigny for winter then we must do it within a month or so. And whatever else you decide to do, then at least some of us will have to move. We can't keep King John here for winter. London is the only safe place to keep him."

Edward nodded, then waved the others away. He needed to write to his beloved wife Joan this night, and for that he needed solitude. Speaking to Joan always managed to clarify his thoughts ... and if he could not speak to her, then the next best thing was to write.

Sweet Jesu, but he could have done with her here!

Margaret had intended to go back to Raby's chamber to snatch what few hours of sleep she could, but was halted just as she reached the quarter of the fortress where most of the nobles' apartments were located.

"Lady Margaret?"

She jerked about, surprised and disconcerted. One of Gloucester's men stood behind her, his face anxious beneath his rounded iron helmet.

"Lady Rivers, the Duchess' time has come. Will you attend her? She has only one other lady, and —"

"Has no one sent for the midwife?" Margaret asked.

The man's face set into hard lines. "No one can find her," he said. "She has found herself a comfortable and warm bed for the night, and we have several thousand such beds and a score of miles of corridors to search through. Madam, hurry, for the Virgin's sake!"

Still Margaret did not move. Her heart was thumping, and she fought down rising panic.

She didn't want to attend the birth.

Unbelievably, Margaret had almost no experience in childbirth. After her own birth, her mother had no other children, none of their serving women had fallen pregnant, and neither Margaret nor her mother had bothered themselves with village births. The local midwife had been more than competent.

Thus Margaret's home had yielded no experience, and there had been no opportunity for any since she'd become a wife. Roger had dragged her about Europe, perpetually travelling from shrine to shrine, holy relic to holy relic, and few of the women pilgrims Margaret had encountered had been with child.

All Margaret knew about birth were the frightening tales she had been confronted with since she was old enough to join the circle of older women about the kitchen fire. Tales of women so wracked by pain they begged their attendants to kill them.

Women so fearful of the knives and hooks of their midwives they locked themselves in attics to give birth alone and unaided.

Tales of blood and dismemberment as husbands sent in butchers to save their heirs in preference to their wives.

"I cannot!" she whispered, her hand on her own belly. *She would not go through that!*

The man grabbed her by the forearm. "You *must*, my lady, or I will march directly to Gloucester and tell him that you refused his wife aid."

Margaret tore her arm out of his grip. "There must be someone else —"

"The Duchess has asked for *you*, my lady."

"But —"

"You *will* attend her, my lady."

There was something in the man's voice, a quiet anger and determination, that told Margaret that he would drag her into the Duchess' birthing chamber if necessary.

Margaret jerked her head in assent, her face set, and the man escorted her towards Gloucester's apartment.

Margaret took a deep breath, then entered the chamber.

Eleanor was calmly walking about the central space of the room, both hands clutched to her sides.

She turned and smiled as Margaret entered. "Ah, I am glad that Walter found you, Margaret. I —"

Eleanor broke off suddenly, her face stilling and paling, and Margaret froze halfway across the floor. The Duchess moaned, closed her eyes, then reopened them, relaxing as the contraction faded.

She looked at Margaret searchingly. "Why so afraid, Margaret? I have birthed three daughters before this. No doubt this child will slither out as easily."

Margaret took a deep breath and tried to relax. Eleanor was right — she had given birth before, and easily at that. There was nothing to be afraid of.

Besides, wouldn't it be best if she went into her own birthing time the better prepared for the experience?

XVII

After Nones on All Souls Day
In the fifty-first year of the reign of Edward III
(late afternoon Tuesday 2nd November 1378)

— ii —

Thomas had managed two hours sleep, and was still scratchy-eyed and irritable as he wandered aimlessly through the narrow, dark streets of Chauvigny. He couldn't find Bolingbroke anywhere, and Raby was, apparently, still closeted with the Black Prince.

There was nothing to do save wander about and look for some amusement.

In itself, that wander had more than enough to interest Thomas. He'd spent too many years as a nobleman not to feel at home in a military environment. Most of the men he paused by were eager enough to chat, and to explain the slight changes in the armour or weapons they carried since Thomas had last ridden to battle.

But there was something wrong, and Thomas couldn't quite work out what it was. It seemed almost as if an invisible miasma had settled over the fortress. A tension. Or was it just him?

"Ah," Thomas mumbled, walking towards a group of

men-at-arms standing about a fire in a small courtyard outside their quarters. "I should have had more sleep."

No ... it wasn't that, and Thomas knew it. He stopped suddenly, as he realised what it was. He felt *needed*, as if someone, somewhere, was calling his name, holding out a desperate hand towards him ...

"Tom! Tom!"

Thomas blinked, and focused on the figure waving to him from the circle of men.

Sweet Jesu! It was Wat Tyler!

Well, that was good. Thomas knew he needed to talk more with the man to see if he could discover his true nature. Demon, demon-controlled, or just plain misguided? A part of Thomas wanted it to be the latter. He and Wat had been close when Thomas was a youth, but time, physical separation and Thomas' holy vows had put a considerable distance between them — nothing demonstrated that more than their meeting in Rome.

Thomas wondered that he hadn't thought about seeking Wat out before this. Wat Tyler had long been Lancaster's man, and it made sense that he was here. Wherever there was a battle, and Lancaster, there would be Wat.

Thomas walked slowly over towards the group of men, wondering about Wat's connection with Lancaster. Should the Black Prince and Lancaster know of the imp they sheltered within their midst? But if he told the princes that ... then he must perforce tell them all.

Thomas slowed even further as another thought occurred to him: Wat had said that Lancaster agreed with the heretical words of Wycliffe.

Who was the imp, Wat ... or Lancaster?

"It is good to see you back within the company of good men," Wat said as Thomas finally joined him. Wat gestured about the circle. Most were free commoners, trained in the arts of sword and lance, who rode in units to back up the knights in battle.

"These are all home county men," Wat said, smiling gently at his companions, "men of my own heart."

Thomas glanced at Wat sharply. *Men of his own heart? Men of heretical inclination?*

He looked back at the circle of watchful eyes — most of the men had some form of chain mail or plate armour on, and all had a weapon ready to hand — and found one among them who was not a soldier at arms.

Thomas nodded to the man, standing just behind the shoulders of two of the men-at-arms.

"Good priest," Thomas said, "I am glad to see you here, ministering to the souls of these soldiers. From what parish do you hail?"

The priest, his robes slightly dishevelled, stepped forward so he could address Thomas directly.

"I come from London, friar. And my parish is the betterment of all good Englishmen."

Thomas frowned. What kind of answer was that? And the priest had no tonsure! His dark brown hair was grown long and curly over his scalp — this man had not shaved a tonsure for many months — and his black eyes burned with a fanatical light that Thomas immediately distrusted.

"My name is John Ball," the priest said, smiling a little at Thomas' obvious distaste, "and I am a true priest."

"What do you mean?"

"He means," Wat said, "that he ministers for the good of our souls, not for the betterment of the Church. Do you understand my meaning, Tom?"

"There is no difference," Thomas said, and would have said more, save that the entire circle of men had burst into laughter.

"The Church strives for *nothing* but its own betterment, friar!" said one man. "So long as we pay our tithes, and mortuary taxes, and coins on feast days and for every service the local priest provides us, then our souls can go to hell for all the Church cares."

"That's sacrilege!" Thomas said. "The Church is —"

"The Church is a fat, lumbering cow," said another. "It cares only for itself, and not for us. I give *that*," he spat into the centre of the circle, "for your *Roman* Church."

"John," said yet another, moving closer to the priest and placing a hand on his shoulder, "cares for our welfare *before* that of the Church. He is our friend, and our helpmeet. He does not speak to us of hell, only of the beauties of salvation."

"The Church brings you salvation, no thing nor no one else!" Thomas said. How far had this rot spread?

"All a man or a woman needs for salvation," John Ball said quietly, "is an understanding of God's word as written in the Scriptures. We don't need a bevy of fat, bejewelled clerics to interpret it for us!"

"This is Wycliffe's doing!" Thomas said.

"Nay, Tom," Wat said quietly. "This is the workings of the mind of any free man. Wycliffe only speaks what many men already believe."

Thomas, his face flushed, was about to say more when a shout halted him.

Everyone looked. A frantic soldier ran towards the group.

"Brother Thomas! Brother Thomas!"

He reached them, and gripped Thomas' sleeve. "The Duchess Eleanor lies a-dying. She has asked for you ... to take her last confession ..."

Thomas stared at him, then without looking at the circle of men, he broke into a run, remembering his earlier feeling that someone, somewhere, had been reaching out for him.

"The Duchess would have done far better," Wat said, watching Thomas' retreating figure, "to ask for a flask of good brandy-wine so that she can see out her last hours in a fog of happiness, instead of a damned Dominican who will speak to her of nothing but the horrors of hell."

Then his face went expressionless as a terrible thought occurred to him.

Was Meg with the Duchess? Oh, sweet Meg, how fare you?

Margaret was trapped by the painful grip of Eleanor's hand; if the Duchess had not held on to her she would have fled long before this.

Eleanor was bleeding to death before her eyes.

She had been in labour a mere twelve hours, but in those hours the pain had worsened until the woman lay writhing and screaming about her bed, and in those twelve the babe had not shifted for all the effort its mother put into its birthing.

The midwife was still nowhere to be found, and Margaret knew that if she ever found the woman, she would personally string her up from the nearest tree.

About midday Eleanor had begun to bleed. At first it was little more than a showing of blood-stained fluid that Margaret hoped indicated that the baby was finally ready to be born, but within the hour this innocuous fluid had become thick blood that clotted and congealed among the twisting sheets.

Neither Margaret, nor the duchess' waiting lady, Mary, had known what to do — and Eleanor herself had panicked at the sight of so much blood.

She had begun to scream, and her screams and writhings had only ceased after two hours when she'd become pale and clammy with the constant loss of blood.

She had clutched at Margaret's hands. "You must save me. I don't want to die ... I don't want to die."

All Margaret could do was to offer useless words. What else could she do?

She'd never had any experience at this kind of birth ... it was so different ... so different ...

"Where is the midwife?" Eleanor whispered.

"Madam, I don't know." *And if the midwife was here, then could she do anything?*

Eleanor lapsed into silence, her skin now grey and cold, her eyes dull, her belly humping reproachfully towards the peak of the chamber. Every so often Mary would take the blood-clotted linens from under Eleanor's body and replace them with fresh ones.

They would be soaked as soon as Mary drew back the sheet to preserve Eleanor's modesty.

Why all this trouble to birth a child? Margaret thought,

cold and shaking with horror. *Why does God make them suffer so?*

Is this what I must go through?

Finally, Eleanor whispered for a priest, asking for Thomas by name, and Margaret screamed through the chamber door for someone to fetch Thomas.

Why Eleanor wanted Thomas of all people, Margaret could not fathom.

Eleanor's pain and suffering was hard enough for her to witness — and especially since Margaret knew that she, too, would have to go through the same in a few short months — but the very worst thing was that no one could help the duchess.

I will not go through this! Margaret thought over and over. *I will not go through this! I care not for the danger, but I will not go through this. I must find my own place, alone, and give birth in the way of my own.*

"My lady?"

Margaret looked up, consciously having to fight to focus on the woman across the bed.

Mary looked almost as bad as Margaret felt, and neither could look at the silent, death-cold woman between them any more.

"My lady," Mary said, "we should say a prayer —"

"I will *not* say a prayer to a God who needs us to beg Him to aid her!" Margaret said. "Why has He allowed Eleanor to suffer so? Didn't she say *enough* prayers to prepare for this moment? *What more could God want from her?*"

"What the Duchess does *not* want," said Thomas directly behind Margaret — she had not even heard him enter the chamber, "is such impious anger surrounding her. She is *dying*, woman, and you should at least aid her to prepare to meet her God if you could not aid her to birth her child!"

Eleanor stirred on the bed, and her grip loosened about Margaret's hand as she caught sight of Thomas. Margaret tore her hand loose, and backed away.

"Brother!" Eleanor whispered. "I thank God you have come."

Margaret slowly inched towards the entrance of the chamber, her eyes still riveted on the dying woman.

She would not go through that! She would not!

Thomas turned about and stared at her. "Margaret, Eleanor needs your prayers! Get back here!"

"I can't," Margaret whispered, staring at Eleanor's form, once more writhing weakly. "I can't!"

And then she turned and fled.

Thomas turned back to the woman, then glanced at Mary, still hovering impotently the other side of the bed. "Fetch my Lord of Gloucester. *Now!*"

As Mary fled, Thomas' face lost its harshness and became soft and compassionate, and he bent down to Eleanor — crying with relief now — and took her final confession.

By the time Gloucester arrived, he was too late to say his final farewells to his wife.

XVIII

Compline on All Souls Day
In the fifty-first year of the reign of Edward III
(night Tuesday 2nd November 1378)

— iii —

Thomas entered the chamber quietly, and largely
unobserved, save by the guards who had nodded him
through.

It was long past dusk: Thomas had spent many hours by
the Duchess' corpse, praying for the salvation of both her
and her child. Gloucester had spent perhaps an hour of that
time with his wife as well, and had then left, stony-faced
with grief and, from what Thomas could see, anger.

That anger was the reason Thomas was here now. He had
not been able to simply walk back to his own quarters
without seeing where Gloucester might direct it.

He stopped just inside the entrance of the chamber, not
yet wanting to be observed. Gloucester was standing before
a brazier, Raby looking uncomfortable and irritated in equal
amounts to one side, the Black Prince in a chair well back in
the shadows, resting his head in one hand as he watched
silently.

Gloucester's face was thin, sensitive, and, currently,
infused with anger. Thomas knew that look well. Most of

the Plantagenet men were tall, sturdy and fair with open and hard faces. Only a few, perhaps harkening back to some timid foreign bride, were born with Gloucester's thin and sensitive mien that often indicated a passion for letters and music. Gloucester was patron of a number of artists and colleges, kept a large and continually expanding library, and could always be relied upon for a philosophical discussion to while away the long, dark hours.

Unfortunately, this sensitivity also generally hid a narrow and intolerant character — and this Gloucester was demonstrating amply now.

Margaret stood before Gloucester, her head bowed, her hands, from what Thomas could see, folded before her. Her hair hung down behind her in a long, thick twist that glinted gold as a lamp high above swung gently in the movement of air caused by the opening and closing of the door. Some part of Thomas' mind also noted that Margaret wore the same pale grey gown he had originally seen her in, and then he realised she had never worn anything else. From his vantage point, and with the light of several lamps shining on Margaret's back, Thomas could see that the seams running down the back of the gown had been repaired and restitched many times.

Thomas frowned. Surely Raby could have dressed his mistress with more care?

"If you had cared better for her then my wife would yet live!" Gloucester said, and Thomas saw that Margaret's shoulders visibly jerked.

"My lord," she said, her voice low and tremulous — was she truly frightened, Thomas thought, or just feigning? — "I am not a midwife, and —"

"Then where was the midwife? Why did you not see that my wife had the care she needed?"

"My lord, I sent for her, but she could not be found!"

"You sent for her? Is that all you can say? Ah!"

"My lord —"

"I will hear no more of your excuses! If you could not find the midwife, then why did you not tear the fortress apart? Why did you not send for me ... my God, woman, I would have mobilised half the army to find her! And when you realised the midwife would not easily be found — and I am not convinced that you made effort to locate her at all — then why not send to one of the closer villages for one of their midwives? God curse you woman, the countryside is crawling with peasants and it must therefore be crawling with midwives to tend their women. Well? Well?"

Margaret shuddered, and sank to her knees. "My lord, I did not think. I was so frightened myself, I did not know what to do —"

"It was your responsibility to know what to do!" Gloucester took a step forward, and raised a hand. Margaret cowered, and Raby made a move as if he would also step forward, then caught himself and melted back into the shadows.

The Black Prince narrowed his eyes, but otherwise made no move.

"My Duchess, and the heir she carried, are dead — and dead because of you!"

Gloucester lifted his hand higher, his face now twisted with hate and retribution.

"My Lord of Gloucester, if anyone should be blamed for the Duchess' death, then surely you should shoulder your share."

Gloucester halted, his eyes raging at the man who now stepped forward.

Margaret tensed, as if she could not believe she'd heard aright.

Thomas strolled forward, hardly believing himself that he'd intervened, especially on behalf of the witch. But something in the scene seriously disturbed him: whether it was Gloucester with his intolerant anger, or his uncle, apparently too afraid of losing favour with the Plantagenet princes to aid the woman he bedded. Raby wasn't slow to defend her against me, Thomas thought, but he would sacrifice her to princely anger.

Besides, the manner of the Duchess' death smacked of

inexperience and some poor or unthinking decisions — not of the malevolent witchcraft Thomas might otherwise have suspected of Margaret. Sweet Jesu! Even a clumsy village midwife could manage the murder of a woman in childbed more competently!

"What did you say?" Gloucester whispered.

Thomas walked completely into the lamplight, glancing at Margaret as he walked past her.

"My Lord of Gloucester," he said, easily holding the prince's furious stare, "every husband has a burden of duty to his wife: to protect her, and to serve her best interests in every way he can. Any husband who brings his wife, close to term with a child, into an army camp, and then does not personally ensure that she would be well cared for, with experienced midwives constantly on hand, has failed dismally in that duty."

"Thomas," the Black Prince said quietly from his shadowed chair. He was now leaning forward slightly. "You speak out of place. Contain yourself."

"I will not!" Thomas said, his own eyes snapping with anger now. "The Lady Rivers was clearly negligent, but she was frightened and she was inexperienced. She was not the right woman to entrust a beloved wife's confinement to, Gloucester. She was a bad choice — but she was *your* choice, through your inaction, if not your spoken decision. What was your Duchess doing birthing your child in an army encampment? Why did you not ensure that she was surrounded with midwives who could be trusted not to wander off seeking pleasures elsewhere?"

Thomas glanced at the Black Prince. "I did not speak out of place, my lord. I was the one to hear the Duchess' final confession, and her last words." Thomas swung his eyes back to the man before him. "My Lord of Gloucester, the Lady Eleanor did not speak of you. Rather, she asked me to console the Lady Margaret who will, in a few months, be approaching her own confinement. The Duchess felt badly that the manner of her own death should so severely affect the Lady Margaret."

Margaret dropped her face into her hands, mortified that she should have abandoned Eleanor.

Gloucester slowly, finally, lowered his hand, but his face was still enraged — his anger now focused on Thomas rather than Margaret.

"I will not forget this, priest," he said quietly.

"We have more important things to be concerned about," said a voice from the entrance, "than who should have sent for the midwife, and when."

Hal of Bolingbroke strolled into the chamber. "My Lady of Gloucester's death is a tragedy," he said, "but for the moment the dictates of war must banish our tears. I have received intelligence from the north." He paused. "Paris is burning."

He glanced at Margaret. "Lady Rivers, you may leave us."

Her face red and shiny with tears and lingering shame, Margaret rose shakily to her feet and fled the chamber.

As she did so, and as most eyes followed her stumbling progress, Hal leaned close to Thomas.

"I am glad to see that my friend has not completely disappeared beneath the cold clerical exterior," he whispered. "That was well done, Tom, and I do thank you."

XIX

The Feast of St Felicity
In the fifty-first year of the reign of Edward III
(Tuesday 23rd November 1378)

— i —

According to Bolingbroke's spies, within a week of Thomas' departure towards Chauvigny Philip and Charles had combined forces in order to regain control of Paris, although whether or not they had managed this successfully was as yet unclear. Whatever, now Philip wanted to push the negotiations, necessarily somewhat secret, with the Black Prince to determine who would gain the French throne. The Black Prince must have received Philip's offer through Thomas by this stage, and Philip would appreciate some response.

Responding was not a simple affair. Messengers had to travel back and forth between Philip and Chauvigny in order to organise a meeting place mutually acceptable to both Philip and Edward.

The haggling over the site itself was a delicate affair, let alone who to bring as escort and advisers and witnesses, what safeguards to have in place to ensure safety and secrecy, and what courtly niceties needed to be observed. Who could be trusted? What alternate arrangements could be made in case of treachery (almost certain treachery, Lancaster observed, in the case of Philip)?

For almost four weeks the two sides bickered and planned, until even the Black Prince's temper frayed and he was heard to mutter on at least one occasion that the French throne was not worth this much trouble. Whatever, the four weeks meant that at least one option was closed to Edward: it was now too close to winter to even consider pushing forward on his own. The delay reduced his choices to two: ally with Philip and smash Charles into the ground ... or winter it out in Chauvigny and recommence the campaign in the spring against a possibly revitalised French army.

In the end the Black Prince acquiesced to Philip's preferred meeting place: an abandoned quarry three miles south of the heavily fortified town of Chatellerault which was itself some twenty miles north of Chauvigny. Philip must travel the furthest, but Chatellerault was not English-controlled, and many within the English camp felt the quarry was a little too close to the town for complete comfort.

The quarry was easily approached across cleared land that stretched for almost a mile in either direction: neither Philip nor the Black Prince would be able to secrete forces in order to ambush the opposing force. The quarry was not open-cut, but consisted of vast underground chambers and tunnels, as so many French quarries did. It had two entrances: one north, which Philip would use, and one to the south-east, which the Black Prince would use. The respective tunnels converged some two hundred feet underground in a great vaulted chamber. When the mine had been operational this chamber had, in turn, branched off into a myriad of other tunnels that led to the chambers where rock was actually mined, but some twenty years ago the floor of this chamber had collapsed into a vast natural cavern which lay beneath it. Now the floor of the cavern was little more than a great, gaping hole that plunged hundreds of feet into the earth. Edward and Philip would have to shout ungraciously at each other over its yawning depths, but at least both would feel some measure of safety at its presence.

Finally, the date was agreed: the Feast of St Felicity. The attendants were agreed. The Black Prince would enter the quarry with only a token force of eight attendants — six men-at-arms, Hal of Bolingbroke and Thomas — although he could leave a larger force to guard the entrance. It had been a difficult decision for the Black Prince as to who to include in the small company allowed inside the quarry. Lancaster, Gloucester and Raby all demanded to attend the Black Prince, as did numerous other nobles. But Edward had not wanted to risk any of them; Bolingbroke would serve as a suitable noble attendant who also knew Philip well from his youth, and Edward had wanted Thomas along as well. The friar, like Bolingbroke, not only knew Philip well, but had recently been in the north of France, and would know better than most whether or not Philip mouthed truth or lies.

Since the scene with Gloucester, Thomas had found himself mildly ostracised by the higher nobility. He'd spoken nothing but truth to Gloucester, and all knew it, but he had spoken harsh words to one of Edward III's sons, and few wanted to ally themselves with a man who had deeply offended one of the Plantagenets. After all, everyone had their own causes to nurture.

Nevertheless, Thomas was not completely proscribed. Bolingbroke kept him company for a number of hours each day, and both the Black Prince and Lancaster, although outwardly chiding Thomas for his outspokenness, also made it apparent that they believed it a husband's duty to ensure his wife had the safest lying-in she could. The Black Prince was well known for his devotion to his wife, Joan of Kent, and Lancaster had adored his first wife, Blanche of Lancaster. His second wife, Constance of Castile, may not have been adored, but at least Lancaster had provided her with everything she'd needed for the birth of their two daughters, and Thomas well knew the love and care Lancaster lavished on his long-time mistress, Katherine Swynford, and their two children.

Thomas had every reason to believe that, in the privacy of

their own brotherly company, both the Black Prince and Lancaster would have had their own harsh words for Gloucester. A wife — especially one with child — was to be cherished and protected.

The two elder Plantagenet princes might treat him with some degree of coldness in public (which also, it must be said, extended in some measure to their private dialogues), but he knew that the Black Prince and his immediate advisers needed Thomas' own intelligence — even intuition — in regard to Philip of Navarre. Thomas was needed, he was useful, and he would not be made the complete outcast.

Besides, Thomas *was* hiding something. The Black Prince and Lancaster, as Bolingbroke, could almost smell his secretiveness. He knew *something* of great import. Why else had he abandoned St Angelo's friary and scampered through the German states and then through half of France, and why else would the Prior General seek aid from almost every nobleman in the western half of Europe to capture him?

The princes, as Raby, had questioned Thomas at great length. And yet, while Thomas had *apparently* answered their queries in candid detail, especially as regards the events he encountered in northern France, Thomas had managed to evade every attempt to discover the reason he had been travelling in the first instance. It was the business of the Church, he would say, and shrug and smile with great charm, and would then further shrug off the observation that it must *not* be the Church's business if the Church was trying so desperately to get him back within its clutches.

"Then it is the Lord's business," Thomas would say, and then would refuse to be drawn further, folding his arms and sliding his hands deep within the sleeves of his robe, and holding the furious princes' gazes with irritating coolness.

At that the Black Prince and Lancaster would lock eyes. *Damn to hell every cleric's assurance that he could brush aside the needs and demands of secular princes!*

Thomas had seen very little of Margaret during the weeks spent negotiating meeting arrangements with Philip. Raby had kept her within his own chamber and, as Thomas now shared quarters with Bolingbroke and, further, was not encouraged to visit his uncle (who Thomas now realised was busily allying himself with the Plantagenets for a reason he could not yet fathom), he had little reason to see her.

Well, he cared little for that. If she was a witch, then she was ineffectual and could largely be ignored. She had been right when she said to Thomas that there was no danger he would lose his soul to her, because Thomas knew that there would never be a time when he would offer it.

She was safe, kept under close scrutiny within Raby's quarters, and Thomas bothered himself little more about her.

What did fret him was the delay in returning to England. Patently, the Black Prince and Lancaster knew he was hiding something, but Thomas was not prepared to trust them with the details — who could he trust? The encounter with the renegade priest, John Ball, had shaken him, as had the realisation that the even-worse-than-renegade priest, John Wycliffe, held a powerful position at court. If heresies were tolerated within court, then Thomas was going to trust no one with his knowledge until he knew who he could have confidence in, and who not.

Unfortunately, that meant that he was not going to be released back to England (and there to the heavy care of Prior General Thoreseby, who would also have to be placated) until the Black Prince and Lancaster believed they had prised every last piece of information out of him that they could.

So Thomas was left to fret in Chauvigny, while waiting to ride to the rendezvous with Philip. He tried reasoning that the demons had already had some thirty years to locate Wynkyn de Worde's casket for themselves, and a few months here and there would make little difference.

On the other hand, they might make all the difference in the world ...

He saw neither demon nor St Michael, but the demons would hardly dare show themselves in their true form amongst the many thousands of men encamped within

Chauvigny and St Michael had no reason to appear. Thomas had his mission, and it was up to him to accomplish it.

Neither did Thomas see Wat Tyler or John Ball during these weeks. Tyler had, apparently, been sent by Lancaster on some mission into the surrounding countryside, and Ball had just ... vanished.

Perhaps, Thomas wondered, he had melted into the thick forests, there to revel with his fellow demons.

Sweet Christ Saviour, how many demons had infiltrated the English court?

And who? Who?

Finally, after so many weeks of waiting, fretting and delicate manoeuvring, Thomas was riding towards the disused quarry surrounded by the six men-at-arms while Bolingbroke and the Black Prince rode slightly ahead. Behind them rode another group of fifty men-at-arms; these men would not progress down the tunnel with the smaller party, but remain as guard to its entrance. The Black Prince's larger escort of a further one hundred men had stayed in camp.

Thomas smiled at the thought of meeting the King of Navarre underground — Philip had ever had a warped sense of humour, and Thomas wondered at the persuasions Philip must have used to make the Black Prince agree to the arrangement.

Perhaps Edward was just the slightest bit curious — he was certainly eager to speak with Philip and hear what he had to say. The English camp was still divided about what to do: ally with Philip and risk his well-known penchant for treachery, or push forward in the spring after waiting out the winter in Chauvigny.

Whatever, this meeting would decide Edward one way or the other.

The day was blustery and grey; winter was closing in. All the horses were skittish, shying and snorting at the leaves and dried vegetation that blew across their paths, and the men had to concentrate as much on keeping their seats as they did on the meeting ahead.

All, save Thomas, were arrayed in armour. The Black Prince and Bolingbroke wore plate armour covering chain mail over their torsos and limbs — both had tunics bearing their respective coats-of-arms over their armour — and visored and considerably bejewelled basinets on their heads. For their part, the men-at-arms (as the fifty riding some twenty paces behind this small group) had metal breast plates over chain mail, and round iron helmets on their heads. The horses, again save for Thomas' gelding, were similarly arrayed in battle gear with shaffrons covering their heads, and peytrals covering their chest. The coat-of-arms of the Black Prince had been embroidered into the hangings that covered the rumps of all horses save Bolingbroke's, which carried his own heraldic devices.

Thomas did not envy them one bit: riding this fast and this distance (although they had come the larger part of the way between Chauvigny and the quarry the previous day) in full armour and in biting wind and difficult conditions would not be easy. For once, Thomas was glad of his simple, yet thick and comfortable robes; only his feet, still clad in open sandals, were cold.

It lacked an hour to midday by the time they approached the quarry.

The Black Prince called a halt, and for several minutes he and Bolingbroke sat their horses, looking intently across the landscape for traps.

Eventually, the Black Prince waved his small retinue forward.

"Thomas!" he called. "Come ride behind me!"

Thomas pushed his gelding forward until he rode a pace or two behind the Black Prince. Bolingbroke acknowledged his presence with a small movement of his helmeted head, but the Black Prince made no sign.

The entrance to the quarry came into view when they were about a quarter of a mile away. The trail sloped down into a great cutting, disappearing into a blackness that would have been all-consuming save that the approaching group could see the first flicker of torches inside.

They halted some fifteen paces from the entrance. "I like it not," said Bolingbroke. "It could be a trap."

"Wait," the Black Prince said.

Bolingbroke shot Thomas what Thomas thought was probably a worried look, although he could not see the man's expression beneath his closed visor, and began to say something, but just then there was a movement at the entrance of the tunnel, and Bolingbroke, as everyone else, stared forwards.

A man in chain mail, leather tunic and round and visorless iron helmet had stepped forth and was now waving his arm.

"Tyler!" Bolingbroke said.

The Black Prince nodded. "Aye. Lancaster sent him forward some time ago to provide some degree of protection. If Tyler indicates that the tunnel is safe, then it is safe."

"My lord," Thomas said, kneeing his horse forward. "Is Tyler entirely trustworthy?"

The Black Prince turned his metal-clad face towards Thomas. "Do you have something to say about Tyler that you think I should know? Well, speak up, man!"

Thomas hesitated. What should he say — that Tyler was likely in consort with demon-controlled men, might even be a demon himself?

"Tyler has strange thoughts," he said, and then wished he'd kept his mouth shut.

Bolingbroke laughed. "Tyler is Tyler, and the man has ever had a strange mouth about him. Nevertheless," Bolingbroke's voice hardened, "I would trust Tyler with my life."

"As would I," the Black Prince added, and then he spurred his horse forward, Bolingbroke to his right and just slightly behind.

Frowning, Thomas followed them, the men-at-arms a heartbeat behind him.

"The way is clear, my lords!" Wat called as they approached. "And the black-hearted King of Navarre is already in position."

The Black Prince raised a mailed hand, but did not slow his mount. "I thank you!" he called, and was then past in a scattering of loose dirt and pebbles thrown up by his horse's hooves.

Thomas tried to measure the expression on Wat's face, but only had the hazy impression of bright eyes and a slight smile as he, too, rode past.

The tunnel was wide and lit with torches, although the incline became steeper as they progressed, and the party had to slow their horses to a sliding walk.

The air was dank, far colder than the outside, and Thomas huddled deeper within his robes while still keeping a wary eye out for traps: he was not going to trust Tyler.

And yet had he not trusted Tyler with his life on many occasions in the past?

No, no, Tyler was likely no longer the same man. He spoke of social disorder and rebellion — he had spoken demon-inspired thoughts.

But there was no place from which hidden troops — or even demons — could launch an ambush. The walls of the tunnel were smooth and solid, and there were no subsidiary tunnels branching off this main one. The fifty men-at-arms had been left at the entrance to provide some warning of a force moving in behind them. Even if the men were overwhelmed (and that was unlikely, as the fifty were battle-hardened and suspicious of eye), then the sound of ringing steel should carry down through the quarry.

They should also, Thomas hoped, be able to keep a potentially dangerous Wat Tyler under some control.

Slowly the incline levelled out a little, and the group urged their horses into a trot. The air was stale and smoky from the torches, shadows flitted across man, beast and walls alike as if a cloud of great moths whispered overhead.

It was an atmosphere carefully calculated to menace. What was Philip's purpose?

The horses had to be kept on a tight rein lest they shied and threw a rider, and the men found they were having to ride knee to knee as the tunnel walls closed in.

Bolingbroke murmured something ahead, and even though Thomas did not catch the individual words, he knew what Hal had said: *I like this not.*

Almost as soon as Hal had spoken, they rode into the cavern that, while not much wider than the tunnel, was some forty or fifty feet high.

In its centre was the yawning mouth of the collapsed floor that plunged down into the unknown.

Did it touch hell itself? wondered Thomas.

In the cavern's far distance were a panoply of blazing torches lighting Philip of Navarre and his retinue. Although the numbers of Philip's men matched the Black Prince's, they gave the impression of far more, for they were arrayed in unmarked white steel armour that had been polished to mirror brightness, and shafts of light from the torches glanced off them and leapt unbounded about the cavern until Philip and his men were surrounded by a golden brilliance.

Philip himself was sitting his destrier to the front of his men, the horse's hooves almost at the edge of the great void. As were his men, he was clad in mirrored steel, and only the golden crown atop his basinet differentiated king from nobleman. His visor was raised, and his handsome face grinned cheerfully. He clutched something in the front of his saddle, but the gap was too wide for any among the Black Prince's party to see what it was.

"Hail, Edward!" Philip called, and lifted his right arm in greeting.

The Black Prince pulled his horse to a halt opposite Philip, and raised his visor. Bolingbroke did the same.

"Philip," the Black Prince said, nodding, and keeping his face impassive. "This is a pretty display."

Philip's grin stretched wider, and he laughed, although it sounded forced.

"You have brought Hal with you," Philip said, "and Thomas. Thomas! Well met, my fellow!"

Thomas nodded from his position directly behind Edward and Bolingbroke — the space between their horses was wide enough to give him a clear view of Philip, as Philip had of him — but did not speak.

"Did you have a pleasant ride?" Philip said.

"Enough!" the Black Prince replied, and Thomas suddenly realised that Edward was very tense, and his face very pinched.

And how tired? The man had just endured two days hard riding, and was not well to begin with.

Philip shrugged. "As you wish. Did Tom relate to you my offer?"

Edward nodded.

"Then what say you, my friend? Do we," he laughed again, "shake hands on the deal? Do we ride together against pretty boy Charlie?"

"I do not think you truly want my response," the Black Prince said, "else you would have picked a fine meadow where we could have shaken hands on the deal. I think, Philip, you do not want to shake hands on it at all."

"Ah," Philip said, "what a suspicious mind. Don't you want to ally yourself with me?"

"I do not trust you, Philip."

Philip affected a distraught expression. "You do not trust me? But —"

"There is no one in Christendom who trusts you Philip, and no one knows that better than yourself. You wanted to see me, and you wanted to say something. What? Not to deal, I think."

Philip's face hardened. "Nay. I do not wish to 'deal' with you, Edward. I wish to inform you of my decision, and I wanted to do that face-to-face. I knew you would appreciate hearing it from my own mouth.

"Edward, most renowned Black Prince, the French have grown mightily disaffected with your incursions into their beloved lands. I have listened to their pleas —"

The Black Prince grunted.

"— and have granted their wishes. I have decided to leave behind any thought of gain —"

Now the Black Prince managed a laugh.

"— and have decided to ally myself with Prince Charles, grandson of the kidnapped King John, and rid this beauteous land of your filthy presence. We —"

"How much did he offer, Philip?" the Black Prince said in a quiet voice that cut across Philip's.

"Offer?"

"Damn you, Philip!" Bolingbroke called, his mount shifting uneasily. "How much did you sell out for?"

"I cannot 'sell out' my own land!" Philip said.

"And how long do you think your 'alliance' will last?" the Black Prince said. "How long before one or the other of you decides the crown of France is within reach and it is time to strike out on your own?"

"Our alliance is God-blessed!" Philip shouted. "We know so!"

"And how is that?" the Black Prince said. "Did He speak to you Himself, or did you bribe one or the other of the popes to speak on His behalf?"

A chill ran down Thomas' spine, and he suddenly realised what Philip would say next.

"We have heard the word of God from a saintly damsel," Philip cried. "She performs miracles in our presence. God will protect the French, and cast out from this land the evil English stench that assails us. I fight on the side of God! I fight on the side of God, not *you*, corruption!"

Both the Black Prince and Bolingbroke tried to smile, but could not. They did not want to believe Philip's words, but there had been such an underlying ring of fanaticism in them that —

Thomas urged his horse close to those of the Black Prince and Bolingbroke.

"Believe him!" he hissed quietly. "I know who this girl is! I know who he speaks of."

The Black Prince stared at him for a heartbeat, then looked back to Philip.

"Your alliance will not hold. You do not have the men to fight back an army that is —"

"Wrong!" Philip said. "We have already performed a

miracle, as the damsel said we would. Between us, Charles and I have retaken Paris and the regions beyond that had rebelled! We control northern France, cur, and soon we will control all of our country!"

"How can we believe you?" Bolingbroke yelled.

Philip smiled, hard and cold. "I am more than glad you touted Thomas along with you," he said, "for he can verify the truth of what I now show you."

Suddenly Philip hefted a black bag from the front of his saddle, and the next instant it was sailing the distance between them.

It landed with a thud between the horses, and all three men had to struggle to control their mounts.

"Thomas," the Black Prince said quietly.

Thomas dismounted, giving the reins of his horse into the outstretched hand of the Black Prince. He walked slowly up to the bag, and he saw that it was black with blood, not dye.

He knew what he would find.

Gingerly he undid the thong about the neck of the bag, and tipped out its contents.

Marcel's head, his eyes staring lifelessly into eternity, rolled out.

"Who was he?" said the Black Prince.

"Etienne Marcel," said Thomas. "He was the ringleader of the Parisian rebels. If he is dead then Paris has indeed fallen."

He looked up, and was surprised to see Hal staring at the head with a tightly-controlled expression as if hiding deep emotion.

Why? Hal could not have known Marcel . . .

"Aye," Philip called across the space. "Paris has fallen, and the north is under our control. Why, Edward, I even have eight thousand men-at-arms in Chatellerault. Should I grow bored this winter, I might be tempted to sally forth to visit you at Chauvigny. Perhaps to toast wassail together? What say you?"

Edward did nothing but stare: *eight thousand men at Chatellerault? Sweet Jesu!*

"Charles sends his regards," Philip continued. "And says

that you may keep his grandfather. At John's age he won't stay ransomable for long!"

And then, laughing, Philip whipped his horse's head about, motioned to his escort, and with a clatter of hooves and a final glinting of golden light, was gone.

XX

After Nones on the Feast of St Felicity
In the fifty-first year of the reign of Edward III
(early afternoon Tuesday 23rd November 1378)

— ii —

The Black Prince halted his entourage the moment they rode back into the open light. He waited until all the men were out of the tunnel, and until the fifty who had waited just outside its mouth — as well as Wat Tyler, who had recovered his own mount from some hiding place — had formed a protective ring about the core party, then he wheeled his destrier's head to the south and spurred him forward.

Bolingbroke pushed his own horse forward, Thomas riding by his side, and the escort fell in behind.

The Black Prince turned slightly to make sure that all was in order, and spoke quickly to Thomas. "When we get back to the main camp, Thomas, you are going to tell us *who* this saintly damsel is that has inspired Charles and the damned Philip."

Then he faced forward again, and urged his mount to greater speed, thundering south across the rolling low hills.

They rode without a break for about an hour, until close to mid-afternoon. Then the Black Prince, still leading, slowed his horses and looked about wonderingly: the day was darkening as if the sun was about to set, but surely there were still some few hours until dusk?

Thomas and Hal, just behind the prince, likewise slowed, and Thomas turned to look behind him.

There were only three men-at arms to be seen. All the others had apparently vanished into a roiling cloud that swept up behind them.

He whipped forward again. "My lord! My lord!"

For a moment he thought the Black Prince hadn't heard, but then the man halted his horse and turned to look.

The prince began to speak, then halted, his mouth partway open as he stared beyond the small group of riders who still accompanied him.

Thomas and Bolingbroke pulled their mounts to a halt, the remaining three men-at-arms with them.

"What has happened to the rest of the escort?" the Black Prince said, his sharp eyes moving between Thomas and Bolingbroke, and then to the other three men. "And what is this mist?"

No one answered immediately, all apparently as shocked as the prince that over fifty men had so easily vanished.

And so quietly.

Edward looked about. The first tendrils of mist were creeping around them now, and they would be enveloped within a few minutes.

"Ah!" the prince said. "We have another hour's riding before us before we reach our camp for the night, and I have no yearning to sit here waiting for that damp fog to envelop us completely. The men will have to find their own way. They no doubt fell behind, and became disorientated ... I have heard no ring of steel, nor the sounds of a battle.

"Come." He waved their small group forward, but rode only at a trot now. The mist was all about them, and to ride faster would risk a horse breaking a leg in a ditch or burrow.

Thomas rode a little closer to Bolingbroke, meaning to ask the man if he was well, for his face seemed pale, and his eyes introspective, when there was a shout from one of the men-at-arms.

"Ware! Ware! Ware to the left!"

Every eye swung in the direction the man pointed.

They were riding through uncultivated grasslands, the dry brown stalks of the meadow reaching almost to the horse's bellies.

Through this tall grass shapes were moving, perhaps some ten paces away in the mist.

Large shapes, tawny, and as fast as the horses.

"And there!" Bolingbroke said, pointing in the opposite direction — they were surrounded by the creatures!

One of the men-at-arms cried out in fear, and the Black Prince angrily hushed him.

"What are they?" the Black Prince said. There was no panic in his voice, nor fear, and his face was calm. Thomas realised that at the first indication of danger the prince had slipped into his famed battle coolness.

For a moment or two no one answered, then Bolingbroke spoke hesitantly. "I remember tales of the Crusades, of when men moved through the grasslands of northern Africa. There they encountered great cats — lions — that stalked their horses, and oft times brought them down. I ... I have heard there are no creatures as fearsomely efficient at killing than these."

The Black Prince turned his horse about in a tight circle, trying to get a better view of the creatures. *Lions? Here in France?*

But what else could they be?

"Bunch up," he said. "And face outwards. There is no beast that a good English soldier cannot best."

"They are not lions," said Thomas quietly, a coldness seeping through him. He knew why they had come. "And they are not beasts such as we know."

The Black Prince glanced at him sharply, while Bolingbroke turned about in his saddle and regarded Thomas with an unreadable expression.

"Then what are they, man?" said the Black Prince. All the

men had bunched into a tight circle, each man facing his horse outwards, his sword drawn.

All save Thomas, who stood his mount slightly apart from the others.

"They are demons," he said. "Come to collect the remains of their brother."

Then, as if to prove the truth of his words, a humped shape rose on its hind legs not four paces from the horsemen. It was clearly no cat, although it had some cat features — the squareness of face, the sharp white fangs, the swishing tail — and resembled nothing so much as the grotesque demons and gargoyles that crawled in lifeless stone over every cathedral in Christendom.

It had luminous orange eyes, shining like corrupted lanterns in the false twilight of the mist.

The men-at-arms murmured, and again one cried out in fear, but the Black Prince — as horrified as everyone else — did nothing to quiet them this time. The horses, terrified, tried to bolt, and the men only barely managed to keep them under control.

The demon grinned — although it could just as well have been a grimace — and spoke in a harsh voice. "Here's Tom, pretty Tom, riding about the countryside without his angel companion. What's wrong, pretty Tom? Have you lost your angel?"

Several other demons now stood up, staring unblinkingly at the horsemen, eyes glowing, tongues drooling between white fangs.

At last, thought Thomas, they have assumed their true forms.

The Black Prince turned and stared at Thomas.

Another demon sidled closer, sneering at the glint of swords pushed in its direction. "Hello, Edward, so handsome in your black armour. Has Tom told you that your world is sidling closer to a conclusion? Has he told you that all you hold dear and sweet will soon be lost ... to us? Has he told you that the day of reckoning is not going to be quite what you've been told by your holy brothers?"

The Black Prince whipped his head around to the demon who had spoken, and then back to Thomas. "Tell me what this means, Thomas!"

"What? What?" Now several score of demons were either standing or circling about, all laughing and howling. "Hasn't Tom told you what's happening, Eddie? Has he left you all in the dark? My, my, you'd best make sure he doesn't work on our behalf."

They screamed with laughter, and Thomas fumbled with the blood-encrusted bag that hung at the back of his saddle. He finally worked the thong free, then stood in his stirrups and threw the loathsome bundle into the midst of the demons.

"Take it!" he screamed. "Take the head of your brother and leave us be ... in God's name!"

The laughter ceased abruptly, and one of the demons, the largest of them all, now hopped to within a pace or two of Thomas. "God means nothing to us," it said. "Nothing! We mean to recreate the world to our needs, Tom, and your God will have little place in it!"

And with that it hissed, dropped down to all fours and bounded away. Thomas, as all the other men, twisted and turned about — all the demons had either disappeared, or were vanishing rapidly into the night.

The Black Prince kneed his horse close to Thomas and leaned over, grabbing Thomas by his robe and pulling his face to within a handspan of his own.

"We are now going to ride in all haste back to Chauvigny," he hissed, "even if it takes all night. And once we get there, you are going to tell us every one of the cursed secrets you harbour!"

He gave Thomas — pale-faced and silent — a hard shake, then let him go, wheeling his horse about. "Bolingbroke! You will guard Thomas with your life. If he escapes between this patch of cursed earth and Chauvigny, then you will die! Believe it!"

Bolingbroke nodded, and would have spoken, but just then a man's voice hailed out of the night, and there was a low rumble of hooves.

The fifty men-at-arms who had apparently vanished now joined the small group about the Black Prince. They were headed by Wat Tyler who appeared wan and exhausted.

"My lord!" Tyler said. "We thought we'd lost you forever!"

"It is not me," the Black Prince said quietly, his eyes not leaving Thomas' face, "who is apparently lost forever."

Then he swung his gaze to Tyler. "What happened?"

Tyler shrugged. "A devilish mist crept in about us, and we took a wrong turning — both sight and sound were warped by the fog. I swear before God we might have ended up in Paris itself if I hadn't realised our error! It took us time to rejoin you. My lord, is anything amiss?"

"The whole world is amiss," the Black Prince said, and rode off.

XXI

The Vigil of the Feast of St Catherine
In the fifty-first year of the reign of Edward III
(Wednesday 24th November 1378)

The ride back to the camp at Chauvigny was hard. It was accomplished at a canter with stops only every few hours to give the horses rest. By the time it was done, dawn had lightened over the Vigil of the Feast of St Catherine, and all the riders and horses were stumbling with weariness. Nevertheless, the Black Prince, who had been struggling with his health the past few weeks, appeared the freshest of all as they finally dismounted.

The Black Prince began shouting the instant he was off his horse. "Ask Lancaster and Raby to attend me in my chamber immediately! Tyler — take the three-men-at arms who hadn't got lost with you and secure them somewhere where they cannot speak to any other men. Hal, Thomas, with me. *Now!*"

Lancaster and Raby were waiting for the Black Prince in his chamber.

"What news?" Lancaster said, striding forward to greet his brother. "You are back much earlier than we expected. Why? Did you manage to deal with Philip? Or are we sworn enemies?"

"Philip has allied himself with Charles, and we shall have to fight without him. Worse, Philip has a force of some eight thousand at Chatellerault and threatened to arrive and bring in the New Year with them at his back."

Lancaster, appalled, began to speak, but Edward hushed him.

"No, all that can wait, believe it or not. There is something else we need to discuss first ... there is something that Thomas needs to *explain*, before we even think about Philip. We have greater forces to worry about than his, I am sure."

Lancaster and Raby glanced at Thomas, Bolingbroke close by his side, then back to the Black Prince.

"Edward?" Lancaster said.

The Black Prince did not answer. Instead he swung about to face Thomas, drew a knife, and thrust it at Thomas' neck until the point nicked his skin.

"*Talk!*" the Black Prince hissed.

"My lord!" Raby said, half moving forward before he thought better of it. "Why —"

"Thomas has been consorting with the Devil, it seems," the Black Prince said, his face tight and fearful beneath his basinet, "and I am *not* going to remove this knife until he tells me the *why* of what we witnessed on the journey back here!"

"Edward" Lancaster said. "You are near exhausted. At least have your valet remove your armour before you —"

"*I will hear what Thomas has to say now!*" the Black Prince all but screamed, and, apart from Thomas, the other three men present froze.

"My gracious lord," Thomas said, his eyes steady on the Black Prince's face, "I work only for your salvation, as for that of every God-fearing man and woman in Christendom. What met us on the journey back here are our true enemies, not Philip or Charles. I am no danger to you, my lord, but, I beseech you, hark what my Lord of Lancaster says — you are near collapse with weariness, and it will only serve our enemies further if you take not the trouble now to remove your armour and fortify yourself with some food and wine. My lord, Bolingbroke can briefly describe to my Lords of Lancaster and Raby what transpired with Philip, and what we encountered in the meadow lands while your valet rids you of your armour. Please, my lord, I beg you. See, I will stand here where you can see me."

The Black Prince stared at him, hissed, then withdrew his knife and shouted for his valet. "And if you move, so help me God, Thomas, I will set the entire army to your slaughter!"

As the valet entered, moving swiftly to divest the Black Prince of his armour, Bolingbroke joined Lancaster and Raby and, motioning them to a corner where the valet would not overhear him, he began to speak quickly, his hands gesturing, his face so earnest the other two men could not doubt what he said. Within a moment or two they were both staring at Thomas, their faces a mix of bewilderment and fear.

As the valet laid aside the last of the metal plate, the Black Prince shrugged into a fur-lined robe and accepted a glass of warmed wine. Then he motioned the valet out, asking him to tell the guards that they were not to be disturbed and, if the friar was seen to leave the chamber unaccompanied, then he was to be killed.

Finally, the Black Prince sank into a chair, and looked at Thomas, still standing in the same spot. "Speak."

In truth, Thomas was relieved that he could now tell someone else of the events of the past few months, although there were some details on which he decided he should remain silent.

He spoke evenly and in a quiet voice, directing both voice and eyes to the Black Prince. He told of his vision when he first arrived at Rome, and of the subsequent times when the archangel had appeared to him.

None disbelieved him. Thomas spoke with the authority of one touched by the messenger of God, and all had been raised since birth to believe in the power and word of God as expressed in miracles, prophecies and supernatural appearances of God's servants.

"That there is evil abroad, my lord, you cannot doubt," Thomas said. "Nothing has been the same since the time of the great pestilence. Men who were once content with their lot now agitate for a greater standing in life, commoners are infected with the noxious idea of personal freedom, and merchants control more wealth and power than good noble men. Every day more men abandon the spiritual in search of greater material comfort and wealth, even, I am sad to say, from within the Church itself."

Lancaster nodded from where he sat. He was a devout man, and the state of the Holy Church had distressed him for many years. "The holy office is in sad disarray," he muttered, "with many bishops and archbishops so wealthy that, if only they gave up their gold and jewels, we could feed the poor for many a year. And, to compound the Church's woes, we have *two* popes, each trailing expensive and corrupt retinues, and I hear that the general council of the Church wants to meet and elect a *third* pope to replace the other two!"

"Yes," Thomas said. "And I have been touched by God in order to try and set right the wrongs which now infest Christendom. I learned of a friar, Wynkyn de Worde . . ."

Thomas related what he knew of de Worde, and then of how he left St Angelo's without permission in order to travel north to Nuremberg — he told them of the encounter he'd had with one of the demons in the Brenner Pass — and from there into the forests of northern Germany.

Here Thomas faltered, and asked for wine.

Bolingbroke handed him a goblet wordlessly.

Thomas took several sips, then spoke of the Cleft.

He did not speak to them of Odile, or of the demon who had told him that Thomas' own soul would be the battlefield.

He told them only that he was to find Wynkyn de Worde's casket — it was secreted, hopefully, in Bramham Moor friary — and that the casket would contain all he needed to know in order to combat the devilish influence of the demons.

"And this saintly damsel that Philip mentioned?" Bolingbroke said. "What of her?"

Thomas shrugged. "When I travelled through the village of Domremy in Lorraine, I encountered a peasant man, Jacques d'Arc, who had a daughter, Jeannette. She ... she also has been blessed by Saint Michael. She said that she was to go to the aid of the French dauphin and rally his spirits. She said," Thomas gave a wry grin, "that evil stalked the land in the guise of an English soldier, and that evil must be destroyed."

The Black Prince, as Lancaster, snorted with laughter.

"She is a true French girl," the Black Prince said. "And this is the one who Philip spoke of as the saintly damsel?"

"I believe so," Thomas said.

"The blessed Saint Michael must have his wits twisted," the Black Prince said, "if he believes that *we* are the force of evil in Christendom!"

To that Thomas said nothing. How could he say to these men that St Michael himself had said that evil stalked in the form of the English king, and that demony had infected the English court? The latter Thomas had no trouble believing ... but that the venerable and ancient Edward III was evil incarnate? Thomas had difficulty believing that, and he certainly wasn't going to suggest the possibility to Edward's sons here in this chamber.

"A peasant girl is a poor choice for an archangel to pick as one of his warriors," Lancaster said. "Tell me, has she the face and form to seduce Charles and Philip into believing her mutterings?"

Thomas smiled. "She is squat, and dark, and would have a difficult time tempting deformed dwarves, my lord."

There was brief, soft laughter, then the Black Prince spoke quietly. "If I had not seen with my own eyes these demons, Tom, I would disbelieve every word you have uttered. But ... *sweet Jesu!* Are these things crawling through England's green fields as well?"

"My lord," Thomas said, his tone urgent. "I believe so. Etienne Marcel was clearly their creature — he advocated a social order of chaos, no less! — and I have heard mutterings among your own men that —"

"What?" the Black Prince sat up, setting his wine goblet down. "*What have you heard?*"

Thomas hesitated, wondering who he could trust among the other three in the chamber. John Ball was patently demon-influenced in his ideas, as was the heretical priest, John Wycliffe, and Thomas had serious doubts about Wat Tyler as well, if only because he frequented the company of Ball, and spoke admiringly of Wycliffe. But Tyler, at least, was well respected among these men, and Wycliffe was influential at court ... did the Black Prince support and protect him? Did Lancaster? And what of Hal?

"Well?" the Black Prince said.

"It is just ... just that I have heard some of the men in this encampment, faceless men, I do not know their names, talk of a world where the Church had been destroyed."

"There *are* some things about the Church that would do well to be destroyed," Lancaster said, and Thomas was glad he'd kept names silent. "Its over-weening wealth, and its ambitions to interfere with the secular state."

Thomas shrugged. "There is a level of disrespect that —"

"Ha!" the Black Prince said. "Do you blame them, Tom? Do you? Have you not just pointed out the corruption that bedevils your blessed Church? Well ... I can see why Prior General Thorseby wants you back in his den for whatever harsh discipline he considers fitting, Thomas. He has never liked you, as well you know. Running off from Saint Angelo's without so much as a by-your-leave from the prior was bound to ignite Thorseby's ire."

"My lord," Thomas half-stepped forward, "if you send me to Thorseby he might confine me for a year or two of solitary prayer in a cell! I might never reach Wynkyn's casket! I —"

"Yes, yes," the Black Prince said. "I well understand your concern, Tom, but for the moment be still. John," he looked at Lancaster, "I fear Philip's news has made our choice about what to do less difficult."

Lancaster, so long an advocate of pushing forward whatever the cost to consolidate their victory at Poitiers, nodded wearily. "He has *eight* thousand men at Chatellerault? Sweet God in heaven, Edward ..."

"Winter approaches," Edward said, "and our men are tired and war-weary. We must wait the winter out, and push forward in spring. But ... we cannot winter here in Chauvigny. It is too close to Philip and whatever men Charles has mustered. So, this is what we shall do ... I will lead the larger part of the army south, to Bordeaux. Our fortifications are stronger there, and we have enough supplies for the winter. There, during winter and while our force rests, I will open negotiations with the Duke of Burgundy — the Lord Saviour knows he has ever been Charles' foe!"

"Aye," Lancaster said wearily. "And King John?"

"Whatever Philip said, John *is* still useful. Brother, I would that you and our brother Gloucester escort him back to London. We cannot risk keeping him this side of the Channel for the entire winter. Bolingbroke can attend you. Thomas, you will attend Lancaster and Gloucester and, once Lancaster determines it can be accomplished without Thorseby's knowledge, you will journey north to this friary where rests de Worde's casket. Lancaster, you will ensure that Thomas does so in all security."

Lancaster nodded yet again, knowing Edward meant that Thomas was to be well escorted on his journey north to Bramham Moor.

"I think," he said, now looking meaningfully at Raby, "that the Lady Rivers should also travel back to England in our retinue. Your camp, brother, will be no place for a lady due to deliver, and in the meantime Lady Rivers will do well to attend my own lady, Katherine."

Thomas was surprised, if only for the reason that at this moment of crisis Lancaster should take so much interest in a fairly unimportant woman. Why? Why was Lancaster so determined to remove the witch from Raby's company?

Well, it mattered not. All it meant was that Thomas would continue to be able to keep an eye on her.

Lancaster remained behind after the others had left the Black Prince's chamber.

"Edward," he said softly, watching his brother slump into his chair, "you are not well. Should you not come home with us? There is no need for you to remain in Bordeaux."

Edward waved a hand tiredly. "I am well enough," he said. "The flux does not weaken me overmuch."

"Let me send for the physician, if nothing else."

Edward hesitated, then nodded. "Very well. Perhaps a dose of wormwood . . ."

Lancaster rested a hand briefly on his brother's shoulder. "We would be lost without you," he said. "*England* will be lost without you."

Edward nodded again, and then Lancaster was gone.

"Meg?"

She was still asleep, and Raby had to shake her shoulder to wake her. "Meg, wake! Your child has made you a laggard!"

Margaret rolled over, and then abruptly sat up as she came to her senses. "Ralph! Has the prince returned? And Bolingbroke?"

"Aye, and the news is not good." Raby sat on the edge of the bed and studied Margaret. Her hair was all sleep tousled, and her eyes dark and dreamy. She was naked under the coverlets, and as she sat her breasts slipped free.

For an instant Raby wondered if he had the time to bed her . . . then the coverlets slipped yet further and he saw the roundness of her belly.

"We are to abandon Chauvigny," he said briskly, standing and drawing on a pair of thick outdoor gloves. "Edward is to move south to Bordeaux, and you will travel back to England with Lancaster, who escorts King John. There. Our bargain is complete. You are to return home."

Margaret threw the covers back completely and slid out of bed.

Raby watched her from the corners of his narrowed eyes, but pretended an interest in the fastening of one of his gloves.

"And you?" she said, moving to stand by him.

"I will remain with Edward for the time," he said, "although no doubt I shall return to court in the New Year."

She smiled. "Then you will be in time for the birth of our —"

He whipped about and stared at her. "I do not believe we shall meet again. You shall spend time attending the Lady Swynford until your time draws nigh, and then you will return to your husband's parents to present them with their grandchild and heir."

Margaret paled. "But I thought you —"

Raby took her shoulders in his hands, his eyes trailing one last time down her body. God, if only she had not fallen with child! How sweet she would have been as his mistress at court!

"Margaret, I will say this one last time. You carry your husband's child. I will never acknowledge it as mine."

"And thus I am to be discarded?"

"Thus you made your choice," Raby said carefully, "and the choices were made plain before I ever bedded you."

Margaret's eyes filled with tears. "Ralph, will you hold me, one last time? I would feel the comfort of your arms about me, and —"

His hands dropped away from her. "I have done with you," he said. "Clothe yourself, for your nakedness proclaims your shamefulness, and pack your belongings."

Raby walked towards the door, then abruptly turned back, lifted a hand and stabbed a finger at Margaret. "Use that child to force my hand, Meg, and I swear before our Lord Christ Saviour that you will regret it!"

Then he was gone, the door slamming shut behind him.

XXII

The Vigil of the Feast of St Andrew the Apostle
In the fifty-first year of the reign of Edward III
(Monday 29th November 1378)

The Black Prince's and Lancaster's retinues were ready to abandon Chauvigny within a few days. King John fumed and argued, but with no success. He was to be transported to the court of his arch-enemy in time for the Nativity of Christ ... no doubt Edward III would make sure John enjoyed a festive Yuletide season.

The Black Prince could not afford to linger. His spies had reported that Chatellerault was, as Philip had said, bristling with men-at-arms, and with such a force so close, Chauvigny was no place to winter or to try and hold the French king.

Of the two leaders, Lancaster was the more likely to have a difficult journey. Philip was sure to know — or, at the least, to guess — that the English would try and take John back to England, and the Black Prince feared he might make some attempt to intercept Lancaster's retinue as it made for the port of la Rochelle. During the inevitable fracas, Edward had no doubt that, most unfortunately, King John would be mortally wounded, leaving the way slightly clearer for Philip's own grab for the French throne.

That thought in itself gave the Black Prince reason to

pause for thought. Would it be worth the internal disarray in the French army to lose his hostage? But ... no. The Black Prince knew that much could be won through diplomatic negotiation if the English had a living French king hostage in London. Not only that, having a French king as hostage would give both commoners and Edward III reason for hearty cheer. The commoners because it would make them feel as if the English army had finally done something worthwhile, while John's presence in his court would give his father good reason to entertain on a lavish scale, and Edward III didn't get enough excuses to do that in a domestic economy ravaged by waging prolonged war across the seas.

Whatever, the Black Prince made sure Lancaster and Gloucester would have enough force alongside them to cope with any attack. He split the English army into two forces: the smaller force to accompany Lancaster back to England, returning to Bordeaux in time for the spring campaign, the larger force to travel with the Black Prince.

Thomas was buoyed by the fact that he now had the aid and protection of Lancaster and the Black Prince — the two most powerful men in England, discounting their aging father — under which to further his search for Wynkyn's casket and to keep Prior General Thoreseby from pursuing him into penitential isolation in a bare and imprisoning cell. He spent the first two days after St Catherine's in preparations for the journey to England. In truth, there was not much to be done. All he had to do physically to ready himself was ensure his gelding had been well fed and groomed, all the horse's gear cleaned and repaired, and that his own clothing was in good enough repair to stand an early winter dash through potentially hostile territory to the port of la Rochelle. He said his goodbyes to Raby, who would ride with the Black Prince, and he spent some time praying to St Michael in one of the chapels of Chauvigny ... but the excitement of the preparations inevitably dragged him back outside within the hour.

He was going home!

Thomas had not thought he would be so excited. His way

ahead now seemed so plain, he had the protection and aid of the most powerful men in England … but most of all, he was going *home*.

Thomas could not wait to see England again.

Contrariwise to Thomas' excitement, Margaret was sad and unsure. At dawn on the Vigil of the Feast of St Andrew, the day that Lancaster and his retinue would finally leave, she stood cloaked and hooded in the chill wind on the parapets of Chauvigny, staring at the cold and dismal land stretched before her, wondering if her future in England would be any less dismal. She had not been home — if home it could be called — for over a decade. Longer, for Roger's house, with his cold and distant parents, could hardly be called a home.

No, she had not been "home" since the day she left her father's house, and that was many, many years even further distant into her past.

Her father. He'd been her adoptive father only, for her real father had abandoned her and her mother before Margaret was born, but he was the only man she had ever known as a father. He had married her mother even though she was with child to another man, and greeted Margaret's birth with joy and pride. Margaret's eyes filled with tears. He had been dead so many years, and at this moment, standing in this cold wind with the early winter fields spreading before her, Margaret would have given anything to feel his arms about her again, and to hear the comfort of his voice.

When would she ever feel that safe again?

Margaret sighed, and rested her hand on her belly. She was almost five months gone with child, halfway through her pregnancy. When she held this child in her arms, she would never let it go, never let another seize it from her, never abandon it. She well knew what it was like to live without love, and she would give her life if it meant her child would never have to know that desolation.

When she held it. If.

If she survived its birth.

Margaret began to cry, great gulping sobs that tore through her entire frame, and they did not stop even when the soldiers came and escorted her to her horse, and Lancaster's retinue began the long ride west to la Rochelle.

Margaret was moving again, but she did not think she'd reach home for many years to come.

ENGLAND

"the time will come, deliuered you must be;
then in the campe you will descredditt mee."
"*Ile goe from thee befor that time shalbee;
when all is well, my loue again Ile see.*"

A Jigge (for Margrett)
Medieval English ballad

I

The Friday within the Octave of the
Conception of the Virgin
In the fifty-first year of the reign of Edward III
(10th December 1378)

*L*a Rochelle was a small, windswept port on the
northern coast of Brittany. It took the Duke ten days
of heckling, shouting and bargaining to get his train of
one French monarch, several English peers, more noblemen,
several hundred knights, a thousand men-at-arms, an equal
number of archers, a score of noblewomen and serving
women, one Dominican friar, a bevy of captive and sullen
French noblemen, and the whole company's riding and pack
horses and gear, from Chauvigny to the coast. Along the
way the Duke had to counter appalling weather — they'd
ridden most days hunched down into cloaks against driving
and icy rain and the horses struggled through knee-deep
mud more often than not — intransigent peasants, sporadic
attacks by bandits and semi-organised bands of French
soldiers still wandering the roads after the disaster of
Poitiers, a lack of food, an even greater lack of shelter, and
one French king who held the entire train up with his
complaining and his damned awkward litter, which
continually threatened to tilt the royal person into the mud
of his realm.

They hardly rested. The third day out Lancaster's spies had reported troop movements to the north and the Duke, fearing that Philip had mobilised against them, had driven them even harder. The party dismounted only for brief meal stops, and an hour or two here and there when it was patently clear that horses were going to drop dead if they weren't given some rest. After five days of hard riding Lancaster had begun to beg, borrow and commandeer mounts wherever he found them, and threatened to tie to the saddle anyone who so drooped from weariness they threatened to fall off. On at least three occasions that Thomas was aware of, Lancaster did just that.

Thomas rode in the group that directly followed the French king's litter, itself drawn by two horses in front, and two at the rear. Here was the heaviest concentration of troops — all of the knights and two-thirds of the men-at-arms — for Lancaster constantly feared that the French would make an attempt to seize back their king.

Apart from the occasional raid from bandits and disorganised soldiers, who were more in search of food than regal flesh, the French made no such attempt.

The noble and serving women in the retinue also travelled close behind John's litter to obtain the maximum benefit from the close proximity of the armed men, and Thomas, much to his chagrin, found himself on several occasions riding next to Margaret.

After the first few days, Thomas felt as though the cold and wet had eaten into his very flesh, and he doubted if he would ever be warm again. And yet he journeyed in luxurious comfort compared to others. The knights and men-at-arms who rode in varying degrees of armour (many had taken the risk of stowing their heavier and more cumbersome pieces of plate on pack horses after a few days of wet chafing misery through the rain) spent much of their time on frequent rest stops to have their valets and pages rub salves into the red and weeping chafes over shoulders and joints. Even some of the women suffered. Margaret looked as if she spent the greater part of each day in abject distress.

Her face had lost its beauty to a wretched pallor, her once clear dark eyes had become clouded and sunken, and her body lurched sickeningly with every stride of her grey palfrey. Sometimes she grabbed at her belly and lurched forward, retching over the side of her mount's neck, and when Lancaster did afford them the luxury of a stop, Margaret refused all the food offered to her, and curled into a doleful ball under whatever shelter she could find.

On the day they reached la Rochelle, Lancaster forced them to ride at almost a gallop the last few miles — little matter now if some of the horses foundered. By daybreak — a thin, weak greyish dawn that brought no cheer — they had been in the saddle since the middle of the night after only a two-hour rest from the previous day's ride. Everyone, from the most inexperienced boy-soldier to the captive king, was exhausted, brittle-tempered and nursing a variety of chills, aching muscles, callused hands and cold-hardened flesh.

Margaret looked as if she was almost dead. She swayed alarmingly in the saddle, her eyes closed in her pallid face, her mouth a thin line of distress, her hands clutching the pommel of her saddle, the reins dangling loose about her palfrey's neck. It looked as if she stayed in the saddle only because her muscles had cramped into position.

Thomas watched her carefully, thinking that she feigned her distress. *Why? Did she hope that he would lean over and lift her into his own saddle? Did she hope that the intimate contact between their bodies, lurching and swaying in the mad ride, might awake in him some uncontrollable lust? Did she think to stimulate his pity, that she might then turn it to love?*

Suddenly, as their horses' hooves clattered over the first cobbles on the road that led into la Rochelle, Margaret gave a low cry, and swayed so alarmingly in the saddle it seemed she might, finally, topple to the ground to be trampled by the hooves of the following horses.

Thomas averted his face. He was not going to allow her to —

"Thomas!"

Thomas looked back to Margaret. Bolingbroke, clad in chain mail and a soaked, thick tunic, had ridden his destrier beside Margaret's palfrey and had lifted the woman into the saddle before him. She swooned, and Thomas saw Bolingbroke's body tense in the effort both to hold her and to control his own horse, shying at the unexpected extra weight.

As soon as Bolingbroke had regained control, he shot Thomas a furious look. "Why did you not aid her, Thomas? Look!"

He dipped his chin down. Margaret's cloak had fallen open, and the rain had plastered her grey gown to the contours of her body, emphasising her five-month rounded belly.

"She is with child!" Bolingbroke said. "She deserved your *care*, Thomas, not your disregard!"

And with that he spurred his horse forward, pulling Margaret's cloak once more about her body.

Thomas' expression hardened, furious at the niggling guilt that he should have aided her himself, and blaming Margaret for both guilt and fury.

La Rochelle was only just stirring when Lancaster's column clattered into the town. It was one of the main ports along the French coast, and was thus well stocked and provisioned by the English — who had held the territory about it for the past year or two — for an emergency such as this. Although there was not housing for the entire party, which numbered several thousand, warehouses close to the pier accommodated most of the men, and several inns took in the higher nobles, a damp and cantankerous French king, and all of the women.

Nine cog vessels bobbed in the grey water at the pier. The ungainly vessels were merchantmen, used for carrying cargo from the Mediterranean ports to the northern waters of Europe and so while not pretty, and a nightmare to sail in, had generous space for both men and horses. Lancaster wasted no time in bargaining a good price for their use, although his threats could hardly be called bargaining, and for their provisioning; the cogs would be ready within two days. Meanwhile all would rest and Lancaster himself finally appeared to relax. His scouts reported that the area for some fifty miles about was secured, and no sizeable force could approach la Rochelle without being seen.

By noon, as lines of men were strung out along the pier shouldering heavy bundles of provisions from town to cogs, a dark ponderous line of clouds moved in from the southwest. A heartbeat after several of the men had stopped and pointed to the clouds, a furious wind blew in, hurling cream-crested waves over the entire pier and washing some eight men out to sea. The next moment hail pelted down from the sky, and men dropped provisions and scattered to whatever shelter they could find.

The storm lasted four full days, developing into an early winter tempest within hours of its arrival. Snow and ice sleeted down from the clouds at vicious angles, and the wind galed so maliciously that the entire town of la Rochelle wailed and groaned as slate was torn from roofs, and nails popped from walls, shutters and doors.

Several outbuildings were destroyed, but the rest of the town remained secure. La Rochelle had endured many such storms in its history, and its homes were, for the greater part, strongly built and heavily reinforced.

No one moved beyond shelter, and Lancaster spent the greater part of an entire day on his knees before a makeshift altar, thanking God that the tempest had not hit them while they were still on the road, or, come to that, after they had put to sea. Having thanked God for their own safety, Lancaster then paced about worrying for his brother. Had the Black Prince been hit by this same tempest? And, if so, had he and his managed to find adequate shelter?

Thomas spent the days confined to his particular accommodation fretting about the time wasted, and wondering if the storm were demon-sent. What better way to prevent him reaching England? Would it hail and gust for the next several months as the demons consolidated their position ... wherever and whatever that was?

After a few days fretting, both at the delay and at the irritation of being confined to the same tiny set of rooms, Thomas persuaded the three men-at-arms who watched over him (or was it guarded him?) to allow him, with them in close tow, to dash across a narrow street to the larger and more commodious inn that housed Lancaster, the French king, and most of the higher nobles.

Even in this narrow alley, the wind picked up the four men and thudded them painfully against the door that opened from kitchens to alley. Thomas and one of the men-at-arms hammered as loudly as they could on the door and, after a nightmarish wait of several moments, it opened inwards, tumbling the men onto the dirty floor of the kitchen.

At least it was warm. Thomas picked himself up, brushed off the worst of the wet and dirt, and asked one of the men in the kitchen where Bolingbroke was.

Having been directed up the narrow stairs that led to the guest apartments, Thomas asked his "companion" men-at-arms to wait in the kitchen for him — they agreed readily enough — and started up the steps. He met Bolingbroke's valet halfway up, and the man pointed him to a door just beyond the top of the stairs.

Thomas stood outside it for a moment, straightening his robe and wishing he'd thought to shave before he came over, then knocked.

Bolingbroke's voice sounded indistinctly, and Thomas opened the door, stopping in disbelief the instant he saw who sat with Bolingbroke before the roaring fire.

Margaret, her eyes startled, the needlework she'd been stitching lying on her lap.

Thomas looked across the other side of the fire. Bolingbroke was settled comfortably into another chair, a glove turning lazily over in his hands.

What? Had the witch found herself a new protector?

"Thomas!" Bolingbroke stood up. "I am glad you have come to visit the Lady Rivers. She has much improved since her troubling ride."

"I —" Thomas said.

"My lord," Margaret said to Bolingbroke. "I, too, am glad the friar has come, for I have need to talk with a priest."

"Ah." Bolingbroke took his cue and bowed slightly in Margaret's direction. "When you take your leave of Brother Thomas, could you direct him to my rooms?"

Margaret nodded, and smiled slightly, and Bolingbroke crossed the room to where Thomas still stood by the open door.

"My friend," Bolingbroke stopped close to Thomas and spoke softly. "I am more than glad you came. The Lady Rivers has been ill, both in body and spirit, and thinks that she has offended you."

Thomas, his face set and ill-tempered, opened his mouth to speak, but Bolingbroke forestalled him.

"We both know she carries Raby's child," Bolingbroke said, "and that his child will be your kinsman or woman. Lady Rivers deserves your respect for that, as well as for her nobility and virtue."

"Virtue?" Thomas hissed, and Bolingbroke grabbed his arm.

"Keep your voice down! You will treat her with respect, Thomas, for she is not the only person, man or woman, who has lost her way in this troubled world of ours. She is troubled, not malicious. She deserves guidance, not condemnation!"

And with that he was gone.

Thomas would have liked nothing better than to have followed him, but fully realised that Bolingbroke was likely to march him straight back in here.

Damn her! How had she managed to get her claws into Hal's clean soul?

Margaret stood as Thomas approached, but he waved her back into her chair.

"As ill as you are," he said, "I would not like you to exert yourself on my behalf."

He sat down opposite her. "You wanted to see a priest?"

"I needed to talk with you," she said, and her voice and gaze were steady. "I need to know why you regard me with so much loathing."

"What? You know why I —"

Margaret leaned forward, dropping her needlework into a basket by her side. "You think me guilty of demony, don't you?"

Thomas was shocked into silence for an instant. Then ...

"And how — what — do you know of demony, my lady?" he said softly.

"I have heard rumours of what entrapped the Black Prince and his party when you rode back from meeting with Philip the Bad."

"How? No one was to speak of that!"

Margaret smiled cynically. "The three men-at-arms who accompanied you —"

"Were isolated on their return and —"

"Had many hours during which to speak to their companions on the ride back before they were isolated! Lord Jesus Saviour, Thomas, the entire camp knew of the demons before we began the ride here!"

She leaned back in her chair, her face pale and frightened now. "You think me party to demonic witchcraft, do you not, Thomas?"

He did not answer. Margaret's face worked, and she briefly covered her eyes with a trembling hand.

"I ask you again," she finally said, "why, if you believe in your own innocence that day you planted this child in my belly, you cannot also believe in mine. Why cannot I be a victim of sorcery also, instead of its engineer?"

"I will never acknowledge that bastard as mine," Thomas said, after a lengthy silence.

"Of course you won't," Margaret said, "because a Dominican friar could never admit to an afternoon spent in sorcerous fornication, could he!

"I wish the child were Raby's!" she continued as Thomas stared at her. "I wish so with every beat of my heart, for then the child would have been conceived in some measure of regard and respect instead of the narrow-minded hatreds you have so embraced. Did the Church teach you such blindness, Tom, or has it been a part of your nature always?"

Whether it was her words, or the distraught expression on her face, Thomas shifted uncomfortably, wondering if it was true that she might, indeed, be as innocent as he.

"If there is witchcraft," Margaret said in a low voice, "then we both share it. If there is guilt, then we both share it. If ... if there is innocence, then we share that as well. Thomas, believe me, I beg you, I am as innocent as you ... I have been used as poorly as you have been used."

Thomas dropped his eyes and studied his hands clenched tightly in his lap. He hated it that her words made sense.

"If there are demons," she said, almost in a whisper, "then I swear before God and all His saints that I am not one of them, nor one of their pawns. I am only Margaret, a poor God-fearing woman left to carry a child whom no one will acknowledge."

There was a long silence, then Thomas raised his eyes. "Where will you go to bear the child?"

Her mouth worked. "My lord Raby tells me that my 'husband's' child will be born at Rivers House in Bratesbridge, Lincolnshire. Roger's parents reside there." She shifted uncomfortably. "They will doubtless be curious to learn that their son, who for ten years was too weak to bed me, somehow managed to arise from his death throes and get this child."

"Raby will no doubt —"

"Raby will not acknowledge the child, nor acknowledge the fact he bedded me for months before I arrived back in England. Raby will provide no support nor benefit to the child. As you once told me, he has sons and bastards enough without this one."

"I am sure that he will do something to —"

"No! No, he will not. He cannot."

"What do you mean?"

She arched an eyebrow. "Have you not heard?"

"What?"

"My Lord of Raby has bargained for the Lady Joan Beaufort's hand in marriage."

Thomas was so shocked he could not immediately speak. Joan Beaufort was Lancaster's bastard daughter by his mistress, Katherine Swynford. Suddenly Lancaster's interest in removing Margaret from Raby's bed became obvious: as a doting father — and all knew how Lancaster doted on both Katherine and their bastard offspring — he would not want a former mistress of Raby's to embarrass his daughter by flaunting her swollen belly and demanding recompense.

No, all would deny that Raby had ever set eyes on the obviously demented Lady Rivers.

But why would Raby want to negotiate a marriage with a bastard, even one fathered by so important a man as Lancaster?

"Lancaster plans to wed Katherine once we have returned to England," Margaret said, watching the emotions play over Thomas' face. "His children by her, Joan and Henry, will be legitimised in return for surrendering any claim to the throne."

Thomas breathed deeply, trying to expel his shock. So ... Lancaster loved Swynford enough to make her his wife. Well, both were aged now, and Lancaster already held enough land and power that he could afford to flaunt expectations and marry a penniless woman.

"How do you know all this?" he asked finally.

"Some from Raby, but not much — only that he wanted me and my belly gone from his life. The rest I heard from his valet, keen to make me realise that his master had no intention of making me his wife."

Thomas nodded. Valets almost knew more of their master's lives than their masters did themselves.

And the rest of her tale also rang true, if only because it would be too easy to prove false.

"Margaret —"

"Please," she said, raising a hand as if to shield herself from him. "Do not fear. I will not impose on you, either."

Thomas stared, angry again now that she forced his guilt to flare anew, then he stood and raised his hand in blessing.

Margaret's despair found some outlet in anger. "Do not bless me, priest! I want nothing from you!"

Thomas hesitated, then he turned and strode out of the room.

II

The Wednesday before the Feast of the
Nativity of Our Lord Jesus Christ
In the fifty-first year of the reign of Edward III
(22nd December 1378)

Late on the afternoon that Thomas spoke with
Margaret the storm abruptly died, and by dusk the
sky was clear and the air calm. Lancaster ordered that
provisioning be resumed immediately and continue through
the night, and that the cogs be readied for departure on the
dawn tide.

The channel crossing was smooth and unadventuresome,
and within a week they arrived safe at Dover. Here the
majority of the men and horses were disembarked, but
Lancaster and his immediate party — his younger brother
Gloucester, Bolingbroke, King John, Thomas and Margaret,
plus a score of ladies and some two score of knights and a
small number of men-at-arms — disembarked only to
immediately re-embark on a stately vessel belonging to King
Edward, and then sail northwards along the coast to
London.

On the afternoon that they sailed off the coastline of
Kent, Hal joined Thomas on the deck. Both men leaned on
the starboard railing and stared across the grey, choppy
waves towards France.

"What is Charles doing over there, do you think?" Hal said.

"Who knows. Trying to keep Philip's knife from his back, no doubt."

Hal smiled, but it died almost as soon as it had formed. "I wonder if his sister managed to escape Paris when he did, or if she fell foul to Marcel's rebels."

"Oh, yes, she escaped. I met her when I met Charles on the road east of Paris."

Hal straightened and stared at Thomas. "You never told me you saw Catherine!"

"I did not think it important."

There was silence for a few minutes, then Hal spoke with a forced disinterest. "How did she appear?"

Thomas looked searchingly at Hal. "Well enough, although thin and tired from her flight. She has an acute mind, and a biting tongue. She spat at me!"

Hal laughed. "She ever had a sharp tongue. Did you know, Tom, that my father spent almost an entire year trying to negotiate a marriage between us?"

"No, I did not. Hal, your family and hers have been at war for years! How was it Lancaster thought all could be forgotten for a marriage between you and she?"

"My father," Hal said, "thought it would make an ideal truce arrangement."

Hal looked as if he would say more, but he abruptly shut his mouth and turned his face back to the grey sea. After a minute or two of silence, he spoke again. "My chance for a match with Catherine is far and gone now, and she is not to be robbed of her maidenhood by one of the Lancaster men. My father now looks to good English blood for a woman I can wed and bed."

Thomas smiled, and they chatted a little about possible matches within the English nobility, and Thomas forgot Hal's interest in Catherine.

They sailed up the Thames on a clear winter's day, approaching London from the east on the high tide. Thomas had taken up position in the prow of the boat, excited beyond measure, not only to be in England at last, but also to be approaching London.

Although he was a northerner born and bred, Thomas loved London as he loved no other place. It was a tangled, dirty city, but nevertheless had a charm and a life that he had not encountered anywhere else.

The Thames wound through fields dusted with snow and hamlets battened down for the winter. A few hardy men braved the reed beds in flat-bottomed punts, searching for salt-tangy fish to augment the rich pork of their Christmastide feasting, and Lancaster's ship passed five or six others sailing in the opposite direction, carrying either wool or pilgrims for the markets and shrines of the continent.

Thomas wrapped his cloak closer about him as they sailed into the straight that led to London. There! The square keep of the White Tower rose glinting in the sunshine, and ... there! ... the curve of the ancient Roman walls as they enclosed the city that sat on the northern bank of the river.

Thomas could not help himself — he grinned. London was awash in smoke from fires, and alive with movement and colour and people. As they sailed closer to London Bridge, Thomas could see scores of people hanging from the windows of the houses atop the bridge waving pennants and ribbons. Others — approaching the southern gate of the bridge, with its constant grisly decoration of criminals' heads stuck on pikes as a moral lesson for all London's good citizens — stood in carts or by the side of the road, waving and shouting.

The English returned with the French king! Hurrah! Hurrah!

Thomas laughed with sheer exuberance. None of this welcome was for Lancaster — God knew the English commoners generally loathed him — but for the fact that the ship bore the hated French monarch as hostage. Nothing could have cheered the English more than having a French king captive in their beloved London where fishwives could throw cabbages at his passing, and drunkards piss on the outer walls of whatever hold King Edward placed him in.

The ship sailed under the bridge, and Thomas ducked as people threw down loaves of bread and parcels of sweetmeats for the heroic English to feast upon.

Once safely under, Thomas stood up again. Banners and pennants flew from every window that he could see, and the bells of St Paul's, and of every parish church within London's walls, pealed out in melodious welcome. Not only was Lancaster bringing home the French king, but this was also Christmastide, and London was in festive dress and mood.

Thomas turned about and looked down the boat. Lancaster, Gloucester and Bolingbroke had arrived on deck, arrayed in finery and jewels, and behind them the bowed and surly figure of King John, accompanied by an escort of good English knights. Lancaster was standing looking forward with an intense gleam in his eyes. Gloucester and Bolingbroke were standing to the side of the boat, waving at the people now thronging the riverbank.

Thomas turned back to the view opening up before him: far in the distance, so far he could only barely discern it, the Thames swung south in a great curve. Nestled on the northern, outer bank of the curve was the city of Westminster, where lay the great abbey as well as the fabulous palace and court of King Edward.

But they were not sailing direct to Westminster. Instead, Lancaster had directed the master of the vessel to dock at the Savoy Palace, his private residence on the Strand, the street that ran south-west from London to Westminster. The official reception and greeting of King John by King Edward, the two aging foes, would take place on the morrow, and for today Lancaster thought to rest himself and his party at the Savoy.

Lancaster's palace was one of the most beauteous buildings in the London vicinity. Perched on the northern bank of the Thames, the wall of the building facing the river rose several storeys high, its stone punctuated with two rows of windows and three massive square towers. Beyond the outer building, which housed supplies and Lancaster's men, rose the palace proper, a huge building that to most eyes resembled a church with great gothic windows filled with stained glass: it was a fit place to receive the French king.

In all his life, Thomas had never been inside of it. He'd spent much of his youth with Bolingbroke, but all of that time had been either on the Neville estates in the north or on Lancaster's own country estates.

The cold wind freshened, and Thomas narrowed his eyes against its sting. The vessel was now slowing as it approached the stairs that ran down to the water's edge from a small gate set in the outer wall. A figure stood there, a woman of late middle years, and as the vessel moored alongside, she ran gracefully down the steps, laughing and holding out her hands.

Lancaster leaped the distant between vessel and steps, and took the woman in his arms.

"Katherine!" he cried.

For an instant the entire world stilled, centreing only on Lancaster and Katherine, and then movement and noise and colour erupted about them. Men-at-arms, knights, squires, pages, valets, sundry servants and ladies, porters, chamberlains, diplomats, noblemen and their ladies as well as countless unidentifiable men and women spilled out of the gateway leading into the Savoy complex. King John raised a smile and a wave to the Londoners who crowded the riverbank and bridge and leaned from high windows, and then descended to the steps in regal style. Lady Katherine Swynford curtsied low in obeisance to the regal hostage and spoke a courtly greeting in a low voice that was, nevertheless, so beautifully modulated it reached above the hubbub of the crowd that thronged about.

Then, her duty as hostess done, she turned to Bolingbroke, who stood to one side of King John, and greeted him with first a curtsey and then, formalities taken care of, with an embrace of genuine warmth.

Thomas, still standing by the railing of the deck, watched, his face quiet. Bolingbroke's mother, the Lady Blanche, had died when he was a toddler, and his father's mistress then became his surrogate mother. Although Lancaster had married again, to Constance of Castile, Hal's stepmother had rarely lived in England, and, on those occasions when she did, showed her young stepson nothing but a cold and distant face. Thomas had only met her once, but Bolingbroke had spoken often of her, and Thomas idly wondered that Lancaster had managed to get *two* daughters on the woman. Thomas had years ago decided that Lancaster had an unusually high tolerance to frostiness.

Now Katherine turned to greet Gloucester, her manner more reserved in the face of his loss.

And then ...

... then Katherine turned, lifted up her face, and saw Thomas.

For an instant her face, still beauteous despite her years, remained expressionless, then she lifted the corners of her mouth in a sweet smile of genuine warmth.

"Thomas!" she called, lifting both hands and shifting her feet a little in excitement. "Thomas!"

Thomas could not help but return her smile. As Katherine had been a surrogate mother to Bolingbroke, she had been the same to him. Thomas' parents had died when he was young, caught in the same returning outbreak of pestilence that had killed the Lady Blanche. Raby's first wife, his aunt, had been too busy with her own brood to spend much time with Thomas and, as he'd spent the greater portion of his youth with Bolingbroke, Katherine had stepped into the role of mother with as much genuine warmth and care as she'd extended to Bolingbroke.

She was riven with sin, for she had fornicated with Lancaster for many years and had born him two bastard children, but Thomas still loved her, and could understand why Lancaster had never given her up and now, if what Margaret said was true, intended to make her his wife.

He waved, and moved down the deck, walking smoothly

through the crowds of disembarking passengers as well as servants who had come on board to assist in unloading supplies and baggage, then hurrying down to where Katherine waited.

She hesitated as he reached her. "I do not know if I should embrace a priest," she said, her smile now uncertain, then her eyes lit mischievously, and she leaned forward, putting her hands on Thomas' shoulders and kissing him softly on his cheek.

"I have not seen you for some six years," she said, leaning back. "You left with Hal to play at some tournament, and you never returned. I mourned you as if you were dead."

"Madam, you cannot infer that entering holy orders equates with death."

"No? I lost you that day, Thomas. We all did. But," she paused to smile a little, "I am glad you are now home, even if so dismally garbed."

Thomas' face hardened, feeling keenly her implied criticism of his decision to join the Dominicans. "You should rejoice, madam, for I have left the world of man to serve God."

Her eyes searched his face. "I *would* rejoice, Thomas, if I felt that love of God had led you to that decision. But regret and guilt do not make good fuel to fire a lifetime of service to God ... do they?"

She had now referred to the unmentionable, Alice's death, the incident that had driven Thomas into the Church in the first instance, and now he drew back from her, stiff and cold. He *would* feel no guilt! Hadn't St Michael absolved him? Hadn't he said he'd acted aright?

"Thomas," Katherine said instantly. "I spoke thoughtlessly and now I must beg your forgiveness. I have been a poor hostess and an unthinking friend."

"My decision to take holy orders must have been seen by many to be —"

"Thomas, we will not speak of it. Not now, not today." Katherine's face brightened. "Why, today I have my lord home with me, and Hal, and *you*! This is a time for rejoicing, for my family is together for Christmastide. Ah," she turned as a servant spoke swiftly in her ear, "I must be off, there is so much to be attended. Tom, will you join us in my lord's private apartments this evening? There will be no formal reception for his grace the king until the morrow, and this evening we will be permitted to relax and laugh as old friends. Come, say you will join us."

She took his hands and laughed merrily. "Yes? Ah, Tom, you make me a contented woman!"

And then she was gone, back through the throng to Lancaster's side, and thence to escort King John to the apartments that had been set aside for him.

Thomas glanced up at the formidable fortifications about the Savoy palace. It was no wonder that the French king would sojourn here during his captivity. The Westminster palace complex where King Edward lived was not so secure and the Tower not so commodious.

King John was to be treated as a guest, not a prisoner.

Lancaster's chamberlain, a man by the name of Simon Kebell, appeared at Thomas' side.

"Brother Thomas, it does my old eyes good to regard you again: I greet you well. My Lord of Lancaster tells me you are to be accommodated within the main apartment complex. Look," Kebell's hand reached out into the crowd and snatched at a passing valet, "Robert will accompany you to your chamber."

The Savoy palace was one of the wonders of London, and certainly constituted its most luxurious private dwelling. Although its heart was the traditional hall, a massive and grand chamber where all formal meals, audiences and entertainments were held, it also had a large number of private apartments and rooms, so that Lancaster and his family, as well as their most favoured guests, could retire to a more informal and comfortable privacy. Not even King Edward enjoyed such comforts in his palace at Westminster. The Painted Chamber, one of the three main halls of

Westminster's palace complex, was not only the place where Edward conducted all audiences and banquets, he also slept there, his bed being curtained off at one end of the hall. Privacy was not a luxury the English kings enjoyed.

Lancaster not only had luxurious privacy and a grand hall to frame his magnificence and wealth, he also enjoyed all the accoutrements of power normally only commanded by monarchs. But then, by virtue of his marriage to Constance, Lancaster was a king (if only titular, now that Constance was dead ... her death rumoured to have been caused by a severe chill brought on by her personality), and by virtue of the lands and properties he owned about not only his native land but also the continent, he was the richest — and thus the most powerful — private individual in England. At any given time he commanded more wealth and could raise more fighting men than could his father, the king.

It was highly significant that King John was to be held in custody (if such a luxurious sojourn could be equated with custody) at the Savoy Palace under the protection of Lancaster. Even far to the north of England, where Thomas had resided in his home friary of Durham before leaving for Rome, there had been rumours that King Edward's mind had softened with his years and, as the Black Prince was so often away (*and now increasingly ill*, Thomas added to himself), John of Gaunt, Duke of Lancaster, was the effective King of England.

Thomas turned away from the window where he had been watching the continued activity in the courtyard as horses, equipment and baggage were still being unloaded and studied his chamber anew. It was small and barely furnished, almost a cell. There was a stool, a small chest in which to stow his belongings (and they were not great: a spare robe, some underclothes and a small, unadorned, but highly cherished book of prayers) and a plain wooden bed to sleep on, and not even a fireplace for warmth. Nevertheless, it was private, something Thomas had not truly expected.

Well, that was all to the good, because he could spend his privacy well in prayer.

He sighed. He was back in England, and another portion of his journey done, but there was yet more to be accomplished. Thomas doubted he would be able to leave London before the Christmas celebrations were done, and that might be a delay of some two or three weeks.

And then there was the Prior General to consider. Had he heard that Thomas was travelling with Lancaster's party? Was the grim-faced man even now riding his mule south from Oxford?

Richard Thorseby had the power to completely sabotage Thomas' plans to move north to Bramham friary where, Thomas prayed daily to God, Wynkyn de Worde's casket still rested undisturbed in some undercroft, and only Lancaster had the power to protect Thomas from the Prior General.

Thomas glanced at the stool. A platter with the remains of some bread and cheese rested on it; Katherine's invitation had not extended to joining the family for the evening meal. Well, it was well past dusk now, and his chamber was growing chill. Time, indeed, to join Lancaster and Katherine for the evening.

As he left the room, noting well the guards placed at intervals down the outside corridor — Lancaster was evidently ensuring Thomas didn't make his own plans to journey north — Thomas wondered what had become of the Lady Margaret.

He soon found out.

Lancaster's private apartments were situated just behind and up from the main hall, and when the guards outside the main door nodded him through into the main chamber, the first person Thomas saw was Margaret.

She sat in the shadows of a leaping fire — its flames had attracted his eyes before anything else — on a stool, her hands occupied with the ever-present needlework to be found close to any noblewoman, and, for the first time since Thomas had met her, wearing something other than the patched grey gown. Katherine, who had known her own youthful years of poverty and neglect, had given Margaret one of her own gowns — Thomas remembered Katherine wearing it — of lemon linen, embroidered about its hem, sleeves and neckline with cornflowers. It suited Margaret's colouring, and its lines somewhat concealed her growing pregnancy.

"Thomas, come join us." Lancaster spoke from a dais set against a soaring arched window filled with delicate stained glass. Katherine was at his side in a smaller chair than Lancaster's all-but-throne, her hand resting gently on his arm, and a smile still on her face.

Katherine, Thomas thought, *looks as if she were the most contented woman in Christendom.*

There was a low table before them, water and wine ewers set upon it, with goblets, and platters of figs and dates. At one end was a chessboard and pieces, and here Bolingbroke sat relaxed upon a stool, a pawn turning over and over in one hand.

A young woman sat to one side of him, her cheeks flushed. She had Katherine's deep auburn hair and sparkling grey eyes and Thomas recognised her instantly as Joan Beaufort, bastard daughter of Lancaster and Katherine.

And, presumably, Thomas' next aunt.

There were several other figures who sat or stood beyond the immediate family circle on the dais; like Margaret, they were minor nobles who served the Lancaster family.

Thomas bowed his head in greeting, and began to move to the chair next to Katherine that Lancaster indicated, when a youth stepped forward from a curtained doorway set in the rounded right wall of the chamber.

Thomas halted, then bowed his head — a little lower this time. "My lord Richard," he said, "it has been many years since we have last conversed, and in this time I find you have turned from a boy into a man."

Richard, eighteen-year-old only child of the Black Prince and his wife, Joan of Kent, moved forward to take the chair.

He was tall and slender — no doubt he would eventually mature into the well-muscled form of most Plantagenet men — and fair of hair, but it was his face that most caught

Thomas' attention. Richard shared the thin, sensitive features of his Uncle Gloucester, and that boded ill, for he would one day be King of England, and England would not well enjoy the narrowness of vision and intolerance that so often went with those features.

"Thomas," Richard said, pausing briefly to look Thomas up and down. "You look quite the inquisitor in those robes and with that sour look upon your face. Have you come to condemn us all to hell, then?"

Thomas froze, then forced a smile to his face. "I am come here in goodwill, Richard, and shall condemn none of you to hell unless you so force my hand."

Lancaster and Katherine laughed, but Hal looked carefully at Thomas' face, and then dropped his eyes to the chess piece he held in his hand.

"We must be careful what we say," Lancaster said, winking at Richard, "lest Thomas hand all our names to the Holy Office of the Inquisition."

Richard smiled, hard and cold. He sat down in a chair and reached for a piece of fruit. "I think this is not a jesting matter, uncle. Thomas' friends do have a habit of ending up in the flames."

Thomas, as all the members of Lancaster's household, froze into a shocked stillness. Margaret, not privy to the story of Alice, merely looked bewildered. Nevertheless, she could see the effect the comment had on everyone else, and she lowered her head to her needlework.

"If my presence so disturbs you," Thomas said, "then perhaps I should leave."

"No," said Richard, waving his half-eaten apple about languidly, "do stay. Perhaps you can entertain us with tales of what penitent peasants whisper in the confessional. Is it true, Thomas, that some peasant men like to fornicate with cows?"

"Richard!" Lancaster said, staring intently at his nephew.

"Forgive me," Richard said to Thomas. "I have spoken out of turn."

He did not sound in the least penitent, and his eyes still contained a spiteful glow.

Thomas bowed, accepting the words of apology, and moved to a stool that Hal had pulled out from behind his own. He hoped that Richard would have many years to grow into a more magnanimous maturity before he finally succeeded both his grandfather and father ...

But Edward was old and ripe for death, and the Black Prince was middle-aged and ill!

Richard was, in all likelihood, closer to succeeding to the throne than anyone would wish.

And here he was in Lancaster's court rather than his grandfather's.

As the group fell into a gentle — if slightly forced — debate about the merits of the various hawks in Lancaster's stable, Thomas studied the duke with deep interest.

Lancaster had ever been known for his ambition ... how much had it rankled in him that he was a fourth son, not a first? The two brothers between himself and the Black Prince were both dead ... and between Lancaster and the throne stood only the prince and his son Richard. Was Lancaster only minding the throne for his nephew, or did he intend to seize it from him?

It was well past Compline — Thomas had heard the bells of St Paul's ring out faintly — when Lancaster and Katherine rose.

As they left the chamber, Lancaster paused and turned to Thomas.

"At midday," he said, "I and my household will escort King John to Westminster to be greeted by my father. Thomas, it will be a lengthy and grandiose occasion, and I expect you will be happier here. Do not think this a rebuff, Tom, for you will be welcome among my household for the Christmastide feasting in the Painted Chamber ... but for now, it is best you stay within these walls."

And then he and Katherine were gone.

III

Matins on the Thursday before the Nativity of
Our Lord Jesus Christ
In the fifty-first year of the reign of Edward III
(pre-dawn 23rd December 1378)

— The Nameless Day —

— i —

*J*ohn lifted back a heavy wave of hair from Katherine's
brow, and, smiling sweetly, kissed her mouth.

*God, he was glad beyond measure to once again have
her in his bed and house.*

They had made love, passionately, each as desperate as
the other, and now were languid and loath to sleep.

The months apart had been too long.

"I have sent messages to my father," John said, his mouth
only barely clear of hers. "We shall be wed on Saint
Stephen's Day, and in his chapel."

Tears filled Katherine's eyes. She was of only minor
nobility and the honour that John did her, and the love that
he showed her, in making her his duchess moved her deeply.
She lifted her hands, and caressed his face.

"There will be many who will not be pleased," she said.

"Then they can be damned!"

"Shush, beloved!" But Katherine giggled anyway, and John lowered his head and kissed her with as much passion as the afternoon they'd first bedded some twenty-five years previous.

She playfully disengaged herself. "My lord, you shall get me with child again!"

John laughed. "If you got with child again at your advanced age, my sweet cherished woman, then the pope would declare it a miracle!"

For a while there was nothing but sweet murmurings and caresses between them, then, as they stilled again, Katherine sighed.

"Tired of me already, beloved?" John said, a decided edge to his tone.

"Oh, nay! I was but thinking of the Lady Margaret."

"One of the greatest peers of the realm shares your bed, and you can think of nothing but a minor lady?"

Katherine smiled, relieved that his tone had slid back into banter. "*The* greatest peer, my darling lord. No, I was thinking of Margaret because of what we'd said about me getting with child."

She paused, knowing they both remembered back to that afternoon twenty-five years ago. Her husband, Hugh de Swynford, had only recently died, and Lancaster had taken advantage of her widowhood to finally coerce her into his bed. He had gotten her with child that afternoon — their first, Henry — and for many years afterwards all had lived with the pretence that Henry had been Hugh's posthumous son.

Now here was Margaret, recently widowed and now pregnant with a lover's child that would be passed off as her husband's posthumous get.

The difference between Margaret's situation and Katherine's was that Margaret's lover would not stand by her.

Katherine understood why Raby had distanced himself from Margaret. Indeed, her maternal instincts applauded him for it, for her daughter Joan would thereby win herself a husband unencumbered with a mistress and bastard child, but Katherine still felt for Margaret.

When the woman had been brought into her presence earlier this afternoon Katherine's heart had instantly gone out to her. Margaret was fearful and looked thin and ill ... *and* ill-cherished in that threadbare robe.

"Perhaps we can find her a husband at court, my sweet," Katherine said.

"Ah! Now I know why I cleave so strong to you. You have spoken well, my dear. Yes," John rolled onto his back and stared at the shadowy vaulted ceiling of their chamber, "we shall find her a husband."

It would not be difficult. Margaret was a beautiful woman, and between them, Lancaster and Raby would ensure she was endowed with enough land to make her doubly desirable. That she had a bastard child (*her husband's posthumous child*) would be no matter at all. Indeed, it would only increase her value, showing as it did her ability to breed heirs.

"But not until she has had the child," John continued. "No man would want to take to his marriage bed a woman so swollen with child he could not top her."

"None of my bellies stopped *you*, my lord!"

"Ah, but there has never been a woman as desirable as you."

She giggled again, and, encouraged, John slid his hand to regions still hot from their previous lust.

She wriggled, heating his desire. "Thomas has much changed."

"Ah!" John rolled away again. *Would she never tilt her mind back to the matter at hand?*

"Alice's death caught him hard," Katherine said.

John was silent some time before he replied. "Thomas behaved badly towards Alice and her husband, and then behaved even more poorly towards his own family as well as his liege lord in escaping into holy orders. He has run far and fast to escape the consequences of his actions. It has not become him."

"And yet ... yet you said that there was some holy duty that he has been charged with? Something of such great import that you have allowed him back into the heart of your court?"

John lay silent again, then, his love and trust of Katherine so strong and true it formed one of the cornerstones of his entire existence, he told of her the demons that had taunted the Black Prince, Hal and Thomas, and of Thomas' desire to find this casket that would contain the secrets to the demons' destruction.

Frightened beyond anything she had yet experienced in her life, Katherine clung close to John.

"What can we do?"

John shrugged slightly. "As much as we can." Then he tightened his arms about her. "As much as we must."

"Thomas is *such* a strange man," she said, not knowing quite what she meant by that.

"Strange indeed," John said, sliding his hand once more into the realms of temptation, "if he gave up the feel of womanly flesh for the scratch of clerical robes."

This time Katherine did not discourage John. Nothing would so ease her fear or make her feel so safe as the weight of John atop her again.

"If what you say is true," she said, then moaned involuntarily as her lover's hand stroked and teased her flesh, "then perhaps Thomas was meant for a life as a priest, after all."

"Enough of Tom and of the Church," John said. "What I have here for you, my lady, has nothing to do with either!"

Thomas spent the night in prayer. He valued the privacy of his chamber, as well as its sparseness that recalled the many years Thomas had spent immersed in spiritual contemplation within the family of the Church.

Over the past weeks and months the constant travelling had meant a deepening distance from the order and discipline of a friary, and Thomas had missed that deeply. He'd become too absorbed in the secular world — its people and intrigues — and had become distracted from his purpose.

Katherine inferred he had taken holy orders in order to escape the guilt he felt for the deaths of Alice and her children.

Had he?

No! No! Their deaths had merely opened a door for him, made him realise that his true purpose in life was not to dabble in the intrigues of the nobility, nor to run his vast estates, nor even to participate in the glorious practice of war, but to serve God as best he could ... to become a soldier for the cause of righteousness.

And hadn't the soundness of that decision been justified by God choosing him to lead the fight against the demons and their infernal conspiracy to create a Godless world? Hadn't St Michael said he'd been forgiven?

But what of Jeannette? Why had God also sent St Michael to prepare her for the same fight? Did God think he needed a reserve in case he failed?

Did God not have faith enough in him?

Thomas bent his head and wept, now completely distracted from the comfort of prayer and contemplation. Perhaps he had failed, for here he was in the worldly luxury of the Savoy Palace and not at Bramham Moor friary, learning the secrets of Wynkyn's casket.

Thomas.

Thomas lifted his head, his face wan and tear-streaked. "Saint Michael?" he whispered.

There was nothing before him save the freezing pre-dawn gloom. Nothing ...

Thomas.

He twisted, looking behind him. Nothing but the bare stone of the outer wall of the chamber.

He turned back, and gasped.

Some two feet before him two hands hung in the air, suspended in a soft golden glow. They were the worn, comforting hands of an old man, held out palm upward as if to offer Thomas their warmth.

Without thinking Thomas reached out his own hands, and at the same moment the archangel reached forward and took Thomas' chilled hands in his.

Thomas, you must not doubt, even though the path seems dark.

"I have wasted so much time, the demons will have snatched the casket, I —"

Thomas, trust. Even if the demons seize the casket, they will not — they cannot — destroy either it or its contents. And while the casket and its secrets survive, the demons can be foiled. You are Wynkyn's successor. You alone can use the casket's mysteries against them. It may take you a month, it may take you a year or more, but they cannot keep that casket from you for much longer. It will be as drawn to you as you are to it. Trust.

Thomas wept anew, but this time for the warmth and comfort of the archangel's touch and words.

"Blessed saint, thank you!"

The archangel's hands tightened about his, and filled Thomas with a sense of urgency and dread.

Thomas, even if the demons cannot destroy the casket, nor keep it from you forever, the means they have chosen by which to work their evil within Christendom is devilish beyond words.

"They use ideas as their weapons, making men discontented with their lot, and with God."

Yes.

"Their persuasions must be great, to have so many willing servants within the realm of mankind."

Thomas felt the archangel hesitate, and now he shifted his grip so that he could grasp the archangel's hands, and give back as much reassurance as he'd received.

There is more, Thomas. The power of the demons has grown, but it has also grown desperate. They fear you, and they fear Jeannette — Joan. For many years they have nurtured within their midst a dark, cancerous mass they call their Crown Prince. Soon they will enthrone him, and he will become the great Demon-King whose task it will be to frustrate you and Joan, and to seize for all time this world for theirs.

Thomas opened his mouth to ask a question, then

remembered something the archangel — and Joan — had said to him when he'd been blessed with a visitation in Domremy.

"The English king ..."

Will be one and the same, yes. In order to give their prince the greatest power possible, the demons will crown him.

"But ... but ... the Black Prince will inherit when Edward dies, and I do not believe him to be a demon."

There is darkness afoot, Thomas. Darkness that I cannot fully fathom. All I know, all I can tell you, is that the ancient throne of the English kings, who are all descended from the line of David himself, will shortly bear the weight of the demon Crown Prince.

"What can I do?"

Prepare yourself, Thomas. The Demon-King will know you for what you are — the weapon of God — and he will actively seek you out. Yours will be the ultimate battle. What he cannot do, even with his power, is to keep you for long from the casket that is yours by right.

Thomas frowned. Who could it be? His mind kept returning to the Black Prince. Edward was old and not likely to live long. The Black Prince would succeed him ... but the prince as the devilish new Demon-King? Somehow that did not seem right at all.

And if the Black Prince did not live long himself? Then who? Richard ... or Lancaster himself?

I regret I cannot aid you more. The demon prince covers himself well.

Thomas remembered something that he'd been turning over in his mind for months. "Blessed Saint Michael ... after I had spoken to the demon at the Cleft, I began to suspect that the demons are sorcerous shape-shifters, and that they take the place of men and women within our society. Is that correct?"

Yes. You have learned well, Thomas. Anyone you meet could be a demon. Their masks are thick ... sometimes not even I can see through to the truth within.

"I can trust no one."

No one, save your God. Thomas ... why did you not tell me of this understanding in Domremy?

Thomas bowed his head. "I did not wish to share this information with the girl."

Then you are a fool, Thomas, and too given to self-pride. Your silence has done you little good — Joan already knew it, and she, unlike you, is far better at seeing through the masks that the demons disguise themselves with.

And with that, the archangel was gone, and Thomas was left alone in his cold, dark cell to consider the fact that Jeannette-grown-to-Joan might well be God's favoured weapon.

IV

Nones on the Thursday before the Nativity of
Our Lord Jesus Christ
In the fifty-first year of the reign of Edward III
(midday 23rd December 1378)

— The Nameless Day —

— ii —

John, Duke of Lancaster, escorted King John to meet
with the English King Edward in Westminster in fine
style, as befitted the rank and power of all concerned.
Just before midday five barges drew up close to the steps
leading down to the Thames from the Savoy Palace.

The barges were elaborately decorated: damasks and
tapestries hung over the vessels' sides, drooping almost to
the waterline; gilded pavilions had been set up on the
leading two barges, with cushioned and well-draped
thrones under each for Lancaster and King John. Slightly
less intricate and gilded pavilions had been raised on
the final three barges, with seating for nobles and knights
who would serve as escort, and from all five fluttered
pennants and standards — a bright, riveting display of
colour, gaiety and power for the Christmastide celebrations
of the Londoners.

From his windy, cold perch high on the parapets of the Savoy's outer wall, Thomas watched Lancaster and his retinue escort King John through the inner courtyard of the palace towards the river gate. Thomas was tired, but was nevertheless much calmer and stronger in spirit than he'd been for many weeks. St Michael's visit — even though it had left many questions in his mind — had fortified him and renewed his resolve, and Thomas blessed the saint for his benevolence.

Lancaster and King John, like those who escorted them, were tiny, bright sparks far below, incongruous summer butterflies proceeding majestically along the flagged courtyard between the Savoy and the gate in the outer wall. Although all of the nobles and knights wore ceremonial swords belted about their velveted and furred robes, none wore armour, for there was no perceived threat from within the environs of London and Westminster.

Thomas smiled sardonically. *No "threat"? But who knew what demons walked among them, smiling and bowing and scheming?*

He leaned on the inner parapet, trying to glimpse faces among those who followed Lancaster and the French king. There was Hal, close behind his father, and Gloucester, who must have arrived earlier in the day from his own palace in London. There was the bishop of London, the weak winter sun glinting off his jewelled mitre, and behind him a black- and brown-robed bobbing train of monks and friars.

Who among them were demons?

Thomas shuddered. Until he discovered the means by which he could tell demon from Christian, he must needs suspect all he met. Furthermore, he knew that as the demons knew him to be the soldier of St Michael and of God, they would necessarily gravitate to him.

Everyone about him might be a demon!

His heart turned cold at the thought. The demons had been loose within Christendom for thirty years. In that time they could have assumed the identity ... of anyone ... anyone ...

Horns sounded, breaking Thomas' reverie. He looked down — Lancaster and his party had entirely disappeared.

Thomas turned, strode the five paces across the top of the wall, and leaned over the river side of the parapet.

The two barges containing first Lancaster, and then King John and their immediate escorts, were just now pulling away from the steps, and the next barges drawing in so the rest of the retinue could board. With a minimum of fuss they embarked, and within a quarter hour the three barges joined the two awaiting them in the centre of the river before all five began their stately progress west towards Westminster.

As he watched, Thomas suddenly became aware that the biting wind had chilled him to the bone. Shivering, and pulling his robes tight about him, he moved to the stairs and walked down to the courtyard.

He wasn't sure what he wanted to do. He'd have liked to talk with Bolingbroke, but Hal had accompanied his father to Westminster. Katherine? No, Thomas wasn't too sure he wanted to talk with her.

He didn't want to be reminded again of the incident that had propelled him towards the Church.

He hadn't done wrong, no, he hadn't. He just didn't want to keep going over an old and valueless episode of his youth.

So Thomas walked briskly towards the gates that led from the Savoy complex into the Strand, but was brought to a rude halt when the guards flanking each side of the gate set their spears to block his path.

"Your pardon, Brother," one of them said, "but our Lord of Lancaster had requested that you remain within the palace grounds."

Thomas gave a low laugh. "For my own safety, I suppose."

Then he realised that the expression on all of the guards' faces were ones of great discomfort, and he understood they were gravely embarrassed by their orders. It was not right to restrict the movements of a man of God, nor to imprison him without the orders of a prelate.

So Thomas smiled more genuinely, and bowed slightly.

"I commend you for your loyalty and duty to your lord. Be assured that I realise this is none of your wishing."

Their expressions relaxed, and one or two smiled.

"I wish you good day," Thomas said, and turned and left them.

The wind bit deeper, strengthening, and Thomas glanced towards the sky. Heavy snow clouds were roiling in from the south-west. He grinned impishly; by now the Thames would be irritable and snappish, and doubtless kings and escort alike were clinging grimly to the arms of their seats and wishing they'd chosen to ride the distance to visit King Edward. Whatever shit and mud the horses' hooves threw up would be vastly preferable to the white-crested wetness of the waves. Lancaster had done him a service in forcing him to remain inside the Savoy.

Seeking somewhere warm, Thomas entered the main hall of the palace. It was huge, stretching a good two hundred paces from east to west, forty from north to south, and another good one hundred towards its soaring hammerbeamed roof. Within the top third of the side walls ran a row of delicately arched gothic windows filled with jewel-like stained glass. The stone walls beneath them were covered with massive and beautiful tapestries, as well as the standards of Lancaster and his retainers.

There was a huge fireplace in the eastern wall, and another in the western, as also six open hearths that ran down the centre of the hall. Both fireplaces and all the hearths contained fiercely burning fires: although there would not be a feast here for at least three days (not until Lancaster and his new bride celebrated their wedding feast here on St Stephen's Day) the fires were needed now to warm the furthest corners of the vast hall in time for the great gathering.

Lancaster would be going through several forests in order to heat his hall ... but then, who could afford it if not he?

Trestle tables were already set up for the wedding feast, for Lancaster was planning for a sizeable number of guests — at least six hundred — and Thomas knew that the kitchens and pantries would already be a flurry of activity.

Here, for the moment, it was serene, with only a few servants quietly attending to their tasks, and it was warm. Thomas slowly paced down from the western end of the hall, where he had entered, towards the dais containing the High Table at the eastern end. His eyes were half closed, his posture relaxed, as he basked in the warmth and the scent of the herbs and spices that had been scattered about the fresh rushes underfoot.

He did not hear the man approach behind him with the silence of a great black crow swooping in for a kill.

"Brother Thomas," said a soft, whispery voice that was, nevertheless, hard with authority, "how well you stride your past haunts. Have you found the thrill of hawking and feasting hard to exchange for the rigours of serving the Lord our God?"

Thomas spun about, almost slipping in the rushes.

Behind him stood an elderly and very tall man, so thin he was almost skeletal, robed in black and wearing the cap of a Master at Oxford. His hair and long straggly beard were thin and grey, the skin of his face pallid and deeply scarred with the marks of an ancient pox, the fervent, feverish brightness of his eyes the only clue as to the fire that raged within.

Thomas stared too long before remembering his manners.

But then, did he need to demonstrate manners before a man who was almost indisputably a demon clothed in man's form?

"Master Wycliffe," Thomas said by way of greeting. He did not bow, nor show any other gesture of respect to a man he should otherwise have humbled himself before.

Wycliffe's mouth stretched in a tight smile, revealing yellowed teeth. "You have no respect left for me, Thomas."

"I had little to begin with."

Wycliffe indicated they should continue to walk towards the top of the hall. "You were ever one of my hottest adversaries at university."

"I remain so now."

"Ah, Thomas, you should learn a little tolerance."

Thomas stopped, forcing Wycliffe to do likewise.

"I do not tolerate your kind," Thomas said.

Wycliffe raised his eyebrows, as if to ask what Thomas meant by that, but he did not speak for a moment. Instead he took a deep breath, folding his arms and slipping his hands inside the sleeves of his robe.

"My Lord of Lancaster asked me to attend you this morning," Wycliffe eventually said, his eyes steady on Thomas' face.

"Lancaster asked you?"

Wycliffe inclined his head. "I am spiritual adviser to my lord, as well as his household."

"You are a heretic!"

Wycliffe showed no outward response at the charge. He was used enough to it.

"What for?" he asked softly. "For suggesting that the Church should release its wealth and secular power and again embrace the values of the Church Fathers — poverty and service?"

"I have heard that you advocate the abandonment of most Church services. Indeed, the abandonment of the entire Church hierarchy."

"I am glad that my poor musings have wandered so wide. But don't you think, Thomas, that if the Scriptures contain all we need to attain salvation, then most of the stinking, corrupt flesh of the Church can be cut away and left to rot of its own volition?"

"Priests are needed to —"

Wycliffe stopped him with a thin hand held up. "Spiritual advisers are needed, yes, but your average fat, corrupt and unlearned priest? The entire top-heavy structure of bishops and archbishops and cardinals and popes? Nay, I think both we and the Lord God Himself can do without them."

"I cannot think why the pope —"

"Of which among the current three popes ... I think it was at the last count ... do you speak?"

"— has not yet ordered your trial on charges of heresy!"

"Perhaps," Wycliffe said quietly, his eyes holding Thomas', "they are afraid of what I should say given the platform of a trial.

"But," Wycliffe turned and began to walk forward again, "we digress. My Lord of Lancaster asked me to interview you to determine your true nature."

What? Thomas walked after Wycliffe. "What do you mean?"

"My lord tells me that you believe yourself to be attempting some kind of divine mission." Wycliffe's mouth curled. "He wants to be sure that this is truly the case, and that you are not suffering from some devilish delusion."

"I serve my God with all my heart and soul ... which is far more than you —"

"I serve the best interests of mankind, my friend, not the best interests of the Church."

"The best interests of mankind are the best interests of the Church!"

They had almost reached the dais, and now they halted again, standing facing each other a few feet apart, Thomas white-faced and angry-eyed, Wycliffe irritatingly calm.

"Lancaster needs to know he can rely on you," Wycliffe said.

Thomas opened his mouth to protest that Lancaster could always depend on him when he stopped, thinking.

But who was Lancaster, and to whom and to what did Lancaster owe his loyalties?

Wycliffe smiled. "There are some scholars within the academies of Florence," he said, "who say that the world is entering a new age ... the age of humanism. The age of man. An age where salvation and fulfilment can be found in this life rather than the next. Where," he dropped his voice, "perhaps a man owes his king and country, even his wife, more loyalty and love than he does a distant, arrogant God."

Thomas' heart thudded. Wycliffe went beyond heresy, beyond treason to God.

"I know who you are!" he whispered.

Wycliffe shook his head, his malevolent smile stretching even further. "No. You know who no one is. I wish you well, Thomas."

He turned, and walked away.

"Wait!" Thomas called. "What will you tell Lancaster?"

Wycliffe paused, and spoke over his shoulder. "I shall tell Lancaster that you pose no danger."

And with that he was gone.

V

After Nones on the Vigil of the Nativity of
Our Lord Jesus Christ
In the fifty-first year of the reign of Edward III
(afternoon Friday 24th December 1378)

— Yuletide Eve —

Lancaster's party had returned late in the evening, by horse, with a litter for the French king. As Thomas had suspected, the Thames had blown up into irritable, choppy waves, and a barge ride back from Westminster had been out of the question. Thomas had seen none of the party. He had been in the chapel praying when they returned, and had then kept to his room for the evening and night until Matins prayers the next morning.

He had not been invited to join Lancaster and his family in the evening.

The Vigil of Christ's Nativity had dawned clear and crispy cold: yesterday's threatening storm had moved eastwards without making good its promise to ruin London's Christmastide festivities. Thomas had attended dawn mass in the Savoy's chapel, an imposing building that abutted the river. Katherine was there, as well as her ladies, including Margaret, several other members of Lancaster's household, and most of the servants who were not immediately needed. Lancaster and Bolingbroke were not present, and Wycliffe seemed to have disappeared back into whatever dark pit he inhabited.

After mass Katherine invited Thomas to break his fast at her table, but he refused. He needed time alone, and time to pray in order to prepare his soul before the morrow's holiness, as also for the coming battle against the demons, and so he bowed politely to her, nodded to the bevy of ladies at her back (Margaret had her face averted and refused to catch his eye), and made his way back to his room and a humble meal of water and bread.

Finally, as the Savoy Palace came to life — men-at-arms tramping along hallways, men and horses moving in courtyards, servants hastening hither and thither, cooks and pantry boys overseeing preparations for Christmas feasts — Thomas sank to his knees on the cold stone floor of his chamber, and folded his hands and bowed his head in prayer.

Thomas prayed three or four hours, finally rising at nones and stretching his stiff and cold limbs. He rubbed a hand across his face and scalp. Both his chin and tonsure were bristly and needed attention. The least Thomas could do to celebrate and honour Christ's birth was to greet the day of his nativity with shaven face and tonsure.

Just as he'd finished shaving — very carefully, with a razor that had seen too much service already — he heard footsteps approach along the corridor outside before someone used their fist to hammer on his door.

"Tom! Tom!" a man's voice called. "I seek Tom Neville!"

Laying the razor to one side, and repressing a grin, Thomas stood, straightened his robes, then stepped to the door and opened it.

There was a tall man outside, of an age with himself. He was lean and fit, wearing a heavily embroidered knee-length and hooded over-tunic of blue and gold wool with streamers dangling from its sleeves. His thick dark hair was cut short over straight eyebrows, a slightly hooked nose and merry brown eyes.

Bolingbroke stood laughing behind the man, similarly (if slightly more richly) dressed in a colourful knee-length tunic embroidered with gems and pearls and with silver-gilt buttons. He had two thick cloaks draped over one arm.

Both men were armed with knives in their belts.

As soon as Thomas opened the door, the man who had hammered and called affected a startled and contrite expression.

He fell to his knees, and clasped his hands in contrition. "Oh, father! Forgive me. I thought my old friend Tom resided here ... but I was misled! Why! Here is a sober priest, ready to condemn me to hellfire's misery for my thoughtlessness."

Thomas grinned over the man's now bowed head at Bolingbroke, then leaned over and shook the kneeling man's shoulder.

"Oh, get up, Hotspur. I still live here, under these sober robes."

Lord Henry Percy, son and heir of the powerful and ambitious Earl of Northumberland, known far and wide as Hotspur for his courage in battle, leaped to his feet and embraced Thomas.

"Ah, my friend, it has been too long! Too long!"

"Hotspur arrived late last night, Tom," Bolingbroke said. "He demanded there and then to be taken to your chamber, but I demurred. I said you'd be in too deep a conversation with your God and would not welcome mere mortal merriment."

Thomas smiled, and gripped Hotspur's forearms with his hands. "You look well ... better than well. How many of the foul Scots have you laid waste with your sword in the past years, Hotspur? I have heard such tales about your exploits!"

Hotspur sobered. "As I have about yours, Thomas."

Thomas locked eyes briefly with Bolingbroke. *What had Hal told Hotspur?*

Hal reassured him with a quick shake of his head. *I have told him nothing of the demons.*

"You have been to Rome, no less!" Hotspur said. "And now I hear you have the monstrous Thorseby panting for your arrest and, doubtless, your execution!"

Although he knew Hotspur had spoken in jest, Thomas narrowed his eyes thoughtfully. *Was the Prior General more than just a man?*

"Ah!" Hotspur said. "But we cannot stand about in this chill corridor, Thomas. I can't imagine why Hal hasn't had you housed more hospitably."

Hal shrugged. "This is what makes Thomas feel most comfortable these days, Hotspur."

"You carry the pretence of priesthood too far," Hotspur said.

"I do not *pretend* at all!" Thomas replied, stung.

Hotspur ignored him. Swivelling, he took one of the cloaks that Hal had been holding, then turned back to Thomas, slinging the cloak about his shoulders. "Do you have a warm cloak? Yes? Then fetch it, man! An adventure awaits us!"

Thomas hesitated. He constantly felt as if he should be *doing* something, going somewhere, but his recent conversation with the archangel and his hours of prayer had made him realise that he could not always be moving, or fighting.

Sometimes he had simply to rest, and observe.

Thomas now understood that a calm observing eye would serve him as well, if not better, than constant agitation to move forward and find Wynkyn's casket. After all, the casket was as much moving towards him, as he should be moving towards it. Yes, he needed to reach it, and discover its secrets ... but Thomas *also* needed to discover the secrets of those about him.

Somehow Lancaster, or someone (or a number of people) within his immediate circle, was involved with the demons. Wycliffe, certainly. Others, most definitely.

Was the heir apparent to the Demon-King's throne among them?

St Michael had told him that the new Demon-King would be as driven to seek him out as would the casket.

If Thomas watched and observed, perhaps he could mark him before he did too much damage.

Beside, it was Christmastide, and there would be no leaving London for two weeks or more until after Plough Monday, the unofficial end of the Christmastide festivities.

It was Christmastide, and there was to be much eating and drinking and merry-making, and perhaps the demons among Lancaster's retinue would relax ... make an error of judgement ... disclose themselves ...

"Thomas?" Hotspur said. "Have you gone to ask your God for permission to indulge in a small Christmastide adventure?"

Thomas grinned, shook his head, and went to fetch his cloak. A small adventure wouldn't do him any harm at all.

Hal and Hotspur had horses waiting in the courtyard.

"Come, come!" Hotspur said, striding ahead of the other two, sliding on thick gloves against the winter chill.

"I am to be allowed to leave?" Thomas said softly to Hal.

Hal slid him an unfathomable glance. "My father merely wants to be sure of you," he said. "There is too much unsurety in these days to risk that which does not need to be risked."

Hotspur had mounted his horse, a showy, fiery grey stallion. "Tom, Hal, do hurry along!"

Grooms held Hal's and Thomas' horses, and the two men mounted.

Thomas still had the brown gelding given him so many months ago by Marcel.

I must be rid of it, he thought, *for this horse is a gift from the Devil himself.* Then he half jerked, wondering further if the horse itself was a demon.

"Don't you even want to know where we're going?" Hotspur said as they clattered towards the gates.

"To where do we go?" Thomas dutifully replied, his eyes still on the gelding beneath him.

"There is to be a tilting match at Smithfield," Hal responded before Hotspur broke in.

"And a wrestling match, and an archery contest, and, some say, fireworks!"

Hal grinned wryly. "Half the household is already there," he said. "We waited only to fetch you ... Thomas, do stop glaring at your horse like that. He is a mediocre animal, to be sure, but I thought priests did not like to mount themselves atop showy, prancing beasts."

Thomas finally raised his eyes. "He was a gift from a man I no longer trust," he said, "and so now I wonder whether I should distrust the gift."

"Trust is something that can all too easily be misconstrued," Hal said. "Sometimes we accept in trust what we should reject, and reject what we should trust."

Hotspur threw up his hands in mock despair, his stallion almost bolting as his rider momentarily relinquished control of the reins. Hotspur regained control, then grinned over his shoulder.

"I did not think you the philosopher, Hal. Now, can we ride?"

Hal smiled back at Hotspur, although his face remained thoughtful, and soon all three were clattering through the crowds in the courtyard of St Paul's. At Cheapside they turned north onto the short street that led through Aldersgate towards the open space in the suburbs beyond the walls where many festivals and markets were held. As they rode through the streets, people stood back, waving and calling out cheerfully to Hal.

Thomas rode closer to him. "If the people had their say, Hal, you would sit the throne before either the Black Prince or Richard!"

Hal did not laugh, as Thomas thought he would. "'Tis treasonous talk, Thomas. I'd not thought it of you."

"It was but a jest," Thomas said, "and between friends."

Hal stared at him. "And are we friends, Thomas? You and I and Hotspur were once inseparable; we sinned and jested and fought together. Now ... ah, forgive me. I grow maudlin."

He looked away, his eyes focused on something in his

thoughts rather than on the still cheering crowds to either side of him. "After yesterday I feel the passing of an age most sorely."

"What happened?"

Hal did not reply for the moment, but waved briefly at the crowds. He waited until they had ridden through Aldersgate before he replied.

"His grace my grandfather has aged since I last saw him some few months previously."

"Edward is old."

"Aye. He still appears strong in body ... but his mind has slipped away. Yesterday ... yesterday during the ceremonies to greet King John he dribbled and whispered, and some of the baser men watching sniggered and jested at his expense. My father had them committed to Ludgate later, but ..."

"Hal."

Hal shrugged. "My grandfather grows old, and inane with age. But he is also a king, and I do fear for what lies before us."

"Has your father heard of the Black Prince?"

"Aye. We know he has reached Bordeaux safely, but little else. My father grows more worried by the hour. He wishes now that he counselled my uncle the more strongly to return to England. My God, Tom, he is the heir, and he should be here, now!"

"Can no message be sent?"

Hal gave a short bark of humourless laughter. "Messengers have been sent night and day, to no avail."

"Hal, there is something I should tell you." Thomas needed to confide in someone ... if only to gain another pair of ears and eyes, and Hal had access to places and people that Thomas did not.

And who could he trust if not Hal?

"Yes?"

"It is about the demons."

Hal now focused sharply on Thomas' face.

"I fear we have badly misjudged their power and abilities. It seems that —"

"Hal! Tom!" Hotspur had reined his horse into a sliding, half-rearing stop as they neared Smithfield, and was now calling back to them. "Why do you lag so! The games have already begun!"

He waved ahead to a field containing thousands of Londoners, scores of tents, and hundreds of leaping, waving standards and banners. In the open centre of the field knights were already tilting to the cheers and cries of the crowd.

Hal reached out and touched Thomas' arm. "Later, my friend. I think this neither the place nor time."

When they arrived at the stand accommodating Lancaster's retinue Thomas saw that both the Duke and Katherine sat throne-like chairs already, laughing and clapping at the display before them.

A few paces behind Katherine stood Margaret, still wearing the same lemon gown, but now with a dark blue cloak wrapped about her.

As Thomas watched, the cloak blew back, momentarily exposing her pregnant belly, and Thomas' mind was instantly, frighteningly, reminded of how good it had felt when Odile had pressed her pregnant body into his, and how it had made his lust rise . . .

"Thomas," Hal said. "Stop gawping at the ladies and dismount. There is a much better view from atop the stand."

VI

After Nones on the Feast of the Nativity of
Our Lord Jesus Christ
In the fifty-first year of the reign of Edward III
(afternoon Saturday 25th December 1378)

— Yuletide —

— i —

"Yes? What is it?" The Black Prince raised his head from the letter he was composing to his wife. Raby had entered his chamber, and was waving a letter of his own from one hand.

"My lord! It is a letter —"

The Black Prince sighed irritably. He was not feeling well, and would rather not have been disturbed.

"— from your lady wife, Joan."

"What?" The Black Prince rose to his feet, stumbled slightly, recovered, then strode to meet Raby halfway across the chamber.

"Wat Tyler brought it to me, my lord," Raby said. "A messenger brought it to the gates of the city, and then left."

The Black Prince glanced at the seal — it was indeed from Joan! — and tore the letter open. They had been in Bordeaux a week or more now, and even that short period had seen the prince grow bored. He missed Joan terribly, and wished he could have been with her for the festive season.

His eyes scanned the letter. "Sweet Jesu! Raby, Joan is on her way here!"

"What? Not true ... surely?"

"True enough!" The Black Prince waggled the letter at Raby. "She left London as soon as Lancaster arrived, swearing she would spend Christmastide with me. It was to be a surprise, save that her ship put in at Blaye because the master had a toothache so sore he could not continue without having his decaying peg pulled. Lord God, Raby, Blaye is only some twenty or so miles north of here! Joan is surely on the road already. Come, man! Let us meet her!"

And before Raby could object, the Black Prince had hastened from the chamber and was shouting for his horse.

VII

Vespers on the Feast of the Nativity of
Our Lord Jesus Christ
In the fifty-first year of the reign of Edward III
(early evening Saturday 25th December 1378)

— Yuletide —

— ii —

Christmastide was the busiest time of year at any
court — surpassed only by the funeral of a king and
the coronation of his successor.

For Lancaster's household the religious rites of
Christmastide began with midnight Angels' Mass in the chapel
of the Savoy, continued with the Shepherds' Mass at daybreak,
and culminated in the Mass of the Divine Word at noon. Apart
from a few guards, the entire household attended all three
masses; even the cooks, for the evening Christmastide feast and
revelries were to be held at Westminster in the great hall,
hosted by King Edward. All three masses were marked with
great joy, and joyous spirituality. Now, at the darkest time of
the year, Christ had been born, signifying the eventual
resurrection of the sun on the grim (yet, even so, joyful) festival
of Easter. The solstice had occurred and winter was here, but
so was the newborn Christ, and with Him, hope was born.

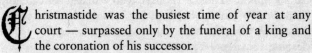

During the Mass of the Divine Word the chapel was filled with light — there were over three thousand lit tapers and candles, as well as the cold midday light that filtered down through the stained glass windows — incense, and the music of the choir. To one side of the altar a nativity scene had been set up under the alabaster statue of the Virgin Mary and the infant Christ: a crib, with a straw cow and ass set beside it. Lancaster, Katherine, Bolingbroke and the immediate members of the household sat on richly decorated pews at the front of the nave. Thomas stood alongside one of the columns that separated nave from aisles on either side. Behind Lancaster's family were a few score knights and their ladies, then a hundred or more men-at-arms, before the mass of servants who made up the bulk of Lancaster's household. To either side of the nave stood sundry monks and friars who were not part of the choir, but were in some manner attached to the Savoy chapel or Lancaster's household. Thomas studied them carefully, but could not see Wycliffe among them.

Margaret stood among the knights and their ladies. She glanced neither to her left nor to her right — she certainly did not appear to notice Thomas, who watched her carefully from time to time — but kept her eyes on the rood screen before the altar, her lips murmuring in prayer, her hands clasping a small prayer book.

Was she merely pretending, or truly devout?

Lancaster's personal chaplain rose to deliver the Christmas homily, a righteous but generally torrid and baffling piece about the rigours of the true Christian life, and Thomas found his attention wandering.

A movement at the very rear of the chapel caught his eyes.

Wycliffe, standing in the shadows, watching Thomas as carefully as Thomas had been watching others.

The man nodded when he saw that Thomas had spotted him, and then melted back into the shadows.

Thomas went cold.

The demon dared show himself, even within God's house, and during this most sacred of masses?

He stared towards the spot where Wycliffe had vanished, but he could not see him, and eventually he turned his eyes back over the rest of the congregation … wondering …

The Black Prince rode from Bordeaux with an escort of several hundred men. The city was deep within English-controlled territory, but he wished to take no chances with the life and health of his beloved wife. If luck were with him he would have her back by nightfall!

But luck was not with him at all. Almost as soon as Bordeaux was out of sight, the rainy weather disintegrated into a winter storm with driving snow and a wind that bit deep into the riders' bones. The Black Prince tried to push on through the storm, but it was not possible, and he reluctantly agreed with Raby that it were best to shelter in the lee of a hill.

Had this storm hit Joan as well? Or had she taken the precaution of waiting for him in Blaye?

Within an hour the Black Prince was in desperate straits. His men had managed to light a small fire for him, and even managed to keep it going, but whatever warmth it threw out was blown away before it could reach the flesh of any who huddled about it. The prince had hunkered down on his haunches, blankets and cloaks thrown about him so that only his eyes and nose emerged from their woollen wrap.

Yet even that small glimpse afforded of his flesh told of nothing but disaster. The prince's eyes were bright with some inner fever that ate away his strength, his flesh so pale it was almost transparent — Raby swore he could see the shape of the prince's bones beneath its inadequate protection.

His form shook and trembled beneath the mound of blankets.

It was almost as if the storm was sucking the life force out of him with every gust.

Raby stood to one side (leaning, more like, in the strength of the wind), feeling utterly useless. He knew he should have persuaded the prince to wait in Bordeaux. *Lord Jesus Christ, the prince's life was more important than that of his wife!*

He was just about to suggest that they try and find a farm, a barn, *anything*, to wait out the storm when a shout came from one side.

"My lord! My lord!"

A man, struggling to keep on his feet as he emerged out of the storm.

Raby wiped his eyes free of clinging snow and stared. Ah, Wat Tyler, one of Lancaster's men who the Duke had left in his brother's force.

"My lord," Tyler said, gasping for breath as he gained Raby's side. "There is something ..."

"What, man?"

"There is something in the storm, my lord. Something evil."

It wasn't until the hour before Vespers that Thomas finally managed to speak privately with Hal in the man's apartments.

"Sweet Jesu!" Hal said as he pulled Thomas in through the door and walked him close to the window. "I have spent half of Christmastide wondering what it is that you must tell me!"

"Forgive me, Hal, but the tilting and entertainments had not seemed appropriate. There were many ears and eyes present."

Bolingbroke looked at Thomas searchingly. "You do not trust Hotspur?"

Thomas spread his hands helplessly. "There are few I can trust. I do not distrust Hotspur specifically ... it is just that I do not yet know if I *can* trust him. Besides, there were *many* people present, not just Hotspur."

"We talked briefly yesterday of trust." Hal had now turned to stare out the window to where grooms readied the numbers of horses necessary to convey Lancaster and his party to Westminster.

"You said that sometimes we accept in trust what we should reject, and reject what we should trust."

Hal turned back to Thomas. "And yet you still trust *me*?"

"What lies between us goes beyond trust. If I cannot trust

you, then there is no reason for me to live. I have few friends, Hal, and those few I have I must treasure."

Hal's eyes filled with tears, and he clasped Thomas' shoulders in his hands. "Thank you ... thank you."

"Yes, well ... um ..."

Grinning now, Hal dropped his hands. "So what is your news?"

Thomas hesitated, dropped his eyes to consider his hands, then looked Hal directly in the face. This was something he should have confided to Joan ... he would not keep it from Hal.

"Hal, the demons are stronger than you realise. Although their true forms are those we saw in the fields outside Chatellerault, the creatures have the power to shape-shift. Hal, they can assume the forms of Godly men and women!"

"Sweet Jesu! But that would mean that any among us ..."

"Yes. Hal, there is worse, far worse. Two mornings ago Saint Michael again appeared to me, bearing devastating tidings. For many years the demons have nurtured within their midst a Crown Prince ... and soon they plan to place him —"

"*Jesu!*"

"— on England's throne. Hal, soon the English will be led by a Demon-King, and led into such devilry that we can hardly imagine!"

Now Hal was shocked into utter silence.

"Hal, I do not know the *who*, and I cannot understand the *how*. I do not accept that the Black Prince is —"

"No, no, I am with you. My uncle is no demon! But ... Tom, I cannot understand this. Was the archangel speaking in metaphors? A new English king is to be the Demon-King? No, no, I cannot believe ..."

Hal could not finish. He stood, his hands half raised as if he meant to grasp something, his eyes still locked into Thomas'.

"I cannot understand it either." Thomas could not tell Hal that he suspected Lancaster as well as Richard. Not yet. Hal must reach that conclusion in his own time.

"But . . ." Hal could not continue past that one word. He finally lowered his eyes, saw that he had his hands half-raised, and thrust them down as well.

"But I *do* know of one of the demons within our midst," Thomas said, watching Hal's face carefully. "John Wycliffe."

Hal slowly nodded. "Aye . . . aye, you do not surprise me. The man has dark ideas to match his dark visage. Does my father know of this?"

"I cannot tell your father," Thomas said evenly.

It took Hal a moment more to grasp Thomas' meaning. "No! No! You cannot suspect that my father . . . no, you go too far!"

Thomas reached out and grasped Hal's arm with a gentle hand. Hal started to pull away, then accepted Thomas' touch.

"I hope before God he is not," Thomas said, "for I respect your father before almost any other man in Christendom. But your father has come under Wycliffe's sway, and it would be inadvisable to tell him that I — we — suspect Wycliffe to be a demon. But there is someone else besides your father who stands close to the throne — Richard. If anything happened to the Black Prince, well . . ."

"Aye. Richard." Hal pulled a face. "Demon or not, he will make a right vile king." He sighed, and rubbed at his eyes as if tired. "What can we do?"

"For the moment, little, for Christmastide is a season when life is given over to enjoyment and revelry. But after the festivities are over, after Plough Monday when the world becomes sane again, will you press your father to allow me to go north? Hal, I *must* find this casket!"

"Yes, for its secrets will illuminate the path to the demons' destruction. Meanwhile —"

"Meanwhile we attend the revelry, and we observe."

Thomas turned to go, but Hal stopped him. "Thomas . . . is there anyone else you suspect as demon rather than man?"

Thomas did not reply immediately.

"Yes," he finally said. "There is. A priest I met among the

English soldiers in France who goes by the name of John Ball. And Wat Tyler."

Hal made a sound as if to contradict what Thomas had just said, but Thomas had not yet finished.

"And the Lady Margaret Rivers."

"Oh, Thomas, no. Why?"

"I cannot say. And I do not truly know if she is or not, or merely a victim of demonic sorcery . . . as I have been."

Hal grunted. "You have never liked her . . . but I thought that to be because you resented her place in your uncle's bed. As for the others . . . this John Ball I do not know . . . but Wat Tyler?"

Thomas shrugged. "There is no specific reason, but just some of the things Wat has said to me . . . and he *did* keep company with John Ball, who is a demon if ever there was one!"

"Many Englishmen speak strange words in these times," Hal said, "not just Wat. Traditional bonds between bondsman and master have weakened since the time of the great pestilence —"

"Aye . . . and we know why that is so, do we not?"

"Hal! Ah, Tom, there you are." Lancaster strode through the door, and both Hal and Thomas jumped guiltily. *How much had he heard?*

"The horses are ready," Lancaster said, "the womenfolk are twinkling in their finest gems and silks, and a great feast awaits us. What do you two here, murmuring as if you plotted to overthrow the throne?"

"Merely planning our Christmastide jest on Hotspur," Hal said easily, and clapped Thomas on the shoulder. "Come, father has spoken wisely. Why do we linger here in this chill room?"

Westminster lay a good mile's ride south along the Strand and past Charing Cross. The palace and abbey complex was a town in its own right, with scores of homes, workshops and dormitories accommodating servants, workers, soldiers and men-at-arms, and the monks; orchards and vegetable gardens lay between and behind many of the buildings. The complex's greatest building, the abbey, was over five hundred years old, and the great hall and palace not much younger. Westminster had been purposely built beyond the walls of London by the last of the Anglo-Saxon kings in order to keep the monarchy safe from interference by the unruly London mobs. No king since then had seen fit to move his principal residence away from the complex.

Nevertheless, the primary palace accommodation was not particularly commodious, being one of three massive but draughty halls of the complex. All of Edward's sons had built or purchased accommodation elsewhere, leaving their aging father to wallow in his arthritis in the pretty, but chilly, hall called the Painted Chamber.

Tonight the festivities were not to be held in the Painted Chamber which, although roomy, could not possibly hold the thousands invited to the banquet. Instead, the great hall of Westminster had been readied.

It was a spectacular sight. Torches lit the way through the streets leading to the hall, and from every part of England, or so it seemed, came hundreds of riders dressed in a rich variety of velvets, silks and furs to keep at bay the winter chill. Others approached the hall on foot.

But all the crowds parted for Lancaster's retinue. There were some cheers, and some hisses, but mostly just silence, and Thomas realised with a jolt just how ambivalent the English were about Lancaster. Why? Was it just his wealth and power, or did they, like he, suspect the man of greater ambitions?

There was a clarion of horns as Lancaster pulled his stallion to a halt before the hall, and the party dismounted with much gaiety and gossip. The ladies, who had ridden sweet-tempered palfrey mares, paused to straighten their headdresses and gowns, and to make eyes at the lords and knights standing about.

Hal, who had by now moved to his father's side, sent Thomas a wink — the chill night ride had given him time to think and to calm — and offered his arm to the Lady Mary

Bohun, heiress to the titles and estates of Hereford, who had wandered by with her own retinue in tow.

Lady Mary was a small woman, her face saved from outright plainness by a pair of lustrous hazel eyes. She smiled nervously at Hal's attentions, one hand fidgeting in her hair, and Thomas thought she looked like a nervous mare about to bolt at any instant.

Hal spoke gently to her, and Mary's face lost some of its apprehension, and she smiled more naturally.

Lancaster watched them carefully, relaxing himself as Mary did also, then he motioned with his hand, and the party moved inside the hall.

Thomas gasped the moment he stepped under the threshold.

The hall looked like a palace from fairyland.

More candles and torches than he could possibly count hung from every beam and stood from every pillar and sconce; golden light filled the entire hall. Greenery — holly, ivy, mistletoe ... everything that *was* green in winter time — had been draped about walls and over the trestle tables, and wound about with silver and golden threads and red balls of wool.

The floor had been strewn with sweet-smelling herbs and spices, and fires of scented apple wood burned cheerily from hearths. A huge Yule log lay at the far end of the hall by the High Table, one end crackling and hissing in the great fireplace.

Along each table were set thousands of yule candles, prettied with ribbons and streamers, and the scent of incense and warmth and revelry filled the air.

Both lords and servants moved quickly to greet the Duke, and he and his party were escorted to the tables set at the very top of the hall.

Unsurprisingly, Lancaster and Katherine both sat at the High Table where Gloucester already waited — Edward had not yet arrived — but Thomas was surprised to find himself seated at the first table on the High Table's right, a few places down from Hal and Mary Bohun.

Then his delight died a little as Margaret was placed directly to his left.

"Thomas," she said as greeting, and smiled a little, and lowered her eyes demurely.

"My lady," he replied. "You look well."

And indeed Margaret did, for she wore a new gown of gold wool, embroidered about with a deep blue thread. It had a wide neckline, which showed the top of her breasts and her shoulders, and a tapered waist, which emphasised her belly: Thomas noted with some little surprise how much bigger she had grown since they had left France. Her beautiful hair was not piled under a cap or veil, nor even atop her head, but had been wound into a thick braid with gold threads and seed pearls which hung down her back.

She looked lovely and virginal and utterly desirable, save that her belly showed indisputably that at least one man had already found her desirable enough to bear down to his bed.

She smiled more naturally now, looking about the hall with wonder-filled eyes. "I feel well, Thomas. The Lady Katherine has been good for my soul, and tales of her own childbed has made me fear my own less."

Margaret paused, and looked back to Thomas, smiling with sheer joy and lightness of spirit, and he could not help but respond.

"My Lady Katherine tells me," she said, "that the mid-months of carrying a child are always the best."

"And the last months?"

Margaret made a face. "Then a woman swells so big she can scarcely walk from stool to table and all avert their eyes from her form. Thomas ... I thank you for taking such an interest in a woman's woes."

"I cannot pretend that I have no interest in this child," he said quietly, then turned to speak to the cheery-faced man on his right before Margaret could respond.

She sat, her face now expressionless, staring at him. Then she refocused on someone further down the table, smiled slightly, and nodded.

"Sweet Jesu!" Raby whispered, watching the barely visible deformed shapes cavort through the driving snow. Wat Tyler had led the baron to the edge of their huddled encampment, and now they stood, grabbing onto the top of a waist-high stone wall for support

"Are these the demons that attacked my lord the Black Prince and yourself on the way back from your meeting with Philip?" Wat Tyler said.

"Aye."

For an instant Raby lifted his eyes from the demons to the waves of snow and ice driving through the night air. "This tempest is not of God's earth."

Tyler mumbled a prayer. "What can we do? How can we defeat such as these?"

His voice cracked, as if he toppled on a knife-edge of despair.

Raby grabbed at him, pulling the man close so he could see his face. "We've got to get the prince out of here! He is near to death as it is, and to allow such as these to get close again ..."

"We should have Thomas Neville here."

Raby peered at Tyler. "Why?"

"Wasn't it he who ordered the demons to depart before? *We need a priest!*"

"We have no priest," Raby said. "Come, Tyler."

And he hauled the soldier back into the camp, past wailing groups of men standing or half-sitting in the snowdrifts, pointing into the night, and calling to their God.

The cheery middle-aged man on Thomas' right now leaned forward and smiled gently at Margaret. He had a round, ruddy face, thinning brown hair, a snub of a nose, and bright eyes whose sharpness belied the otherwise genial conviviality of his expression.

"My lady, I fear I have not yet had the privilege ..."

Thomas sighed. "The Lady Margaret Rivers," he said. "Recently arrived from France, where she lost her husband to the wasting illness. Lady Margaret currently serves Lady Katherine Swynford."

"Ah!" the man said. "My lady, I am deeply honoured to make your acquaintance, for I know the Lady Katherine well. My name is Geoffrey Chaucer, and I make my way through this world as a humble poet."

Margaret's face lit up. "I have heard some of your work, Master Chaucer. My Lady Katherine often causes your poems to be read aloud to her and her ladies as we sit at our needlework."

Chaucer beamed. "Both my Lady Katherine and my Lord of Lancaster have been good to me. If it were not for them, I should have starved many years previous."

"Master Chaucer's wife, Pippa, is Katherine's sister," Thomas said. "Is she not with you this night, Master Chaucer?"

"Nay. My sweet Pippa has an ague, and has preferred to stay before her fire at home." Chaucer again caught Margaret's eyes, and winked. "I shall have a fine evening without her company!"

Then Chaucer's expression sobered. "My lady, I am grieved to hear of the loss of your husband. And to think that he shall not know his child. Tell me, how long has he been dead?"

The question was so impolite, and so direct, that it bordered on the impudent.

Margaret was fixated by Chaucer's sharp and very direct stare. "He, ah, he died last, um ..."

Thomas could almost hear her counting frantically in her mind. "He died but a few months ago, Master Chaucer, after a long and incapacitating illness."

"Not too incapacitating, I note," Chaucer said.

"I kept my husband warm and comfortable through the long nights of his suffering," Margaret said, her voice now steady, "as all good wives should do. *I* would not leave my spouse alone by the fire."

Chaucer's mouth quirked. "Well said, my dear. Margaret ... I am not unaware of your situation, few at court are, but it would aid your cause if you were a little more prepared for the inevitable questions and comment."

She inclined her head and changed the subject, demonstrating she was not so unskilled at court conversation as Chaucer had intimated. "Master Chaucer, much of your work interests me deeply. I confess myself amazed that some of your commentary on social injustice, particularly the plight of the poor, and the parasitic nature of many of the wandering clergy, should find such favour at court."

Chaucer shot a glance at Thomas, amused that the woman had so needled the friar. Chaucer was not loath to caricature the fat, corrupt clergy who lived off the poor and needy, and his work *had* caused him some official reprimand. If it had not been for Lancaster's protection ...

"My Lord of Lancaster supports a great many writers and philosophers, my lady. Without him, no doubt many of us would by now have long starved, or —"

"Been burned at the stake," Thomas said, but with a grin. He liked Chaucer, and if some of his work did overly satirise the more corrupt members of the clergy, well ... criticism of sin had never gone astray, from whichever mouth it came.

"There are many who now speak against the overweening ambition and wealth of the Church," Chaucer said, watching Thomas carefully. "Many who criticise. You have, of course, heard of John Wycliffe ..."

Thomas' face closed over completely. There were, however, *some* voices that should be silenced rather than allowed free rein.

Margaret waved a hand, as if to dismiss Wycliffe. "Have you heard the new dissident poem, Master Chaucer, called 'God Speed the Plough'?"

"Yes! Yes! Magnificent, isn't it? I cannot think who can be the author, but he deserves his place in heaven for it."

"I have not heard of it," Thomas said, "Perhaps ..."

"As a husbandman drives his plough and team through a muddy field," Margaret said, "he is disturbed by a never-ending stream of clerics — friars, monks, priests, bishops, university students — as well as those who live off charity — beggars, freed prisoners, disbanded soldiers, lepers — all of whom demand of him money and food. As you know, Thomas, we are all supposed to give charitably to wandering clerics, as to those in need. Those of us in this great hall," she motioned about the glittering display, "can well afford it. But the poor ploughman who has the food snatched out of his babe's mouth to feed the needy? He *has* a reason to complain, do you not think?"

"We are all obliged to partake in good works," Thomas said.

"Yes, but to the point where our 'good works' starve the families of the poor?" Chaucer asked. "There are some who believe that our entire society is so corrupt a new order is needed to alleviate the plight of the mass of poor labourers and husbandmen. Their voices, as you know, are growing."

To this Thomas said nothing. His eyes were fixed on some distant point, appalled that the demons had planted their ideas so successfully. What they complained of was true enough — there were members of the clergy, and religious orders within the Church, who were clearly corrupt — but to plant the idea of an overwhelming social upheaval to fix what could be cured by an internal Church investigation, to question God's order of things, that was unprecedented.

"Ah," Chaucer said, "this is a joyous occasion, and we have talked of nothing but want and starvation. I am sure, indeed I am positive, that every Englishman tonight enjoys a table as laden as ours."

Thomas gave him a black look, but whatever he wanted to say was interrupted by the sound of bells, and bright voices, and the ringing tones of horn.

"Our king!" Chaucer said, and rose with every other member of the assembly.

King Edward III of England entered from a side door in the hall to be greeted with a deep bow and a kiss on his cheek by his most senior son present, Lancaster.

Thomas watched the king curiously. This was the first time he had seen him in six or seven years. In that time Edward seemed to have aged twenty years. When Thomas had last seen him — at a tournament staged in Durham — the king had been strong and vibrant and lusty, belying his age. Now the king was clearly close to death, in spirit if not in body.

He had thinned, and his richly bejewelled and furred robes, although carefully tailored, hung unbecomingly from his gaunt frame. His gait was uncertain and Lancaster had to take the old man's arm from the valet who had led him this far to get him safely to his throne on the dais. His hair had grown scant, and his beard was streaked and straggled, and his yellowing skin, like his robes, hung slack and carelessly from the bones of his skull.

His mouth hung open, revealing a few blackened teeth amid a greater expanse of reddened gum. If he were not a king, Edward would be snugged down into a chair by a fire and left with a child-minder to make sure he didn't fall into the flames.

Chaucer glanced at the expressions on both Thomas' and Margaret's faces.

"He is not the man he once was," he said.

"How long has he been like this?"

"Some four or five months. His physicians have bled him, and administered a multitude of purges, but they cannot cleanse his mind of the shadows that inhabit it."

Thomas watched as Lancaster led Edward to his throne and sat him down, bending to speak briefly with the Black Prince's son, Richard, who sat on the king's right hand.

If Edward was incapacitated, and the Black Prince in France, and Richard of yet tender years, then that meant Lancaster was effectively king.

"Pray God the Black Prince returns soon," he said, and all those within hearing distance of Thomas mumbled agreement.

"Tyler!" Raby shouted above the howling wind. "Get the prince's horse saddled, as mine and yours, and as many spare destriers as we can safely lead."

"Aye, my lord!" and Tyler had, with two steps, disappeared into the swirling snow.

Raby struggled towards where he *thought* the Black Prince's position was, occasionally falling over men half buried within snowdrifts.

God damn this devil-driven tempest! he thought for the tenth or eleventh time as he regained his feet and stumbled a few steps further. There was nothing for it but to get the prince out — now! — and to give the rest of the party (what still survived of it, for several of the men Raby had tripped over were stone cold dead) permission to scatter and find what shelter they could.

He could not let the prince drown in this cold, nor could he risk the demons sinking their talons into him.

Trying to get the prince to safety with only himself and Tyler as escort was risky, but Raby was prepared to take that risk. For every extra man as escort Raby must sacrifice speed, and the prince's condition now meant that speed was of paramount importance.

Besides, Raby was certain the storm existed for one reason only — to kill the Black Prince. The more he thought about it, the more likely it seemed that the letter from Joan had been a ruse, meant to lure the prince out of his stronghold in Bordeaux. If Raby moved the prince, although he might still be encased in its fury, there was good reason to think the rest of the men might be saved.

Raby finally reached the prince's fire — now damp, grey ashes — just as Tyler arrived with the horses (how had he managed so quickly?).

"My lord!" Raby leaned down and shook the prince's shoulder.

There was no response.

"Edward!" Raby screamed, and now the prince stirred slightly, and moaned.

"I have ropes, my lord," Tyler said. "And blankets. We'll have to tie him on and rope together all the horses, otherwise we'll lose ourselves in the storm."

Raby nodded, relieved that Tyler had thought so well and so quickly, then turned to the man huddled the other side of the Black Prince.

"Robert!" he yelled. "Spread the word. Tell the men to scatter and find what shelter they can. Now. It is the only way any will survive. Robert ... tell them I wish them Godspeed."

Robert nodded, struggled stiffly to his feet, and moved away.

Tyler stepped close to Raby, and between them the two managed to get the Black Prince onto his horse and secured with blankets and ropes.

It was only then, as Raby stepped back and finally found the time to wipe the ice away from his cheeks, that he realised he'd been crying.

Now that the king had made his entrance, as unstately and unregal as it might have been, the festivities could begin.

Scattered groups of musicians took up their lutes and pipes, and heady music filled the hall. Servants scurried in from service entrance ways, some bearing cloths and bowls for the washing of hands, others laden with Gascon wines, and foods of every description: meats, fishes, poultry and puddings and pastries whose shape and variety defied the imagination.

Margaret, looking about, leaned close to Thomas. "The French king is not to join the revelry?"

A wry look crossed Thomas' face. "No doubt it was felt that two inane kings was one too many. Doubtless John is back in the Savoy enjoying his own feast, and with enough warm ladies to keep him busy for the entire night."

He looked back to Edward. The old man was ignoring the food servants had laden on to his plate, and was in animated conversation with Richard, although Thomas could see that the youth was barely managing to humour his grandfather and was proving somewhat inept at trying to hide his boredom.

Richard's thin, pale face was set into an expression of utter irritation, and his eyes (*his sly eyes*, Thomas thought) were sliding this way and that through the hall, as if he were trying to size up support for whatever intrigue his secretive mind considered.

Just down from Richard was his mother, the Black Prince's beloved wife. Joan of Kent, or the Fair Maid of Kent as she'd been known in her youth, was a massively overweight woman with hair dyed a bright straw colour. She sat for the most part eating, drinking, and dabbing delicately with a square of linen at the beads of perspiration that appeared in the folds of her cheeks and neck, not speaking to any about her save, occasionally, her son.

Lancaster, on Edward's left, had turned to Katherine, and was serving her the juiciest pieces of meat from his own platter.

Whether or not they were soon to be married, it was an indication of Lancaster's extraordinary power that he could bring his long-time mistress to sit at his side at High Table.

Gloucester, further down the table — the Lord Mayor of London on one side and the Archbishop of Canterbury, Simon Sudbury, on the other — appeared profoundly ill at ease.

The Plantagenet family, as represented at High Table by its most senior members, looked as if it were about to implode through the force of its own disharmony.

Thomas' eyes moved from the High Table to the top of his own table.

There, Hal Bolingbroke, ignoring the attentions of the Earl's daughter, was watching the High Table as carefully as Thomas had just been.

How many demons, and how many men?

And was there a demon prince among them?

"Mawmenny!" Chaucer cried as a servant set down a dish of heavily spiced and sugared ground meats, fruit and almonds, and Thomas jerked slightly, his reverie broken.

The Black Prince was the only one on horseback. The other two men walked, as wrapped as they could be in cloaks and blankets and still be able to move their legs, on the sheltered side of the horses, making as much use as they could of the beasts' powerful bodies to block out the wind.

The camp had long disappeared behind them, and Raby had no idea how far they'd come, or if they were even heading west towards the coast.

All he could do was take one step, then concentrate on lifting the next foot forward.

Suddenly the horses stopped, and one of them snorted.

"Tyler," Raby croaked. "Can you see more than a hand's length before you?"

There was a lengthy silence before Tyler replied, and Raby thought his face might have frozen, rendering speech impossible.

"Aye," Tyler finally said. "But I wish I could not see what I can."

Raby raised a hand — appalled at the effort it took — and rubbed his eyes, trying to clear them of the ice that had collected there.

He blinked, blinked again, then peered forward.

He cursed, and stumbled a little as he tried to see to the sides and behind him as well.

Demons had moved in so close they had formed an impenetrable ring about the men and horses, and now they were shuffling forward, apparently unaffected by the storm, their snouts lifted towards the still form of the Black Prince.

The banquet progressed with course after course. From each platter diners took only a few slivers of meat, for if they gorged themselves on the first courses, they would have had no room left for the thirty-odd more to come.

Mummers moved into the centre spaces between the tables, dancing and performing short plays. All of them hid their faces behind strange animal masks, and their hands covered with gloves fashioned to resemble the claws of wild beasts. Their robes were made of colourful materials that fluttered and flowed in the draughts caused by the many entrances to the hall and fires that roared throughout its length.

As the night lengthened, the never-ending supply of Gascony wine took hold, and some of the revellers took to the floor with the mummers, forming carol rings, and singing songs of cheer and ribaldry. One group of dancers, mummers cavorting within the centre of their circle, took up a popular Christmastide ballad at the top of their voices.

Man, be glad in hall and bower,
This time was born our saviour.
In this time a child was born,
To save those souls that went forlorn,
For he wore garland of thorn,
All it was for our honour.

Many at the tables close by laughed, clapping their hands, and joining in, for this was a much-loved song.

Jesu, for your courtesy,
Ye be our help and our succour.
On Whitsunday you down do send,
Wit and wisdom us to a-mend;
Jesu, bring us to that end,
With-out delay, our saviour!

There was general applause as the ballad ended, and the leader of the carol circle jumped up and down several times and shouted: "Bring us in good ale!"

There were screams of delight, and even Edward III banged his fist on the table.

"Bring us in good ale!" he roared. "Bring us in good ale!"

Bring us in good ale, and bring us in good ale;
For our Blessed Lady's sake, bring us in good ale.
Bring us in no brown bread, for that is made of bran,
Nor bring us in no white bread, for therein is no gain.
But bring us in good ale.
Bring us in no beef, for there is many bones,
But bring us in good ale, for that goes down at once;
And bring us in good ale.
Bring us in no bacon, for that is passing fat,
But bring us in good ale, and give us enough of that;
And bring us in good ale.
Bring us in no mutton, for that is often lean,
Nor bring us in no tripes, for that be seldom clean,
But bring us in good ale.

Now many hundreds in the hall were singing, and the sound of the ballad soared into the rafters.

Bring us in no eggs, for there are many shells,
But bring us in good ale and give us nothing else,
And bring us in good ale.
Bring us in no butter, for therin are many hairs;
Nor bring us in no pig's flesh for that will make us
  boars;
But bring us in good ale.
Bring us in no puddings, for therein is all God's good;
Nor bring us in no venison, for that is not for our
  blood;
But bring us in good ale.
Bring us in no capons' flesh, for that is often dear;
Nor bring us in no duck's flesh, for they slobber in the
  mere;
But bring us in good ale.

Edward III leaped to his feet — to the evident consternation of Lancaster — and capered about, as if dancing. Just as his son reached out a hand, the king darted behind his chair, and half ran, half stumbled towards the singers and dancers.

"The prince!" Raby screamed, and he and Tyler stumbled to where the prince sat still, huddled over his horse.

Raby fumbled with the knots tying the man to his saddle. "Tyler, take him, I'll hold back the demons."

"My lord, there are too many!"

Raby risked a glance. The demons were closer in now, circling, dancing to and fro with delight.

"You must!" he said. "For if you don't then we are all dead for certain."

The last knot slipped free, and as it did, the prince lurched to the side, fortunately in Raby's direction.

The baron grunted under the weight, and would have fallen himself had not Tyler helped.

Raby hefted the prince up, intending to throw him over Tyler's shoulder, but just as he did the prince moaned, shuddered, and rolled away. He half fell, half jumped to the ground, but somehow managed to maintain his feet.

The prince looked up. His face was stark white, his eyes shining a stunning blue.

"Raby," he said, hoarsely.

"My lord, we must get you out of here!"

In answer, the Black Prince threw off most of his blankets, and stumbled against Raby.

When he stepped back, he had Raby's sword in his hand, and then, before either Raby or Tyler could act, he lurched out to greet the demons. Raby started after him but Tyler, surprisingly strong, held him still.

"We're all dead if we try to pull him back," he said.

Edward III had picked up the hem of his trailing robe and, dribbling and giggling, was trying to shuffle a dance. The carollers and the masked mummers had surrounded him, forming concentric circles of dancers, cheering him on.

"More song," Edward cried. "More song!"

Lancaster, swearing under his breath, moved down from the dais, Gloucester at his side.

Richard, sitting slouched in his chair with hooded eyes, was watching his grandfather, a finger on his right hand slowly moving back and forth with the beat of the music, as if he were conducting the maddened dance before him.

"Drink today and drown all sorrow!" Edward cried, and immediately carollers and mummers burst into song.

> Drink today, and drown all sorrow,
> You shall perhaps not do it tomorrow:
> Best, while you still have it, use your breath;
> There is no drinking after death.
> Wine works the heart up, wakes the wit,
> There is no cure 'gainst age but it:
> It helps the head-ache, cough and tisic,
> And is for all diseases physic.

Lancaster and Gloucester reached the floor and tried to elbow their way through the throng of dancers towards their gibbering father. A bull-masked woman tripped and fell headlong into Lancaster, and the duke fell over, pulling Gloucester down with him.

The dancers ignored the two princes struggling on the floor, leaping over them as if it were part of the dance, their quick feet slamming time and time again into the two men's heads, sending them floorward again.

> Then let us swill, boys, for our health;
> Who drinks well, loves the commonwealth;
> And he that will go to bed sober,
> Falls with the leaf still in October.

The Black Prince hefted the sword and lunged at the first of the demons which had surrounded him.

The demon ducked, as graceful as the most accomplished dancer, and the blade swept harmlessly over its head.

"Damn you!" Raby swore, trying to get away from Tyler.

"We can do nothing ... nothing," Tyler yelled. "It is out of our hands now!"

The Black Prince, clearly close to collapse, took a deep breath, steadied himself by leaning the blade momentarily on the ground, then lifted it into a huge sweep through the air that should have taken off five demons' heads.

The blade swung through the air, the sound of its passing a sweet and clear song.

Edward capered and gambolled as if he were a yearling colt let loose into the field for the first time.

The dancers screamed with enthusiasm. Indeed, the entire hall was on its feet, roaring and cheering the ancient king in his dance of stupidity.

Lancaster and Gloucester finally managed to get to their feet and pushed roughly through the infernal mummers.

Edward turned, and saw them.

"My boys!" he yelled. "Come join my dance!"

He threw up his hands, kicked up his heels, and bellowed forth again:

Drink today, and drown all sorrow,
You shall perhaps not do it tomorrow:
Best, while you still have it, use your breath;
There is no drinking after death.

He stopped suddenly, a stunned expression on his face, his cheeks draining of all colour.

For an instant his eyes appeared to have regained their sanity, and he blinked.

"Edward?" he said, his voice puzzled. "What do you there?"

The Black Prince could no longer maintain his grip on his sword. It dropped from his hand, and he wavered on his feet.

"*Edward!*" Raby screamed.

The Black Prince blinked, as if surprised to find himself surrounded by demons.

"Father?" he said.

And then he jerked, and dropped to the ground.

"Edward!" the king screamed. "No!"

He made as if to take a step forward, but then he contorted in a massive convulsion, and fell with a horrible thud to the floor.

Lancaster dropped to his knees beside his father, but he was too late. Edward III had abandoned his earthly realm.

The demon closest to Raby and Tyler turned, its face twisted and malevolent.

"Drink today," it hissed, "and drown all sorrow, for there shall be no drinking tomorrow."

And then all the demons were gone, and the storm was abating, and Raby and Tyler were left alone with their milling horses to stare at the Black Prince's body half buried in the cold, cold snow.

"Drink today," the mummer whispered, turning to stare at Thomas, "and drown all sorrow, for there shall be no drinking tomorrow."

The circle of carollers and mummers drew back and silence filled the hall with its cold, horrible weight as every eye fell on the body of Edward III.

VIII

Midnight of the Feast of the Nativity of
Our Lord Jesus Christ
In the first year of the reign of Richard II
(Saturday 25th December 1378)

— Yuletide —

— iii —

There was such a complete silence and stillness that some distant, disassociated part of Thomas' shocked mind wondered who would be brave enough to first break the icy enchantment.

Who else, but Lancaster.

Still on his knees before his father's body, the duke looked up, stared, then noticed the hundreds of people staring shocked and silent at the corpse.

"Get out!" he yelled, his face contorting so violently the veins corded the length of his neck. "Get out!"

The circles of carollers and masked mummers broke first, running madly in every direction for whatever exit they could find.

Then the assembled revellers murmured, like a storm rustling through a sapling forest, and abandoned their laden tables with a great sigh.

Hal Bolingbroke was one of the few not to move. He stood a few places up the table from Thomas, staring at the tragic tableau before him: his grandfather's corpse, his father still kneeling before it, his uncle, Gloucester, standing and slowly wringing his hands in grief and indecision.

"No," Hal murmured.

"No!" he suddenly yelled, and, leaping over the table, made several ineffective lunges at the last of the departing mummers and carollers in an attempt to seize their sleeves.

"No!" he cried again, trying to get his father's attention. "Don't let them leave! Who, *what*, lies behind those masks?"

Lancaster stared, then leaped to his feet. "Seize the mummers!" he yelled to the guards.

But it was too late. They had melted into the crowds, and flowed through the doorways.

They had gone as if they had never been.

Westminster Hall had not completely emptied; many stayed to further witness the unfolding tragedy, and perhaps determine how best they might use it to their advantage.

Prince Richard, who had sat — apparently — whey-faced and stunned as his grandfather collapsed and died, moved from his place on the dais towards where Lancaster and Gloucester now stood a few feet from the body.

His eyes were narrowed and thoughtful.

He was, after all, one corpse closer to the throne.

Simon Sudbury, the Archbishop of Canterbury, hurried past Richard, intent on giving Edward whatever last rites might benefit his cooling flesh and departing soul.

Katherine still sat at her place at the High Table, both hands clasped to her cheeks, her grey eyes wide and shocked. She was trembling so badly her entire form shook.

Margaret quickly regained her composure and, as Richard and Sudbury joined Lancaster and Gloucester, she moved towards Katherine, murmuring to Thomas as she passed that her lady needed comforting.

Geoffrey Chaucer stood with arms folded, his head tilted to one side. His eyes regarded the entire scene with sharp intelligence, as if he were storing away images and words to be used, perhaps, in a commemorative poem.

There were six or seven other nobles who had stayed, peers of the realm. A king had died, and a new one must be crowned, but in the meantime the realm would be governed by council.

Thomas stood where he had first risen, absolutely still save for his eyes which flitted from one person to the next.

Who man, who demon?

As Lancaster sighed, rubbed his eyes, and prepared to speak, Thomas' eyes settled on one figure, lurking in the shadows at the rear of the hall where many candles and torches had blown out as doors were hastily thrown open for the horrified exit of the revellers.

John Wycliffe, standing with burning eyes, thinking only the Devil knew what.

"The king is dead," Lancaster said, "and only God knows when the Black Prince will arrive to claim his heritage. We must move, and fast, to maintain order within the realm. I call a meeting of the Privy Council for dawn. Gloucester, will you see that guards are sent out to fetch those councillors not present here in this hall?"

Gloucester, glad to have something to do, nodded and moved away.

"I shall attend as well!" Richard said, his voice shrill and demanding.

Lancaster began to shake his head, then changed his mind. "Yes, you must attend. My Lord Archbishop," he turned to Sudbury, "will you and yours see to my lord father's body?"

As the group broke up, Lancaster spoke quietly to Bolingbroke. "Hal, do whatever you must to find those mummers. Use our spies, and our paid eyes and ears. Do you understand?"

Hal nodded, and, as he walked away, stopped briefly by Thomas. "We must talk," he said. "You and I, and, I think, my father."

Then he was gone.

There was little Thomas could do for the moment. He could take no part in the meetings and whisperings that attended the death of a king, even if he believed he knew who — or what — might be behind it.

Not for the moment.

Lancaster, Hal at his side, would need to ensure that rapid, practical measures were taken to prevent any outbreak of disorder. But once they had been attended to, then Thomas knew he must talk to Lancaster and persuade the duke to grant permission for Thomas to move north to Bramham Moor friary.

IX

The Feast of St Silvester
In the First Year of the Reign of Richard II
(Thursday 30th December 1378)

— i —

*I*n the days after the death of Edward III, Lancaster laboured from early morning until late each night, working with the members of the Privy Council to secure England for the Black Prince. Until the prince arrived home, Lancaster would act as regent. Urgent messengers were sent to Bordeaux, and it was expected that the Black Prince would arrive in London by mid-January at the latest.

One of Lancaster's first actions was to put out word that King Edward had died a natural death of old age, hastened by his drunken participation in the Yuletide celebrations. Whatever Lancaster and his immediate confidantes suspected, no word was mentioned of demony, or any unnaturalness associated with the king's demise. On behalf of his father, Bolingbroke undertook an exhaustive search for the mummers who had surrounded the king at his death: none were ever found.

The preparations for a great funeral were begun, and Edward's body was embalmed and laid to rest on a bier before the altar of Westminster Abbey.

Lancaster also quietly began the preparations necessary for a renewed spring campaign in France. No doubt the Black Prince was also likewise engaged, but Lancaster was a prudent man, and knew that it took many months to arrange an army of invasion.

There was also one other matter Lancaster attended to in these days: his wedding to Katherine. He had waited many years to make Katherine his wife, and not even the death of his father or the possible unrest of England would prevent him realising his ambition, even if it must needs be a few days delayed.

St Stephen's Chapel, attached to Westminster palace, was possibly the most beautiful building in England. The spires of its clerestory, the soaring upper roof of the nave, rose almost to the height of the spires and towers of Westminster Abbey, and certainly far above those of Westminster Hall.

But if St Stephen's did not quite eclipse Westminster Abbey in the height of its spires, it far outstripped it in the beauty and magnificence of its adornment. This was the chapel of kings, and it had been constructed and decorated to enhance the power and glory of England's monarchs. Light flooded down from the stained glass windows set high in the clerestory, washing over the silver and gold and gems set into and about the high altar. The nave was characterised by a delicate arcading of elegant arches and columns, exquisitely painted and gilded. The entire floor was not the usual stone flagging of gothic cathedrals, but consisted of brilliantly patterned tiles of azure, scarlet and ivory. Over the past thirty years the best of English painters had embellished all the chapel's walls, depicting the lives and devotions of past generations of English royalty, as well as complete cycles of scenes from the bible, angels holding draperies and the lives of warrior saints.

St Stephen's was a space of the most serene spirituality, as well as the grandiose majesty of the deeds of English kings and princes.

Here John of Gaunt, Duke of Lancaster, took as his third

wife, Lady Katherine Swynford, on the evening of St Silvester's Day in a quiet and subdued ceremony.

The nuptials were short, the mass markedly attenuated, and the bride and groom pale and weary — but still desiring to legitimise their love match.

The immediate members of their households were present. Hal Bolingbroke; Lancaster and Katherine's bastard children, Henry and Joan Beaufort; Prince Richard (who had slept well and looked alert and excited); his mother Joan of Kent who, due to her degree of fatness, was one of the few to sit throughout the ceremony; six or seven of Lancaster's most senior retainers; his and Katherine's personal servants — valets, pages and ladies; John Wycliffe, who was there to act as witness to a degree of religious ceremony he publicly deplored; and Thomas, who stood back a little from the assembly to, again, observe as much as listen.

During the ceremony, Margaret, who stood in the group of Katherine's ladies at the bride's back, turned and glanced at Thomas. Her expression was unreadable, but Thomas thought he saw tears in her eyes, and wondered if she hoped that somehow she also might find a husband to legitimise her own shame.

He looked to Joan Beaufort, rumoured to be Raby's intended wife. She was dressed plainly, but with arm and finger rings bejewelled with exquisite gems. Thomas wondered what she felt, watching a rite that, together with an Act of Parliament, would make her not only legitimate, but one of the most eligible women in England.

And she was to be given to Raby?

The ceremony was almost finished when Thomas heard the door at the end of the nave open and close and hurried footsteps move up towards the wedding group.

He turned and looked.

A messenger, smeared all over with the mud of his travel and the consternation of the news he carried, was heading straight for Lancaster.

Thomas grabbed the man's arm as he passed. "Stop!" he whispered. "Whatever news you have can wait a little longer!"

The man trembled, as if he considered tearing himself free of Thomas' grip, then nodded reluctantly.

Thomas, keeping his grip on the man's arm, looked back to Lancaster and Katherine.

The chaplain was intoning the final words over them and, as Thomas watched, Lancaster turned to his new duchess and kissed her gently.

Thomas leaned close to the messenger. "Go to Bolingbroke," he said. "Tell him what news you have. He will then pick the best time to tell Lancaster."

Again the man hesitated, then nodded. He moved hurriedly towards Bolingbroke, murmuring apologies as he pushed past several of Lancaster's retainers, then caught Bolingbroke's attention and whispered frantically in his ear.

Thomas' eyes narrowed. The man's news must be devastating, for Bolingbroke visibly shuddered, and turned pale.

Lancaster and Katherine turned away from the chaplain and began to accept the congratulations and well wishes of those about them when Bolingbroke stepped up and caught his father's attention.

"Yes?" Lancaster said.

"My lord ..." Bolingbroke hesitated, as if the news he bore was so grievous he could hardly annunciate it. "My lord, this man has just ridden from the port of Dover, where a fishing vessel has brought such lamentable tidings I fear this will prove to be one of the darkest days in —"

"What tidings?" Lancaster said, grasping his son's shoulders and staring him in the eye.

"Your brother Edward, heir to the throne, is dead."

Lancaster's hands tightened, and a tremor shuddered over his face. "What?" he whispered.

"A storm," Hal continued, also almost in a whisper, "and more that in this gathering I should not discuss, has stolen breath and warmth from the Black Prince."

There was a faint cry, and then a mighty thump, as Joan of Kent fainted.

Instantly, there was a scurry of activity, but Thomas, as appalled as anyone else, noticed that amid all this action, only one person remained still and calm.

Richard.

As Thomas became aware of it, so also did Lancaster. He turned from Bolingbroke to Richard, and dropped to one knee before the youth.

"My liege," he said.

Richard's eyes flared with excitement ... and something else.

Triumph, Thomas realised, and then dread as he had never felt before swept through him, body and soul.

Soon both England and the demons would crown their new King ... and he would be one and the same man.

Thomas turned slightly, and saw Wycliffe.

He was grinning with as much triumph as Richard.

X

Compline on the Feast of St Silvester
In the first year of the reign of Richard II
(night Thursday 30th December 1378)

— ii —

Westminster Palace was quiet and still. The approaching New Year's festivities had been irretrievably dampened by the twin deaths of Edward III and his heir, the Black Prince. Edward had sat the throne for over fifty years and, loved as he was, most people had accepted that he was reaching the final years of his life. But all had thought the Black Prince, another Edward, would reign after Edward III. The Black Prince was a known quantity: courageous, splendid, just. He would have made an admirable king.

But this boy, Richard? Few Londoners knew much about him. He had been a pale-faced youth they could have begun to know at their leisure once his father had assumed the throne.

The Lancastrian party had remained at Westminster after the wedding, although on the morrow Katherine and her retinue would depart back to the Savoy Palace.

For now Thomas and Hal stood close together in the quiet and warmth of the stables in the alley behind the palace of Westminster. All the grooms and stable boys had bedded down for the night, and Bolingbroke and Thomas, unsure whether demons could horse-shift as well, had moved to an empty stall twenty paces from the nearest living creature.

They spoke in hushed but urgent tones.

"Hal, you must have realised that both the king and the Black Prince's deaths were unnatural!"

"Aye. Demons attended both." The messenger had told of the devilish tempest and encircling demons who taunted the prince to his death. Hal and Thomas did not doubt for one moment that the masked mummers who had encircled Edward III had been demons as well.

"Thomas ... do you still suspect my father?"

Thomas hesitated. "No," he eventually said. "I had wondered if he were to be the new Demon-King ... but his grief at his father's death is genuine, and in the days since Edward's inhuman end he has done nothing but that which any mortal man bound by loyalty and duty should. If ... if he had been the new Demon-King he would have acted differently."

"Seized power himself."

"Yes." *And if he* had, *Hal, that would have made you heir to the throne.*

If nothing else, the events and actions of the past twenty-four hours had relieved Thomas' mind regarding both Lancaster *and* Hal. If they had been demons themselves, or in the employ or thrall of demons, they would not have acted as they did.

No demon would leave the path to all-encompassing power untrod.

No, Lancaster and Hal had both acted with loyalty and righteousness.

Hal studied Thomas' face. "You think Richard will be the Demon-King, don't you."

Thomas nodded. "There were only three people to gain from the simultaneous deaths of Edward and the Black Prince," Thomas said. "Your father, you, and Richard.

Neither you nor your father have taken any advantage of their deaths ..."

"But Richard can scarce contain his joy at his fortune."

"Aye. He has not shed a tear for either grandfather or father."

Hal half turned away, his handsome face shadowed, and mouthed an obscenity.

Then he looked back at Thomas. "We must tell my father."

Apart from Richard, no one save Bolingbroke could have gained access to Lancaster at such a late hour and during such trying times as these ... and certainly no one save Bolingbroke could have managed an interview with Lancaster on the man's wedding night. Hal and Thomas waited in a small chamber within the apartments of the palace complex that Lancaster had hurriedly selected for himself, watching Lancaster's back as he stared out a window.

He had stood, silent and watchful, as Thomas and then Hal had spoken, and had then turned and walked away to think.

His hands, held behind his back, suddenly twitched, and the duke turned around.

His face was ravaged, grey, and horribly old. For Lancaster, the past few days had been solid shock and grief, save for those brief, sweet moments when he had wed Katherine.

"I refuse to believe you," he said.

"Father," Hal said, stepping forward, "who else could it be? Saint Michael said that —"

"I care not what Saint Michael has said!" Lancaster said. "You may or may not be correct in believing there is a Demon-King in our midst, but I do know it is not Richard!"

He walked stiffly to a table and poured himself a goblet of wine, and then left the wine untouched. "I owe my father and my brother loyalty, and through that loyalty — which has been the mainstay of my entire life — I owe loyalty to Richard!"

"Perhaps," Hal said softly, knowing he risked his life saying this, but knowing that it had to be said anyway, "it would be better if you took the throne yourself, and —"

Lancaster whipped about and stared at his son. "Is your ambition so overweening, Hal?"

"Would you place a demon on the throne of England, father?"

"Prove it! Prove to me he is a demon!"

"I believe ..." Thomas said with some hesitation, "I believe that I might be able to."

Now both Lancaster and Bolingbroke turned and stared at Thomas.

"Wynkyn de Worde's casket," Thomas said.

"It will tell you?" Lancaster said.

"Perhaps," Thomas said, "for who knows the extent and breadth of the secrets it contains. But it will also draw the Demon-King out, for he will do all he can to prevent me finding it. My lord Duke, let me ride north. Please. I am useless in London."

Silence, save for the angry breathing of Lancaster.

Thomas held the duke's stare. "Grant me your permission to ride north, my lord."

Lancaster finally took a swallow of his wine. "You cannot leave until after my father's funeral rites."

Thomas bowed his head. It would look too strange; no one would leave London until after the king had been interred.

"And you will return with your 'proof' before Richard is crowned in the spring."

"Aye, my lord."

Lancaster stared a little longer, then his shoulders slumped and he waved his hand dismissively. "Get out. Both of you."

As Bolingbroke and Thomas moved towards the door, Lancaster added quietly: "If I didn't believe your mission was angel-inspired, Thomas, both you and Hal would be in the Tower now for your treasonous words."

XI

Matins on the Second Sunday after Christmas
In the first year of the reign of Richard II
(pre-dawn Sunday 2nd January 1379)

"Tom?"

He jerked awake, his mind still fogged. Where was he? Westminster or ... no, back in his chamber at the Savoy, where he had returned the previous afternoon after the subdued New Year's celebrations at Westminster.

"Tom? Tom?"

His mind would not clear. All he could think of was Lancaster, speaking words of treachery and imprisonment.

"Tom?"

Sweet Jesu! That was Margaret! He leaped out of bed and was almost to the door when the cold air crawling over his skin finally made him realise he was naked. He snatched at his white robe, sliding it over his head, cursing as the woollen cloth caught and rucked over his shoulders.

"Tom!"

Thomas threw open the door. "For the sweet Lord's sake, woman! You'll wake half the palace!"

"Tom."

She was standing shivering in her thin nightgown, a red wool cloak flung over her shoulders.

Her hair was unbound, and Thomas' mind found the time and energy to note he had never seen it thus before.

"What are you doing here?" he hissed, keeping the doorway blocked with his body.

Her hands clenched at the cloak, trying to pull it tighter closed. Her shivering had increased and she had to make a visible effort to speak.

"Tom. I have heard rumours about the fate of the Black Prince in France ..."

"And?"

She winced at the cold dismissal in his voice. "Ralph ... what has happened to him?"

"My uncle? But —"

"Just because this is not *his* child I bear, it does not mean I have no regard or affection for him. Tom, please, what do you know?"

He sighed, glanced along the corridor, then pulled her inside his chamber.

As the door closed, John Wycliffe stood forth from a darkened niche. He smiled slightly, and stepped back into his lair.

"Sit down." Thomas indicated the narrow bed, and Margaret, having given the stark chamber a cursory glance, did as she was told.

She pulled the cloak yet closer about her and stared up at Thomas with pleading eyes. "What have you heard —"

"Why aren't you with the Lady Katherine?"

"She has been badly upset by the events of the past day. Her husband's physician —"

Thomas noted wryly the way she said "husband".

"— gave her a sleeping draught. She does not need me. But, oh, Thomas, all I have heard is that the Black Prince and his force were decimated by a tempest driven by the Devil's breath, and the Black Prince is dead. But I have heard nothing of Raby!"

"I know little ... but Raby is alive."

Margaret let out a great breath of relief, and her hands loosened somewhat their hold on her cloak.

"He and a soldier, leading a horse carrying the prince's body, stumbled into Blaye at dawn on Saint Stephen's Day, just as a fishing vessel bound for Dover was leaving. Once it had landed, a messenger set out immediately for London."

"And Raby? Where is he?"

"He remained in Dover for a day or so. He was sick unto death — no, do not fear, he is well now, but needed to rest. He will be here in a day or so with the prince's body. Lancaster has sent Gloucester with an escort to bring them home."

Margaret nodded, her fears alleviated, and looked at her hands, now in her lap. "And are you going soon, Tom?"

He wondered where she thought he might be going. *What did she know?* "Why? Do you seek to stop me?"

She jerked her head up, her eyes angry or hurt, Thomas knew not which.

"Nay. I do not seek to stop you. I ..." she dropped her gaze again, "I am a woman without friend. My lover ignores me, and the father of my child fears my 'devilish enchantments'."

Her mouth curled.

"You should not be here," Thomas said. "Someone in the duchess' apartments will realise your absence."

"I should not be here? Why not?"

"Sweet Jesu, Margaret. No woman should wander into a friar's chamber in the darkest hours of the night!"

She raised her head, grinning softly. "I did not 'wander in', Tom. You invited me. Besides, I think you less the friar now than the man, Tom Neville."

"I am still a man of God!"

"That is not what I said. I think that somewhere along your journey in the past months you have abandoned the Church, although you remain a committed man of God."

Thomas was about to remonstrate with her when he realised the truth of her words. His commitment to God was no less — indeed, it was far stronger than it had ever been — but his commitment to the Church? Wavering, at best. Since he'd been in England he'd hardly attended regular canonical services ... and here it was Matins, and he'd been sound asleep in bed. He hadn't even kept the company of priests. Instead he'd fallen back in with old friends and acquaintances: Lancaster, Hal, Hotspur. True, that had been partly due to circumstance, but he hadn't fought against it, either.

Was he more Lord Thomas Neville now than Brother Thomas?

And which would serve God and St Michael best?

"Oh!" Margaret said, and Thomas looked down.

She had her hands softly clasped about her belly — the cloak now fallen open to reveal the soft thin material of her nightgown — and she was looking up at Thomas with black eyes soft with emotion.

"The child," she whispered, and then reached out and took one of Thomas' hands.

He almost pulled back, but then he let her draw it down to her belly, and place it gently over its firm roundness.

"Do you feel?" she said.

Thomas was now squatting before her in order to rest his hand comfortably. "What is it?"

"The babe is shifting."

He could feel the child, but it meant nothing to him. All he could truly *feel* was her, her roundness and warmth, and the scent of her hair as it fell over her shoulders.

He put his other hand on her belly, and felt her arch her body very slightly towards him.

Her cloak had fallen completely back now, and the material of her nightgown was very, very thin.

"This is sin," he said.

"This is nothing but what happens between a man and a woman."

She paused. "I cannot harm you unless you allow it. Do you fear yourself, Tom?"

He looked up into her eyes.

"No." He felt very strong. He lifted a hand to the neckline of her gown, and unlaced it, placing his hand flat against the creamy skin of her chest.

"Why did you come here, Margaret?"

"To learn of Raby's fate, for I do truly care for him —"

Thomas felt a surge of emotion sweep through him. But as he could not identify it, he ignored it.

"— and to see you. I am so cold, Tom, and alone in the world."

"What can I do?"

"You can warm me, just this one night, just for a short hour."

He lifted his hand to her face, and pulled it to his, hesitating slightly before he put his mouth to hers.

Her kiss was very sweet, and very tender, but Thomas only savoured her, he did not perceive her, nor realise her tenderness for what it was.

His hands tightened in her hair.

She slid down before him on the floor — her nightgown and cloak had gone, he did not know how — and pressed her body against his.

Her pregnant belly pressed through the wool of his robe against his own belly, and he groaned.

"Your robe," she whispered, and he fumbled in his haste to rid himself of it, and to press his belly back against hers.

"Do you love me, sweet Tom?" she said.

"No."

"No matter," she whispered, and leaned back in his arms as his mouth sought her breasts.

Soon his child would suckle there as now he did . . . ah!

Margaret cried out, and writhed against him, her hands clutching to his shoulders.

They were both fumbling now, desperate to ease their lust, moaning and thrusting hip against hip. He set her on the edge of the bed — it was too narrow for them both to lie its length — and kneeled before her.

"Now *this* is sin," she said, "for the Church teaches it is not the natural way to take a woman . . . oh, *Tom*!"

"Too late," he said. "Are you warm enough now, Lady Rivers?"

"Yes," she whispered, again arching back in his arms so his mouth could once more suckle at her breasts and her belly press against his, "Oh . . . yes."

When the door closed behind her, Thomas pulled on his robe and stood by the window, uncaring about the pre-dawn chill.

His mind and soul were peaceful.

She — whatever "she" was — would never be a danger to him. He knew that now.

Margaret Rivers was a common whore — she'd had no shame, no modesty! — who had doubtless spread her legs through the entire English encampment. He would never love her.

His mouth curled. And the demons thought that *she* could steal his soul . . . ?

He had bedded her — if such animal rutting could even be dignified with such a title — but there was no stain on him. No guilt. Neither God nor St Michael were displeased.

Thomas thought on the child. It was probably his, for Margaret had been a virgin when the sorcery had thrust them together, but he felt no responsibility for it.

Indeed, he felt nothing for it.

Perhaps it should be killed. Smothered at birth. After all, it *was* the child of witchcraft. The midwife could tell Margaret it had been strangled with the birth cord . . . Margaret would know no better . . . and would never grieve.

Thomas sighed, content, and turned to find a cloth with which to wash himself.

Margaret paused by the shadowy niche, and John Wycliffe stepped forward so she could see his face and know him for what he was.

Then he bowed deeply. "Beloved Mistress," he said. "Did he . . ."

"Yes, John. I shall ache for many days to come."

But he did not smile at her poor attempt at a jest.

Instead Wycliffe's face assumed the most infinite of

sadnesses, and he dared reach forward and caress her cheek with the back of his fingers. "Lady, do not love him."

She smiled, her expression now as sorrowful as Wycliffe's. "He is not a man who can be loved, John. He will not allow it."

And then she was gone.

XII

The Monday within the Octave of the Circumcision
In the first year of the reign of Richard II
(3rd January 1379)

Ralph, Baron of Raby, stood in the chilled interior of
Westminster Abbey, staring at the two coffins set
before the high altar. Both were draped in black, and
both were guarded by knights standing in armour dulled by
a dusting of ashes.

Raby could hardly comprehend what he saw. Even now,
even after he'd spent so many days escorting the Black
Prince's body home through France and then across the
seas to England, he found it hard to accept that the man
was dead.

And the prince's father.

And in such similar, demonic, circumstances.

Raby crossed himself, and murmured a prayer, wishing
that it could comfort him, but he wondered if anything
would ever comfort him again in this suddenly bleak and
dismal world.

On the morrow both the king and his heir would be laid
to rest, and somehow England would move on. It had a new
king, an untried lad who should have had another ten years
at least before he assumed the throne.

Ten years where he could have learned, matured ... and been tested for his strength and integrity.

Now it was all too late. Far too late.

"My lord? Ralph?"

Raby jumped, surprised and angered by the intrusion into his grief.

He turned slightly.

Margaret.

He turned his back on her. "Leave me."

"My lord ... I must speak with you."

"Damn you, Margaret!" Raby hissed, wheeling about to face her. "There is nothing we have to say to each other! You are safe home in England, and there is nothing to bind us!"

"There is this to bind us!" Margaret placed both her hands on her six-month belly. Her face, naturally pale, was made even more colourless by a drapery of soft white linen over her hair that she wore as a mark of respect for the dead.

"Do you think to use that child to bind me? You know I will never own it."

"Nevertheless," Margaret said in a quiet voice, "everyone knew you lay with me between summer and winter of last year. Whatever pretences are mouthed about court, all know you put this child in me, not some long-dead husband."

"For the love of Jesus Christ, Margaret, what do you want?"

"A father for my child. Recompense for my labour pains. A house for shelter, and an income for life. A settlement, on the child and on me."

Raby went white with anger. "You self-seeking whore!"

"I want you to acknowledge this child, and to give it — and me — a name. You cannot abandon us."

"You want me to marry you?" Raby started to laugh, then stopped as two of the knights standing guard about the coffins stared in his direction.

"I will not," he continued. "My betrothal to the Lady Joan Beaufort will be announced within the month."

"I did not say I wanted *you*," Margaret said, still very calm. "I said I wanted a husband and a name ... and a husband and a name that will give this child good rank within society."

"You will return to your husband's parents, and there you will give birth to your husband's child. Our bargain was that I should enable you to return to England in return for your warmth in my bed. A simple transaction. Don't try to raise the price now."

"And when I ask for audience with your new wife in her comfortable castle of Raby with a mewling fatherless infant in my arms? How will she feel, presented with her new husband's bastard as a wedding gift? If I have to, Ralph, I will gift the child to her. The Neville name and heritage is its natural right, and I will fight tooth and nail to —"

Raby stepped forward and grabbed her wrist, pulling her close to him.

"I do not take threats kindly!" he hissed in her face. "And you will not humiliate me before my wife or her family!"

"Perhaps you should have thought of that before you mounted me, my lord."

He breathed deeply, angry beyond measure. The whore had chosen her site of confrontation carefully, for he could do little here save whisper furiously at her.

Sweet Jesu, all he wanted to do was to lift his hand and send her sprawling across the cold, hard stone. Perhaps that might shock the child out of her, and solve his dilemma here and now.

His hand tightened about her wrist, and she gasped.

"Hear me now," he said, "and hear me before God as my witness. I will never acknowledge the child, and I will take every means possible — do you understand me? — to ensure that you never present your bulging belly or its contents at my court."

It took all of Margaret's willpower not to try and wrench her wrist from his furious grip. "Do you threaten me before God, my lord?"

"Did you not threaten me first, bitch?"

Raby let her go, and Margaret took a step back, rubbing her reddened wrist.

"I think it more than time," he said, "that you return to your husband's home to inform his parents of your happy tidings. I shall speak to Lancaster this day, to suggest that you are not fit company for his wife's retinue."

"Lancaster has ever stood by his mistress and his bastards," Margaret said quietly. "At least he is a man of honour."

They stared silently and angrily at each other for a long minute, then, almost as one, they turned to face the draped coffins, bowed, made the sign of the cross, and turned to walk down the great nave of the abbey, the footsteps echoing high above to disturb the cobwebs among the beams of the vaulted roof.

They would not speak again for a very long time.

XIII

The Feast of St Valentine
In the first year of the reign of Richard II
(Monday 14th February 1379)

Northern Lincolnshire was a harsh and forbidding place, and even more so in the late winter. An arctic wind swept down over the Humber estuary and river and then whistled between the low hills below Barton towards the small village of Saxbye, adding bone-chilling misery to the late February hunger. The bounty of Christmastide was long past, and all that most households had to sustain themselves before the first of the spring vegetable crops were a few meagre handfuls of half rotten grain and legumes. Even the occasional poached rabbit or hare was hardly worth the effort of its entrapment — below the sparse, winter-matted fur lay nothing but bones and empty entrails. In the old language February was Hungry-month, and in the peasants' yearly agricultural cycle the month was notable for two things besides belly-aching hunger: birth and the beginning of the spring ploughing.

Many peasant women timed the birth of their children — generally through selective abortion — for February so that they could be back in the fields working by May at the latest. May through to October were the busiest months of the year, and few peasant women could afford to spend the summer months labouring with a big belly. The members of the party from London that wound its slow way through Cambridgeshire and then southern Lincolnshire grew used to seeing thin, hunger-ravaged women with tiny, squalling infants in their arms. They also grew used to the newly turned earth of village graveyards as both infants and mothers succumbed to the rigours of childbirth and of the leanness of the year.

As their women struggled — and often died — in childbed, so husbandmen abandoned the warmth of their hearths to struggle with their heavy-wheeled ploughs and dim-witted oxen in the frozen fields. Now was the time to turn the soil before it thawed and became impassable mud, now the time to cart manure from winter stables and spread it over fields in preparation for the planting of the spring crops.

What should have been a joyous time of the year — the time of birth and the first forays into the field — was made miserable and disheartening by bone-deep cold and hunger.

At least, as the fields were frozen, so too were the roads, and that made the way easier for the horses. Nevertheless, the riders were almost as miserable as the local peasantry who struggled for their lives and livelihood in the hovels and fields. No number of cloaks or wraps could keep the cold at bay, and there was nothing in the frozen land to please the eye.

There was merely the bone-jolting jar of every stride of their mounts, the unceasing sting of the wind, and the chilling silence between the riders.

Edward III and his son, the Black Prince, had been interred in Westminster Abbey in the second week of January. The ceremonies, whether the official rites in Westminster or the unofficial grievings across London, were as cheerless and cold as the time of the year.

Richard's coronation would not take place until May. England needed time to grieve for two well-beloved men, and the bureaucracy needed time to prepare for a new king. There were new seals to be fashioned, new coins to be made, new appointments to fight over, and intricate plans laid for the first coronation England had witnessed in over fifty years.

All this would take time, and in this time, Thomas could finally head north to Bramham Moor friary in Yorkshire to there, God willing, discover Wynkyn de Worde's casket and its secrets. Thomas was grateful for these months that always intervened between the death of one monarch and the coronation of the next, simply because it gave him the time he needed to find the proof that Richard was indeed the next Demon-King.

Every gut instinct, every strange, sidling glance Richard sent his way, every damned *event* since Edward and the Black Prince had died, told Thomas that Richard would be the Demon-King.

Yet none of that was enough to convince the only man who had a chance of preventing Richard taking the throne: Lancaster. The duke was letting nothing stand in the way of his loyalties. He had promised both his father and elder brother that he would fight for Richard's right to take the throne, and he would listen to none of Bolingbroke's or Thomas' suspicions.

"Show me the proof," he demanded, and Thomas was finally on his way to do just that.

Unfortunately, he was not allowed to ride directly to Bramham Moor, nor was he allowed to ride alone, which is what he would have preferred.

Lancaster would not let Thomas ride north without an escort, and so now here he was, trotting along the wintry northern Lincolnshire lanes with five men-at-arms men led, to Thomas' irritation, by Wat Tyler himself.

Lancaster had insisted on Tyler. The man was a long-time retainer in Lancaster's retinue, and the duke trusted the man deeply. Besides, Thomas and Tyler had been acquainted for many years — indeed, Tyler had fought with Thomas when the man had been a noble and not a friar — and Lancaster could see no reason why Tyler shouldn't be the perfect sergeant to lead Thomas' escort.

Thomas could say nothing. He did not trust Tyler, but he had no proof against him.

As Lancaster demanded Thomas ride with an escort, so he also demanded Thomas abandon his clerical robes. Thus Thomas rode, not as a friar, but as a knight returning to his estates in Yorkshire.

The Prior General of the Dominicans in England, Father Richard Thorseby, had discovered that Thomas was back in England, and the man's influence was particularly strong in northern England. If Thorseby discovered that Thomas was in the north, then he would have no trouble finding a lord to arrest the friar for him. The north was both home and trap for Thomas.

So Thomas must needs ride in disguise. He found it discomforting to once again wear the habit of the man he thought he had abandoned. It reminded him of what Margaret had said to him: *You are less the friar now than the man, Tom Neville.*

And so here he was, his tonsure grown out, and a three-week old black beard covering his lower face. About his body he wore an expensive tunic of green velvet with silver gilt buttons over a fine linen under-tunic, black leggings and boots, fine-grained leather gloves with fur trimming, and a double thickness cloak of rich blue around his shoulders.

While it was warmer than riding in open-toed sandals and friar's robe, Thomas was nonetheless uncomfortable at how "at home" he felt in the clothes.

He found he did not miss his robe and sandals at all.

But, of all things Thomas had to ride with, the most discomforting was Margaret.

Lancaster had insisted that, as Thomas was already heading north with a sizeable escort, he might as well escort the Lady Margaret Rivers to her husband's parental home just south of Saxbye in northern Lincolnshire.

There she could give birth to her — her *husband's* — child. Lancaster had been grimly insistent that Margaret ride with Thomas, and Thomas thought he knew why.

Raby's wedding had been planned for mid-February —
indeed, it would have been accomplished sometime last
week, when Thomas and Margaret and their escort had been
riding the northern Cambridgeshire roads — and both Raby
and his soon-to-be father-in-law wanted Margaret and her
swelling belly out of the way.

Fast.

Thomas had not wanted to be burdened with Margaret
for many reasons, but primarily because she would delay
them on the road — Lord Jesus! she was almost seven
months gone with child — and because the detour needed to
get her to Saxbye would add many days to Thomas' own
journey.

Nevertheless, he was burdened with her, and he must bear
his burden as well as he might.

Surprisingly, Margaret was little trouble. Unlike their ride
through western France to reach the port of la Rochelle,
Margaret coped well with the long days in the saddle. In the
evenings, when they halted at an inn or the welcoming house
of one of Lancaster's vassals, Margaret ate quickly and then
retired to bed, tired from her long hours on the road. She
rarely talked with Thomas, and then mostly only a brief
commentary on the countryside they passed through, or the
pleasantries that a particular occasion demanded. She did
not attempt to seduce him again, nor flaunt her pregnancy.

They did not mention the child.

In fact, Thomas thought Margaret was somewhat
subdued, and wondered what had passed between her and
Raby. But perhaps that was merely the natural habit of a
woman fast approaching her childbed, and more concerned
with thoughts of pain and death than of seduction and love.

At dusk on St Valentine's Day they rode through the small
village of Saxbye, peasant women peering through doorways,
their husbands pausing from unyoking their plough teams
to wonder at the strangers.

A mile past Saxbye, nestled in the hollow of the foothills
rising towards the ranges that separated Lincolnshire from
the Humber Estuary, stood Rivers Hall. It was a fortified

house rather than a castle, sitting by a frozen pond in meadows that, Thomas thought, would be particularly pleasant in springtime.

The gates to the courtyard were open — no one in this part of England suspected any trouble — and Thomas led his party straight into the court of the house, their horses' clattering hooves bringing surprised servants from kitchen and barn doors.

"Well, Margaret," he said as he swung down from his horse. "You are finally home."

She sat her horse, her face strained under the hood of her scarlet cloak.

She was staring at the walls of the house rising about her.

"This will never be my home," she said.

The Prior General of the Dominican Order in England, Father Richard Thorseby, sat gratefully before his fire in his chamber. He had spent much of the day inspecting and questioning the members of his Order who taught at Oxford, and it had been a cold and tiresome affair.

But there was one more item of business to be attended to before he could finally relax.

The letter.

It had arrived this morning, and Thorseby had left it to one side the entire day. Well, God would not be mocked, and he supposed he finally must read it and see what heresies it contained.

Thorseby picked it up, idly turning it over in his hands. He had not needed to see the seal to know who had sent it: this crabbed writing was as well known to him as his own.

Well, what apostasies had Master Wycliffe decided to write him now?

Because of their mutual association with the colleges of Oxford, Thorseby knew Wycliffe well.

Unfortunately.

The man had abandoned God years ago, and now ran riot in London, protected by Lancaster, spouting forth ever more horrendous ideas.

If it hadn't been for Lancaster ... Thorseby sighed, and broke the seal.

His eyes scanned the brief letter inside, then his face went purple and he leapt to his feet shouting for his secretary.

An aged man, a shock of wiry white hair over a sallow and sunken face, rushed out of the main entrance way in such a hurry he had forgotten to grab a cloak. Behind him came a stout woman, of a similar age to the man, with badly dyed brown hair and a russet robe straining about her ample body. She, at least, had remembered to lay hand to a wrap, and now she was hurriedly throwing it about her shoulders.

"Good sir," the man said as he stopped before Thomas. His eyes briefly noted the Lancastrian emblems on the soldiers' tunics and the horses' saddlecloths, and his manner became even more deferential. "Good lord, may I offer you the hospitality of my house this night? My name is Egdon Rivers, and this," he indicated the woman, "is my wife, the Lady Jacquetta."

"I thank you, Sir Egdon and Lady Rivers," said Thomas, pulling off his gloves as a stable lad rushed to take the reins of his horse. "Your hospitality would be most welcome, for the road has been long and cold. My name is Thomas Neville, kinsman of Baron Raby, and I escort home to you your daughter-in-law, the Lady Margaret Rivers."

Sir Egdon and Lady Jacquetta stared unbelieving at Thomas a moment longer, then their eyes slowly settled on Margaret, sitting her horse a few feet behind Thomas.

"Margaret?" Sir Egdon said hesitatingly. "Where ... where is Roger?"

Thomas swung about to stare at Margaret. *She had sent no word?*

Margaret made a helpless face. "My lord, my lady, I am so sorry. Roger ... Roger died this past six months. In Bordeaux, where we rested after having visited Santiago de Compostella."

Still shocked and angry that she hadn't had the courtesy to let the Rivers know that their son was dead, Thomas still noted somewhat wryly that at least Margaret had now got her dates in correct order. Roger had been dead six months, and here she was with a seven-month belly.

Jacquetta began to keen, a thin and grating wail that wove in and out of the men and horses crowding the courtyard. Sir Egdon, still staring at Margaret, put an arm about his wife's shoulders and pulled her to him.

It muffled, but did not stop, the Lady Jacquetta's wailing.

"The Lady Margaret also bears good news, my lord," Thomas said, suppressing a grin, "for she is seven months gone with your son's child."

Sir Egdon's brow lined with suspicion. "I don't believe it," he said.

Margaret winced. "It was a miracle sent by God," she said.

The expression on Sir Egdon's face did not alter, and after a moment he motioned to the waiting servants to show his visitors inside and turned his back on his daughter-in-law.

Sir Egdon and Lady Jacquetta had never liked Margaret. She had not come from a good family — scarce anyone knew of her father and mother, who were reported to have died in an outbreak of pestilence in 1357 — she hardly had a dowry worth mentioning, she had no land to her name, and she was so beautiful that they knew she would prove temptation incarnate.

She would be a husband's nightmare.

Yet Roger had eyes for no one else. He'd seen her in York when he attended the Easter celebrations at York Minster over ten years ago. Margaret had been there with her guardian, an elderly woman of even less distinguished family than Margaret's, and the girl had wasted no time in gaining Roger's trust and love.

She'd been but fifteen, but the Rivers thought her more skilled in the arts of manipulating the hearts of men than the most-married widow.

But Roger had been ailing even then — he'd attended York Minster in the hope of a miracle — and neither Egdon nor Jacquetta could refuse him. Roger and Margaret had married but a half year later, just as Margaret turned sixteen years, and within a month she'd convinced her doting husband that the only way to find a cure for his worsening wasting sickness was to take to the road as a pilgrim.

For years they'd attended every shrine in England. Then, five years ago, Margaret had persuaded Roger to attempt the shrines of Europe.

Sir Egdon and Lady Jacquetta had never seen him since.

And now, never would.

They sat in the hall of their house, the fire blazing, Lord Thomas Neville to one side, and their daughter-in-law to the other. The meal — an abstemious affair of stringy rabbit and coarse-ground bread — had been left an hour or more ago, and it was now late at night.

Margaret was clearly tired, but the Rivers were in no mood to let her rest just yet. They asked her question after question about their son, and about the child.

To each question Margaret answered apparently clearly and honestly, but Thomas could see that the Rivers' suspicion of the woman had not abated.

"It puzzles me," Sir Egdon said, the shadows flung by the fire scattering over his face, his eyes steady on Margaret, "that you took so many months to return home to England. Why?"

"There was war throughout France," Margaret said, visibly rousing herself from lethargy. "Travel was difficult."

"But why stay with the army?" Jacquetta said. Her tone clearly indicated what she thought about any woman that journeyed about with an army.

Margaret shrugged a little. "Baron Raby kindly vouchsafed me protection. And where better to seek safety than in an armed force of one's own countrymen?"

Sir Egdon's gaze never faltered. "I find it difficult to believe that the child is my son's. He found it nigh impossible to sup at soup, let alone mount a woman."

Margaret's cheeks reddened. "It was a miracle," she said. "How else can I explain it?"

Sir Egdon switched his gaze to Thomas. "Lord Neville ... can you verify Margaret's words?"

"Good sir," Thomas said. "I act only as escort to Lady Margaret for my uncle's sake. When I arrived in the English camp Lady Margaret was already there and, I believe, some months gone with child even then."

"And in whose chamber did she reside?" Sir Egdon asked.

"She served our Lady of Gloucester."

"Humph." Sir Egdon shuffled about in his chair a little, then turned back to Margaret. "I wonder, Margaret, if you could tell us how ..."

And so on it went, late into the night, so late it was almost Matins before Sir Egdon finally allowed his weary guest, his daughter-in-law and his wife to retire to their beds.

Thomas left the next morning after only a few hours' sleep, impatient to reach Bramham Moor.

Just as he mounted his horse and swung its head towards the courtyard gate, a cloak-wrapped Margaret appeared in the doorway of the house, and hurried over to him.

Her face was white and her eyes circled with lack of sleep.

"Tom," she said quietly once she had gained the side of his horse.

"Be careful what you say," he responded as quietly. "Sir Egdon and his lady wife are not far behind you."

She turned her head slightly. Her in-laws were standing a few steps out from the doorway, watching her.

"Do not leave me here," she said, turning back to Thomas.

"Where would you have me leave you?" he said. "You have no coin, and no friends."

"They despise me," she whispered.

"I'm not surprised," Thomas responded, his tone hardening, "considering you did not bother to grace them with the news of their son's death."

"This is your child!" she hissed, taking a half step forwards.

"Don't expect me to acknowledge it," Thomas said.

"You are a Neville born and bred, aren't you?"

Thomas lifted his head and smiled and saluted the Rivers. "Good day to you sir, and to you, my lady. I thank you for your hospitality."

And then, without another word, he signalled Wat Tyler at the head of his escort, and they trotted out of the Rivers' courtyard.

XIV

Nones on the Feast of St Mathias
In the first year of the reign of Richard II
(midday Thursday 24th February 1379)

— i —

It took Thomas and his escort another ten days to reach
Bramham Moor. A fierce storm closed in two days after
they'd left Saxbye, and they'd been forced to shelter in
a monastery guest house for three days. But once it had
passed the weather turned clear, if frosty, and the party
made good time.

In the initial week or two after leaving London, Thomas
had found Wat Tyler's presence disturbing. He did not quite
know what to make of the man, and he did not know
whether to trust or mistrust him. In Thomas' youth and
early manhood, when he had been such a part of Lancaster's
household through his close friendship with Bolingbroke,
Wat Tyler had been a familiar face. It seemed as if he'd been
with Lancaster as a sergeant-at-arms ever since either
Thomas or Bolingbroke could remember, although he was
but some six or seven years older than they, and he was one
of Lancaster's most trusted men.

As part of his duties to the duke, Wat had been one of the
boys' trainers in the skills of warfare. What Thomas knew of

close combat with sword and knife he largely knew through Wat's tutorship.

And when both Bolingbroke and Thomas had first ventured onto the battlefield, Wat had been there, gruff and reassuring during the bloodshed, loud and jocular during the drinking once the bloodshed was done.

But the Wat whom Thomas had met in Rome, and had then talked to at various times over succeeding months, seemed somehow different, and it was not only the views Wat espoused, or the heretical company he kept. Thomas was not sure if the difference was because Wat had changed, or because he had. Before he'd left London, Thomas would have sworn before God that it was because Wat had changed.

But now ...

The fact was that since Thomas had abandoned his clerical garb in favour of the noble clothes he had once worn, he and Wat seemed to have fallen back into their easy friendship of years past. If Wat voiced any views that were critical of the Church or the established structure of society, then they seemed nothing but the ill-chosen words of a rough-edged and illiterate man of war.

Thomas even found himself nodding once or twice when Wat spoke of the burden of taxes the ordinary man had to bear.

Perhaps it was the northern air, Thomas mused, that made him distrust Wat less. Every day's ride brought him closer to his home county ... and perhaps even closer to the person he once had been.

Mayhap it had been a mistake to so easily agree to Lancaster's order that he abandon his clerical garb. It had probably been another, gigantic, step in the process Margaret had pointed out to him: Thomas, while still a man of God, was becoming every day less a man of the Church.

He was certainly enjoying the comfort and warmth of his linens and wools, and of the thick and well-tooled leather boots which encased his feet and calves. He had enjoyed the Rivers' hospitality, not only for watching Margaret's conspicuous discomfort, but because of the respect Sir Egdon and his wife had accorded him as a noble kinsman of Baron Raby.

He enjoyed the fine stallion he rode, a chestnut from Lancaster's own stable.

And most of all, he enjoyed the freedom of not having to live his entire life, hour by hour, day by day, year by year, in the rigid regulations and restrictions and formulations of clerical life.

Thomas had forgotten that once he had found spiritual comfort in these very regulations and restrictions and formulations.

What he *did* remember was that St Michael had told him that both his and Joan's paths would appear strange to them.

Well ... maybe this is what the archangel meant.

Whatever, by the time they rode down the track leading to Bramham Moor friary, Thomas had decided not to re-garb himself as a cleric, which had been his original intention.

Somehow it just didn't seem worthwhile ridding himself of his beard and reshaving his tonsure when both beard and hair had taken so many weeks to regrow back into their black, curly thickness.

Before he left London Thomas had made some discreet inquiries about the friary. It had been founded some hundred years previously through the donation of money and land by a local wealthy lord who hoped thereby to ease his path to salvation. The friary was only superficially Dominican; in fact, the Dominican Order had little to do with it. The friary, it appeared, and those brothers who lived and worshipped within it, were largely left to their own ways.

In truth, no one and no chapter within the Church cared much about the friary. It was tiny, boasting no more than four brothers at any one time (and, once, only one), men who came from the local population of shepherds and farmers and who were, most likely, completely illiterate. The friary certainly wasn't rich. The original benefactor had given enough to establish the foundation, but little towards its daily upkeep, and the sparse population of Bramham Moor itself hardly generated enough income to keep the brothers in luxury.

Basically, Bramham Moor friary was poor, and contained no more than four illiterate brothers who had little training, no education, and who collectively could undoubtedly manage to remember no more than three commandments of the ten. It would have been totally unremarkable but for two things: it had produced Wynkyn de Worde (*How?* Thomas wondered), and it harboured Wynkyn de Worde's casket.

The moor in which the friary was situated was typical for this part of Yorkshire: low rolling hills with few trees, tough grasses and heath that somehow withstood the constant blowing winds, and little in the way of human presence or cheer. What houses existed were of local stone, thick-walled, low-roofed and often windowless abodes that were as grim and dour as the landscape.

This was a land where a man planted his staff and stood, head bowed, hoping somehow to weather the elements and the loneliness.

It made Thomas understand Wynkyn de Worde a little better. If this was where he had grown to manhood, it was no wonder that his character had reflected the grimness and determination of the moors, and likewise it was no wonder that he had been the kind of man who could stare a demon in the eye and never flinch.

The friary stood five miles from the nearest village, a dreadful isolation for the brothers. Thomas had asked directions from the villagers, and had been pointed down a barely visible track — no more than an overgrown rut — winding over the moor.

Neither Thomas nor his escort had occasioned more than a few brief disinterested stares from the village folk. Thomas supposed the harsh struggle to survive had sapped them of any unnecessary emotions or curiosities.

It took less than an hour to ride down the track, and by noon of St Mathias' Day they approached the friary itself. It was little more than a larger version of the local hovels: a long, low, stone building with a doorway in the centre of one of the long side walls, a single window in one of the end walls, a gap in the roof for the smoke from a central hearth to exit, and not even a separate chapel for the brothers to worship in.

Thomas felt a knot of excitement and fear in his belly. He was here at last.

He pushed his heels into his stallion, and the horse snorted and jumped into a canter for the last hundred yards, Wat and the rest of the escort not far behind.

As Thomas' horse clattered to a halt before the door, it opened, and a dirty-robed brother stepped out.

His watery blue eyes opened in amazement at the visitors, and he began to shuffle from foot to foot, wringing his hands in excitement.

"Brothers!" he cried. "Brothers! We have guests!"

Two other brothers emerged from the dark interior of the building, another hurried around a corner from a latrine situated behind a dung heap — his robes were still about his thighs as he hastily tried to rearrange himself.

Thomas slid down from his horse, wondering if he had the patience to get through the necessary politenesses before he asked for the casket.

"My lord!" the first brother said, "greetings! My name is Brother Simon, and this is Brother Fulke, and Brother Paul, and this," he nodded to the brother who had emerged from the latrine, and had only now got his robes back down to his ankles, "is Brother Alfred. May we offer you our hospitality? I am afraid it will be but meagre, and —"

"Pray do not bother yourselves on my account," Thomas said, "for I and my escort are but passing through. Some water for our horses will be all we require. My name is Thomas Neville —"

All four brothers oohed and aahed, for the Neville name was well known in the north.

"— and I come here on an errand that, I pray to God, will take but a few short minutes to accomplish."

The brothers' faces fell, and Thomas immediately regretted he had not accepted their offer of hospitality. Obviously they had few visitors, and now that a lord had ridden by, they must be beside themselves with joy.

"Well," Thomas said, "perhaps I can stay for just a while."

The brothers' faces brightened as one, and Simon beckoned Thomas inside. "Alfred will see to your men," he said. "Please, enter."

The interior of the friary — if it truly deserved such a name — was as poor as its exterior, save in one respect.

At one end was a hearth and the implements and dishes for cooking, together with a few small chests, a trestle table and benches, and sleeping mats for the brothers. At the other end of the building was what served as an altar: a stone platform with a crude stone altar, but bedecked with some of the most beautiful and finely-crafted gold plate and goblets that Thomas had ever seen.

On the wall behind the altar hung a superb gold cross decorated with rubies, emeralds and pearls that stood a full four feet high.

It was worth a small fortune.

Thomas suddenly felt very cold.

"What brings you to these distant parts?" Simon said. Behind him Paul and Fulke were bustling about the kitchen area, pouring out water into cups and bowls, and spreading out bread and cheese on platters.

Thomas was certain now that his trip had been in vain. "I seek a casket belonging to a brother who originally came from this friary," he said. "It belonged to Wynkyn de Worde."

Simon's face fell, and Paul and Fulke stopped their bustling and stared at Thomas.

"My lord," Simon stammered, "I am so sorry, but it has gone."

Thomas had not believed he could get this cold and still remain able to think and speak. "When? And by whom?"

"But a bare seven or eight weeks ago, my lord. I do so apologise ... After all these years that the casket had remained forgotten in our store cellar, and now to have two lords ask after it in such a short space of time —"

"*Who took it?*"

Simon looked to the other two brothers for help, but they were having none of it, and had faded back to the far wall.

"Why ... he was a mighty lord, much as yourself —"

"*Who?*"

"Why, ah, I believe he said his name was Robert ... or was it Edward? No, I am wrong ... I think ... it may have been —"

"My lord," Paul now stood forth. "We cannot remember his name, but we recognised the emblem on his tunic, and on the clothing of his escort."

Thomas stared, waiting.

"It was the emblem of Lancaster, my lord."

Time halted for a while, but finally Thomas overcame his anger and bitter frustration and collected himself enough to ask the brothers to tell their tale in detail.

None of the brothers were over the age of thirty: Bramham Moor was a harsh place, and men, whether friar or shepherd, tended to wither and die not long after middle age. Until so very recently the name Wynkyn de Worde had been unknown to them. The four brothers were hard put to remember the names of the brothers who had inhabited the friary immediately prior to them.

But, almost two months ago, a young lord had ridden to their door and, a charming smile about his mouth and politenesses tumbling from his tongue, had asked them of this Wynkyn de Worde.

They had professed ignorance.

The young lord — so fair of hair and face! — had not been angry, but had told them of what he sought: a casket, of oak wood, bound about with bands of iron and probably locked. The brothers had sat silent, blinking slowly in a state of perplexity.

The fair young lord had waited.

The brothers fell to whispering among themselves, chasing this thought and that, until Paul had remembered that there was an old casket of some description, lying almost hidden behind a jumble of rubble and rubbish in their cellar.

There was excitement — could this be it?

The young lord had smiled, and nodded, and asked if perhaps they could look.

After some heaving and ho-ing, and some barely muffled curses, the brothers had pulled the surprisingly heavy casket out from the detritus of generations of incurious brothers and had hefted it into the ground level room.

They had never looked inside? asked the young lord.

Well, no, the brothers had answered, and had blinked in confusion when the young lord had insisted that perhaps they had been curious, and surely they had wondered . . .

No. The casket had merely been there, covered with dust, and they had never wondered at all . . .

Listening to this tale, Thomas could understand why this "young lord" had accepted their professions of incuriosity: these brothers lived in a world of almost total mental dullness. They were local men who had joined the friary as a means of subsistence when they had failed in their careers as shepherds. The friary gave them shelter and some food. They asked no more of it, and certainly did not investigate its secrets.

So the young lord had smiled all the more, and had praised their efforts, and had told them that the casket had been left at the friary many years previous by his father, who had always meant to return for it.

The brothers had murmured, doubt penetrating their murky minds.

The young lord reassured them, saying that his father was most assuredly grateful for the brothers' care of the casket, and would pay accordingly.

The brothers' doubts fell away. The young lord motioned to his servants, who bought in the gold now displayed about the altar, and then he packed up the casket, said his farewells, and departed.

"And you cannot remember his name?" Thomas asked, bitterly.

"No," Simon said. "It is here," he tapped his head, "but refuses to come forth."

Well, Thomas thought, no doubt the demons have left spells to addle his mind.

And so, in his turn, he stood, made his farewells, and departed.

When Wat Tyler, waiting with the horses outside, asked where they went now, Thomas merely snapped, "London," and, mounting his horse, turned it back to the track they had only just ridden down.

XV

Vespers on the Feast of St Mathias
In the First Year of the Reign of Richard II
(early evening Thursday 24th February 1379)

— ii —

Margaret set her needlework to one side and surreptitiously eased her back — it had begun to ache abominably in the past few hours. Her pregnancy was becoming ever more uncomfortable, and she hardly slept at night with the child squirming and kicking as if it, like its mother, loathed the Rivers' household so much it wanted to leave as soon as possible.

Jacquetta sent her daughter-in-law a cold glance. Neither she nor her husband had quite decided what to do with the woman. It was tempting to believe that her child was Roger's ... but they weren't that guileless! Nay, the whore had got herself thick with another man's babe, and then, no doubt, sought to murder their Roger in order to pretend it was his. There was a convent close by ... perhaps they could sequester her there until the child was born, and even after, for a life spent under the veil would do the harlot no harm at all.

"Madam," Margaret said, finally becoming so uncomfortable she had to move or scream, but got no further, for just then came the sound of horses in the courtyard, and voices as Sir Egdon greeted the newcomers.

Jacquetta looked to the door, and held up a hand to Margaret. "Stay where you are."

Margaret squirmed, one hand on her belly, and would have spoken save that just then Sir Egdon entered with a Dominican friar of short height but great presence.

Margaret stilled completely, her dark eyes watchful.

"Madam," Sir Egdon said to his wife, "we have a most distinguished visitor. This is Father Richard Thorseby, Prior General of the Dominican Order in England."

Thorseby bowed elegantly to Jacquetta, then fixed Margaret with his eyes.

"There is no need to speak of this one," he said, "for I know her well. I fear you harbour a Jezebel within your midst, good sir and madam."

Margaret stared at him, but he held her gaze easily. Thorseby was short and stocky, but his face was all sharp angles and hooked nose, and his brown eyes as sharp and cunning as those of a fox.

Jacquetta drew in a sharp breath and glanced triumphantly at her husband before speaking to Thorseby. "Father, we suspected she was wicked, but we did not know the true nature of it. Will you sit, and take refreshment?"

"Gladly, madam." Thorseby sat, and Margaret had to endure an uncomfortable few minutes as a servant brought wine — she refused — and then withdrew. She knew what the next hour or so would bring, but that did not lessen the dread.

Eventually, Thorseby set his goblet aside, and, turning slightly in his chair, addressed himself to Margaret.

"Whatever you say now will be said before God, do you understand, woman?"

She nodded, her eyes lidded so he could not see their expression.

"What have you told your hosts regarding your child."

Margaret hesitated, then spoke softly. "That it is the child of my late husband and their son, Roger."

"She lies," Thorseby said, not taking his eyes from Margaret.

The only sign of her distress was a slight tightening of her hands on the arms of her chair.

"We thought her a harlot the first day we saw her," Sir Egdon remarked.

"I was never a harlot to your son!" Margaret said, bright spots of pink in her cheeks. She was now staring defiantly at the other three.

"But you were to his memory," Thorseby said. "Woman, if you do not want to burn in hell eternal, name the true father of your child now!"

She was silent.

Thorseby drew out a piece of folded parchment from a pocket in his robe and waved it at her. "I have proof! Witnesses who saw you disport yourself with your lover!"

Margaret's face deepened in colour, but still she did not speak.

"This 'man'," Thorseby said, now talking to the Rivers, "has already brought untold grief to another family through his defilement of the lady of the house. He swore to me that he had repented, but this woman's belly is proof of his shame! I say to you, that the father of that child is none other than Brother Thomas Neville!"

He had finally disconcerted Sir Egdon and Lady Jacquetta.

"'Brother' Thomas?" said Sir Egdon. "But a Lord Thomas Neville escorted her here ..."

"He was not wearing his clerical garb?" Thorseby said, finally aghast. "He has abandoned all his vows?"

Jacquetta jerked out of her chair, took the two steps between her chair and Margaret's, and struck Margaret a great blow across the cheek.

Margaret slumped to the side, but none moved to aid her.

"Whore!" Jacquetta said. "Deceiver! Get you gone from this house!"

"Am I to be allowed no response at all?" Margaret said, managing to straighten herself with some considerable effort.

"Do you deny the child was fathered by Thomas Neville?" Thorseby said.

Margaret said nothing.

"She even fornicated with him under the Duke of Lancaster's roof," Thorseby said to his hosts. "There are witnesses. I would not be surprised that if Neville spent so much as one night here he spent it disporting with his wanton before the fire while you slept innocently."

Sir Egdon's and Lady Jacquetta's expressions were now a curious mixture of horror and triumph. *They had her ... the harlot!*

"Do you deny," Thorseby asked Margaret, "that Thomas Neville fathered your child?"

"No."

Sir Egdon and Lady Jacquetta both affected great, horrified breaths.

"I did not deceive your son," she said to them. "Never. I loved Roger. We —"

"Hold your tongue!" Sir Egdon said. "You have no shame!"

Margaret averted her face, and wished the gloom would reach out from the corners of this chill hall and gather her in its embrace. She was tired of these people, their jaded beliefs and their shrill, useless denunciations. She wanted a warm fire and a soft bed, and someone to tell her that she was finally safe. She wanted a home, finally, after so many years keeping a sick man company on his ramblings about Christendom.

She wanted her father, but he was gone forever.

She wanted her brother, but he could not acknowledge her.

She wanted to be loved, but no one would risk it.

She closed her eyes against the tears that had suddenly formed, and wished her child was in her arms, and that she would not have to endure the agony of childbed to achieve even that small wish.

"See," Thorseby said softly, "the whore harbours regrets. As well she might, for the fires of hell will eventually consume her, and the worms of retribution shall gnaw at her lustful privy members throughout eternity, and —"

"The fires and the worms of eternity," Margaret said, her eyes still closed, "would be a blessed relief after enduring but an hour of your sorry prating."

Now she had truly shocked her erstwhile parents-in-law, and they turned their heads, unable to look upon her.

Thorseby remained unruffled. He regarded Margaret a moment longer, then called for the sergeant of his escort.

"You need fear her no longer," he told Sir Egdon and Lady Jacquetta.

XVI

The Wednesday before the third Sunday in Lent
In the first year of the reign of Richard II
(9th March 1379)

*L*ancaster ... Lancaster ... Lancaster.
The name tumbled over and over in Thomas' mind as
they rode south.

Lancaster.

Who had been the fair young lord, wearing the badge of
Lancaster, who had spirited away the casket *in the weeks after*
he and Lancaster and Bolingbroke had returned to England?

The casket had been safe ... until he had told the Black
Prince, Lancaster, Bolingbroke and Raby about its existence.

No, no, the demons already knew of its existence ... but
they *hadn't known of its location until he told those four!*

But just because the man had worn the badge of
Lancaster didn't mean he had been one of Lancaster's
retainers or vassals — Lancaster's badge was so well known
throughout England anyone could have tricked themselves
out as one of the duke's men.

Had Lancaster told someone about the demons? Richard?
God knew that the two were close. Had Richard caused the
casket to be taken and, perhaps knowing that Thomas
suspected Lancaster, tried to trick him into blaming the duke?

Lancaster would never have sent his men so plainly apparelled ... would he?

Thomas ached all over from trying to resolve this nightmare: his head, his body, his heart and his soul.

He did not doubt that Richard was the new Demon-King — he was the only one to have so profited from the obviously demonically-aided deaths of Edward and the Black Prince — but Thomas did not, and could not, know if Lancaster was also a part of the demonic conspiracy.

Originally Thomas had suspected that Lancaster was the new Demon-King ... but when Lancaster had made his support of Richard's succession so apparent Thomas had believed the duke above suspicion.

But if Lancaster was not the new Demon-King, then he nevertheless could well be one of the new king's demonic supporters and servants. That would explain Lancaster's championship of Richard just as easily as thinking he was merely a highly loyal, mortal subject. Ah! Whoever and whatever Lancaster was, the fact remained that Thomas was seemingly no closer to achieving his quest for the casket than he had been six months ago.

All he knew was that the casket was now in the hands of the demons ... and that the demons lurked somewhere within either the Lancastrian family or among the duke's retainers at court.

And Lancaster, being the richest and most powerful man in England, had a court as large as a king.

They rode south towards Lincoln along the ancient Roman roadway still known as Ermine Street. Around them the countryside opened up to spring: birds were returning in flocks from their winter feeding grounds, trees were beginning to bud, and peasants put more and more fields to the plough.

The weather was finally warming, and winter-thin livestock were turned back into fields and fruit trees were pruned and grafted. But of none of this did Thomas take note. All he could think about was the Lancastrian household, who within it he should trust, and how, and *if*, he could prevent Richard taking the throne.

A demon sitting the throne of England? It was inconceivable!

Lincoln straddled two of England's most ancient highways, Ermine Street and the Fosse Way, and had long been an important trading and market town, particularly for the wool industry. Its magnificent Norman cathedral and castle, with the attendant needs of the attached clergy and retainers, brought wealth and influence the town's way. Lincoln was a vibrant, colourful and still expanding community. It was not walled — townsfolk could always seek protection within the castle or cathedral — and so Thomas, Wat and their small escort approached the town along the open northern approaches. There was a small Dominican community situated on the northern outskirts of the town, but Thomas had no intention of staying there. An inn would do as well, and in an inn he would not be bothered with the tiresome bells and chants of a religious order.

It was close to dusk and they had been on the road all day, and so, as they rode tired and inattentive, they did not see the group of some score of horsemen riding towards them until it was too late.

Thomas, in fact, was so absorbed in his thoughts he did not raise his head until he heard Wat Tyler mutter an expletive and rein his horse in.

The next instant Thomas' own horse slowed, and Thomas was forced to take note of his surroundings.

To either side of the road were fenced yards holding cattle and sheep for the markets. Immediately before him, sitting a dark horse and backed by a solid wall of horsed men-at-arms, was Richard Thorseby, Prior General of England.

"Well, well," Thorseby said in a quiet voice. "If you decided to abandon the Order, Thomas, you could perhaps have informed me so that I would not have had to spend so much of my time chasing across England after you."

Thomas could, for the moment, do nothing but stare. He'd been so engrossed in his thoughts that he found it difficult to comprehend that Thorseby now sat a horse before him, blocking his way.

Thomas was by now so far from the Church and the influence of the Dominican Order that he actually found it difficult to remember *why* it was that Thorseby might have been chasing across England after him.

"Tom?" Wat said, and Thomas glanced at Tyler. The man was tense, one hand on the hilt of his sword.

He looked back at Thorseby. The man had at least twenty heavily armed men-at-arms with him — probably sequestered from a lord who owed Thorseby a weighty favour.

"Stand down, Wat," he said, not shifting his eyes from Thorseby. "I will not have you waste your life on this black devil."

Thorseby kicked his horse forward until he was but a few feet from Thomas and could look him directly in the eye.

"As you have not yet formally abandoned your vows, Brother Thomas," Thorseby said, "you still remain under my authority. I hereby arrest you for a variety of grievous offences ranging from disobedience to fornication to suspicion of heresy —"

"For the love of God, Thorseby, *heresy*?"

"— and hereby command you to place yourself under my authority and care ... if you still remember what it is to submit yourself to the authority of the Church, that is. If you do not, then, as you see, I have the means to force you to submit. *Will* you come?"

Thomas sat a long moment, his eyes locked into Thorseby's, his horse fidgeting beneath him.

"Is my escort also under arrest?" he finally said.

"Of course not. Unless they have also willingly aided you in your —"

"They are innocent."

"Then they may leave."

Without moving his eyes from Thorseby, Thomas spoke quietly to Wat. "Ride south. Fast. Tell Lancaster that if he wants to know what I have discovered then he shall need to free me from the claws of this black bird."

Thorseby's mouth twisted derisively, but he said nothing.

Wat nodded, and moved his horse forward a little, the other five men of Thomas' escort close behind.

Thorseby — still holding Thomas' stare — signalled his men, and they parted, allowing Wat and his men free passage.

As his escort closed ranks behind him again, Thorseby said, "We shall spend the night at the friary here in Lincoln, then on the morrow we shall move south towards Oxford. There I shall have you placed on trial."

He started to turn away, then looked back at Thomas with a strange smile on his face. "I think you shall find this evening's company more than stimulating."

Thorseby's grin stretched a little wider, then he beckoned to his escort, and they surrounded Thomas. Within a few short minutes Thomas was being escorted securely along the short stretch of road towards the Dominican friary on the outskirts of Lincoln.

Dusk slipped into night, and Thorseby and Thomas discovered that the time for surprises and ambushes was not yet past. As the Prior General led Thomas and the men-at-arms down the laneway which led to the friary, he in turn found his way blocked by an even larger and better-equipped party of armed men.

Sitting their horses before these armed men — some three score, at least — were the Duke of Lancaster, the Baron of Raby, the new Baroness, Joan Beaufort, and a very smug Wat Tyler, who had run into Lancaster's party almost the minute he'd ridden into Lincoln itself.

This was, after all, a world in which miracles were an everyday occurrence.

Thorseby reined his horse to a halt, absolutely stunned — a reaction that mirrored Thomas'.

"My lord!" Thorseby said. "I . . . I . . ."

"My man," Lancaster said, nodding to Wat, "informs me that you hold one of my men as prisoner."

"I was not aware that Thomas Neville was *your* man, my

lord. Surely you know he is a Dominican friar, and thus under my authority."

"Nevertheless," Lancaster said, "he was under my instruction in riding north, and thus I ask that you release him into my care."

Thorseby's face hardened. "As Dominican and a member of the Church, Brother Thomas is *not* yours to command, my lord! I beg you, step aside, and allow us to pass."

"Thomas Neville," Lancaster said, "is my kinsman, by virtue of the fact that his uncle is married to my daughter, and I take a hearty interest in the welfare of all my kin. I suggest, Father Thorseby, that we do not continue this discussion here in the chill air — we have ridden far this day, and are weary and hungry — but perhaps retire to the friary ... where I am sure you will be happy to explain what you are doing with my *kinsman* in custody."

Thomas sat silent throughout this exchange, still stunned by Lancaster's utterly unexpected appearance.

Chance? Or design?

Raby sat his horse slightly to one side, as watchful as Thomas was ... and apparently as surprised. His uncle had obviously made the most of his presence in London to secure the hand of Joan Beaufort. She sat a pretty, dapple grey palfrey close to Raby, heavily cloaked against the chill, but with enough of her face showing to allow Thomas to glimpse her irritation at this turn of events.

Well, as Lancaster said, no doubt she was tired, and now eager to warm herself in her new husband's bed.

And no doubt her marriage was Lancaster's excuse for travelling north. He needed to see for himself that his beloved daughter was safely installed in Raby's home base of Sheriff Hutton castle in Yorkshire.

Thorseby gave in with some considerable ill-grace. "The friary shall be poor accommodation for those used to considerable riches —" he began.

"I have bedded down in my cloak in the battlefield," Lancaster said. "A draughty friary shall be luxury indeed."

"It cannot accommodate your entire escort!"

"But doubtless the inns of Lincoln can." Lancaster twisted in his saddle and spoke to one of the nobles behind him.

The man nodded, then turned his horse and began organising Lancaster's escort so that the majority of them turned back into Lincoln.

"My lord!" Thorseby tried again. "I must protest vehemently against your interference in the workings of the Holy Church!"

Lancaster swung back to face the Prior General, his face flushed with anger. "And I, as regent of England, do protest on behalf of the new king that you take such a free hand with his subjects! Now, Father Thorseby, if you would care to show us the way into the friary ..."

"A friary will be poor lodging indeed for my lady," Thorseby said, indicating the Lady Joan, "and I fear the night's events might prove distressing. Brother Thomas has been most vile in the manner of his disobediences."

Lady Joan inclined her head, and spoke in a low and sweet voice. "Thomas is also my kinsman now, Father Thorseby, and I take as keen an interest in him as my father. Besides," she gave Raby a tender glance, "I am as yet disinclined to part with my husband."

Thorseby gave up, and led the way into the friary.

Despite what Thorseby had intimated, the friary was reasonably large, situated as it was in one of the richest towns in England. Besides the church itself, there was a long line of individual cells for the brothers, two refectories, a guest house, guest refectory and hall, an infirmary, cloisters, gardens, and sundry store rooms.

Once the party — now consisting of Thorseby, Thomas, Lancaster, Raby, Joan, and some remaining twelve men-at-arms from Lancaster's train (Thorseby's men had ridden to quarters situated just beyond the friary itself) — had dismounted in the courtyard and been greeted by a flustered prior (not only had he to entertain the Prior General, but here was the Duke of Lancaster as well!), Thorseby led the way into the hall of the guest quarters attached to the friary.

It was relatively commodious, and a fire burned bright in the hearth.

At first, as the arrivals shook off the night dew from their cloaks and drew gloves from their hands, it was the fire that caught their attention, but as, one by one, they turned from the fire, their attention was caught by a figure sitting in a chair further back in the hall.

Lady Margaret Rivers.

Thorseby, noting with some considerable satisfaction the surprise and consternation on Thomas' face, was nevertheless surprised himself to note similar consternation on the faces of Lancaster and Raby.

He frowned, wondering if there were further secrets here that could be exploited.

XVII

Matins on the Thursday before the
third Sunday in Lent
In the first year of the reign of Richard II
(pre-dawn 10th March 1379)

— i —

Margaret was pale, and trembled a little as she rose,
grabbing at the arm of the chair for support.

She swallowed, curtsied clumsily to Lancaster and
then to Raby and his wife, then stood, one hand to her side
and her eyes on Thomas.

"There stands Thomas' whore," Thorseby said, "her
swelling belly proof enough that he has abandoned his vows."

"*What?*" Raby and Lancaster said together.

Lady Joan merely averted her eyes and blushed,
uncomfortable only with being in the presence of such lechery.

Thomas sighed, and averted his face slightly, rubbing his
eyes. *Sweet Jesu, as if he didn't have enough mischief in his life.*

"Do you deny that you fornicated with the Lady Rivers in
Lancaster's residence in London?" Thorseby thundered.

Thomas dropped his hand from his face and straightened.
"No," he said softly.

"*What?*" Raby and Lancaster said again, then looked at
each other.

Raby took a half step back, allowing Lancaster the stage.

The duke turned to Thomas. "Is this true?"

Thomas nodded.

"The Lady Rivers has further confessed to me that Thomas fathered her child," Thorseby said.

Lancaster shot a look at Raby, who was staring gape-mouthed at Margaret, then addressed Thomas.

"*Do* you admit to fathering the Lady Margaret's child?" he said, enunciating each word very carefully.

His eyes bored into Thomas'. *Admit it, and save my daughter's pride.*

Thomas hesitated, then looked to Raby, now also looking intently at him. "Yes," he said.

For the moment, the truth would cause less harm than a lie.

A welter of emotions flitted across Raby's face: continued shock, surprise, pain, but, most of all, relief.

"You have dishonoured my name and my house!" Lancaster roared at Thomas, making everyone flinch. The duke turned to face Thomas so that his face was hidden from Thorseby, and clapped a hand on Thomas' shoulder.

"For this," Lancaster whispered, his face losing its fury and showing only gratitude, "I will reward you well. I thank you, Tom."

Then he raised his voice. "You have also dishonoured the Lady Margaret. I insist that you —"

He got no further, for just as he spoke Margaret whimpered, and collapsed to the floor.

Joan Beaufort reacted instantly. She moved to Margaret's side, and stooped beside her.

"Lady?" she whispered. "What ails you ... is it the child?"

Margaret, her eyes wide with pain and fear, nodded, and Joan looked up at the group of men standing helplessly by.

"Her time has come," she said. "I beg you. Someone send for a midwife."

Margaret paced back and forth, supported on one side by Lady Raby, and the other by one of the town's midwives, Maude Fiston.

She could not believe the pain she was enduring, nor could she believe the platitudes her two companions fed her every time she moaned or wailed.

Margaret *knew* she was not doing well, nor was she being a good girl. Neither was the child ever going to slip out like a greased lambkin, nor was it all going to be over in a minute, sweeting.

No, she was being torn apart, and she was going to die in the tearing.

Margaret was also aware of the worried looks the Lady Raby (oh, if only she knew she was supporting her husband's mistress!) and Maude shared over the top of her bowed head.

This labour was progressing badly, and all three women in the chamber knew it, even if none of them spoke it.

After Margaret had collapsed in the guest hall, Raby had helped his wife walk Margaret to one of the private guest chambers in the friary.

Here Raby, doubtless feeling acutely the irony of the situation, had left his wife and Margaret, and Joan had done her best to keep Margaret cheered until Maude bustled in an hour later.

That had been twelve hours ago. And in that twelve hours, neither Joan nor Maude had left the chamber.

All Margaret wanted was some solitude. *All she needed was to be left alone for half an hour to birth this child her way, but neither of the cursed women would go!*

And, in the meantime, both she and the child were dying.

Margaret doubled over and screamed, tearing herself from Joan and Maude's grip and falling to the floor.

The scream wailed through the entire guest complex, and Lancaster, Raby, Thomas and Thorseby, still in the hall, reflexively twitched at the dreadful sound.

"My lady!" Maude said, squatting down by the writhing Margaret. "My lady — you must get to your feet, the babe will never be born this way, and —"

"The babe is not going to be born anyway, you cow-faced harlot!" Margaret yelled, and then curled up into a tight ball about her belly, moaning and shrieking at the same time.

Joan took a step backwards, unsure. What was wrong with the baby? Why wouldn't it come forth? She locked eyes with Maude, but the midwife shrugged helplessly.

"We have to get her up," Maude said.

Exhausted and emotionally drained herself, Joan stepped up and leaned down to take Margaret's arm.

Just then Margaret gave a great groan, and blood stained the skirts of the linen shift she wore.

"She bleeds!" Joan said, freezing in the act of bending down. "Maude ... what is there to be done?"

Maude looked helplessly at the blood, pooling in ever greater amounts about Margaret, then looked up to Joan.

"Fetch a priest, my lady," she said tonelessly. "There is only that one thing to be done."

Joan's hands flew to her face, her eyes horrified, then she nodded, stepped around Maude and Margaret and left the chamber. Joan was in such a hurry, she did not close the door behind her.

Maude started to rise herself and, just at that moment when she was the most unbalanced, Margaret suddenly lurched up and shoved the midwife with all the strength she could summon.

Giving a faint cry of surprise, Maude tumbled over, falling through the door into the passage outside.

She rolled over, and found herself eye to eye with a fierce-faced Margaret still lying on the floor of the chamber. Then, before Maude could react, Margaret somehow managed to get to her knees, and then fell forward with her arms outstretched, catching the edge of the door, and slamming it shut in Maude's startled face.

There was a faint thump, as if something — Margaret, perhaps — had fallen against the door.

Maude scrambled to her feet, as much angry as she was concerned. *What was the woman doing? Did she think to die unshriven?*

Maude put her shoulder to the door and shoved, but it did not budge.

Grunting, Maude tried again.

Nothing.

Maude took a deep breath and tried one more time, putting all her not inconsiderable weight and strength into the effort.

The door did not move.

Instead, there was a further thump from the other side, as if something very heavy indeed had thrown itself against it.

Then a cry sounded, faint, but distinct, and Maude reeled away from the door.

It had sounded partway between the warbling of a bird and the growling of a cat.

Maude turned, and would have run, save at that moment Joan reappeared, this time with Raby, Thomas and Thorseby.

"Maude?" Joan said. "What ... why ... "

"She threw me out, the minx!" Maude said. "And now she lies blocking the door, and I cannot get in, and something ... something ... something is wrong!"

"What do you mean, 'wrong'?" asked Raby.

"The birth is not going well," Joan said quietly.

"Nay," said Maude, "and it should, for that babe is barely seven-month along and should slip out with no trouble at all. But ..."

"She began to bleed," Joan said, looking at her husband. "Maude sent me for a priest."

Raby groaned. "Oh, poor Margaret!" He looked at his wife. "She attended Gloucester's wife when she died a-bleeding in childbed. Margaret was so scared the same would happen to her ..."

Joan did not think to wonder why Margaret should have confided this to Raby, but merely took his arm, and bit her lip. "Someone must break that door down," she said. "If only that Margaret may not die unshriven."

"And have you nothing to say?" Thorseby said to Thomas, who was standing slightly behind Raby, staring at the closed door. "If you had not forced the woman to your bed, she would not even now —"

"Oh, hold your tongue!" Thomas snapped, then addressed Raby, ignoring Thorseby's furious face. "If we both put our shoulders to that door, uncle, we must be able to break it open."

"Yes, yes!"

But just as they moved to the door, a scream echoed that sounded as if it had come from another world, or from the throat of a being from another world.

And then the sound of something very heavy and very wet shifting across the floor.

Utter silence.

Raby and Thomas could not move. They stared at the door, as if transfixed.

The heavy, wet noise came again, and then the sound of something huge thrashing about.

The door creaked slightly, as if it were about to crack.

No one could move.

"Margaret?" Raby whispered.

Nothing ... then a sob ... then the thin wail of a child.

"Margaret!" Raby yelled, then he was battering away at the door with his shoulder, Thomas beside him.

Slowly, protestingly, it gave way, and the men pushed more gently, knowing they were pushing against Margaret's body.

"Sweet Jesu!" Raby said as he managed to step through the gap they'd opened.

Thomas was a heartbeat behind him.

Margaret lay on the floor, naked now, her torn shift lying tossed to one side, her hair tangled about her, her limbs lying akimbo.

The very first thought that entered both men's minds was how beautiful she looked, even like this.

The next was that she was dead.

Everything appeared to be covered in blood: Margaret, the floor, the stuff was even spattered against the door and walls.

Maude pushed past both men, wailed at the sight that met her eyes, but bent down to Margaret instantly. She put a hand to a pouch at her belt, took out some twine and a small knife, and busied herself with something between Margaret's legs.

Then she stood up.

"Take this," she said to Thomas, and bundled something warm and damp into his arms, "and go baptise it in the name of our Lord. It will not stay long in this world.

"My lord?" Maude said to Raby. "Will you assist me lift the lady to the bed?"

As Raby moved to aid Maude, Thomas looked down at what he held in his arms.

It was a baby girl, so tiny she could almost have fitted in the palm of one of his hands. Her naked body — it was so scrawny! — was clotted with Margaret's blood; a length of their shared umbilical cord, roughly tied off with twine, still dangled from her belly.

"Go take that thing away!" Maude said to him. "It is of no use to its mother now, and we might still save her life."

"Come," Joan murmured in Thomas' ear. She put her hands on his shoulders, and gently steered him out of the room.

Once he was outside, Joan closed the door on herself, Maude, Raby and Margaret, and Thomas found himself standing in the corridor with his tiny, dying daughter in his arms, and Thorseby, for once so shocked he was unable to speak, staring between them.

XVIII

Prime on the Thursday before the
third Sunday in Lent
In the first year of the reign of Richard II
(daybreak 10th March 1379)

— ii —

The girl drew in a breath, and it was so laboured that her entire body shook with the effort.

It broke Thomas' shocked reverie, and broke through the facade of cold heartlessness he had so assiduously cultivated since Alice's death.

Sweet Jesu, he had to warm her!

Thomas pushed past Thorseby and almost ran in his rush to get back to the hall. Lancaster was still there, standing with the prior who had returned.

Both stared as Thomas strode into the hall, the tiny bloody scrap of flesh in his hands.

Thomas looked at Lancaster, then at the prior. "Help me!" he said.

It was the prior who acted first. He grabbed a linen cloth from a table close by and held it out to Thomas.

"Wrap her in this," he said. "Now!"

Thomas fumbled with the linen and the girl, but finally managed to get it about her, praying with every fibre of his being that he did not break one of her fragile limbs as he did so.

"Brother Harold runs the infirmary here," the prior said. "He will know better than anyone what to do. Thomas, come with me, please."

Brother Harold was a lean, wispy man with the sweetest smile Thomas had ever seen.

"Give the child to me," he said, as soon as he entered the infirmary where Thomas and the prior waited.

There was already a fire blazing in a hearth, and Harold sat on a stool with the baby in his lap. He carefully unfolded the linen from about her, then pursed his lips in concern.

"This is not a full-term infant."

"No," Thomas said. "I think Margaret was some seven months gone."

Harold shook his head. "The child will not live. See, even now she struggles to breathe. Her lungs will be wet and ill-formed. Look."

One blunt-ended finger rested gently against the girl's chest wall. "See how she labours with each breath? She cannot get enough air in. I'm sorry, my son, but she is slowly suffocating. She will not live past noon."

"But —" Thomas lifted a hand, helplessly.

"I'm sorry," Harold repeated, then he looked to the prior. "Has she been baptised?"

The prior shook his head, then lifted a small vial of holy water that hung from his belt. He unstoppered it, dipped in a finger, then made the sign of the cross over the girl's head and touched his damp fingertip to her forehead.

"I baptise you in the name of the Father, the Son, and the Holy Ghost," he said. It was a perfunctory baptism only, for she should have had salt placed in her mouth and godparents named who could speak for her ... but under the circumstances it was the best that could be done. And, all things considered, it was enough.

He looked to Thomas. "What is her name?"

"What is her name? Ah ..." Thomas thought frantically,

for he felt as if he should, at the least, get her name right. "Her name is Rosalind."

The prior smiled gently, feeling sorry for the man. He might be a corrupt friar, but he was a father also, and, as a father, he currently was living a nightmare.

"It is a good name," he said, and placed his fingers gently on the girl's face. "I baptise thee Rosalind."

Thomas looked back to Harold. "Help her, please!"

"There is nothing I can do, my son! Ah ... well ... at the least I can wash her and find her some soft woollens to be wrapped in. Here, you can aid me."

Harold fetched some warm water and, as Thomas held her in his hands, gently sponged away the birth blood. Once the girl was dry, Harold wrapped in her a square of creamy woollen cloth and handed her back to Thomas.

She was now hardly breathing at all.

Thomas looked up to Harold. "What can I do?" he whispered.

"Pray," said Harold.

Thomas cradled the tiny girl close to his chest and walked back to Margaret's chamber. He had thought about the chapel, but had abandoned the idea. Perhaps the baby would respond to Margaret's voice and warmth more than she would to the cold impersonality of a stone church.

Maude and Lady Joan were still with Margaret, and looked mildly surprised when Thomas entered with the child, as if they had truly forgotten its existence.

"The babe still lives?" Maude said, then shrugged her shoulders without waiting for an answer. She didn't care one way or the other.

Joan stood and smiled at Thomas, then lifted the wrap away from the baby's face with one gentle finger.

"She's so tiny," she whispered.

Thomas looked at Margaret.

She was unconscious, lying flat on her back on the bed with the coverlets pulled up to her shoulders. Her hair was unbound, and lay neatly brushed over one shoulder.

Her face was gaunt and grey, her cheeks and closed eyes looking as if they were on the point of collapse.

Thomas looked back at Joan, the question in his eyes.

"We do not think she will live," Joan said in a low voice. "She has lost most of her blood. Perhaps one of the Brothers from the infirmary might help."

"Harold? That cursed Brother could do little for a mouse with a thorn in its tail," said Thomas. "I will sit with Margaret a while. Alone, if you please."

Joan regarded him a moment, then nodded. "Maude," she said. "Come."

There was a stool by the bed, and Thomas hooked it close with one foot and sat down as near to Margaret as he could.

He very gently lifted one of her arms free of the covers — it was so thin! — and then rested it down, setting the baby girl to nestle in the crook of her arm.

Margaret made no sound, nor stirred, and for long minutes the only sound in the chamber was that of the baby's rucking, tortured breaths.

Oh, sweet Jesu, he wanted her to live! An urge to protect the child, so violent it was almost an anger, swept through Thomas. *She could not die! She could not!*

For a long time Thomas sat and stared at mother and child. Already one woman had died because of a child he'd put in her, now another lay close to death.

It was even more painful knowing that the child had been born, because, seeing the baby, watching her frightful fight for life, Thomas found himself desperately wanting her to live. He wanted to see her grow, surrounded by both safety and love ... and Thomas could not say *why* he wanted so desperately for her to experience both safety and love.

And Margaret. He wanted Margaret to live, also.

He didn't care who or what she was. He didn't care that she had trapped him via Thorseby. He wanted her to live ... if only for the baby's sake. Every child needed both mother and father ...

His daughter.

My God, she could not die!

He reached out and stroked the child's tiny forehead. Her skin was wrinkled and red, but still so amazingly soft. Her face was scrawny, and further wizened by her horrible battle to breathe, but if only she would open her eyes, Thomas knew they would be alive with personality.

A child of sorcery?

Maybe so, but surely the sin of the begetting should never be visited on the child.

How could he ever have planned to have her smothered the instant she was born?

"Rosalind," he whispered, and the baby whimpered.

Margaret continued to lay cold and still.

Thomas, his hand still outstretched to touch his child, bent his head and silently wept, his shoulders shaking.

It was a long while after, that Thomas realised he was no longer alone with the dying mother and child.

He raised his head.

Thomas.

The archangel stood in a glow of reddish gold light at the foot of the bed, his form almost obscured by the strength of the light he emitted.

"Blessed Saint Michael," Thomas whispered. "Help her!"

I will not do that.

"Why not? Why not?"

I am here only to guide you.

"I want her to live!"

Thomas, you are one of God's Beloved. You are His chosen, but you must choose your own path.

"What do you mean? What has that to do with this tiny child and her fight for life?"

It is better she die, Thomas. Better for you.

"No!"

Better for her.

"No!" Thomas whispered. "She *must* live!"

Thomas, how can you serve God when you cannot recognise the tests set before you? How is it that you can't see that she is —

There was a knock on the door, gentle at first, then louder and more insistent.

The archangel hissed, making Thomas jump, and the light about him flared so brilliantly that Thomas cried out.

The archangel roared, and Thomas had the impression of two fists, clenched and raised in anger ...

... and then St Michael was gone, and Thomas was left with Margaret and the baby, and the increasing tempo of someone's fist at the door.

Thomas sprang to his feet and threw open the door.

"What do you want?" he snarled.

Wat Tyler stood there, looking almost as grey and haggard as Margaret. With him was a portly, bald man with round, popping, startled blue eyes.

"I knew the Lady Margaret was in need," Wat said, shifting a little on his feet so he could see around Thomas to where Margaret lay. "All could hear her screams as she gave birth."

He looked back to Thomas, and Thomas was truly surprised to see real concern in Wat's face. "I ran into Lincoln, and beat on doors until one man directed me to a physician's house. Tom, this is Garland Hooper. He will help Margaret and her child."

"A physician?" *Sweet Jesu, physicians existed only to fatten graveyards!*

"My lord," Garland Hooper said gravely, "I *can* help her. I spent many years journeying through the Arab lands, and —"

"You think to practise infidel magic on her?"

Hooper drew a deep breath, held it, closed his eyes briefly, then resumed speaking. "And if I said, my good sir, that infidel magic will save her life, and that of her child, would you still stand there, blocking my way?"

Thomas stood, staring at Hooper, uncertain.

"I *can* save her," Hooper said, "and her child. *Your* child, this good man tells me. I can save her when all others cannot. Or will not."

It is better she die, the archangel had said.

"I can save her," Hooper said yet again, his eyes remaining steady on Thomas.

In the heavens angels raised their fists, and raged, while the Demon God turned to His Father, and said: "You may have trapped me, but she will yet run free."

Thomas suddenly felt the power and anger of St Michael crashing about his entire being, wanting him to say, *No. Go away. Let her die.* But the urge to *save* her, to *protect* her, was so overwhelming that Thomas somehow found the strength to fight the archangel back.

"Save her," Thomas said, stepping aside and setting to one side the screams of the angels in heaven. "Save them both."

Hooper brushed past Thomas, Wat a breath behind, and Thomas wearily closed the door, only to have a hand push it back again.

The Lady Joan.

She looked at Hooper and Wat Tyler, then raised her eyebrows at Thomas.

He shrugged. "A physician. He says he can save her."

Joan pursed her lips. "'Tis better she have a priest," she said.

"Oh, I don't believe so," Thomas said, his tone bitter, "for God has abandoned both mother and child."

And ignoring Joan's startled look, he moved over to Margaret.

"Sit here," Hooper said to him, pointing at the head of the bed, "and support the lady's head. I am going to give her an elixir that will strengthen her heart."

Thomas moved the stool around to the head of the bed, and sat down.

As he took Margaret's head between his hands, he felt Joan move behind him, and lay her hands on his shoulders for support.

Hooper busied himself in the large cloth bag he had carried with him, withdrawing a phial of a peculiarly translucent marbled green stone. Unstoppering it carefully, Hooper poured a small amount of deep red liquid into a cup so tiny it was almost the size of a thimble, then nodded to Thomas.

Thomas lifted Margaret's head up, and Hooper carefully put the cup to her lips, increasing the pressure until her lips opened slightly.

He poured the liquid in, then stroked her throat, stimulating her swallowing reflex.

"Good," Hooper said. "That will work within a few minutes. While we wait ... the child."

He rummaged about in his bag again, withdrawing this time a tiny mask made of leather and cloth. This he fitted over the child's face, pouring from another vial a few drops of a golden liquid over the cloth parts of the mask. Then, pushing the vial to one side, Hooper leaned down, put his own mouth over the mask encasing the child's face, and blew gently.

Then he stood up, lifting the mask off her face as he did so.

Thomas, who had let Margaret's head rest on the pillow, stared at the child.

Nothing. Still the same tortured breaths. He lifted his head to say something to Hooper when he was forestalled by a sudden intake of breath by the baby, and then a loud squall as she began to cry.

Thomas jerked his eyes back to the baby. She was screaming now, her face screwed up even more, but she was screaming easily.

Lord God, she hadn't even had the strength to mew before this!

Hooper grinned at the expression on Thomas' face, then nodded at Margaret.

"Look," he said.

But Thomas had felt it even before he looked. Margaret had shifted her head towards the sound of the crying baby, and now her eyes fluttered open, and her arm tightened fractionally about her daughter.

"Infidel magic," Hooper said, and then both he and Wat Tyler were laughing softly.

XIX

Vespers on the Thursday before the
third Sunday in Lent
In the first year of the reign of Richard II
(early evening 10th March 1379)

— iii —

"Ah, Tom," Lancaster said, and beckoned him over. "Sit down. How is Margaret?"

Thomas bowed, then sat down in the fourth chair pulled up before the fire in the guest hall. Raby sat to Lancaster's right, and the Prior General in a chair opposite them. Thomas' placing was halfway between Lancaster and Raby to one side, and Thorseby to the other. He glanced warily at Thorseby — the man's face was stiff and obviously furious — and then answered Lancaster's query.

"Margaret is very weak, my lord, but both Brother Harold and the physician Garland Hooper say that rest and care will see her well within a few weeks."

"And her . . . ah . . . your child?"

"Unbelievably, she also seems well. Brother Harold is amazed, for he says he has never before seen a seven-month child survive more than a few hours of life."

Lancaster and Raby nodded and smiled, and Thomas thought he also saw relief in his uncle's expression.

How does Raby truly feel about Margaret? he wondered. *I think that if she had died last night, Raby would have been the one to keen the loudest.*

"Lady Joan remains with them now," Thomas said. He smiled at Lancaster and then Raby. "Without her I do not know how anyone could have managed. Lady Joan kept a steady head when all others about her panicked."

Both Lancaster and Raby smiled as well, acknowledging his thanks and his compliment.

"I am glad to hear the woman and child do well," Thorseby said. "But then, sin has always imbued flesh with strength. Only the innocent embrace death with ease and gladness."

"I pity you," Lancaster said, his hands visibly tightening about the armrests of his chair, "that you so begrudge Margaret and her child their lives.

"Tom, your uncle and I both have things to say to you, but first we have to deal with Father Thorseby's accusations."

Thorseby sprang out of his chair, standing rigid with anger, staring first at Lancaster and then at Thomas.

"Brother Thomas has abandoned all semblance of his clerical duties and demeanour! He has broken every one of his vows! He has —"

"Been a very bad boy," Lancaster said, staring at Thorseby. "For God's sake, man, get to the point."

"I humbly request, my lord," Thorseby said through clenched teeth, "that you release Brother Thomas from your custody and give him into mine so that I may administer full discipline under Church and Dominican law."

"As you remarked," Lancaster said, "Tom has apparently abandoned all semblance of a Dominican friar, and has broken all his vows. Poverty? Yes, for see the fine tunic and boots he wears. Obedience? Most definitely, for he has lived in disobedience these past several months. Chastity?" Lancaster laughed. "Oh, most positively, I think. My point, Father Thorseby, is that Thomas has effectively left the priesthood — he has no tonsure, and does not dress nor act in priestly fashion — and thus he has removed himself from your jurisdiction. Thomas, is this so? Do you formally renounce your vows and your ties to the Dominican Order?"

Thomas sighed, and massaged his forehead with his fingers in order to delay his answer a moment or two. He was physically exhausted, for he had not slept, and was emotionally drained by watching both Margaret's, and their child's, struggle for life. At any other time he would have had to ask for an interval to think ... but now he was so tired ...

Margaret was right. He was no longer a man of the Church.

"Yes," he said. "I do so renounce my vows to the Church."

"Then that's settled," Lancaster said.

"No!" Thorseby said, still standing and staring between Thomas and Lancaster. "It is not settled! He can't just leave whenever —"

"He has renounced his vows!" Lancaster roared, leaping to his feet and making both Raby and Thomas jump. "Accept it!"

Thorseby stared up at Lancaster — the duke was a good foot taller than he — a muscle twitching in one cheek. "There is the small matter of heresy," he said. "And that is my provenance!"

"Heresy?" Lancaster said. "Heresy? What heresy?"

"It is rumoured," Thorseby said, grinding each word out, "that Thomas claims to have been visited by the archangel Saint Michael."

"Where is the heresy in that?" Lancaster said. His eyes narrowed. "Or is it that you are accusing Saint Michael of heresy for appearing without your permission?"

Raby laughed, and even Thomas had to suppress a smile. Lancaster couldn't have torn Thorseby apart more effectively if he'd taken an axe to him.

"If Saint Michael has appeared to Thomas then the man is blessed," Lancaster continued, a smile now also playing about his own mouth. "Has Thomas incited the hordes to follow a deviancy? No? Has Thomas made any statement at all that counters the Church's holy law? No?" Lancaster's smile faded away. "Then I put it to you, Father Thorseby, that even though Tom has been a very, very bad friar, he is no heretic. Now ... get out!"

Thorseby flinched, but still he stood his ground. He opened his mouth, but Lancaster allowed him to get no further.

"I may have no jurisdiction over the Church in England," he said, his tone now low and poisonous, "but believe me, Thorseby, when I say that I have the power to make your life hell on earth if you cross me. Thomas' only sin has been to irritate you, and I don't believe that sin is enough to persuade me to allow you to hound him from coast to coast. Now ... get out!"

Thorseby's eyes bulged, and his face flushed a mottled red. He flashed Thomas a look of pure venom, then he turned on his heel and marched out of the hall, slamming the door as he went through.

"My lord," Thomas said, his voice full of genuine relief and gratitude. "I do thank you."

Lancaster grunted and sat down. "Then thank me by pouring me some wine from that pitcher over there."

As Thomas poured out the wine and handed the duke a goblet, Lancaster looked him in the eye. "Welcome home, Tom."

Thomas nodded, poured out some wine for Raby and himself, then sat down.

He *was* home.

"And now," Raby said, staring down into his goblet, "*I* must thank you, Tom."

He raised his dark eyes and regarded Thomas. "You did not need to accept responsibility for my child with Margaret, but in doing so, you have eased my own path and ensured my wife's peace of mind. It was well done, Tom."

"Well done, indeed," Lancaster said, then he smiled gently, conspiratorially. "Did you truly bed Margaret in my palace?"

"Aye." Thomas shifted uncomfortably, not because of Lancaster's scrutiny, but because of the way his uncle stared at him. "She came to my room one night, scared and uncertain about her future. I tried to comfort her, and we found ourselves . . ."

He shrugged helplessly.

"Did she deliberately trap you?" Raby asked.

Thomas hesitated over his reply, not knowing which answer his uncle wanted. "My lust for her overcame me," he finally said. "She is a beautiful woman, even when big with child."

"Tom," Lancaster said, "we must plan for your future. In leaving the Church you have, perhaps, walked into a different trap. Having publicly acknowledged yourself the sire of Margaret's child you must now assume responsibility for it . . . and for Margaret."

Raby put his goblet down and leaned forward. "When you took clerical orders, Tom, you deeded the properties and estates you inherited from your parents to me. You now have them back. I will instruct the clerks to redraw the deeds once I return to Sheriff Hutton."

Thomas stared at his uncle. He hadn't expected . . .

"And for me," Lancaster said softly, drawing Thomas' eye to him, "I also give you estates. Your family estates are far to the north, and I am thinking that I will need you closer to me, and to court."

"But —" Thomas began.

"When you take Margaret to wife," Lancaster said, an edge of steel creeping into his voice, "I would that you both join Hal's household. When Margaret is not child bearing, your wife will do well to serve as a lady to Hal's wife — Lord God, he cannot remain unwed much longer! To do this effectively it is best that you settle closer to London. As a wedding gift I will deed to you two of my manors in Devon, as well as Halstow Hall in Kent. Do you know it? 'Tis but a few miles beyond Gravesend on the Thames estuary. The lands abutting the Hall make only middling farming, for they are salty and windswept, but the estate comes with a goodly portion of the revenue from the fishing industries of the estuary and, combined with the revenues from your estates in Yorkshire and Devon, will give you and Margaret and your children a good living. Now, what say you?"

In truth, Thomas was not sure what to say. Between them Raby and Lancaster had made him a rich man ... and ensured that Margaret would be kept well enough away from Joan.

It was just that he had not quite embraced the concept of marriage in his mind. Over the past night Thomas had realised he must somehow take responsibility for Margaret and the child, yes ... but marriage?

Raby and Lancaster watched him with steely eyes. The past twelve hours had presented them with the perfect solution for their "what to do with Margaret" problem. The past twelve hours and Thomas. If he hadn't admitted he was the father ...

Rosalind ... Thomas suddenly found himself swamped with an almost overwhelming protective urge. Marriage to Margaret, with all the attendant riches gratefully endowed by Raby and Lancaster, would be the most effective way of ensuring Rosalind's safety.

He didn't pause to think, safety from what?

"It is difficult," Thomas said, with a rueful smile, "to wrap my mind about the concept that one moment I am a friar sworn to poverty and chastity, the next I find myself a rich man with a beautiful wife." His smile widened slightly. "I think I should sin more often, if this is the result."

Raby and Lancaster relaxed.

"There is something else we need to discuss," Thomas said.

Lancaster's face lost its good humour.

"Bramham Moor friary," he said. Lancaster shot Thomas a warning glance: I have not told Raby about what you think about Richard.

"Yes. My lord, I am sorry, but the casket has gone. It was taken in December last year ... by a 'fair young lord' wearing the Lancaster emblem."

"What?" Lancaster jerked forward. Thomas knew he was utterly surprised — no one could pretend such flushed startlement.

"You don't know who ...?" Thomas had to ask.

"Nay!" Lancaster's face had continued to darken, now colouring with anger rather than surprise. "Who would dare pretend to be one of my retainers? A member of my household?"

Lancaster got out of his chair and began to pace back and forth before the fire. "I will have his balls when I find him!" he muttered.

He swung back to Thomas. "So ... you have not knowledge of the contents of the casket?"

"No, my lord. But ... the casket must still be in England. I feel it!"

"And this man was a lord, you say?"

"He spoke well, and acted with the demeanour of a lord."

Lancaster shook his head, thinking. "No man can pretend nobility. It must be bred into him. Who can it be? Well, Tom, it is as well that I shall have you at court with me, for you must ferret out this coward who does not dare wear his own arms." He fixed Thomas with his keen eyes. "I do hope that you shall not be reticent in demonstrating your full loyalty to Richard."

Thomas knew to what Lancaster referred. He'd failed to furnish "proof" that Richard was the Demon-King, and now Lancaster would make no move against Richard's coronation. "Not until I know better, my lord."

Raby was glancing between them, curious. "Tom, what do you mean?"

"I'm sure," Thomas said, "that my Lord of Lancaster meant I must give my full loyalty to my king now that I no longer place my loyalty in the pope."

"Well," Lancaster said. "I think you must snatch some sleep, Tom. In the morning we will stay to witness your betrothal to Margaret, then we must hasten north."

XX

Terce on the Vigil of the Feast of St Gregory
In the first year of the reign of Richard II
(9 a.m. Friday 11th March 1379)

Thomas rose early, breaking his fast alone in the hall, and chewing his food slowly as he thought over the plans Lancaster and Raby had made for his future. Shortly, Lancaster and Raby would join him in Margaret's chamber, to witness his and Margaret's betrothal, and then all save Margaret and her newborn would depart for the north: Lancaster to escort his daughter to her new home, and ensure that the often rebellious north would not fail in its loyalty to its new king; Raby to settle his new bride in his main castle of Sheriff Hutton, and, presumably, also introduce her to his eleven children from his previous wife; and Thomas to tour the estates that his uncle would deed back to him so he could refresh his memory of their revenues and expenses.

Lancaster would be the first to return south, not wanting to long linger in the north. Raby and Thomas would follow in mid-April after the Easter celebrations, arriving in London well ahead of Richard's coronation on May Day. On their way south, they would collect Margaret and she and Thomas would take their final vows in London in a quiet ceremony after Richard's coronation.

Then Halstow Hall for Margaret and court life for Thomas.

Lancaster was offering Thomas the perfect opportunity to not only discover which lord it was who had stolen de Worde's casket out from under Thomas' nose, but to also discover and mark the demons within England's highest and most influential circles. Thomas could work the archangel's will much better as a lord than as a humble friar. Doors would open and mouths would loosen for a convivial lord when they would slam shut for a judgemental friar. Understanding would be quicker reached when he stood as one of the decision-makers in the privy chambers of the king rather than hearing of the decisions third- or fourth-hand. The archangel had been wrong in wanting the baby girl to die, for, alive, Rosalind gave Thomas the perfect opportunity to infiltrate the demonic coterie at court.

Thomas supposed even archangels made errors in judgement from time to time.

Neither could Thomas pretend to be dismayed at the arrangements that would propel him back into the magnificence of courtly and chivalric ritual. He sat back from the table a little, running his fingers gently over the rich fabric of his tunic and the stiff gold embroidery at its hem and cuffs. Thomas stilled, his gaze lingering over his fingers, wondering if Raby still had the topaz and garnet rings Thomas had surrendered into his uncle's safe keeping when he'd taken holy orders.

It would be good to come home.

Thomas sighed, and stood up. Lancaster and Raby would be here soon, and Thomas supposed he'd best talk to Margaret, and tell her of those arrangements which most concerned her.

He smiled as he walked — unwittingly in the loose-limbed arrogance of his former noble life — down the corridor towards her chamber. Thomas knew what she was; or at least, he thought he did. Margaret was no ordinary woman. Thomas was more than sure that Margaret had links to the demonic coterie at court, and might well be a demon herself. Whatever, Thomas knew that Margaret was one of the crucial clues in the puzzle that he must solve. Marriage to her would not only keep her close and under strict scrutiny (and was that not what God meant for all women? To be confined within the walls of marriage to repress their natural aptitude for evil?), she would also serve as a lodestone to the demons.

Margaret would be as important to Thomas as any other device he might use.

He frowned, hesitating at her door. He must make sure, however, that the mother's aptitude for evil and sorcery did not touch the child.

Thomas knocked, then entered.

Maude was standing by the bed, and she dropped Thomas a curtsey.

Thomas nodded to her, then glanced at Margaret. She was awake, her head rolled on the pillow towards him, the blanket-wrapped child clasped in her arms.

"You may leave," Thomas said to Maude, and the woman gave Margaret a small smile, then left, closing the door gently behind her.

Thomas sat down on the stool by Margaret's bedside, remaining silent as he studied her. She was still white, and the flesh on her face still sunken, but she had the spark of life in her dark eyes, and her hands did not tremble as she cradled the child closer to her.

Thomas leaned closer and drew back a corner of the blanket that covered Rosalind's face.

In contrast to her mother's face, Rosalind's had filled out a little overnight, and much of the redness and wrinkling had gone. Her breathing was easy and soft ... but she was still so tiny, so vulnerable.

"I had her baptised Rosalind," Thomas said. "We thought she was to die."

"Rosalind is as good a name as any other," Margaret said, watching Thomas' face intently.

"It seems," said Thomas, leaning back from the child, "that we are to be married."

The corners of Margaret's mouth tilted in a small, cynical smile. "So I am to be a Neville, after all."

"The child needs a father, and a home."

Margaret's face softened as she looked down at her daughter. "Aye, that she does, and for both the name and the home, I do thank you, Thomas."

"How is it, Margaret, that Prior General Thorseby knew that you and I had fornicated in Lancaster's London palace?"

"Fornicate? I had not thought that is what we did."

"Answer my question."

Margaret lowered her eyes to the child. "I was seen as I went back to the Duchess' apartments."

"By whom?"

"By Master Wycliffe."

Thomas gave a short bark of harsh laughter. "He has served your purposes well, my lady."

"Tom," her eyes lifted back to his, "I do beg your forgiveness for the manner in which I have trapped you. I needed protection, for both myself and the child."

"When I was a priest, Margaret, you refused to beg forgiveness for anything. But when I am a man, the plea falls readily from your lips."

"The man is a state more honest to who he truly is. The priest was not. Tell me, Tom, what do you feel, knowing you must be my husband?"

"Lust," he said, without hesitation, and watched her eyes wince with pain. "I do not deny that I lust for you, and marriage to you allows me to indulge that lust with honesty. But I also distrust you, Margaret, and that you must know also. Our bodies may join, but never our souls. You have not truly trapped me."

Now her entire face flinched. "You do not love me?"

"No."

"No matter," she whispered, and turned her face aside.

"Margaret, soon Lancaster and Raby will be here, no doubt with one of the friars in tow, to witness our betrothal. Then I must depart, for I am to go north to reclaim my estates from my uncle."

At that, Margaret turned her face back to him, a peculiar light in her eyes.

Thomas remembered the way Raby had fretted for Margaret this last night, and the way he'd rushed to her side, and again a peculiar and unrecognisable emotion ravaged through him.

"But the north will not be our home," Thomas continued, and watched with even greater emotion as the light died from her eyes. "Lancaster will give us Halstow Hall in Kent as a wedding gift, and there we will make our residence. Raby must be left to enjoy his own wedded bliss, Margaret, without interference from you."

Her face tightened. "I will not cuckold you, Thomas. I know you think me the whore, but I am not, nor have ever been."

Thomas leaned over the bed, and tightly clasped her right wrist in his hand. "If ever I find that you have betrayed me with another, Margaret, I will drag you screaming down to the salt flats of the Thames estuary and there hold you face down in the briny silt until your whoring soul drowns."

Margaret's eyes filled with tears, not so much at the threat, but at his need to mouth it. "Then I will enjoy a long life, Thomas, for I shall be a true wife to you."

Thomas was going to say more, but then a knock sounded at the door, and Maude poked her head in.

"The lords Lancaster and Raby, my lord, and Brother Harold."

"Then show them in, Maude, for this is indeed a joyous day."

XXI

Low Sunday
In the first year of the reign of Richard II
(17th April 1379)

homas spent four weeks in the north — barely enough
time to accomplish what he needed — before he
resumed his travel south again. His uncle had made
good his offer to transfer back to Thomas the estates that
had been his from his father, although the deeds would not
receive their final signature until Thomas also made good his
promise to wed Margaret.

Thomas' father, Robert, had been Raby's younger
brother by some eighteen months. While Raby, as elder son,
had inherited the vast ancestral estates of the Nevilles,
Robert had inherited the manors that their mother had
brought into the family as her dowry. These had, on
Robert's and his wife's deaths during an outbreak of the
pestilence in 1353, then passed to their five-year-old son,
Thomas, who had in turn deeded them to his uncle on
entering holy orders.

Now these manors were back in Thomas' hands ... or
soon would be. The five manors were scattered in a rough
semi-circle extending from the small town of Pickering,
skirting the southern edges of the Pickering Forest, to the

coastal port of Scarborough. Between them they would give Thomas a comfortable income. Lancaster's gift of the Devon estates and Halstow Hall, as well as the influence and preferments to be gained within the Lancastrian court, would make Thomas a rich man. Thomas had spent a bare four days at Sheriff Hutton before riding out to make a tour of his northern manors.

He'd spent a few days at each manor, speaking with the stewards and reeves, and going over the accounts and tallies of livestock and grain. Raby, understandably, had not taken a great interest in the manors during the past five or six years they'd been in his care, and Thomas had spent most of the daylight hours walking over the manors, talking with the bondsmen and free tenants, inspecting livestock, and discussing improvements for the land and stock and possible new markets for their produce, making fuller use of the port and market facilities at Scarborough.

If nothing else, Thomas' time spent travelling about as a friar had opened his eyes to the possibilities of the European fairs and trading guilds.

Thomas had returned to Sheriff Hutton in time to spend Easter with his uncle and his new wife and had then ridden south on Easter Monday.

Thomas did not ride in the company of his uncle. Raby and the Lady Joan would return to London in time for Richard's coronation and Thomas' wedding, but Thomas preferred to ride ahead of them.

Best, perhaps, to keep Margaret and Raby apart until she was safely wedded.

If Thomas did not ride with Raby, then he did not ride alone. In York he had joined up with the Earl of Northumberland, Henry Percy, his son Hotspur, and the Northumberland retinue, all on their way down from the far north for the coronation. Indeed, it seemed half of northern England was on the road to London.

Thomas enjoyed the company of Northumberland and his son, but the week they spent on the road before they reached Lincoln had its uncomfortable moments.

Northumberland was highly suspicious of Raby's new marriage, and questioned Thomas at length about it. The Northumberlands and Nevilles had long been rivals for power in the north of England, a wild and independent region far enough from Westminster's control to make whoever held the title of Lord of the North almost as powerful in the northern counties as the king himself. For many years Northumberland had held the upper hand, as also the title Lord of the North. But now that Raby had allied himself so strongly with Lancaster, and Lancaster wielded such influence over Richard, Northumberland could see his power being whittled away.

Hotspur was almost as suspicious as his father. Not only had Raby secured a marriage which would almost guarantee him greater preferment, Thomas had also re-emerged as a potential rival. As boys, Hotspur and Thomas, together with Hal Bolingbroke, had been inseparable. They had formed a clique which defended itself against all outsiders.

But as the boys grew into men, matters changed. Hotspur had inherited his father's ambition. One day he, too, expected to be Lord of the North. This brought him into inevitable conflict with Hal, who would one day succeed to the estates and titles of his father and would become a natural rival for power with Hotspur at the English court and Privy Council.

Thomas had removed himself entirely from the political and dynastic ambitions of Hotspur and Bolingbroke when he had taken holy orders. But now here he was again, not only back with his family estates, but also the goodwill and patronage of Lancaster and Bolingbroke, *and* three of the personal manors of the duke himself. The friendship between Hotspur and Thomas was still there, but it was not as it had been. There was a coolness, almost a suspicion, that had not existed when they'd been mere boys dreaming of bedding their first girl.

Thomas learned as much from the Percys as they learned from him, and principally what he learned was that the father had ambitions for the son that extended well beyond the north. Edward had reigned for over fifty years and had been, apart from the early years when he'd been in his minority and his final months of senility, a strong ruler who had kept his nobles under firm control.

Could Richard do the same? Even with Lancaster behind him? It was notoriously difficult for any youthful king to retain a firm grip on power, and certainly not unknown for another high-ranking noble to try and seize power. Lancaster was loyal ... but were the Percys?

As Hotspur eyed Thomas suspiciously, so also did Thomas watch Hotspur, and wonder ...

Thomas rode into the Dominican friary outside Lincoln just after midday on Low Sunday, the first Sunday following Easter. The great festival of death and resurrection always heralded the onset of spring, and today was mild and clear. The snows and biting winds of winter seemed finally to have given polite way to flowers and tender grasses. The Percys and their retinue had ridden on into Lincoln; Thomas and Margaret and their child would join them on the morrow to recommence the journey into London.

He dismounted his horse in the courtyard, and a lay brother, who took his mount from him, smiled and pointed to the gate leading to the friary garden when Thomas asked after Margaret.

Thomas thanked him, then turned and looked at the gate. It was high and of solid wood ... and closed.

He hesitated, using the excuse of slowly drawing off his gloves, staring at the gate. Beyond there she sat, his future wife, the mother of his child ... and his potential nemesis.

But only if he allowed it.

Thomas took a deep breath, tucked the gloves into his belt, and walked over to the gate, unlatching it quietly and pushing it open.

At first he did not see her. The garden was extensive, laid out in large, raised rectangular beds containing vegetables and herbs. Fruit trees, staked berry shrubs and trellised vines bordered the walks and beds, breaking up the view and making the garden a series of rooms rather than an extended vista the eye could absorb in its entirety.

The sun shone down from almost directly overhead, so that anyone or anything sheltered within the garden's arbours sat secreted within deep shade, and it was only when Thomas had closed the gate and walked a few steps down the main path that he saw Margaret.

She sat under a rose arbour, totally absorbed in the child she held nestled to her breast. Her hair was unbound, hanging girlishly over her shoulders, and she wore a very simple gown that would not have looked astray on a dairy maid.

Margaret's head jerked up as she heard Thomas' step on the path. For an instant her face registered total surprise, then she composed herself, and smiled as he stepped up and sat beside her on the bench.

"Hello, Margaret," he said.

"Thomas," she answered.

Now that he was close, and his eyes adjusted to the patterns of light and shade, Thomas realised that Margaret had regained her beauty and health. Her face had lost its grey sunkenness and was full of colour and vibrancy, and her dark eyes danced with merriment.

Thomas stared, his own face expressionless, and Margaret's smile faded. Her eyes grew uncertain.

"I have no horns, Thomas," she said softly.

Thomas continued to study her for a moment longer, then he dropped his gaze to Rosalind, his face relaxing into a smile for the first time. If Margaret had regained her health, then the change in the infant was remarkable.

Rosalind had lost all her scrawny redness, and was now plump and creamy-skinned. She was still small, very small for a baby almost two months old, but that she was healthy and had taken a firm grasp on life could not be doubted.

Thomas reached out a hand, and touched her cheek gently.

"See," Margaret said, and drew the blanket a little way back from Rosalind's head. "She has the Neville hair."

Thomas remembered that when she was born Rosalind had had a few strands of dark hair across her scalp. Now those few strands had increased and thickened into a cap of wavy black hair.

As his finger traced softly over her head, Rosalind twisted her head away from Margaret's breast and blinked at him.

"She wonders who you are," Margaret said, drawing the linen of her bodice closed over her breast and wrapping Rosalind a little more securely in her blanket.

Then she lifted the baby and placed her in Thomas' arms.

As on the night he'd first held her, so now Thomas again was overwhelmed with the urge to protect and nurture the child. He held her close, and rocked her a little.

"She shall have a good life," he said. "The sin of her begetting shall not stain her."

Margaret bit back a tart answer. *And do you mean by that the sin of her mother?*

"She was born beyond marriage, Tom. Bastardy shall always stain her."

"She shall not suffer for it. I will not allow it."

"There are some," Margaret said very softly, watching Thomas' face carefully, "who think she would be better dead."

Thomas' face jerked up to hers. *Had she been more aware than he realised when he had talked to the archangel St Michael?*

"I will protect her, Margaret. I would give my life for her."

Margaret smiled — *would you give your soul, Tom?* — and tilted her eyes back to her daughter. "She shall have a good life."

"Aye," Thomas said.

"And a long one."

"Aye."

Again Margaret regarded Thomas. "A long life for a beloved daughter is an easy thing to promise here among the roses," she said, "but harder, sometimes, to accomplish in reality. Sometimes other loyalties intrude."

Thomas felt discomforted, not wanting to ask Margaret to explain what she'd meant ... the only image her words had conjured was the archangel, arguing the girl should die when Thomas had so desperately wanted her to live.

Better she die, Thomas, better for her, better for you.

St Michael had implied that the giving and taking of Rosalind's life was a test, a test to prove that Thomas served God before all others.

But how could her death serve God?

"It is no sin to love your daughter," Margaret said.

"No," Thomas whispered. "No sin."

Then he sighed, and roused himself, turning the conversation. "Margaret ... why did you lock out the midwife to give birth alone?"

"Guilt."

"Guilt?"

"I have never forgotten the manner of Lady Eleanor's death, nor forgotten that had I acted more suitably, she could yet be alive today."

"But —"

"No, let me finish. For me the birth was a test, a way for God to punish me, if you like. If I was truly guilty of Eleanor's death, then I should die, too. I locked Maude out so that God should have every opportunity to take me if He so willed."

"I had not thought you the woman to so offer herself to God." *Sweet Jesu, that was as transparent a lie as ever he'd heard!*

"Nevertheless ..."

"There was a strange cry come out from the chamber where you lay," Thomas said. "A cry as if of a beast of the woods, or even of something darker. Why lock us out, Margaret?"

"See!" she said, casting out her arm at the ground before them. "Does my shadow cast horns? Do I hide a forked tail beneath my skirts? I am no demonic fiend, Thomas. Believe me!"

She leaned closer, speaking fiercely. "If you think me a demon, or worse ... then what does that make Rosalind?"

Thomas' eyes jerked to her face, startled.

"She is your daughter as much mine, Tom. And she is no demon."

"No ... no, she isn't."

Margaret's face and body lost some of their tension, and she leaned back in the seat, content for some minutes to watch Thomas continue to nurse the baby. When it seemed he had truly relaxed, Margaret spoke again. "Tell me of Alice."

"What?"

"You know my sins, Tom ... you have reminded me of them often enough. Now tell me of yours, for I would know the darknesses hiding within my husband."

"Where did you hear that name?"

"My lady Katherine spoke of her, just briefly, not knowing then that it was your child I carried. She implied that this Alice, and the wrong you'd done her, was the reason you'd entered holy orders."

The child in his arms forgotten, Thomas let his eyes drift away from Margaret and settle on the garden. Look, there sprang a clump of foxglove, used no doubt to strengthen the failing hearts of the brothers. And there some corn honeywort, used to cool painful swellings.

"Who was Alice, Tom?"

Thomas' eyes now followed a bee that dipped and rose over the garden, wondering if it belonged to a hive maintained by the brothers, or by some nearby peasant. It was a fat bee, and doubtless cheerful to be released from the bonds of winter.

"Who was Alice, Tom?"

Oh, merciful Lord ... Alice!

"She was my paramour," he said. "My mistress."

"Your whore."

Thomas flinched, wishing he'd never thought to call Margaret a whore.

"She was a virtuous lady, and her husband a gentle and chivalric knight."

"And the presence of a husband imbued Alice with virtue where a lack of one made me a harlot?"

"She was a beautiful and accomplished woman, and fascinated me where no other woman had. I was only a young man, barely old enough for my spurs, when first we met. I wanted her, and made my want known. For a year or more she resisted, but finally her own lust overcame her doubts. She and I bedded for over a year, whenever we had the opportunity."

"And her husband?"

"He did not know." Thomas paused, his eyes still roaming over the garden. "One day King Edward sent him to the court of the Flemish count on some matter concerning wool exports. He was gone eight months."

"And in those eight months Alice fell pregnant to you."

"Aye. I could not bear the shame that would grow with the child."

"And so you abandoned her."

"You are right virtuous all of a sudden!" Thomas snapped, finally looking at Margaret. He was surprised to see her face full of pity rather than any degree of satisfaction.

He jerked his eyes away, lest she should see the tears that had suddenly filled them. "But, yes, I abandoned her, and would not acknowledge the child."

Margaret was silent, knowing what must come next.

"And ... and so she murdered herself," Thomas finally said, his voice almost a whisper as if he could barely force the words out. "Herself and the child she carried ... and her three daughters by her husband."

"Oh, Tom! No!"

"She locked herself and her children in an abandoned water mill — the stream it was built on had dried up — and spread straw about. Then she set fire to it."

Margaret had her hands over her mouth, her eyes wide and staring. She had thought there to be a tragedy, but this? *No wonder the man had fled his entire life and sought to appease his guilt within the Church!*

"She sent herself and her children to hell," Thomas whispered, "and I lifted not a finger to save them."

He turned on the seat so he looked Margaret directly in the eye. "I will never allow anyone to take this child," he said. "Never."

Margaret turned her head and closed her eyes, still so appalled and saddened that she could not even savour her victory.

How could the angels, normally so careful, have misjudged so badly this one, critical time?

Had they misjudged, or was there even yet a trap she could not see?

XXII

The Thursday and Friday before the Feast of
the Blessed SS Philip and James
In the first year of the reign of Richard II
(28th and 29th April 1379)

Lancaster stretched out his long legs, leaned back in his chair and regarded Thomas over his steepled fingers.

"Richard has my every support," he said. "I have watched him grow from infancy. He is no demon and you can show me no proof to change my mind."

"Nevertheless," Thomas said, "I cannot imagine how he is *not*! Who else would have the nerve to send his man to Bramham Moor friary wearing your livery? *He* was the one to benefit from the demonic deaths of his grandfather and father."

"Stay your words, Tom!" Bolingbroke leaned the distance between them and placed a cautionary hand on Thomas' arm. "We shall find the casket eventually. Until then ..."

Thomas forced himself to relax. Hal was right, and there was certainly no point in antagonising Lancaster. To do so would see him sent as far from court as was possible ... and it was only at court that he had a chance of finding the casket.

Where had Richard secreted it?

"I apologise," he said to Lancaster. "I had fought so long to reach Bramham Moor, and when I did, it was only to find the casket so recently gone."

"Well," Lancaster said, still watching Thomas carefully, "I can assure you it is *not* under Richard's bed."

"We know," Hal said, and winked conspiratorially, "because we crept into his bedchamber one night last week and lifted the covers to look!"

Both Lancaster and Thomas laughed, lifting the mood.

Lancaster sat up straight, glancing at the window. "Ah, see how late we have tarried talking, and there is yet more to be said before I can join my Katherine in our bed. Thomas, is Margaret quite recovered from the journey?"

"Aye." Thomas and Margaret, with a nurse to carry Rosalind, had rejoined Northumberland on the morning after Low Sunday, and the entire train had then made its way south to London over the next ten days. Despite her recovery, the journey had tired Margaret, and caused her to lose her milk, which had given her deep distress. She had not liked to hand Rosalind over to a wet nurse, but there was no help for it.

They had been at the Savoy now for some two days, time enough for Margaret to recover her spirits, if not her milk. Tomorrow at Vespers they would be wed in a quiet ceremony in the palace chapel. Neither wanted nor expected a grand ceremony, and even had they wanted it, London was in such a fever over the imminent coronation that their wedding would have been ignored anyway.

"Good." Lancaster delayed a moment, lifting a honeyed fig from a platter on a nearby table. He took a bite, chewed, swallowed, then resumed speaking. "Once the coronation is done, and Richard has held his first court, it would be best to take Margaret and the child to Halstow Hall. You will need to inspect your new home in any case."

Thomas bowed his head.

"Then," Lancaster said, toying with the remaining portion of fig, "I and Hal would that you join his household, perhaps as Hal's secretary, but also, I hope, as his friend."

Hal broke into a broad smile. "Well?"

Thomas was truly stunned by the offer. The position of secretary to a nobleman as powerful as Hal was potentially a preferment of great influence. Thomas would control access to Hal, be his ambassador and spokesman, and supervise his estates and manors.

"I do thank you," Thomas said, his gaze taking in both men, "and I do accept. But —"

The other two stilled.

"— it shall be a tiresome task, running about after my Lord of Bolingbroke day and night."

Lancaster laughed, catching and holding his son's eye. "Bolingbroke is about to be tamed," he said, "for this summer he is to take the Lady Mary Bohun to wife."

Thomas turned to Hal, offering his congratulations. Lady Mary Bohun was one of the richest heiresses in England, and her lands and titles and estates would only add to Hal's power base. He remembered Hal's attentions to her at the ill-fated Christmastide banquet, and realised that negotiations must have been going on for many months.

Hal pretended dismay, rolling his eyes and giving a heart-rending groan. "You are not the only one to be led ring in nose to the altar, Tom," he said. "But at the least we can console each other."

They talked of other things for a few minutes, then Thomas asked after news of France. He had been so long in the north that little information worthy of relating had reached him.

Both Lancaster's and Hal's faces lost some of their good humour.

"Charles and Philip continue to be the best of bedmates," Lancaster said. "I have heard reports that they have so strengthened their arms that they may well attempt to retake the south this summer."

"Intelligence also reports that the maid Joan continues at Charles' right hand," Hal put in. "Apparently Charles will not even empty his bowels without her advice."

"And us?" Thomas said. "Can we ..."

Lancaster sighed heavily. "The loss of both my father and brother have crippled us for this year. As with any new and untested king, Richard must consolidate his hold on his own realm before he attempts to snatch another. I do not think we will be able to mount another aggressive campaign until ... oh, perhaps spring of *next* year at the earliest. God has dealt us a poor hand."

"And all we can do in the meantime," Hal said, his face dark, "is to pray this Joan of Arc does not inspire Charles towards *too* many acts of heroism. France will be ours yet. It *must* be."

There were few people in the chapel to witness Thomas and Margaret's nuptials. Lancaster and his wife, Katherine; Raby and his wife, Joan; Hal; and, surprisingly, Geoffrey Chaucer, who had said he was in town for the coronation and might as well attend a wedding as well.

Lancaster's chaplain conducted the service with the minimum of fuss, and what dignity he did assume was totally negated by Hal, who stood to one side grinning as if Thomas' marriage had been something he'd accomplished himself.

Margaret was quiet and pale, speaking her responses in a low voice. She wore a dress of dark green velvet, edged with scarlet at the hem and along the tippets of her sleeves. It was low cut and tight fitted, revealing that her recent pregnancy had not in the least affected her figure. She hardly looked at Thomas, and would not look at anyone else. Thomas had been concerned that she might embarrass herself with a display at Raby, but to his relief she hardly seemed aware that the baron was there.

She had said she would be the good wife and so, it appeared, she intended to be.

Thomas sighed with relief when the chaplain finally pronounced them man and wife, and bent to kiss Margaret.

As she lifted her face to his, Thomas was stunned to read fear in her eyes, and as a result the kiss he gave her was more tender than he'd actually meant.

There was a round of congratulations as the witnesses stepped forth, the women kissing her on the cheek, and the men kissing Margaret on the mouth as was the custom. Thomas watched Margaret's reaction carefully as Raby placed his mouth over hers, and then watched with some amazement as Hal kissed Margaret with surprising tenderness. Then, just as Lancaster jovially suggested they repair to his private apartments to share a simple wedding supper, a youth stepped forward from the shadows of the aisle, clapping his hands slowly.

Richard.

He was dressed all in green from the short and tightly fitted fur-trimmed tunic that revealed the bulge of his privy members to the equally tightly fitted leggings about his thin legs.

"Well, well, Neville," Richard said as he finally lowered his hands. "I did surely think we'd lost you to the priesthood ... and yet here you be, married to a woman any man would lust to bed. May I offer my own congratulations to those of my uncle and his family?"

"Your grace," Thomas said, bowing, but Richard paid him no attention. He caught Margaret in the midst of her curtsey, placing both his hands on her shoulders and raising her up so that he could plant a lingering kiss on her mouth.

Thomas barely restrained himself from placing his own hands on the king's shoulders and wrenching him off his wife.

"She tastes sweet," Richard said, finally leaning back from Margaret. "I envy you your bedding. I must take my own wife soon, methinks."

He glanced slyly at Thomas. "After all, I could hardly take another man's, could I? Nay, only tragedy would lie in that action."

He bent to kiss Margaret again, and her face wrinkled in either disgust or fear, Thomas could not tell which. At that point Thomas thought he might truly have ruined his entire life by striking Richard — *how dare he sully Margaret and refer to Alice in the same moment?* — but Hal stepped between them, took Margaret by the arm, and handed her over to Thomas.

"We must not keep the happy couple apart for too much longer," he murmured. "Your grace, perhaps you will join us for a simple wedding supper?"

"Nay," Richard said, his eyes not leaving Thomas' face, "I think not. The Abbot of Westminster thinks he needs to spend yet another evening with me to ensure I don't put a foot wrong at my coronation. I merely rode here to offer Thomas my congratulations, and to tell him how pleased I am that he is to be so close to my court rather than lost in the wilds of the Dominican family. Thomas, you and your delightful wife will stay to attend my coronation court, will you not?"

"Aye, your grace. It will be our pleasure."

Richard glanced again at Margaret. "And mine, too. Well, be off with you now. Best sate your wedding appetites while you have a mind to."

And with that he turned and walked away, taking his gloves from his belt and idly swinging them to and fro as he went.

"Tom," Hal said quietly in his ear. "Ignore him. He has not the manners of the lowest serf."

"And to think that he shall be our king," Thomas said. "*And* of the —"

"Tom!" Hal's hand dug into his arm. "Do not say that here!"

Thomas lay awake late into the night, his hands behind his head on the pillow, staring at the low ceiling of their chamber. Margaret was asleep on her side beside him, her back a graceful pale blur in the darkness. They were wedded and bedded, and yet when he *had* finally bedded her, Thomas' mind could not let go of the image of Richard with his hands on Margaret's shoulders, and his mouth on hers. From that image his mind would sidle forward to a point where he could see Richard casually offering him money, or a preferment perhaps, so he could sate his lust on Thomas' wife.

After all, Richard would say with just the hint of glee in his grey eyes, *I know you would understand the need to bed another man's wife.*

He must get Margaret away as soon as possible. She and Rosalind would be safe at Halstow Hall.

He rolled his head slightly, and reached out a hand, running his fingers with gossamer gentleness over her unbound hair, and from there down over her shoulders.

He knew why Richard was taunting him. He was displaying his power — *you think to stop me, thrust me back into hell, and yet here am I with the power to call your wife to my bed with a click of my fingers* — and revelling in that display.

He did not want Richard, not Richard, of all creatures, bedding his wife. But then, he did not want Raby to bed Margaret, either.

Did his uncle think to resume his affair with her, now that any resulting child could be safely accredited to his nephew?

Thomas was jealous, and that rankled with him. He tried to reason that he merely did not want anyone to cuckold him with Margaret — a man had his honour, after all. But was that enough to explain his jealousy?

How did Margaret feel? She had looked at him with fear in her eyes this past evening, and yet had been wanton enough in their bed. Had she pretended it was Raby hunching over her in the dim light?

Did she love Raby?

Frustrated and angered by his confused feelings, Thomas rolled out of the bed and walked softly over to Rosalind's cradle. Margaret had wanted her in their chamber, and he certainly had no objection to it.

Thomas' face softened as he gazed down at his child. She was asleep on her back, wrapped tight in a blanket.

"Tom?"

He looked over to the bed. Margaret had risen on an elbow.

"Is she well?"

"Aye, she is well. I had only thought to see that she slept."

He walked back to the bed and sat down beside Margaret. "You still fear me, I can see it in your face."

She lay back against the pillows, and pulled a sheet over her nakedness. "You are my husband, and yet I know you not. Who are you, Tom?"

Thomas sighed. "That is partly what marriage is for, to enable husband and wife to come to know each other over the years."

"Will you promise to know me, Tom? You do not respect me, and you doubt me, and yet what I want most of all is to be respected and trusted ... is that not what marriage is about?"

He hesitated. "I thought you would want me to love you."

She smiled, sadly. "Love is of no matter when it comes to you and I."

"Meg, this marriage can only be but a very small part of my life."

"Oh, aye, I know that."

"There is something else I must do."

"And aye again. I know something of that matter, too."

Thomas reached down and pulled the sheet away from her body. "And how do you know of that matter, Meg?"

"You were the one to tell me. You fight against evil, for all mankind, and yet evil will win if you allow yourself to hand your soul over to a woman."

"Then you understand the stakes, Meg. You are my wife, but you will never be my lover."

And as he bent down to her, Margaret began to weep — softly, so he would not know. She was his wife, she was his property; she would never share his soul.

But she could still manipulate it.

XXIII

Before Matins on the Saturday before the Feast of
the Blessed SS Philip and James
In the first year of the reign of Richard II
(after midnight 30th April 1379)

She lay quiet, her eyes closed, and listened to his
breathing. It was an age, almost a lifetime, before she
heard him slip into deep sleep.

Margaret sighed, careful to keep it silent, and opened her
eyes. She had not thought he would sleep at all this night,
and that would have been a disaster, because this was the
only night — their wedding night — when she would have
this much power.

If she could not accomplish what she must this night, then
all could yet fail.

Very carefully, and yet not furtively (for that would wake
him), she rolled close, snuggling her body against his so that
they lay touching their entire lengths.

Her body was still sticky and damp from the fluids of
their recent bedding, and that was good, for it would prove
the vital link between his soul and hers.

She lay, waiting again, for a few minutes to make sure he
had not wakened. Her eyes travelled slowly the length of his
body. He was a handsome man, in face and form, and an

accomplished — if not particularly tender — lover. She knew he would also be a demanding lover — had he not admitted his lust for her body? — and that was also pleasing to her, because she enjoyed bedding with him.

But she must make sure she delayed her next pregnancy. Neither of them was ready for the horrors the next birth would bring ... and yet neither could avoid it.

She could, and must, prevent conceiving for a time. Margaret mourned the loss of her milk not only because she missed having Rosalind suckle at her breast, but because the suckling of one child often delayed the onset of the next. Well, there was nothing for it now but to roam the fields of Halstow Hall and find those herbs — stinking gladwin, pennyroyal and hercules woundwort — each of which could stimulate a woman's courses, and expel any child which had taken root.

Thomas' breathing had now slowed and deepened even further, and Margaret raised herself on one elbow so she could see his face.

"Tom?" she whispered.

There was no response.

"Sweet Tom," she whispered, and lifted an arm, resting it along his shoulder.

He stirred, very slightly, but fell back into unknowing sleep within a moment.

She laid her hand in his hair, sliding her fingers deep into his black curls.

He stirred again, and rested his weight back against her body.

"Dear Tom," she whispered, and kissed his forehead. "Dream sweetly."

He stood before the Cleft again, but it was very different from his previous visitation.

It was awake now. Open.

Flames leaped from amid the boulders in great hissing spouts. Sulphuric clouds boiled forth, stinking the entire air. Screams and wails and pleas for mercy filled the night.

The Gates of Hell were unbarred.

Thomas threw his arm over his face, almost overcome by the heat and stench. He stumbled back, felt a boulder against his legs, and almost fell in his haste to find some protection behind it.

More wails filled the air, but they came from down the valley rather than from within Hell. Thomas edged about the boulder, and peered down the track.

A group of children, about five or six, and utterly naked, were being herded towards the Gates of Hell by a semi-circle of shadowy, dancing demons. The demons carried pitchforks and sharpened stumps of wood with which they prodded and slashed, pushing the screaming children further and further towards Hell.

There was a man behind the group of children and demons, capering in joy as the children screamed. His features constantly flowed from those of a youth into those of a grinning demon and back again. His face was so fluid, so constantly in motion, that his man-face was difficult to make out.

But Thomas knew who he was. He was dressed in green clothes, obscenely skimpy and tight-fitting. He wore a crown on his head, and in one hand he brandished a sceptre.

The Demon-King. Richard.

Thomas tensed, frightened beyond anything he'd ever known, but also knowing that he was the only one who could save the children. He crouched, waiting for Richard to draw close, then he would spring, and tear the sceptre from Richard's hand, and beat him into death with it.

Then he must deal with the other demons, the shadowy ones who were too sly to reveal their true forms.

The children — such sweet children! Five boys and two girls — were now close, and their cries of terror and hopelessness tore at Thomas' heart.

How dare the demons deprive them of life, and throw their innocence into eternal Hell!

Thomas' hands clutched at the boulder as the children and demons passed, and he prepared to spring.

But he did not, for even as Richard cavorted close to him, there came another voice, and another footstep, and it made *both demons and Richard halt their maddened dancing, and turn to stare back down the track towards the forest.*

A man had stood forth from the trees. A knight. Dressed in armour so white it shone. He bore in one hand, not a sword, nor a mace, nor even an axe, but a longbow, and as Thomas watched, the knight lifted the bow and fitted an arrow to it.

"You wouldn't dare!" screamed Richard.

"I dare," said the knight, and Thomas wept, for he knew that voice, "because I have the right."

And he shot forth the arrow, and it skewered Richard in the belly, projecting forth from his lower back in red-tipped victory.

Richard howled, and doubled over, and then collapsed to the ground, and as he did so the shadowy demons screamed, and vanished, and the children, blinking with surprise, ran back down the path towards the shining knight.

Thomas also stood, walking towards the knight.

As the children gathered about him, clinging to his legs and hips, the knight raised the visor of his basinet, so all could see his face.

It was a face of extraordinary beauty — creamy and smooth-skinned, with great cerulean eyes that took up half as much space again as did most human eyes.

And yet this knight was no human. He was an angel, and yet not an angel.

He was Hal Bolingbroke.

"Hal," Thomas whispered, coming to a halt before him.

"Tom," said Hal, and extended his mailed hand. "Will you serve as my man?"

"Yes," Thomas said. "Yes!"

"Will you swear me homage and loyalty?"

"Yes, I do so swear!"

And then Hal Bolingbroke took Thomas' face between his hands, and, leaning forth over the children still clustered about him, leaned forward and kissed Thomas on the mouth with a loving and lingering grace.

XXIV

The third Sunday after Easter
In the first year of the reign of Richard II
(1st May 1379)

— May Day —

— i —

It was Coronation Day and London was hot with revelry. This, the third Sunday after Easter, was also May Day, the traditional popular festival celebrating the resurrection of Spring after the long dark days of winter. Across the land young men and women had spent the night in the forests and woodlands, hunting the sapling they would cut down for their maypole ... and also enjoying some of the lusts that youth and spring inflamed.

Now the saplings, denuded of their branches, were being hauled back to village and market squares, the revellers decked in greenery and ribbons, so that young women could dance about the pole in homage to the Green Man, the ancient pagan god of the trees and forests. For centuries the Church had banned and vilified the May Day revelries, and yet nothing had stopped them, and, today of all days, nothing could.

May Day in 1379 marked not only the rebirth of the

land, but also the coronation of a new king, the youthful and handsome Richard. The old king, with the winter, was dead and buried; now was the springtime of youth and new beginnings.

None missed the symbolism.

At first light young girls, their hair unbound, had taken to the fields beyond the walls of the city to dance about the maypoles. Around them gathered young men, their eyes and bodies hot and drunken from the copious ale at hand from table and barrel. Husbands and wives also stood about, clapping and laughing, their children — oft products of previous May Day revelries — clinging to skirts and tunics.

As the sun rose in the sky, and grew as hot as the lust and revelries below, the crowds departed back into London, still laughing and singing and dancing. There they lined the main streets and thoroughfares as, at noon, with all the bells of London ringing, Richard made his way in stately procession from the Tower of London, through Cheapside, past St Paul's (its bells pealing frantically) and then down the Strand, lifting his head to smile and wave at Lancaster's servants and retainers waving ribbons and pennants from the windows of the Savoy Palace.

Richard walked under a richly embroidered canopy of scarlet and azure and gold, which was supported by the four highest noblemen in England; John of Gaunt, Duke of Lancaster, carried the pole supporting the front right-hand corner of the canopy.

The soon-to-be-crowned king wore opulent clothing — furs, velvets, silks — and in his gloved hands he carried a small branch of greenery, symbol of both spring and his own coronation. He waved and laughed at the screaming crowds, but what words he spoke were lost amid the tolling of the parish church bells and the roar of his subjects.

Flowers and ribbons filled the air and tumbled down on the train of horsed noblemen — the greatest peers of the realm — who followed Richard.

At Richard's heels capered his five companion hounds: slim, sly creatures, who snapped at the noise and tumult about them, and bit the hands of at least three children along the great processional route.

At Charing Cross, which marked the turning point from the Strand onto the road down to Westminster, stood a deputation of twelve young maidens, all freshly garlanded and frocked. They held flowers in their hands and, as Richard stopped before them, began to sing:

> Good morning, ladies and gentlemen
> We wish you a happy May
> We've come to show you our garland
> Because it's the first of May.
> A May garland I have brought you,
> And at your door I stand.
> It looks very nice
> And smells very sweet
> And it came from the Lord's right hand.

Richard accepted a posy from the eldest and prettiest girl, and then the girls stood aside as a servant led forth Richard's white stallion, all bedecked in green tracery. He mounted, and rode the last distance into Westminster followed by the great nobles, now mounted, who had previously carried his canopy. The procession did not turn straight to the Abbey, but to Westminster Hall, where Richard dismounted and entered to be ritually bathed by the Abbey monks.

Washed of sin, he could now be crowned.

In another procession, solemn where the previous had been riotous, Richard walked to the Abbey along a pathway of red cloth. Again he walked under a canopy, this one of silver gilt and edged with tiny bells, and carried by the four Barons of the Cinque Ports. Behind him walked the prior of the Abbey, as well as several monks, carrying the altar cross, the sceptre and the orb.

The instant Richard set foot inside the Abbey, the choir broke into an anthem of praise and joy.

Richard proceeded to a chair set to one side of the throne — a great wooden seat that had borne the weight of the kings of

England since late the previous century when it had been specially built to house the Stone of Scone.

Once Richard had sat, Simon Sudbury, the Archbishop of Canterbury, stepped forth and asked in loud voice the will of the people touching the coronation.

Richard! roared the assembled lords.

And so Richard moved now to his throne, where he stood, and where the ceremony continued apace.

Thomas stood to one side of the nave, grouped among members of Lancaster's and Bolingbroke's households. In accord with every other person in the abbey, he was richly apparelled and jewelled; unlike most other people, his face was set into a carefully neutral expression.

Margaret, also richly dressed in a gown and headpiece of azure-embroidered ivory cloth, stood among the ladies of the Duchess of Lancaster, watching Thomas far more than she watched Richard's triumph.

Lancaster and his son, Bolingbroke, were far closer to the proceedings, among the other high nobles seated on the cushions that had been scattered about the throne.

After two more anthems and a hymn, the archbishop solemnly anointed Richard, who had laid aside his tunic to receive the holy blessing in his shirt and bare feet.

Then the Abbot of Westminster, aided by two monks, dressed Richard in the robes of state. Once he had done, the bishops presented Richard with his sword, which he girded about his body.

Richard then sat upon his throne as the archbishop blessed the crown of state, and set it upon his head. Then the archbishop leaned forward, and kissed Richard, and as he stepped back, so did all the great men of England, led by Lancaster, step forth and do their new king homage.

To Thomas it all seemed surreal. He waited throughout the entire ceremony, half expecting Hal, as he stepped up to the new king, to run him through with his sword, but Hal merely leaned forward, bowed, kissed the new king's ring, and spoke the oath of homage and fealty.

Having received both crown and oaths of fealty from the great nobles, Richard then sat back on the throne, swearing his own oaths as prompted by the archbishop: firstly, that he would keep full peace according to God's law; secondly, that he would rule his realm with mercy and truth; thirdly, that he would defend the rightful laws and customs of his people.

And then the final oath, spoken in both English and French: "I become your liege man in life and limb and truth and earthly honours, bearing to you against all men that love, move or die, so help me God and the Holy Dame."

And so, after yet more anthems and hymns and sundry other oaths and promises and the bearing of numerous swords and spears and ceremonial cloths, Richard II began his formal reign as King of England.

As Richard finally left the Abbey in grand and solemn procession, he turned his head, saw Thomas, and smiled.

Today Richard had enjoyed his own wedding, to his throne and to power, so long as he should live.

XXV

After Vespers on the third Sunday after Easter
In the first year of the reign of Richard II
(evening 1st May 1379)

— May Day —

— ii —

Richard held his coronation court in the Painted
Chamber that evening. It was not to be an overly long
nor grand affair — everyone from Richard to the
lowliest page was exhausted after the day's ceremonies —
but there were the niceties to be observed, and the
traditional gestures of goodwill to be made by the newly
installed monarch.

The Painted Chamber was one of the three main halls of
the Westminster Palace complex, and the traditional
domicile of the king while in London. It was a vast chamber
— although still smaller than the main Westminster Hall —
and of such surpassing beauty that visiting ambassadors had
declared it one of the wonders of Europe. On the left-hand
side of the entry door was a long wall whose entire length
was pierced with graceful, arched windows filled with the
best examples of English stained glass. Three windows
pierced the wall which ran across the head of the chamber

above the royal dais. The two larger windows took up the lower two-thirds of the wall, and a smaller but no less beauteous window sat between the arches of these two lower ones filling the centre of the top third of the wall and leading the eye to the wooden ceiling decorated with cunningly-carved rosettes.

But it was the decorations along the right-hand wall that gave the chamber its name, and which made new visitors gasp.

The entire length of the wall — some three hundred feet — had been painted with glorious enamels to depict all the tales of war contained within the Bible. French text accompanied all the painted scenes, explaining their meaning and purpose. Above the dais and beneath the three windows at the top of the hall were scenes depicting the life and coronation of the royal saint, Edward the Confessor. Sundry other saints looked down on gatherings within the chamber from the very top of the long wall.

Filled with light, whether natural, or candle and torch, the chamber formed an extraordinary framework for the power of the English monarchs.

Although Thomas had been here previously, the evening court was Margaret's first experience of the chamber.

Thomas physically had to pull her to one side as she paused in the entrance doorway to gasp in astonishment.

"It's so wondrous!" she said.

"Isn't it?" Hal said. He was just behind the Nevilles, accompanied by several squires and servants. He waved them on as he paused to talk with Thomas and Margaret.

"Lady Margaret," he said, smiling gently, "not even this chamber can outshine you for beauty."

Thomas looked at him sharply, then studied Margaret closely; she was returning Hal's smile with something far more than courtly politeness.

"Tom," Hal said, turning away from Margaret, "I congratulate you once again on your choice of bride."

He looked back to Margaret. "And I congratulate you, my dear, on tearing him free from the Church when none of us could provide enough persuasions to turn him."

Again Thomas noted the look that passed between them, and remembered the tenderness with which Hal had kissed her at the conclusion of their marriage in the chapel ... and the concern with which he had lifted her, fainting, from her horse to his on that exhausting ride into la Rochelle.

"You must take Margaret to Halstow Hall soon," Hal said to Thomas. "The court shall prove a dangerous place for her, I think."

"Yes," said Margaret, turning a little so she could take Thomas' arm in hers and look him in the eye. "This is no place for a wife, nor for a daughter."

Whatever suspicions had been fermenting in Thomas' mind dissipated. They were both right. Margaret should be taken to Halstow Hall soon ... away from Richard.

And away from Raby ... and Hal.

"Do not fear Richard's reaction," Hal said, watching Thomas' face as if he could truly read the thoughts within. "You are my man, and answer to me. You have a new wife, and daughter too-soon born; both need to rest awhile away from the tumult of court life. You also have a new manor and estates to inspect. I shall therefore inform Richard that I have asked you to escort them home before you return into my service. He cannot object without creating a fuss.

"And when you do return into my service," Hal suddenly grinned, his eyes mischievous, "I shall give you leave to take as many liberties with my new wife as I have taken with yours."

Thomas and Margaret laughed, and Thomas would have spoken, save that Lady Jane Keate, one of the Duchess of Lancaster's ladies, joined them and asked Margaret to join the Duchess at her request.

Margaret smiled, looked at Thomas for his permission, then took her leave of the men and followed Lady Jane.

Thomas moved close to Hal as they, in their turn, moved through the crowds thronging the chamber towards the dais.

"You smiled prettily enough as you made your oaths to Richard this afternoon, my lord," Thomas said quietly.

"Why 'my lord' so suddenly, Tom?"

"I am your servant now."

"But still my friend, and I am still Hal away from courtly protocol. But, as to this afternoon, why, yes, I smiled prettily. I had no choice."

Hal looked about them, making sure that the people in their immediate vicinity were involved in conversations other than that taking place between Bolingbroke and his new secretary.

"Tom ..." Hal drew Thomas close to one of the great stained glass windows, pretending an interest in a craftily executed scene of Noah's Ark, "we can do nothing about Richard until we find proof."

"The casket."

"Aye, the casket. Tom," Hal stared his friend in the eye. "I swear to you on the friendship that binds us that I will do whatever is in my power to see that the casket is placed in your hands. To have Richard on the throne appals me, but neither of us can touch him at the moment."

"What was it that appals you, friend?"

Thomas and Hal both jerked in surprise, and turned about.

Hotspur had joined them, looking rakishly secretive in a black velvet tunic embroidered all about with seed pearls.

"Richard's lack of a wife," Hal said with no hesitation. "He has handled Tom's Margaret too roughly, and I fear for the chastity of my own wife-to-be if Richard lays his lustful eye upon her. We must find him a queen, Hotspur. Any suggestions?"

Hotspur raised an eyebrow at Thomas. "'Tis no great tragedy, surely, if a king's eye falls upon one's wife? There are many preferments and honours to be got from the guilty, and thankful, conscience of a king."

"I would suggest you offer your own wife for Richard's bed," Thomas said, "save that you have none of your own. But there's always your mother, Hotspur. Why don't you dress her in the clothes of a harlot and parade her before the king? As you say, the benefits will far outweigh the sniggers."

Hotspur's face tightened.

"And for that dagger," Hal said, "you have no one to blame but yourself, Hotspur. Come, I hear from the murmur of the crowds that Richard approaches. Let us hear no more of the whoring of one's wife or mother."

Hotspur shot Thomas a further angry glance, but turned to follow Hal as he once more made his way through the crowd towards the dais. Thomas, having checked to make sure that Margaret was safely in Katherine's entourage, trailed a few steps behind, thinking on how friendships altered, blossoming into a different flower, when minds turned to the acquisition of power.

Richard entered the Painted Chamber, riding a wave of trumpet and bonhomie. This was his day, and there were yet some hours left to be enjoyed.

He had put to one side his coronation robes, again affecting a suit of green — amply laden with gold and gems.

As with the robes of state, Richard had dispensed with the crown of Edward the Confessor — a weighty item that was better worn for stately processions than the gaieties of post-coronation celebrations — and wore a simple coronet of gold and silver. The Plantagenet dynasty had ruled England for centuries, and all those centuries of arrogance and power revealed themselves in Richard's every step and movement.

He had succeeded to the throne of England when only a youth, he controlled the fate of a nation in his hands, and Richard intended to enjoy every moment of what he hoped would be a long life.

The king was dead, long live the king.

Trailed by a line of attendants and servants, almost as richly dressed as the king himself, Richard made his way to the throne which had been set upon the dais and sat himself down. He waved magnanimously as the assembled crowd bowed or curtsied, saying in his high voice that the time for stately protocol was over — at least for this evening — and that he wished his subjects to be at ease in his presence.

As the crowd straightened from their collective obeisance (despite their king's words, it was difficult to be totally at ease when there were no seats), Richard began a speech, thanking all and sundry for the goodwill and effort which had gone into making his coronation ceremony such a success.

"And all for the want of a simple oaken casket," Hal murmured into Thomas' ear.

"As you have so freely given of your goodwill," Richard continued, his eyes flickering towards Hal and Thomas, "so now I give of mine. It is traditional that a new king gift as his people have so freely gifted him, and this gifting is more a joy to me than a burden of practise."

Richard beckoned to a clerk standing to one side, and the man handed his king a roll of parchment.

"The appropriate offices within my administration will hastily draw up the following deeds and devices for those men I intend to honour here tonight."

Richard began to read from the parchment, listing names and the honours he bestowed on them.

To nine of his attendants, who had so faithfully served in his household, he gave knighthoods with the lands attendant upon each title.

To his tutor, Sir Guichard d'Angle, Richard bestowed the title of Earl of Huntingdon.

"If I had known he would so richly reward his tutor," Hotspur whispered behind Hal and Thomas, "I would have taught him his numbers many a year ago."

Despite their earlier ill-feeling, both Hal and Thomas grinned.

To his beloved uncle, Thomas of Woodstock, Duke of Gloucester, Richard also gave the lands and titles of Earl of Buckingham.

"To Lancaster's faithful retainer, Ralph, Baron of Raby," Richard said, "I bestow the lands and title of Earl of Westmorland."

"What?" Hotspur hissed, and Hal had to turn about and restrain him from saying any more.

Hotspur, shaking off Hal's cautionary hand, shared a look of smouldering resentment with his father, the Earl of

Northumberland. Was the Percy power in the north to be threatened by the Nevilles?

"And to my beloved cousin," Richard continued, again looking at Hal, "Prince Henry of Bolingbroke, I give the lands and titles of the Earldom of Derby and the Dukedom of Hereford."

Thomas looked at Hal, who, patently shaken, was staring at Richard.

"He thinks to curry your favour," Thomas whispered in Hal's ear.

Hal did not reply for a moment, but eventually he turned and whispered back in Thomas' ear. "Yet what he does not realise, does he, is that he has given me the lands, wealth and power that will enable me to form, in time, an effective power base to rival that of the throne."

"Lancaster did well," Hotspur said bitterly, and loudly, to a nobleman on his left, "to nurture the boy-heir within his own household, for tonight that household has been enriched beyond measure for their foresight."

And then, with a smouldering look of utter enmity towards Hal, Hotspur moved off through the crowd to join his father.

Thomas looked back to Richard, and saw the youth staring towards Hal with evident satisfaction.

Had Richard just rewarded Hal and Raby, or had he purposefully ensured inevitable animosity between the houses of Lancaster, Neville and Percy, three of the most powerful families in England? If so, then Richard had nurtured a conflict that would ensure the fragmentation of any effective opposition against his power.

Richard grinned, and tossed the parchment back to the clerk.

The Demon-King had done good work in his first hours on the throne.

Epilogue

Vigil of the Nativity of St John the Baptist
In the first year of the reign of Richard II
(Thursday 23rd June 1379)

— Midsummer's Eve —

Margaret stood in the meadow land of Halstow Hall, a warm wind gently lifting both her skirts and her hair. The grass had been mown three weeks ago, but in that time the cornflowers had resprouted and blossomed, and a bunch of them now hung from her belt.

This was a peaceful, beautiful land. To the north lay the Thames estuary with its flocks of wheeling gulls and white-capped waves; to the south lay the Medway River and the town of Rochester, and in between stretched the tranquil fields of the Hoo Peninsula. A half mile away from where Margaret stood was the house of Halstow Hall. It was a commodious and agreeable building, full of light and warm wood and soaring hammerbeam ceilings, and Margaret hoped that one day her daughter would clamber, laughing, down the great central staircase, and spend the long winter evenings warm and comfortable before the great fireplace in the hall.

If she had the chance. So much had to pass before that dream could become a reality.

She turned a little, shading her eyes against the noonday sun. There walked her husband, Thomas, some ten or eleven paces distant.

Here in Halstow Thomas had abandoned the clothes of the courtier, and was dressed comfortably in a country linen tunic and leggings. He was looking north towards the Thames estuary and river. Soon, surely, he would leave her and Rosalind, and depart back to court, there to resume his friendship and service with Hal.

Margaret smiled. Dear, beloved Hal.

Then her face sobered, and she drew in a deep breath. She and her brethren hated Midsummer's Eve as much as they hated the Nameless Day. Even though tonight would be harmless — Thomas had not yet found the casket, nor read its contents — the turning of both summer and winter solstices kindled such horrifying memories that Margaret knew she would wake Thomas this night with the whimpering of her nightmares.

And when Thomas did find the casket, as he inevitably would, then her nightmares would become reality. A walking, daylight vengeance.

Margaret watched as Thomas lowered his head and smiled at the four-month child he carried in his arms.

"Don't condemn us to hell," Margaret whispered, staring at her husband. "Don't do to me what you did to Alice and her child."

Thomas turned, almost as if he had heard Margaret's plea, and then he began to walk slowly toward her through the sweet, mown field.

Glossary

ALPINE PASSES: all travellers and trade between Europe and Italy had to use the great alpine passes in order to get to and from Italy — unless they wanted to risk the greater uncertainties of a sea voyage. The main passes were the Brenner Pass, the St Gothard Pass and the Greater St Bernard Pass. Travellers could only access the passes in summer or winter, as avalanches in autumn and spring made passage too dangerous. Thomas Neville's journey through the Brenner Pass is an accurate description of the travails of medieval and early modern travellers. A significant percentage of men and horses died on the way through.

AQUITAINE: a large and rich province covering much of the south-west of France. Aquitaine was not only independent of France, it was ruled by the English kings after Eleanor of Aquitaine brought the province as part of her dowry to her marriage with Henry II.

ARMOUR: the armouring of a knight was a complex affair, done in different ways in different countries and generations. Generally, knights wore either chain mail or plate armour or a combination of both, depending on fashion or the military activity involved. Chain mail was formed of thousands of tiny iron or steel rings riveted together to form a loose tunic (sometimes with arms); plate armour consisted of a series of metal plates fashioned to fit a knight's body and joints — the full suit of armour was rarely seen before the fifteenth century. Helmets (whether BASINETS or the full-visored helms), mail or plate gloves, and weapons completed the knight's outfitting. See also HAUBERK, SHAFFRON and PEYTRAL.

ASTERLADEN: a prosperous village a day's ride north of Nuremberg.

AUDE: a peasant woman of Asterladen, wife to Rainard.

AVIGNON: now part of France, in the medieval period the city was nominally independent. However, its citizens spoke French, and the city was surrounded by French lands. In the early fourteenth century, Pope Clement V, who had gained the papal throne through the aid of the French King, Philip IV, removed the entire papacy, all its servants, officials and administration, to the city of Avignon, where the papacy remained until 1377. This period of French 'subjection' was known as the Babylonian Captivity when most Europeans believed the French monarchs exercised an undue degree of influence over the popes.

BABYLONIAN CAPTIVITY: see AVIGNON.

BALLADS: all the ballads in *The Crucible* are traditional medieval English songs and carols.

BASINET: an open-faced helmet (although many knights wore them with a visor attached) that was either rounded (globular) or conical in shape. See also ARMOUR.

BEAUFORT, HENRY: illegitimate son of JOHN OF GAUNT and his mistress, KATHERINE SWYNFORD, Henry became the Bishop of Winchester.

BEAUFORT, JOAN: illegitimate daughter of JOHN OF GAUNT and his mistress KATHERINE SWYNFORD.

BERTRAND: prior of St Angelo's friary in Rome.

BIERMAN, CHRISTOFFEL: a Flemish cloth merchant.

BIERMAN, JOHAN: son of Christoffel Bierman.

BLACK PRINCE: Edward, Prince of Wales and Duke of Cornwall, eldest son of EDWARD III.

BLAYE: a small coastal town just to the north of BORDEAUX.

BOHUN, MARY: heiress to the dukedom and lands of Hereford.

BOLINGBROKE, HENRY of (HAL): son of JOHN OF GAUNT and his first wife, Blanche of Lancaster.

BORDEAUX: a port on the Garonne estuary in south-west France and capital of the duchy of Aquitaine. Bordeaux is the BLACK PRINCE'S base in France (and in fact his son, Richard, was born there).

BRENNER PASS: see ALPINE PASSES.

BRAMHAM MOOR FRIARY: a small and poor friary located on the edge of Bramham Moor to the south-west of York, England.

CASTEL ST ANGELO: an ancient fortification in Rome in the walls of the LEONINE (Vatican) CITY at which it is said the archangel St Michael once appeared. According to rumour, there is a tunnel running from the papal apartments in the LEONINE CITY to the fortress.

CATHERINE: daughter of Prince Louis of France and Isabeau de Bavière, younger sister to the Dauphin, Charles.

CHARLES, THE DAUPHIN: grandson of the French King John, son of Prince Louis and Isabeau de Bavière and heir to the French throne. Older brother of Catherine.

CHATELLERAULT: a heavily fortified town some twenty miles north of CHAUVIGNY in central France.

CHAUCER, GEOFFREY: a popular English poet and writer. Married to Phillipa Roet, sister of KATHERINE SWYNFORD.

CHAUVIGNY: a town consisting of five interlaced castles situated on a hill overlooking the Vienne River. It is just to the east of Poitiers and some two hundred and twenty miles south of Paris.

CINQUE PORTS: the five (thus 'cinque') important medieval south-eastern ports of England: Dover, Hastings, Hythe, Romney and Sandwich. The barons of the Cinque Ports, as the Lord Warden of the Cinque Ports, were very powerful offices.

CLEMENT VII: the man elected by the breakaway cardinals to the papal throne after the election of Urban VI was declared void because of the interference of the Roman mob. Clement rules from Avignon while Urban, who refused to resign, continues to rule from Rome.

D'ARC, JACQUES: sergeant of the village of Domremy, in the province of Lorraine, France.

D'ARC, JEANNETTE (JEANNE, or JOAN): second daughter of JACQUES D'ARC.

D'ARC, ZABILLET (ISABELLE): wife of JACQUES D'ARC and mother of JEANNETTE D'ARC.

DATING: medieval Europeans almost never used calendar dates; they orientated themselves within the year by the religious cycle of Church festivals, holy days and saints' days. Although there were saints' days every day of the year, most regions observed only a few of them. The average number of holy days observed within the English year, for example, was between forty and sixty. In Florence it was as high as 120. Years tended to be dated by the length of a monarch's reign, each successive year starting on the date the monarch was crowned — EDWARD III was crowned on 1 February 1327, so, according to popular use, each new year during his reign would begin on 1st February. The legal year in England was calculated from Lady Day (25th March), so for legal purposes the new year began on 26th March. See also HOURS, and my web page on medieval time for a full explanation on calculating the medieval year (http://www.saradouglass.com/medtime.html).

DAUPHIN: the official title of the heir to the French throne, Prince CHARLES, grandson of King JOHN.

EDWARD III: King of England.

GASCONY: a province in the south of France famed for its wine and horses.

GERARDO: Italian man, keeper of the northern gate (the Porta del Popolo) of Rome.

GISETTE: wife of RAYMOND, a Parisian carpenter.

GLOUCESTER, ELEANOR, Duchess of: wife of THOMAS OF WOODSTOCK, Duke of Gloucester.

GREGORY XI: pope of the Roman Church. He died in 1378.

HANSEATIC LEAGUE: group of northern European cities, banded together in a trading consortium. The Hanseatic League was second only to the great Italian trading cities as the most powerful trading organisation in medieval Europe.

HAUBERK: a tunic made of chain mail. Generally it had sleeves (sometimes of chain mail, sometimes of plate armour) and reached to a knight's knees. See also ARMOUR.

HOLY ROMAN EMPIRE: a loose conglomeration of some three hundred virtually independent states in central Europe. The Holy Roman Emperor had once been a mighty office until its power was broken in a protracted war with the papacy in the eleventh and twelfth centuries.

HOTSPUR: see PERCY, HENRY.

HOURS OF THE DAY: although clock time was slowly spreading by the end of the fourteenth century (clock time used an evenly divided twenty-four hour day), most people within hearing of church or monastic bells orientated themselves within the day by the canonical hours. The Church divided the day into seven hours, according to the seven hours of prayer:

- The day began with *Matins*, usually an hour or two before dawn.
- The second of the hours was *Prime* — daybreak.
- The third hour was *Terce*, set at about 9 a.m.
- The fourth hour was *Sext* at mid-morning (originally midday).
- The fifth hour was *Nones*, set at about three in the afternoon, but, in the thirteenth century, moved closer to midday.
- The sixth hour was *Vespers*, normally early evening.
- The seventh hour was *Compline*, bedtime.

These hours were irregular both within the day and within the year, because the hours orientated themselves around the rising and setting of the sun. Thus the hours contracted and expanded according to the season.

HUNDRED YEARS WAR: a period of intense war between France and England that lasted from roughly the mid-fourteenth to mid-fifteenth century. It was caused by many factors, but primarily by EDWARD III's insistence that he was the true heir to the French throne. The English and French royal families had intermarried for generations, and Edward was, in fact, the closest male heir. However, his claim was through his mother, who was the daughter of a French king, and Salic law did not recognise claims through the female line. The war was also the result of hundreds of years of tension over the amount of land the English held in France (often over a third of the realm).

ISABEAU DE BAVIÈRE: wife of Prince LOUIS of France, mother of CHARLES and CATHERINE.

JOAN OF KENT: wife of the BLACK PRINCE, and a famed beauty in her youth.

JOHN, King: elderly King of France.

JOHN OF GAUNT, Duke of Lancaster and Aquitaine, Earl of Richmond, King of Castile, and prince of the Plantagenet dynasty: fourth son of EDWARD III (Edward Plantagenet) and his queen, PHILIPPA, John of Gaunt was the most powerful and wealthy English nobleman of the medieval period. The name Gaunt (his popular nickname) derives from Ghent, where he was born. Married first to Blanche of Lancaster, then to Constance of Castile; both dead. By Blanche he had a son, HENRY (HAL) BOLINGBROKE, by Constance two daughters (who became the queens of Castile and Portugal), and by his long-time mistress, KATHERINE SWYNFORD, two illegitimate children, HENRY and JOAN BEAUFORT.

HOOPER, GARLAND: a physician in Lincoln.

KARLE, WILLIAM: a Parisian merchant.

LESCOLOPIER, Sir HUGH: a French nobleman.

LANCASTER, Duke of: see JOHN OF GAUNT.

LA ROCHELLE: one of the ports on the coast of France, held by the English for many years.

LEONINE CITY: the walled papal city on Vatican Hill across the western bank of the Tiber from Rome containing ST PETER'S BASILICA, papal apartments and sundry papal administrative buildings. Now known as the Vatican City.

LONDON BRIDGE: for centuries there was only one bridge crossing the Thames. It crossed from Southwark on the southern bank into London itself, linking up with Watling Street, one of the great Roman roads in England. As with most bridges in medieval Europe, it was built over with tenement buildings and shops.

LOUIS: only son of King JOHN of France. Louis suffered an unfortunate encounter with a peacock which drove him insane, and now his son, CHARLES, is heir to King JOHN.

LUDGATE: a building set into the west wall of London which serves as both a gate and a gaol.

MARCEL, ETIENNE: a rich and influential Parisian cloth merchant and Provost of the Merchants of Paris, an office somewhat like that of a Lord Mayor.

MARCOALDI, GIULIO: a Florentine banker.

NAVARRE: a rich kingdom in the extreme north-west of Spain, it has been in the control of French nobles and kings for generations. Until the early fourteenth century the King of France had also held the title King of Navarre, but a complicated succession crisis witnessed the separation of the two kingdoms into separate branches of the same family. Currently ruled by PHILIP, known as Philip the Bad.

NEVILLE, RALPH, Baron of Raby: a powerful baron from the north of England.

NEVILLE, THOMAS: a Dominican friar.

NOYES, Sir GILLES DE: a French nobleman.

ODILE: a peasant wife from ASTERLADEN, married to Conrad, and mother of Wolfram.

PERCY, HENRY (HOTSPUR): son and heir of the Earl of Northumberland, and a powerful nobleman in his own right.

PÉRIGORD, Cardinal: a French cardinal.

PEYTRAL: plate armour covering a horse's chest. See also ARMOUR.

PHILIP THE BAD: King of Navarre and Count of Evreux, cousin to King JOHN and a powerful figure in French politics. As well as ruling Navarre, Philip holds extensive lands in the west of France.

PHILIPPA, Queen of England: wife to EDWARD III, who died some years before the events in this book.

POITIERS: a town in central France, and site of one of the Black Prince's greatest victories during the HUNDRED YEARS WAR.

RABY, Baron RALPH NEVILLE: see NEVILLE, RALPH.

RAINARD: peasant of the village of Asterladen, husband to AUDE.

RAYMOND: a Parisian carpenter, husband to GISETTE.

RICHARD, Prince: only son of the BLACK PRINCE and his wife, JOAN OF KENT.

RIVERS, Sir EGDON: father-in-law of MARGARET RIVERS.

RIVERS, LADY JACQUETTA: wife of Sir Egdon.

RIVERS, MARGARET, Lady: widow of Lord Roger Rivers.

ST ANGELO'S FRIARY: a friary in Rome. It is located just across the Tiber River from the CASTEL ST ANGELO, from which it takes its name. Its current prior is BERTRAND.

ST PETER: first among the apostles, and founder of the Christian Church in Rome, where he was martyred about 67AD by the Emperor Nero in the "field of blood", Caligula's Circus. He was crucified upside down by his own request.

ST PETER'S BASILICA: the great church built on Vatican Hill over St Peter's supposed grave in an ancient Roman cemetery. The great Basilica was first built by the Roman Emperor Constantine in the fourth century and remained, with various alterations and additions, until it was demolished during the period of great reconstruction begun during the fifteenth century. THOMAS NEVILLE worshipped in Constantine's basilica, while the Basilica now standing is the result of rebuilding during the late Renaissance and early modern periods.

SAXBYE: a small village in the very north of medieval Lincolnshire.

SHAFFRON: plate armour covering a horse's head. See also ARMOUR.

SHERIFF HUTTON: Baron RALPH RABY'S main castle and residence some ten miles north-east of York.

SAVOY PALACE: the Duke of Lancaster's residence on the Strand just outside London's western walls.

SMITHFIELD (or Smoothfield): a large open space or field in London's northern suburbs, just beyond Aldersgate. For many centuries it was the site of games, tournaments, and trading, craft and pleasure fairs.

STRAND, The: an important street running from London along the northern bank of the Thames down to Westminster, lined by palaces of the nobles.

SWYNFORD, KATHERINE, Lady: mistress to JOHN OF GAUNT, Duke of Lancaster. Her husband, now dead, was Sir Hugh de Swynford, a member of the retinue of JOHN OF GAUNT. Katherine is sister-in-law to GEOFFREY CHAUCER. By JOHN OF GAUNT she has two children, HENRY and JOAN BEAUFORT.

THORSEBY, RICHARD: the Prior General of England, administering all Dominicans and their friaries in the realm of England.

TONSURE: a round, shaved patch on the crown of a cleric's head.

TYLER, WAT: an English soldier.

URBAN VI: the man elected by the College of Cardinals to the papal throne after the death of GREGORY XI in 1378.

WESTMINSTER: in medieval England Westminster was an important municipality in its own right, separate from London, although intricately linked to it. Most of medieval Westminster was destroyed by fire in the early nineteenth century, but it consisted of a large palace complex boasting three halls (only one of which still stands) as well the abbey.

WOODSTOCK, THOMAS of: Earl of Buckingham and Duke of Gloucester, seventh and youngest son of EDWARD III of England. Constable of England, married to ELEANOR OF GLOUCESTOR.

WORDE, WYNKYN DE: a mysterious friar from St Angelo's.

WYCLIFFE, JOHN: an eccentric English cleric and master of Balliol College, Oxford.

A JIGGE (FOR MARGRETT)

"Margrett, my sweetest margrett! I must goe!
most dere to mee that neuer may be soo;
as Fortune willes, I cannott itt deny."
*"then know thy loue, thy Margrett, shee must
dye."*
"Not for the gold that euer Croesus hadd,
wold I once see they sweetest lookes soe fade;
nor for all that my eyes did euer see,
wold I once part thy sweetest loue from mee;
"The King comands, and I must to the warres."
"thers others more enow to end those cares."
"but I am one appointed for to goe,
And I dare not for my liffe once say noe."
*"O marry me, and you may stay att home!
Full 30 wekes you know that I am gone."*
"theres time enough; another Father take;
heele loue thee well, and not thy child forsake."
*"And haue I doted ouer thy sweetest face?
And dost infring the things I haue in chase,
thy faith, I meane? but I will wend with thee."*
"itt is to farr for Pegg to goe with mee."
*"I will goe with thee, my loue, both night and
day,
and I will beare thy sword like lakyney; Lead the
way!"*
"but we must ride, and will you follow then
amongst a troope of vs thats armed men?"
*"Ile beare thy Lance, and grinde thy stirrup too,
Ile rub thy horsse, and more then that Ile doo."*
"but Margretts fingars, they be all to fine
to stand and waite when she shall see mee dine."

"*Ile see you dine, and wayte still att your backe,*
Ile giue you wine or any thing you Lacke."
"but youle repine when you shall see mee haue
a dainty wench that is both fine and braue."
"*Ile love thy wench, my sweetest loue, I vow,*
Ile watch the time when she may pleasure you!"
"but you will greeue to see vs lye in bedd;
And you must watch still in anothers steede."
"*Ile watch my loue to see you take your rest;*
And when you sleepe, then shall I thinke me
blest."
"the time will come, deliuered you must be;
then in the campe you will descredditt mee."
"*Ile goe from thee befor that time shalbee;*
when all is well, my loue again Ile see."
"all will not serue, for Margarett may not goe;
then doe resolue, my loue, what else to doe."
"*Must I not goe? why then sweete loue, adew!*
needs must I dye, but yet in dying trew!"
"a! stay my loue! I loue my Margarett well,
And heere I vow with Margarett still to dwell!"
"*Giue me thy hand! thy Margarett liues againe!*"
"heeres my hand! Ile neuer breed thee paine!
I kisse my loue in token that is soe;
wee will be wedd: come, Margarett, let us go."

Medieval English Ballad

A JIGGE (FOR MARGRETT)

(MODERNISED VERSION)

"Margaret, my sweetest Margaret! I must go!
Most dear to me that never may be so;
As Fortune wills, I cannot it deny."

"Then know thy love, thy Margaret, she must die."

"Not for the gold that ever Croesus had,
Would I once see thy sweetest looks so fade;
Nor for all that my eyes did ever see,
Would I once part my sweetest love from me;
The King commands, and I must to the wars."

"There's others more enough to end those cares."

"But I am one appointed for to go,
And dare not for my life once say no."

*"Oh, marry me, and you may stay at home!
Full thirty weeks you know that I am gone."*

"There's time enough, another father take,
He'll love thee well, and not thy child forsake."

*"And have I doted over thy sweetest face?
And dost infringe the things I have in chase,
Thy faith, I mean? But I will wend with thee."*

"It is too far for Peg to go with me."

*"I will go with thee, my love, both night and day,
And I will bear thy sword like a lackey; Lead the
way!"*

"But we must ride, and will you follow then
Among a troop of us that are armed men?"

*"I'll bear thy lance, and attend thy stirrup too,
I'll rub thy horse, and more than that I'll do."*

"But Margaret's fingers, they be all too fine
To stand and wait when she shall see me dine."

*"I'll see you dine, and wait still at your back,
I'll give you wine or anything you lack."*

"But you'll repine when you shall see me have
A dainty wench that is both fine and brave."

*"I'll love thy wench, my sweetest love, I vow,
I'll watch the time when she may pleasure you!"*

"But you will grieve to see us lie in bed;
And you must watch still in another's stead."

*"I'll watch my love to see you take your rest;
And when you sleep, then shall I think me blessed."*

"All will not serve, for Margaret may not go;
Then do resolve, my love, what else to do."

*"Must I not go? When then, sweet love, adieu!
Needs must I die, but yet in dying true!"*

"Ah! Stay, my love! I love my Margaret well.
And here I vow with Margaret still to dwell."

"Give me thy hand! Thy Margaret lives again!"

"Here's my hand! I'll never breed thee pain!
I kiss my love in token that is so;
We will be wed: come, Margaret, let us go."